"What young lady's room were you trying to break into, may I ask?" said Cassandra.

"I wasn't breaking in," Philip responded, stung. "I was accepting an invitation."

"I should have known." Cassandra's voice was dry, and she arched an eyebrow. "I am sure that Sir Philip Neville has ample invitations to enter women's bedrooms. Exactly why are you in my room?"

Neville grimaced. "I must have taken a wrong turn somewhere." Taking out a note from his pocket, he unfolded it and reread it.

Cassandra gasped as she recognized the blotted, sloppy handwriting. "My God, that's Joanna's!"

Neville turned to glare at her, crumpling the note in his fist. "This is a private correspondence. It would be the death of her reputation if this were known."

"I think that my reputation is of more concern at the moment, since you are in *my* bedroom."

"Candace Camp is renowned as a storyteller who touches the heart of her readers time and again."

—Romantic Times

Also available from MIRA Books and
CANDACE CAMP

SUDDENLY
SCANDALOUS
IMPULSE
INDISCREET

And watch for CANDACE CAMP's
next MIRA title,

TEMPTING

June 1999

CANDACE CAMP

IMPETUOUS

MIRA®

If you purchased this book without a cover you should be aware
that this book is stolen property. It was reported as "unsold and
destroyed" to the publisher, and neither the author nor the
publisher has received any payment for this "stripped book."

ISBN 1-55166-450-X

IMPETUOUS

Copyright © 1998 by Candace Camp.

All rights reserved. Except for use in any review, the reproduction or
utilization of this work in whole or in part in any form by any electronic,
mechanical or other means, now known or hereafter invented, including
xerography, photocopying and recording, or in any information storage or
retrieval system, is forbidden without the written permission of the publisher,
MIRA Books, 225 Duncan Mill Road, Don Mills, Ontario, Canada M3B 3K9.

All characters in this book have no existence outside the imagination of the
author and have no relation whatsoever to anyone bearing the same name
or names. They are not even distantly inspired by any individual known or
unknown to the author, and all incidents are pure invention.

MIRA and the Star Colophon are trademarks used under license and registered
in Australia, New Zealand, Philippines, United States Patent and Trademark
Office and in other countries.

Printed in U.S.A.

IMPETUOUS

Prologue

The door to her room opened softly, and a man slipped in. The candle in his hand barely penetrated the darkness, but he could make out the bed, and he glided toward it.

The woman in the bed lay turned away from him, her feminine curves concealed by the covers. He stopped, a little uncertain. He had expected her to be awake, to turn toward him with the eager welcome that she had displayed earlier this evening in the conservatory. He held the candle closer to the bed. Its light glinted off the pale fall of her hair as it tumbled across the covers and pillow. It was that light gold hair which had caught his interest this afternoon, more than the perfect features.

He set down the candle and blew it out, slipped out of his shoes, and crawled across the bed to the woman. She said nothing, and he wondered whether she had actually fallen asleep or was merely feigning it. It seemed peculiar that she would simply have gone to sleep when she had made this assignation with him for midnight. It occurred to him that she was pretending to sleep in order to some-how retain an illusion of her innocence in the whole mat-ter—or perhaps she thought that he would find it arousing. He had to admit that there was something rather intriguing

about lying beside her warm body, pliant and all defenses
down, even that of consciousness.

He nuzzled into the mass of sweet-scented hair, gently
looping his arm across her. Desire flickered through him,
immediate and piercing. The faint aroma of roses teased
at his senses. He found it more arousing than the heavier
scent she had worn this afternoon. He lifted her hair and
placed his lips tenderly against the nape of her neck.

She let out a little shuddery sigh, and he smiled against
her skin. He trailed soft, warm kisses across her neck and
up onto her jaw, finding her ear and nibbling at it, tracing
the gentle whorls with the tip of his tongue, rubbing the
lobe between his lips. His hand slid beneath the covers,
shoving them down, revealing her clad in a plain white
cotton nightgown. The demure gown surprised him, but he
found it intensely, immediately arousing in a way that a
more suggestive gown would not have been. He almost
chuckled. *He would not have thought the chit had such
understanding or expertise. Perhaps this would be much
better than he had thought.* He was glad that he had
changed his mind and decided to accept Joanna's invitation
after all.

His hands roamed her body as his mouth continued to
play with her ear. He caressed her breasts and the feminine
swell of her hips through the cloth of her nightgown. His
fingers played over her thighs, her stomach. His blood
thrummed as he kissed his way down from her ear, across
the soft skin of her neck, until he was stopped by the cloth
of her gown. Impatiently he unbuttoned the first few buttons until it fell open enough that he could pull the gown
down onto her arm, exposing a tantalizing expanse of skin
down to her shoulder. He gazed at the creamy skin for a
moment, feeling himself harden and throb. He trailed a
finger, shaking slightly, across the smooth flesh. It was like

touching rose petals, and it sent a spear of desire straight down into his loins. He bent his head and kissed the point of her shoulder.

His breath came faster in his throat as he kissed his way back across her collarbone and up her neck. He snuggled up closely behind her, pressing his body against hers all the way up and down, letting his desire pulse against her rounded derriere. His hand slid down her abdomen, pushing her tightly against him, and delved between her legs. She let out a soft moan and moved her legs, opening for him. He caught his breath, stirred by the sound of her passion. He was certain now that she must be awake, though her only acknowledgment had been that sound. There was something infinitely arousing in her silent acquiescence, in the way her breath grew faster and louder, as though her most basic needs were betraying her, breaking through her self-imposed quiet. His fingers moved rhythmically, pressing and releasing, sliding across her nether lips through the cloth, and he was rewarded with another low groan that seemed to rise from deep within her.

Eyes closed, luxuriating in the petal softness of her skin, he kissed his way across her cheek. Letting out a murmur of pleasure, she turned instinctively toward him, and their lips met. Her mouth was soft and warm, yielding to the pressure of his, and her lips opened to his questing tongue. Her arms came up and curled around his neck as he kissed her deeply. Desire shuddered through him.

He pulled and tugged at her nightgown, rucking the skirt of it up until finally his fingers were on the soft flesh of her thighs. He caressed the delicate skin, his fingers creeping upward until they encountered the moisture of her desire, which only fed his own. He slipped across the slick, satiny flesh, her pearly dew wetting his fingers. She jerked a little, startled, as he touched that most intimate part of her, but then she moved, inviting his touch, and his fingers began to stroke her.

Need was pounding in him. He wanted to taste her, touch her, everywhere. He would have liked to part her legs and slide between them, plunge deep within her and carry them both to satisfaction. But even more, he wanted to prolong this moment, to explore and taste and suck every ounce of pleasure from this coupling. He had not expected anything like this when he had responded to the Moulton girl's invitation. She had seemed a blatant hussy, and he had not planned at first to even come to her bedchamber. Only restlessness had finally sent him from his room and down the hall to Joanna's. But now...

Now, touching her, breathing in her scent, taking her mouth with his—there was none of the casual, premeditated passion he had expected. Her body was like fire beneath him. Her kisses and the way she responded to his touch, the unstudied moans and sighs, all spoke of a blend of passion and inexperience that was more enticing than any practiced touch. He could not remember the last time he had felt so quickly aroused, so intensely alive, in a woman's arms.

She writhed beneath him, moaning as his fingers worked their magic. He felt as if he might explode. His mouth left hers and trailed down her neck onto the white expanse of her chest. His lips touched the quivering softness of her breast. Gently he kissed her flesh, and her body arched up a little, as though seeking his kiss. Obligingly, he took her nipple into the hot, wet cave of his mouth and began to suckle.

She let out a moan, and her hips moved fiercely beneath his hand. Suddenly she jerked and cried out, her eyes flying open, and he realized with intense satisfaction that he had brought her to release. He raised his head and smiled down into her face. He saw the blank confusion in her eyes, wide-open and staring at him. He saw the horror dawning in them. He also saw, with the feeling of stepping off a cliff into nothing but air, that the girl who lay beneath him was not Joanna Moulton.

1

Cassandra was awash in pleasure. She had never experienced anything like it, dreaming or awake. She had been dreaming lush, colorful dreams from the moment she fell asleep. Somehow she knew they were dreams, and yet she was unable to awaken from them. She had been walking through her house—the old mansion of Chesilworth, not her aunt's more habitable, yet far less pleasant, home—and she had been warm and happy. Her father was still alive and puttering downstairs in his library. The walls were a warm, buttery tint, touched by the rays of the sun, and she passed a bedroom, where a jewel-toned red velvet spread covered the bed. Candles burned inside, beckoning her. She started into the room, but then somehow she was outside in a cool, vibrantly green bower. The leaves of the hedges were dark and waxy, smooth to the touch. A breeze swept over her, lifting her hair and tickling the back of her neck. She shivered a little in delight. The sun was warm upon her shoulders, the breeze caressed her. She closed her eyes, luxuriating in the feeling.

Pleasure welled up inside her as the wind played over her cheek and neck. She was aware that now she had on no clothes, but strangely this fact did not seem to bother

her. She loved the way the sun felt on her naked skin, the way the air drifted over her. Now there was a man with her. But that did not bother her, either. She knew him, though she could not see his face or say his name. He put his hands on her, and her loins turned to warm wax. She felt weak and shaky as he kissed her over and over again. His lips pressed against her mouth, ~pening it to his questing tongue, and she jerked with the violent, unexpected pleasure of it. Warm moisture pooled between her legs, and she squeezed them together, trying to satisfy the ache that had arisen there.

His kisses filled her even as they consumed her. She clung to him in a maelstrom of pleasure. His hand traveled down over her body and delved between her legs, sending waves of pleasure through her. She moaned and moved her hips against his hand, instinctively seeking something, though she wasn't sure what. Then, suddenly, a pleasure more intense that anything she had ever felt seemed to burst within her.

Cassandra jerked, and her eyes flew open. She was awake. And a man she had never met was leaning over her, staring down into her face.

For an instant, she simply stared at him in stupefaction that matched the stunned expression on his face. Then horror rushed through her as her befogged mind began to function. She drew breath to scream. He saw her intent and quickly covered her mouth with his hand, which frightened her even more. She grabbed his arm, trying to pull his hand away, and at the same time, she struggled to sit up. He pushed her back down firmly, and she swung her hand up, hitting him sharply on the ear. He winced and grabbed for her wrist with his free hand, but she swung the other at him, too, and kicked, trying to wriggle off the bed. He threw his weight upon her to pin her down, and she was aware of every hard line of muscle and bone.

He was stronger than she, but Cassandra was not one to give up, and she had an advantage in that he had to keep one hand pressed across her mouth to keep her from screaming. She rained blows on his head and shoulders and back, and thrashed her legs, trying to land a kick that would do some harm. It took him a good while to finally get his legs wrapped tightly around hers and his hand clenched around both her wrists, pinning them to the bed above her. He was lying completely atop her, bearing her down into the mattress. Cassandra could not help but be aware of the intruder's power, of his very maleness. The position frightened her, yet at the same time she was confusedly aware of the heat that sizzled through her veins and lay pooled and heavy in her abdomen.

She wished that she could think better. *Why was her head so heavy and groggy? And what was a man of the wealth and position of Sir Philip Neville doing assaulting a woman in her bedroom at a house party in the country?*

He was breathing heavily, and Cassandra saw that sweat glistened in the hollow of his throat, just above the undone button of his shirt. Cassandra pulled both her eyes and her mind away from that tanned hollow of flesh that was visibly pulsing with each beat of his heart.

"Don't scream!" he whispered, leaning down close to her face. "I promise you I mean you no harm. I will let you go, if you will promise not to scream."

She gazed at him, wide-eyed, and nodded her head. He looked at her for a long, doubtful moment, then eased his hand from her mouth, moving in tiny increments, always ready to clamp it back down if she showed signs of screaming. Cassandra said nothing, merely watched him steadily.

He relaxed a little. "I swear to you that I mean you no harm. I will leave this room. I won't harm you. Do you understand?"

"Of course I understand!" Cassandra hissed back in the same undertone. "I'm not an idiot."

He moved off her with a groan. "Bloody hell! What a tangle." He looked at her, frowning. "You're the wrong one."

"I should certainly hope so," Cassandra retorted acidly, sitting up. "Oh, my head! I feel as if a thousand hammers were banging away inside it." *Why was she so groggy? And why did she feel strangely hot and tingly inside?*

She looked at the man sitting cross-legged on the bed beside her. She supposed she ought to be frightened, but, once that initial spurt of terror was past, once she recognized the stranger for Sir Philip Neville, she had not been scared, only stunned and confused.

The lingering emotions from her dream unsettled her, and she took refuge in sarcasm. "What young lady's room were you trying to break into, may I ask?"

"I wasn't breaking in," he responded, stung. "I was accepting an invitation."

"Of course. I should have known." Cassandra's voice was dry, and she arched an eyebrow. "I am sure that Sir Philip Neville has ample invitations to enter women's bedrooms."

Neville gazed at her for a long moment. "You are a most unusual female."

"So I've been told." Cassandra did not deceive herself that his words were a compliment.

"I would think a young lady would be...rather more distraught in this situation than you are."

"Would you rather that I were?" Cassandra retorted. "I

fail to see how it would help matters any if I were to fall into hysterics.''

"I didn't say it would help. It just seems more…natural.''

"I must be an unnatural female, then. It is what my aunt and cousin tell me. They say it is why I never caught a husband. But I think that had more to do with the sad state of our finances than with my attitude, for I have seen odder women than myself marry well, as long as they had a wealthy father. Wouldn't you say?''

"I daresay you are correct.'' Sir Philip gazed at her in a sort of dazed fascination. He had never before met a woman who spoke in the candid, no-nonsense way this woman did. Indeed, it was something of an oddity to speak to a woman who did not immediately set to flirting with him. He had found that an income of one hundred thousand pounds a year acted as a powerful aphrodisiac.

"To return to the subject at hand,'' Cassandra continued crisply, "exactly why are you in my room rather than that of the female who issued the invitation?''

Neville grimaced. "I must have taken a wrong turn somewhere.'' He turned to light the candle he had set down on the bedside table earlier. Taking out a note from his pocket, he unfolded it and reread it. "Though I don't see how. It's quite clear—the fifth door on the right from the stairs. Isn't this the fifth door?''

Cassandra thought for a moment. "Yes.'' Curious, she rose onto her knees and looked over his shoulder at the note. She gasped as she recognized the blotted, sloppy handwriting and the distinctive looping initials at the bottom of the paper. "My God, that's Joanna's script!''

Neville turned to glare at her, crumpling the note in his fist. "I beg your pardon, madam. This is a private correspondence.''

"Mm. I think it's hardly a private matter, considering that you are sitting in my bed reading it."

"It would be the death of her reputation if this were known," he countered grimly.

"I think that my reputation is of more concern at the moment, since you are in *my* bedroom."

"I would trust, madam, that you would have enough sense not to bandy it about that you were entertaining a man in your room, and since I have no intention of revealing it, I think it is clear that your reputation is safe."

"Of course *I* have enough sense to keep quiet," Cassandra retorted, nettled by what she considered a rather excessive concern on his part over Joanna's reputation. "The one you ought to be concerned with is Joanna, since she is obviously so hare-witted that she directed you to the wrong room."

She reached over and plucked the ball of paper from his hand and smoothed it out, bending close to read it in the dim light of the candle. "Ah, yes, I see. She didn't say fifth door, she wrote fourth. You see? It's just her abominable handwriting, and she left out the *u*. She never was much good at spelling, I'm afraid. I can see how you made the mistake—especially with, ah, your undoubted *eagerness* clouding your thinking. I have had a bit more experience with reading her notes."

"Then it is too bad that I did not consult with you first," Neville snarled, "but, you see, I was not aware that I needed an interpreter."

"There is no need to be testy," Cassandra stated. "And you needn't worry for your, uh, for the lady's reputation. I'm not likely to besmirch my family by telling anyone that Joanna makes assignations with men in her bedchamber. She is my cousin, you see."

"Your cousin?" Neville studied her face in the candle-light. "That's odd. I don't recall seeing you with her."

"That is often the case." Cassandra kept her voice light. She was used, after all, to being overshadowed by her beautiful, flirtatious cousin. Joanna's guinea gold hair and large blue eyes generally captured all male attention when she was around.

Cassandra, at the ripe old age of twenty-seven, knew that she was on the shelf and, indeed, had never been popular with men. She had not "taken" one during her season, and her father had not been able to afford more than one. Cassandra knew, anyway, that any number of social seasons would not have seen her married. For one thing, she had no knack for flirtation and even less interest in it. For another, while she was not precisely plain, her features lacked the even perfection of a true beauty. Her cheek-bones were too high, her jaw too firm, and her mouth was much too wide for the popular rosebud look. Even her eyes, which she felt to be her best feature, were a quiet gray rather than a soulful brown or a sparkling blue, and she did not use them to her advantage, instead gazing at the world in a straightforward, clear way that did not lure men.

So she had retired from the social world after one year, not really displeased that she had not made a successful marriage. She had done the season as a duty for her family. They were, as always, in desperate need of money, and she would have gritted her teeth and said yes if an eligible man had asked for her hand. But she had found no man during the year of her debut whom she had accounted as anything but boring, and she was, frankly, quite glad to return to the bosom of her family at Chesilworth unen-gaged and unlikely ever to be so. With relief, she had donned her old clothes, wound her hair up into the familiar bun and jumped back into the management of her father's household, which had fallen into a woeful state in her absence. She found contentment in raising her younger brothers and sister, and intellectual companionship with her father, and if there was anything missing in her life—other than a chronic lack of money—she had not felt it, or at least had not allowed the feeling to dwell long. At social functions, she sat with the matrons overseeing the antics of the youngsters, rather than with the giggling, hopeful maidens, whose conversations she found stultifying, and in the last couple of years, she had even taken to wearing a small cap over her hair in acknowledgement of her spinster status. It was just as well, she thought, that men's eyes slid past her indifferently. It was much less trying not to have to make conversation about nothing.

Still…she could not help but feel a twinge of hurt at the thought that Sir Philip had not even noticed her when he was standing not three feet away from her, chatting with Aunt Ardis and her cousin Joanna.

"You were otherwise occupied," she continued, not without a sting.

"I see." He turned and looked at her. It puzzled him that he could have missed noticing this creature with the wide eyes and tumbling mass of bright hair and…other, entrancing features. His gaze dropped down to her torso, where her nightgown, still unbuttoned, had once again slipped off her shoulder and down her arm, revealing a high, firm white breast with its enticing pinkish brown nipple. *Even fully clothed and with her hair done up in proper midday form, how could he not have noticed her?*

Cassandra, following the direction of his gaze, glanced down and saw with horror that her breast was exposed. Blushing furiously, she jerked up the neck of her nightgown and began buttoning it up, keeping her eyes turned down. *This was the worst thing that had ever happened to her! How could she face him again?* No man had ever seen more of her than what was bared by the neckline of an evening gown. Now this man, this stranger to her, had seen her with the intimacy of a husband. *Worse—what was she doing with half the buttons of her gown undone?* She thought of the wild, swirling emotions of her dream, the startling sensations and the heat in her abdomen. *What had happened? Had it been not a dream lover but a real man touching her in those intimate ways? Had this man caused that fierce, primeval jolt of pleasure that had finally dragged her from her slumber?*

She looked up at him, color still staining her cheeks. She was embarrassed, but Cassandra Verrere was not one to flinch from the truth. "What happened? Here, tonight, I mean. I—I feel so strange. I dreamed, well, bizarre things, things that I— Were they real? What did you— what did I do?"

Sir Philip hesitated, then he leaned over and took her hand gently. "You did nothing. I assure you. I entered your room, thinking you were another. You were in the midst of a fevered dream. I—you were tossing and turning. Thinking you were Joanna, I came over and, ah, took your arms. I tried to wake you, but you were very heavily asleep. I...kissed you. And you woke up. That is when I realized that you were not Miss Moulton."

"And that is all?"

His eyebrows rose lazily. "Yes. Of course. What else could there be?"

Cassandra let out a sigh of relief. "Nothing. It was just peculiar. I felt as if I were not quite asleep, yet I could not seem to pull myself out of my slumber."

"No doubt you had a tiring day."

"Mm." Cassandra knew it had not been at all tiring

physically. But the social interaction that a large house party involved was rather wearying. Still… "I think you had better leave now."

"Yes. You're right." He slid off the bed and walked toward the door. Cassandra followed him. He paused and turned toward her. "Thank you."

"You're welcome," she responded automatically, then added, "What are you thanking me for?"

"For being a most calm and reasonable young woman. There are not many who would have reacted as you did."

"Oh." Cassandra nodded matter-of-factly. "I am afraid I haven't much sensibility."

He reached for the doorknob, but Cassandra laid a restraining hand on his arm. "No. You had better let me see if anyone happens to be out in the hall first."

"Of course." He nodded and stepped back.

Cassandra eased the door open a crack and put her eye to it. She gasped and jerked back, closing the door hastily. She turned to Sir Philip, her eyes huge.

"What is it?" He made a move toward the door, but she raised her hand.

"Don't!" she cautioned. "Shh. It's my aunt!"

Almost without thinking, she reached down and turned the key in the lock. The last thing she wanted was for Aunt Ardis to barge into her room.

"What is *she* doing here?" he whispered.

"I have no idea. Could she have seen you enter my room? If she knocks on the door, you will have to hide." She looked speculatively toward the window. "I wonder if you could escape out the window."

"We are on the second floor," he reminded her.

"There might be a trellis or a tree."

He raised one brow sardonically. "You seem awfully familiar with this sort of predicament."

"Don't be absurd."

Their discussion was interrupted at that moment by heavy pounding on a door, not Cassandra's, but the one next door. Cassandra jumped at the sound, then relaxed with a heartfelt sigh. "Thank God. She's at Joanna's room."

"Joanna!" Aunt Ardis bellowed, her voice carrying clearly through the walls. "Open this door. This is your mother! Open this door at once, I say!"

"Is your aunt in the habit of waking everyone up in the middle of the night this way?"

Cassandra shook her head, puzzled. "No. I cannot imagine what has possessed her. She is always in bed by ten."

"Joanna!"

Cassandra stealthily unlocked her door and opened it a fraction, peering out at the spectacle of her aunt. Aunt Ardis was a sizable woman, with a large bosom that thrust out like the prow of a ship when she was corseted. It did so now, despite the fact that Aunt Ardis wore a red velvet dressing gown and bedroom slippers. Cassandra noticed, too, that her hair was still coiled up into its usual flat braided bun, not hanging loose down her back. Cassandra frowned, wondering what could have happened to put her aunt into such a state.

"Joanna! Open up I say. Who's in there with you? I heard voices."

"Voices!" Cassandra exclaimed softly and looked back at Sir Philip. "Oh, dear, do you think she could have heard us?"

Neville shook his head, his eyes narrowing thoughtfully. Cassandra had to admit that it seemed unlikely, given the fact that her aunt's room was on the other side of Joanna's.

At that moment Joanna's door was wrenched open, and

Joanna cried out in a carrying whisper, "Hush! It's too early! He's not here yet!"

Aunt Ardis's jaw dropped, and she stared at her daughter in horror. All up and down the hall, doors were opening and heads were popping out, their expressions variously sleepy, irritated or avid, and some all three.

"I say, what's going on?" Colonel Rivington, across the hall from Joanna's room, called out. "What is all this commotion?"

"Uh." Aunt Ardis's mouth opened and closed like that of a landed fish.

"I'm so sorry." Joanna smiled sweetly at the man. "Please forgive my mother. She was, uh, she was just…"

"Worried!" Aunt Ardis found her voice. "That's it. I was worried. I heard Joanna crying out in her sleep. She must have been having a bad dream."

"Yes," Joanna agreed quickly. "A nightmare. I was having a nightmare."

Cassandra eased the door shut and turned toward Sir Philip, frowning in puzzlement. "How odd. Why are they—" She stopped short at the forbidding expression on his face. "What is it?"

"I understand now." His words were short and clipped, his mouth thinned with distaste. "I was surprised when Miss Moulton threw herself at me this afternoon. Before that she had been acting like the usual coy, flirtatious maiden. Then suddenly she turned into a brazen woman of the world." He remembered his faint surprise as she had "accidentally" brushed against him three times this afternoon in the conservatory and the seductive looks she had sent him, the long, promising kiss behind a palm tree as she slipped the note into his hand.

"I don't understand. What are you talking about?"

"Your cousin's scheme. Your aunt's. She wrote me that

note asking me to come to her room tonight at midnight. She gave every indication of welcoming quite dishonorable attentions. And her mother was primed to come barging in after I was in the room, rousing everyone on the floor with her loud comments."

Cassandra stared. "You mean, she lured you up to her room so that her mother could catch you in a compromising position with her? But why? Why would she want to destroy her reputation like that?"

A faint smile flickered across Neville's face. Her lack of comprehension of her relatives' scheme spoke volumes about her own honest character. "My dear girl, I doubt very much that she cared about her reputation being shredded, as long as it brought her wealth and an old name. Her reputation would not have been ruined, in any case, since she and I would immediately have become engaged."

Cassandra gasped. "You mean—they wanted to force you into marrying Joanna? I can't believe it!" But she could; it took only a moment's reflection to bring her around. *Why else would her aunt have been pounding on Joanna's door so loudly and virtually shouting, except to bring out several interested observers? Why else would her aunt, usually early to bed, still have been up at midnight— and still wearing her corset, her hair done up? She was expecting everyone to look at her, and she had been unable to bring herself to be in true deshabille.*

"That's why I was so groggy..." Cassandra murmured. "Aunt Ardis must have put some of her laudanum in my drink tonight. I should have known she was up to something when she came in here with that warm milk to help me sleep. She knows how lightly I sleep and the difficulty I often have going to bed. She wanted me deep in slumber so I wouldn't investigate any noise I heard—like you slipping into Joanna's room."

"No doubt you're right. It is merely my good luck that Miss Moulton's handwriting is so illegible, or you would have found yourself forced into cousinship with me."

"Oh." Cassandra raised her hands to her burning cheeks. She wasn't sure whether she was more humiliated or furious. *How could her aunt and cousin have acted in such a despicable way?* Somehow the thought of Joanna trying to tie this man to her for life made Cassandra long to slap her cousin. "I am so ashamed. Sir Philip, I apologize for my family. I cannot imagine what made them do such a thing."

"I have found that the lure of money often causes people to act in a bizarre fashion."

"That is no excuse for—for such a lack of principles. I am sorry, so dreadfully sorry." Her eyes shone with angry, embarrassed tears. "You must think we are awful."

He smiled and took her hand, gallantly bowing over it and brushing the back of her hand with his lips . "My dear lady, I do not think you are awful at all. Indeed, you almost restore my faith in humanity."

The touch of his lips on her skin sent an unaccustomed thrill through Cassandra, reminding her of the fevered, pulse-racing condition in which she had awakened. That odd melting-wax sensation deep in her abdomen had still not completely gone away. Cassandra swallowed and turned away.

"I, ah, I shall see if everyone has gone back inside." She opened the door a crack and looked out. When she saw no one, she stuck her head out the door and peered up and down the hall.

She turned back to Sir Philip. "There is no one out there now."

He nodded. "Then I shall take my leave of you." He

smiled, sketching her another elegant bow. "Thank you for a most interesting evening, Miss Moulton."

"Oh, I'm—" Cassandra stopped. Now was not the time to go into an explanation that her name was not Moulton. "I'm just sorry for what my cousin and aunt did."

"And I apologize for…my most ungentlemanly behavior."

Cassandra felt another blush beginning to rise in her cheeks. She turned away and made another check out the door, then stepped aside for Sir Philip to pass. She closed the door behind him and waited a few tense moments for the sounds of voices that would indicate that he had been caught. There was nothing. Again she ventured a peek out and saw that the hall was empty. Sir Philip had gone.

She closed the door and leaned against it, letting out a sigh. *Oh, God! Why had this had to happen? Tonight, of all nights, and with Sir Philip Neville, of all people?*

Cassandra made her way over to her bed and sat down heavily. She had schemed so hard to get her aunt to take her along on this visit when she had heard that Sir Philip was going to be here. It had taken numerous careful, subtle hints about the difficulty of chaperoning an active young girl like Joanna on the sort of outdoors amusements that one tended to go on at large house parties, painting a picture of liveliness that was guaranteed not to appeal to Aunt Ardis's sluggish nature. Concealing any desire on her own part to attend such a function, she had worked her aunt around to realizing that the ideal solution would be to take Cassandra along to chaperon Joanna on the activities Aunt Ardis found too taxing. Reluctantly, Cassandra had let herself be persuaded.

It had been, she thought, a superb performance on her part, especially given the fact that her decisive, straightforward nature did not run naturally toward subterfuge.

And now her effort was in all likelihood wasted. How could she even face Sir Philip again, knowing what Joanna had tried to do to him? And knowing, too, in what an intimate situation he had met Cassandra herself?

Heat flooded her just at the memory of the things she had dreamed—the deep, passionate kisses, the sensual caresses. *Had those things really happened? Had her drugged mind just turned them into a dream?* She groaned in despair, covering her face with her hands. She could never live it down if she had moaned and writhed in Sir Philip's arms the way she had in her dream. He had told her that nothing had happened, but perhaps he was merely being gentlemanly.

She flopped back on her bed, unconsciously running her hand down her front as she remembered the hot, pulsing sensations that had assaulted her in her dreams…the intense explosion of pleasure that had propelled her out of her sleep finally. *What had that been? That deep, hard jolt of pure sensation that had left her feeling weak and quietly throbbing?* Nothing in her experience had ever even come close to that feeling.

Was she a wanton woman? The idea seemed absurd. She had had very few dealings with men, really. She did not seem to know how to talk to them. The straightforward way she had talked to her father had seemed to make young men quickly leave her side. Aunt Ardis had told her that young girls did not make conversation about such boring topics as history or politics, much less offer their strong—and often quite radical—opinions. Young ladies, Aunt Ardis had pointed out, were supposed to giggle and flirt, to flutter a fan coyly in front of their faces and let their eyes speak volumes above it. Cassandra had found the whole notion absurd, and she could scarcely believe that a gentleman could decide whether he loved a woman or could even stand to be married to her on the basis of giggles and inane conversation.

Of course, *she* had had no beaux, whereas the flirtatious Joanna, who had never uttered a sensible word to a man in her life, was flooded with them at every party. It proved, she supposed, the truth of Aunt Ardis's advice. Cassandra had realized that she was not romantic enough or not interested enough in men to act the part of a ninny in order to snare one. If her aunt was correct, Cassandra thought, then most men were too foolish for her to want to spend the rest of her life with one. It was far better to remain a spinster and her own woman. With such an unromantic, practical nature, she found it difficult to believe that there was a streak of wantonness running through her. If there was, then her earlier dream had been the only manifestation of it she had ever noticed.

This was nonsense, she told herself, sitting up straight. Sir Philip had not been trying to protect her when he said nothing had happened. He had merely been telling the truth. It was absurd to think anything else. Of course he had done nothing except climb into her bed, thinking that she was Joanna. Then he had seen her face and realized that she was not. He would not have been kissing and caressing her for several minutes before he realized that he did not know her.

Cassandra let out a sigh of relief. She had been letting her imagination run away with her. The peculiar sensations she had experienced were doubtless part of the peculiarity of her dreams. She was sure that Aunt Ardis or Joanna must have dosed her with some of her aunt's laudanum. The sleeping potion had obviously affected her dreams as well as made her sleep, and no doubt it was responsible for the odd sensations she had dreamed—things that had been entirely in her head, not really physical.

Sir Philip would not assume she was wanton. Indeed, he had told her that he appreciated her integrity. She told herself that she need not be embarrassed to face him. And the fact was, she had to talk to him. Her family's whole future rested on getting him to agree to her plan. Her cousin's behavior was irksome and embarrassing, of course, but Cassandra told herself that she would have to rise above it. She had to think of her brothers and their future. It was imperative to get their family inheritance, and only Sir Philip could help her do that. She could not let a few well-bred qualms deter her from her course. She had to talk to Sir Philip tomorrow.

Cassandra gave a short, decisive nod, as if she had been arguing with another person. Then she slid beneath her covers, reaching over to blow out the candle. She felt much more like herself now. And tomorrow she would proceed with her plan.

2

Sir Philip Neville strolled through the rose garden, scarcely noticing the sweet aroma or the heavy, colorful heads of flowers nodding in the morning sun. His mind was on the young woman he had met in such bizarre fashion the night before. He had been thinking of her for much of the morning—indeed, for much of the night before, too, after he had made his secretive way back to his bedroom. *To think that she was related to the scheming Moultons!*

He had trouble seeing any resemblance to Joanna in her open face. He supposed that others would say Joanna was lovelier; indeed, before last night, he might have said the same thing himself. Joanna's sparkling blue eyes and pouting, rosebud lips were far more what was acknowledged as beauty than her cousin's luminous, intelligent gray eyes or generous mouth. But as he thought of the woman's creamy complexion and the firm lines of her cheek and jaw, the softer outlines of Joanna's face blurred in his mind. And that glorious light gold curtain of hair—*how could he possibly have failed to notice her yesterday?*

That question had been plaguing him for hours. He could not believe that he had been so dazzled by Joanna's beauty that he had noticed nothing else. Joanna was a pretty little minx, all right, and her bold looks and smiles had aroused his sexual interest, but he had not been rendered thoughtless by her. Even given her obvious invitation to share her favors, he had originally intended not to go to her room. He found her prattle boring, as he did most women's, particularly the young ladies of quality who pursued him, hoping for marriage, and he had not been sure that the momentary pleasure of her body would be worth the effort of making the sort of sweet assurances she would expect, much less having to listen to her prate on about her hair or clothes or whatever inane thought entered her head.

Thank God he had gone, though, or he would not have met the other Miss Moulton. He found Joanna's cousin a much more interesting prospect than the nubile Joanna. He thought back to the day before, when Lady Arrabeck had introduced him to Mrs. Moulton and her daughter. He vaguely remembered that there had been another woman in the room, standing at some distance from Joanna and her mother. He had received the hazy impression of an older woman, turned slightly away from him, looking out the window. *Surely that had not been Joanna's cousin.*

He tried to remember why he had assumed she was not a young woman. Her clothes had been dark and plain, and he thought he recalled that a matronly sort of cap had sat on her head. *Yes, that was it.* Her tall, slender figure had been encased in dark clothes, unremarkable except for their lack of fashion or appeal, and that glorious fall of bright hair must have been caught up under a spinster's cap. He wondered why she had hidden her best feature that way. His sister, he knew, would give anything to have that thick fall of light gold hair.

Sir Philip could almost feel the satin smoothness of her hair as it had trickled through his fingers, and his abdomen contracted with a swift stab of hunger. He remembered the way her mouth had tasted beneath his, the smooth glide of his fingers over her skin, the unconcealed pleasure she had experienced from his lovemaking. Philip smiled. This was one woman whose pleasure at his hands had not, he was sure, been artifice.

True, other women had smiled and moaned and writhed beneath his kisses and caresses, apparently in the throes of passion. But with his mistresses, he had never been sure whether their desire and delight were real or merely a show they put on to please him so that he would continue to keep them in high style.

Sir Philip had come into a great deal of money at an early age, inheriting from his mother's father a sizable fortune. His father's death some years later had only increased his wealth, adding the substantial Neville properties. While his title was only that of a baronet, the Neville family boasted one of the oldest and most blue-blooded lineages, with countless connections to dukes, earls and viscounts throughout its history. The combination of both great wealth and good name had made him from an early age a prize for predatory females—from aristocratic mamas searching for a husband for their daughters to common ladies of the night to elegant actresses or ballet dancers prepared to accept a carte blanche. He had learned to be cynical about their attraction to him before he reached his twenties.

On the whole, Sir Philip preferred the more straightforward business arrangements of a kept mistress to the coy flirtations of society maidens, all of whom, he was sure, would have smiled at him and fluttered their eyelashes and hung on his every word even if he had been a cross-eyed stuttering fool, as long as they might acquire the Neville name and fortune by doing so.

But even with the elegant, attractive women whom he had kept as his mistresses, he had always known that they earned their living by pleasing him, and he had never been able to trust their protestations of love or even the elementary sounds of their passions.

But last night, there had been no artifice, no deception. The young lady had responded unconsciously, instinctively, and her arousal at his touch had been immediate and unmistakable. Such honest desire intrigued him. Indeed, just thinking about it now, he could feel himself hardening once again.

He stopped and turned to look back toward the house, searching, he had to admit, for the sight of Miss Moulton. He had been doing so most of the morning. He wanted to talk to her again, to hear her warm, pleasant voice, free of the soft, babyish affectations toward which young women of his acquaintance were so often prone. He wanted to see her in the daylight, to assure himself that her creamy skin and luminous eyes were as he remembered them from last night. So far, however, the young lady had been disappointingly absent, though he had met several other young women who had been more than happy to stroll with him in the fragrant garden, annoying him with their chatter.

He wondered if she was simply a late riser or if he should perhaps seek her inside. It was possible, he supposed, that she was one of those delicate creatures who never ventured out into the sun.

As he stood searching the garden and the distant terrace, there was the crunch of a footstep behind him on the gravel, and a woman's voice said, "Ah! Sir Philip. We meet again."

It was her voice. He whirled to face her. She was tall and carried herself with pride, seemingly unaware or uncaring that she loomed over many men. She was slender, with high, enticing breasts, though her figure was concealed in a brown bombazine gown that Sir Philip would have expected to see on a governess rather than on Ardis Moulton's niece. Her hair was hidden beneath a straw hat, and its wide brim shadowed her face, as well.

He stepped forward, unaware of the smile that touched his usually impassive face. He looked down into her face, seeing once again the firm, generous mouth, smiling unaffectedly at him, and the wide, intelligent gray eyes under curving dark brows. He knew that her facial bones were too strong for her to be considered a proper beauty, but their lines appealed to him. Hers was the sort of face one did not easily forget, and he knew that he had been guilty of not really looking at her the day before, for he would not have forgotten that face. He wished she was not wearing the bonnet, so that he could see her hair in the sunlight. His fingers itched to take it off her head.

"Miss Moulton, what a pleasant surprise. I fear my walk in the morning is usually a dull affair, but you, I am sure, will enliven it. If you will walk with me…?" His voice trailed off questioningly, and he offered his arm.

Cassandra took it, smiling. She hoped that the heightened color in her face would not betray her. She had spotted Sir Philip in the garden some minutes earlier, and she had been walking around, working up her courage to speak to him, ever since. When she had finally approached him, and he had turned to her and smiled, her heart had done the most unusual flip-flop in her chest, and her lungs seemed to have forgotten how to breathe. She had never before felt this way when she talked to a man, nor had she ever had the silly desire to grin at a man for no reason, as she feared she was doing now. It was, she told herself, some odd reaction caused by her trepidation at speaking to him.

She tried to ignore the way her heart pounded in her chest as they strolled through a vine arbor and out into the less formally restrained yard at the rear of the gardens. "My name is not Moulton," she began.

"I beg your pardon. I had thought, since your aunt's name was Moulton—"

"Of course. But she is the wife of my *mother's* brother."

"I see. Then I am afraid you have the advantage of me. What is your name?"

Her courage failed her at the last minute, and she said only, "Cassandra."

"Cassandra!" Amusement lit his eyes, and Cassandra noticed that in the sunlight they looked more gold than brown. "A rather gloomy name to put on a child, isn't it?"

"I don't know. Perhaps Papa and Mama thought it would give me prophetic powers. Papa was in his Greek period then, so I suppose that I am lucky that they didn't decide to name me Persephone or Electra."

"Mm. Quite true." He looked much struck by the thought.

"Of course, my brothers and sister call me Cassie. That's not so bad."

"Neither is bad. I assure you, I didn't mean that. Cassandra is a lovely name. It is just not—"

"I know. The sort of name most people would inflict on a baby."

He smiled faintly. "I wouldn't have put it quite that way."

"Only because you are too polite."

"And was your father in his 'Greek period' when your brothers and sister were born?" he asked delicately.

Laughter bubbled up out of Cassandra's throat, a deli-

cious sound that Sir Philip found sizzled along his nerves.
"You mean, are they named Ajax, Agamemnon and De-
meter?"

"Precisely." His eyes twinkled down at her.

"My sister's name is Olivia. That is close, I suppose. It
comes from Latin, does it not? But I think he had left that
phase by the time the twins were born. Their names are
Crispin and Hart. Not exactly Ned or Tom, but at least
they are not classical."

"No. Proper British names, both of them."

They were nearing the maze, and Cassandra nodded toward it. "Would you like to go in the maze? I explored it
yesterday and worked it out. There is a lovely fountain in
the center."

Philip thought of wandering through the high green
walls of the maze with Cassandra, alone in its quiet seclu-
sion, and his loins tightened. "Yes," he replied a little
huskily. He cleared his throat. "It sounds delightful."

"It is nice—though it's not terribly difficult. The one
we had at home was dreadfully complicated. It was easy
to get lost in it, even for us. Once, when Hart and Crispin
were little, they went in, and it took us hours to realize
where they were. Papa threatened to close it off, but I
persuaded him merely to block the entrance until they were
older."

She did not add that in the past few years the maze had
been let go; the once-trimmed shrubs had in many places
grown together, with grass and even weeds cropping up
everywhere. They had not had the money to continue to
pay a gardener to keep it in proper form.

"Where is your home?"

"In the Cotswolds, near Fairbourne. Actually, we live
with Aunt Ardis now, since Papa died. It's not far away
from our home, but we do miss it." She smiled, her jaw

setting in a determined way. "But our circumstances are about to change, and then we will be able to go home again."

They turned into the maze and began to follow its twistings and turnings. The air was still within its corridors, and hushed, with only the occasional twittering of a bird. Enclosed by the high, waxy green walls, it seemed almost as if they were in a different world from the rest of the estate. They walked silently for a time, both of them loath to disturb the hush.

But when they were deep within the maze, Cassandra drew a deep breath and looked up at Sir Philip earnestly. "I did not tell you my last name."

"No, so you didn't." He had noticed the omission and wondered at it. Now his curiosity grew even stronger.

"Well, as I said, I am not a Moulton. That was my mother's name. *My* name is Verrere."

He stopped abruptly, startled, and looked at her. His eyes grew a little wary, and he said in a soft voice, "Ah...a faithless Verrere."

Cassandra planted her hands on her hips and glared at him. "A ruthless Neville," she responded.

For a long moment they simply stood, looking at one another. Finally Sir Philip started forward again, saying only, "And what does a Verrere want with a Neville?"

Cassandra cast about in her mind for exactly the right words to say. She had been waiting for this moment for months now. It was the only opportunity she was likely to have, and she had to get it right.

"I know that our families have for some years now been, well..."

"Enemies?" he suggested.

"I would say that *enemies* is rather a strong word to

use," Cassandra demurred. "It has been over a hundred years since a Verrere or Neville tried to kill each other."

"Mm. A remarkable achievement."

At one time the two families had, indeed, been constantly at the point of drawing swords. Any comment by a Neville about a Verrere was immediately interpreted to be a deadly slur and vice versa. Over the years the hard enmity between them had declined to a social one-upsmanship, with each striving to outdo the other in terms of parties, carriages and racehorses. During this century, even that degree of rancor had died down, so that hostesses became able to invite a Neville and a Verrere to the same function without fearing that neither would ever speak to her again.

Cassandra suspected that the intense rivalry had diminished largely because the Verreres' fortunes had declined, while the Nevilles' had kept on growing, as always. The Verreres had simply been unable to compete any longer in any comparison of possessions or parties, leaving them with little to lord over the Nevilles except the Verrere title, Chesilworth. Indeed, during Cassandra's father's lifetime, the Verreres had retired from the lists, socially speaking. Cassandra's grandfather had long ago had to sell the London house to pay debts, and the expense of clothes and rent for a London season was beyond them. Her father, Rupert, had been a bookish man, anyway, and he had been more pleased than not to give up the season in London each year. He had preferred to spend what money he had on his books and art.

"I trust that you are not so narrow-minded as to hold my name against me," Cassandra continued, looking up at Philip challengingly.

His mouth quirked sardonically. "I was taught as a child that if I was bad, the Verreres would get me. However, I do trust that I will be able to hold my own against this particular Verrere.''

"I have come for your help, not to fight.''

His brows soared. ''My help? A Verrere asking a Neville for help?''

Cassandra frowned. ''Do you plan to continue playing the fool in this fashion? I came to this house party specifically to talk to you, but I can see that I have wasted my time if you are unable to drop your petty prejudices long enough to listen.''

He could not help but grin at her tart words and tone. ''I beg your pardon, Miss Verrere.'' He pulled his face back into somber lines. ''I will endeavor to be serious, since my levity displeases you. However, I have to tell you I find it bizarre that a Verrere would even think of asking me for help, let alone believe that I would be willing to extend that help.''

"Well, as for your helpfulness, I have no way of knowing that, of course. But I would hope that you are a reasonable enough man to see that it would be profitable for both of us.''

"I am afraid you have lost me before we have even started. *What* would be profitable?''

"That is what I am about to tell you. Ah, here is the center of the maze. Isn't it a tranquil spot? Why don't we sit down on the bench, and I will explain myself?''

"By all means.''

Neville politely dusted off the bench with his handkerchief, and they sat down. They looked at each other assessingly. Finally Cassandra began. ''I am searching for the Spanish dowry.''

Neville gazed back at her blankly. ''The what?''

Cassandra frowned. ''Surely you have heard of it. It was what started the whole bitterness between our families.''

Late in the seventeenth century, the Nevilles and Verreres had decided to ally their families by marriage. Sir
Edric Neville was contracted to marry the daughter of
Richard Verrere, Lord Chesilworth. The girl's name was
Margaret, and she, rather than marrying Sir Edric, had
stolen out of the Neville estate on the eve of her wedding
and run off with the man she truly loved. It had been a
scandal of immense proportions, heightened by the fact
that the substantial dowry which she had brought to the
Nevilles was missing, as well. The incident had set the two
families at odds for the next two hundred years.

"You mean Black Maggie's dowry?" Philip exclaimed.

She gave him a disapproving look. "If you mean Margaret Verrere, then, yes, it is her dowry I am speaking of.
A collection of Spanish treasure seized by Colin Verrere
in the late sixteenth century."

Philip snorted. "Stolen, you mean. Colin Verrere was
an out-and-out pirate."

"He sailed with letters of marque from Queen Elizabeth
herself," Cassandra retorted hotly. "He was a patriot, as
well as an excellent sailor and fighter."

"Legalized piracy. I suspect that the Spanish sailors he
killed had some difficulty telling the difference."

"It was a war," Cassandra reminded him coldly. "Spain
was our enemy, and any damage done to her economy was
a blow for England and the queen."

"Yes, and was it not convenient that Lord Chesilworth's
own pockets were so well-lined by his 'patriotism'?"

Cassandra regarded him with irritation. "I fail to understand why an Englishman should have so much sympathy for a country that tried to invade his own."

Neville shrugged. "I have no particular love for Spain,
Miss Verrere. However, I do believe in telling the truth,

rather than masking ordinary, everyday greed with a patina of 'God, queen, and country.'"

She looked at him for a long moment. "Frankly, Sir Philip, I think it is more that you simply enjoy being difficult."

Her words startled a chuckle from him. "Perhaps you are right." He paused, then added, "It doesn't matter, anyway. There is no dowry. It is only a legend."

"A legend! Of course it's not a legend. The Spanish dowry was real. Why else would your Neville ancestor have pursued the matter so assiduously in and out of court? Why did he keep insisting that the dowry by rights belonged to him, if there was not really a dowry?"

"Oh, I grant you that Chesilworth had some jewels and things that his grandfather took from Spanish ships, but the size and value of it has been greatly increased by the years and distance from the actual thing. Who is to say that the dowry was that valuable, and who is to say that Chesilworth even really sent the dowry with his daughter? It could have been an elaborate ruse to defraud Sir Edric."

"Oh, poppycock!" Cassandra said bluntly, color flaring in her cheeks. "I have read the list recorded in the Verrere estate books when they loaded the trunk into Margaret's baggage train. Unset emeralds and rubies from South America, gold coins, gold jewelry, emerald earrings—and, the pièce de résistance, the most beautiful and precious piece of treasure—a 'solid gold leopard of cunning workmanship with eyes of emeralds and a collar of rubies.'"

Cassandra's eyes glistened as she thought of the stunning beauty of the statue. "It was a work of art, as well as being of great monetary value. It was the crown jewel of Colin Verrere's Spanish collection."

"*If* the treasure was actually loaded into the baggage train and sent to Haverly House with Margaret Verrere,"

Sir Philip said firmly, "then Black Maggie took the dowry with her when she ran away. Sir Edric obviously did not have it, or he would not have pursued Chesilworth so about it, and Chesilworth claimed that he did not have it. So either Chesilworth was lying, and she left it with him all along, or Black Maggie took it with her to help set up herself and her lover in the colonies."

"Would you stop calling her that? Margaret Verrere was not a thief, and she did not take the Spanish treasure with her. She left it behind at the Neville estate when she eloped."

Sir Philip gave her an odd look. "You speak as if you knew the woman. She has been dead for at least a hundred and fifty years."

"One hundred and fifty-five, to be exact," Cassandra corrected him. "But I do feel as if I know her. You see, I have been reading her diaries."

There was a moment of stunned silence. Sir Philip stared at her.

"This tale grows more fantastic by the moment," he said at last. "Miss Verrere, if that really is your name, I am beginning to get the feeling that someone has set me up for an elaborate jest."

"Really, Sir Philip." Cassandra looked at him with aggravation, the same look she bent on her brothers when they had been misbehaving and which generally had the effect of making them suddenly stand straighter. Unfortunately, it seemed to have little effect on Philip Neville. "You are the most suspicious human being I have ever had the misfortune to meet. First you don't believe that a dowry, which is recorded in ledgers and which one of your own ancestors pursued with great diligence all his life, ever really existed. Then you don't believe that it was actually delivered to the Neville estate. Now you are saying that you do not believe that I am who I say I am. I don't understand. Are you this suspicious by nature, or have you met so many liars and cheats that you are a sadly disillusioned man?''

Neville grimaced. ''I am suspicious of your story, my dear lady, because it is a highly unbelievable tale. As for the so-called Spanish dowry, I am simply saying that it happened so long ago, and so many stories have been spread about it, that we really have no way of telling what is the truth.''

''But we do. That is what I am trying to tell you, if you would only pay attention. I am in possession of Margaret Verrere's diaries.''

''How did you come to acquire these diaries?'' Neville settled his hands, crossed in his lap, the expression on his face that of one who is preparing to hear a long and entertaining story.

''From Mr. Simons. Perryman Simons—he is a book dealer in London. He sold the diaries to my father. Probably you were not aware of it, but my father, the late Lord Chesilworth, was intensely interested in the stories of the Spanish dowry all his life.''

''I had heard it was a…a continuing passion with him.''

''From the studiously impassive expression on your face, I assume that you heard he was obsessed on the subject. *Cracked,* I believe is the common vernacular.'' She shrugged. ''Pray do not bother to spare my feelings. I am not a woman of high sensibility. Besides, I have heard it all before, and probably worse. But whatever people might have said about my father, he was an intelligent man, a scholar. He based his reasonings on sound facts, not wishful thinking. Of course, he also had access to the family records and the stories that had been handed down from generation to generation. He knew that Margaret Verrere was not the sort of woman to take the dowry with her. The Verreres have always prided themselves on their honor, you see.''

"A thing that Margaret seems to have forgotten when she broke her marriage contract and left Sir Edric standing at the altar.''

"She was in love with another!" Cassandra flared. "She had every right to marry the man she loved instead of being forced into a loveless marriage simply for the sake of family alliances. Sir Edric may have been wealthy and powerful, but everyone knows how the Nevilles acquired their money and influence—they have a history of ruthless, insensitive, predatory behavior, and doubtless Sir Edric was like all the rest of them.''

"Yes, a far cry from looting Spanish shipping, as the first Lord Chesilworth did," Neville countered sardonically.

"Colin Verrere was a man of action, true." Cassandra drew herself up as straight and tall as she could, glaring at the man sitting on the opposite end of the bench. "But he was also the Queen's man, fighting the Queen's enemy. It was a code of loyalty and honor he followed. The Verreres, at least, have never been powermongers, doing whatever it took to acquire land and money, with no regard for anyone else. They did not amass a fortune in land during the Middle Ages by waging war on everyone whose land they coveted. They did not dwell at court, currying every favor they could from the king.''

"You are implying that the Nevilles did?" Sir Philip sprang to his feet, his eyes suddenly flaming with a hot, gold light. "That they made their money off the sorrows of others, from dishonorable conflicts? From gifts from kings? The Nevilles have always been shrewd. But they did not act without honor, and it was more often *they* whom the king asked for money than the other way around. They were good warriors, that is true, and I am proud of that fact. But they did not fight without just cause. They invested their money where it would bring them more and did not fritter it away on dubious works of art or fantastic parties or architectural conceits.'' He looked pointedly at Cassandra. ''The Verreres are dreamers—feckless and generally incapable of making an intelligent business decision.''

''As if that were all that was important in life!'' Cassandra retorted, her eyes flashing. ''Yes, the Verreres *were* dreamers. Still are dreamers. There is nothing wrong with dreaming. It is dreamers who build empires and create masterpieces. Verreres are scholars, and they are interested in things of beauty more than in the price of tea or tobacco.''

''Ah, but the prices of tea and tobacco are useful things to know if one wants to continue to be able to spend one's money on beautiful things.''

Cassandra's cheeks colored. *Obviously he knew about her family's straitened financial circumstances.* No doubt her father's poor investments in various marvelous inventions and enterprises had been the gossip of the town. ''No doubt you are right,'' she said in a tight voice. ''But scholarly enthusiasm and business acumen do not seem to run together.''

Neville sighed, his anger slipping away. His irritation with Cassandra had led him to say something far blunter than was polite. Of course he knew about poor old Chesilworth's idiotic business schemes and their failures, but he would not normally have been so boorish as to shove that knowledge in the man's daughter's face.

''Forgive me,'' he said quickly. ''I did not mean—''

Cassandra sighed. ''Of course you did.'' She looked

Philip in the eye. "I know my father was not good with money. Neither was my grandfather. It is obvious, after what has happened to the Verreres over the years. You are right. A love of beauty and scholarship do not bring in money. But still..." she squared her shoulders proudly "...I would never have wished for my father to be any other way. He was a fine man, and I loved him very much."

"He was a fortunate man to have a daughter such as yourself."

Cassandra smiled faintly. "I hope he thought so."

"I am sure he did. Everyone knows that Chesilworth was a family man."

"Yes. He did love us." Cassandra swallowed, blinking away the sudden tears that threatened at the thought of her father. "I'm sorry. I am afraid that I still miss him very much."

Sir Philip moved uncomfortably. "Forgive me. I—"

Cassandra shook her head, smiling. "No. It is I who must apologize, for straying from the subject. We were discussing the journals."

"Ah, yes, the journals." The faintly sardonic look returned to Sir Philip's face, but he took his seat beside her on the bench again. "Of course."

"They are the journals which Margaret Verrere kept all her life after she ran away to America. There were seven of them in all, and Mr. Simons sold them to my father not long before...before his death." Cassandra did not see fit to add that her father had spent more money than they could afford in order to acquire the journals, leaving them in even worse financial shape when he died. Cassandra had perfectly understood his reasons for doing so. "Unfortunately, Papa did not get to read a great deal of the journals before he was taken ill. His lungs were always weak, I'm afraid. After—well, afterward, I read the journals." She squared her shoulders, seeming to thrust sorrow behind her, and leaned forward eagerly. "In them, Margaret said that she left the dowry at the Neville estate. Not only that, she left instructions on how to get it. If we work together, you and I can find the Spanish dowry."

3

Cassandra gave a triumphant smile and leaned back, waiting expectantly.

Sir Philip gazed back at her shining eyes, and after a long moment, he said carefully, "Miss Verrere, don't you find it a trifle...convenient, shall we say, that these lifelong journals of a woman who lived in the colonies should now turn up here in England?"

Cassandra sighed. "I was afraid that working with a Neville would be like this. Have you no adventurous spirit? No interest in a treasure hidden for generations?"

"I have no interest in fairy tales," he retorted flatly. "Really, Miss Verrere...surely you can see that this is a hoax. The journals—after all these years—happen to turn up in England, even though they've been in the United States all this time. *And* they happen to fall into the hands of Mr. Simons, who happens to be your father's favorite book dealer. I am sorry, but you are asking me to suspend disbelief a trifle too much."

Cassandra took a firm grip on her temper, reminding herself that she had known what it would be like to try to convince a Neville of her plan. She had hoped that Sir Philip would be less stodgy than his father, Sir Thomas, had been reputed to be. Cassandra's father had, by turn, characterized that man as a "dull dog" and a "cold fish." Certainly Sir Philip's entrance into her room last night had been anything but dull, and she had hoped that it had indicated a more adventurous character, but it was clear to her now that his was a typically Neville mind.

Pleasantly, she explained, "I don't find it at all odd. Mr. Simons said that an American, a descendant of Margaret Verrere's, had brought the journals to him. The man is a merchant who sometimes sails to England on business, and when he decided to sell the journals, which had been kept in his family all this time, he thought that since Margaret was from England, the books would fetch a better price here than in America. Americans, I believe, haven't as much respect for old things."

"Mm. No doubt they haven't the imagination or the adventurous spirit for treasure hunting, either."

Cassandra frowned repressively and went on. "Mr. Simons was not the only book dealer this man went to. He tried several. But Simons, you see, was more interested than the others simply because he *was* Papa's book dealer. He knew that Papa would want to buy the journals, given his interest in Margaret and the dowry. So Mr. Simons was willing to buy the journals when other dealers were not."

"Miss Verrere, I think it is much more likely that this Simons fellow or some crony of his made the journals himself, knowing that he would be able to sell them to your father."

"Sir Philip!" Cassandra looked shocked. "Perryman Simons is a reputable London book dealer. My father traded with him many times in the past. Mr. Simons would not have tried to sell him a forgery! And even if he had, why would he put in all those things about the dowry? That makes him no money."

"No? Tales of a hidden treasure doubtless made the journals easier to sell. I'll warrant that he charged your father a hefty sum."

"It *was* rather large," Cassandra admitted reluctantly. "But these are historical documents of great significance to my family. Papa would have bought the journals even if there had been no reference to the dowry."

"The dealer could not be sure of that. Miss Verrere, I am afraid that your father and you were the victims of an unscrupulous hoax."

Cassandra's mouth twisted in exasperation. "I hate to think what must have happened in your life for you to have become such a cynic."

"Think back to last night, and you will know one of those things."

Cassandra thought about her aunt's and cousin's trick to force Neville into marrying Joanna. "Oh."

"I have simply seen more of the world than you, Miss Verrere. I fear you are too trusting, and probably your father was, as well. Scholars often are, especially where their special fields of interest are concerned."

"My father did not have such a highly developed mistrust of people as you," Cassandra admitted. "But he knew Mr. Simons. He had dealt with him for years."

"I am not wedded to the theory that Simons forged the journals. He could have been an unwitting victim, also. Perhaps the man who sold them to him was the real culprit."

"That would mean that this forger was so good at his work that he was able to deceive both my father, a lover of antique books, and Mr. Simons, one of the country's best dealers. Neither of them voiced any suspicion that the journals were anything but genuinely old—the paper, the ink, the bindings. Unless, of course, you are suggesting that the journals were forged a hundred and fifty years ago or more, so that some day one of their descendants could palm off this forgery on my father?''

''No. Of course not.''

''My father knew a great deal about books. Perhaps he was naive, but he was not stupid. He would have known if the journals had been written in the last few months. He would have noticed if the paper was not old or the ink not faded. Whoever forged the diaries would have had to work very hard to make the books look authentically old enough to fool Papa. I cannot imagine that it would have been worthwhile to do all that for the price Papa paid—let alone all the hours it would have taken making up and writing all the things that were in the journals. It would have been a mammoth task and would have taken a great deal of time. It is much more likely that these really are Margaret Verrere's diaries.''

''I find it hard to believe that a woman writing in her journals would have laid out instructions on how to find a treasure. A journal is something one writes to oneself, and *she* knew were the treasure was.''

''She did not write out instructions, as you say. Her remarks about the dowry were spread throughout the book, and they were small, often indirect, things. You see, in the first journal, which she started soon after they arrived in America, she now and again would mention how worried she was because she had heard nothing from her father. She had mailed him a letter, and she had not heard anything back from him to indicate that he had received it. At one point she says something about the letter having the secret to the dowry. That was why she had sent it to him.''

''Then I would think it obvious that Chesilworth got the letter, followed her instructions and found the dowry. He just never bothered to write and let her know he had it.

Probably still miffed over the fact that she had made his name synonymous with treachery.''

"Sir Philip, I am afraid that we are going to find it very difficult to work together if you continue to refer to what happened in that way. I should think that a modern man would be able to admit that a woman has the right to marry whom she pleases.''

"I have no quarrel with that, only the manner in which it was handled. Becoming betrothed, then scampering off the night before the wedding, is not what I would consider correct behavior.''

"Yes,'' Cassandra agreed dryly, '''tis far worse than breaking into young ladies' bedrooms at night and mauling them.''

"I did not maul you!'' Neville looked aggrieved. "And you know that was a mistake.''

"Then give poor Margaret Verrere allowance for making a mistake, too. You don't know what was involved or how afraid she was of her father and Sir Edric. I do. I read the remnants of that fear in her journal entries months later. She still was concerned that her father might track her down to the colonies and try to force her to go back. Perhaps it was not all neat and tidy and polite enough for you, but Margaret Verrere was only a seventeen-year-old girl at the time, desperate and alone. She did the only thing she could think of to do.''

Neville looked into Cassandra's face, animated with emotion for the long-dead girl, and he had to smile. Argumentative and stubborn she might be, but when her face was alight with enthusiasm, her gray eyes luminous, she was almost beautiful. No, something more than beautiful, he thought; she was intriguing…quite out of the ordinary. He thought about the taste of her mouth last night, and a shaft of pure desire speared through him. He wanted to taste her again, he realized—and this time alone in some quiet spot, where he could kiss her at his leisure. It occurred to him that they were in that perfect place, that perfect moment—except that the lady in question was obsessed with discussing lost treasure.

"All right," he agreed, tamping down his burgeoning desire. "I will grant you that Bla—Margaret Verrere was not an evil person, merely a confused and frightened young girl. And I will even, for the moment, accept her journals as genuine. How are we to find this dowry?"

"Well, from what I pieced together, apparently she hid the dowry somewhere on the Neville estate. Then she hid instructions on how to find it in the Neville house and also sent instructions to her father in a letter. Since she never heard from him, she sent him another letter with the same information, and finally, much later in her life, a third. She didn't receive a reply from him, but she was sure that one, at least, of the letters was bound to have reached him. She feared that he had not opened the letters because he was such a stubborn man and that, therefore, he would not have found the treasure."

"Perhaps my Neville ancestor found it," Sir Philip suggested. "Sir Edric or one of his descendants. You said she left instructions at Haverly House, as well."

"Wouldn't you know about it, then?" Cassandra argued. "I would think it would be part of your family lore."

"Probably." He shrugged. "But I have no idea what the man was like. He could have been a sneaky chap who never wanted to admit that he had discovered the treasure—afraid he might have to give it back to the Verreres, you know. He might have quietly sold the gems and so forth and pocketed the money."

"No doubt you know your relatives better than I," Cassandra responded dryly. "However, I doubt that he would

have been able to. Whatever Margaret left at Haverly
House was apparently not enough to lead one to the treasure.''

"But I thought you said—''

"Yes, I know. She did leave instructions, and she did
send them to her father, but she indicated quite clearly in
her journals that neither of the men would be able to find
the dowry alone. That was part of her purpose, you see,
in hiding the treasure. She wanted the two families to have
to work together to retrieve it. She felt very bad about the
rift that she knew her departure would create between the
Nevilles and the Verreres. She wanted to make it up to
them, to force them to cooperate. That was the other thing
that worried her, that even if her father opened her letter,
he might not be willing to work with Sir Edric and so
would never find the fortune.''

"So you need both what she left at Haverly House and
what she sent to her father in order to find the dowry?''
Neville couldn't keep from feeling a prickle of interest at
the mystery, even though he knew that the whole story
was in all likelihood made up.

"Yes. I think perhaps they are two halves of a map or
something. I'm not sure what. But she seemed certain that
one could not find the dowry box without both.''

"Intriguing.'' Neville rubbed his forefinger thoughtfully
against his lip. Cassandra watched, hiding the little smile
of triumph that threatened to break out. He turned to Cassandra. "Where in Haverly House is it located?''

"I'm not sure.''

His eyebrows soared. "I thought you said the journals
told you.''

"Only in a vague way. Apparently the instructions are
hidden in a book.''

"A book!'' he groaned. "Isn't that a trifle vague? There

must be thousands of books in the library. What if it's been thrown away over the years?"

Cassandra frowned. The thought had occurred to her, also. "I think she would have tried to put it in a valuable book, one that would not be thrown away."

"During the course of two hundred years?" he asked skeptically.

"Well, of course, she would not have expected it to take that long for someone to try to find it."

"And that's all you know? That it is hidden in some book?"

"She did not give a title," Cassandra answered carefully. Her ancestor had been more specific about the book, but she was not sure that she was ready to tell Sir Philip exactly what Margaret had written. He was, after all, a Neville, and she was not entirely sure that she could trust him not to go off hunting on his own.

"Aha." Neville apparently saw the flicker of distrust in her eyes, for he gave her a sardonic look as he crossed his arms. "So you know more than you are telling."

"You can hardly expect me to tell you everything when you have not agreed to help me yet," Cassandra said reasonably. "You haven't even admitted that the journals are real. I can assure you that I will be entirely open and forthright with you once we have started our project. I have no taste for sly dealings."

Sir Philip did not add *unlike your aunt and cousin,* but both of them were thinking it. He got up and began to pace, considering Cassandra's madcap scheme. "So you are suggesting that if I agree, we will go to Haverly House, and there we will search the house for this book that you're not exactly sure of in a location that you don't know. And if by some miracle we should find it, then I am to help you find the treasure on my land and give it to you?"

"Half," Cassandra corrected. "I thought it would be fair to split it."

"My dear Miss Verrere, it would seem to me that the entire dowry should be mine," he said, his golden eyes alight with amusement. "It is my land, after all, my house where you hope to find both the instructions and the treasure—which, I might point out, belonged to the Nevilles anyway."

"Nonsense." Cassandra bounced to her feet, hands clenched at her sides and color flying high in her cheeks. "Sir Edric never won the rights to the dowry, and you know it. There was no marriage. The treasure belonged to Chesilworth by rights." She noticed then the laughter in his eyes and realized that Sir Philip was teasing her. She went on with an air of unconcern, "Besides, as I said, the instructions or map or whatever it is at your home is not enough. And I am the one who possesses the other half."

He stiffened and stared at her in amazement. "Are you serious? You found one of these letters your ancestor wrote?"

"Well…not yet."

The surprise dropped from his face and he grimaced. "I see."

"But I will get it," Cassandra insisted. "I would have waited to tell you until I had found the letter, but this opportunity to meet you dropped into my lap, and I had to take advantage of it. I didn't know if I would ever have such a chance to talk to you again. I hardly move in Society, you see. But I am already working on the problem. I have been searching the Chesilworth attics for some weeks now. They are chock-full of old trunks with clothes and papers and, oh, all sorts of things. We are back to the time of the Prince Regent now, and there is plenty of attic left. I am sure we will be able to find it."

"Indeed? And who are 'we'? Is there some third party involved in this harebrained scheme?"

"My brothers and sister and I. They are helping me look. It is for them that I really want to find the dowry. Even half of the fortune would be worth a great deal to-day—imagine those large, uncut gems and the old coins, the golden leopard! I am sure it would be enough money to put Chesilworth back into shape, and then we would be able to stop living on the charity of my aunt. Crispin would inherit a house that is at least worth something. Maybe there would even be enough to help Hart start some sort of career when he is grown, and to give Olivia a proper season."

"You have great plans, I see, for this fortune you have not found yet."

Cassandra looked at him a little defiantly. "You, no doubt disapprove. Verrere dreams again."

"You have an odd picture of me, Miss Verrere, one that I think I have done little to deserve. I have nothing against dreams. I am simply afraid that you will be sadly disappointed when yours do not come true."

"Should that happen, I will have to deal with my disappointment. But, you see, I don't believe that I am going to be disappointed. I am sure I will find the letters."

Neville sighed, looking down at her. He found himself, quite badly, wanting to help her—but the whole idea was too absurd. "Miss Verrere, doesn't this whole thing seem a trifle melodramatic? I mean, star-crossed lovers, feuding families, buried treasure, long-hidden maps…"

"Yes, it does." Cassandra did not seem disturbed by the fact. Her eyes shone as she talked. "Isn't it wonderful?"

He paused, nonplussed. "What I mean is, it seems too

dramatic to be real, too much like a story. It sounds as if someone made it up.''

"But we know that most of it is true," Cassandra protested. "Margaret did elope with another man on the eve of her wedding. She did have a fabulous dowry, which disappeared at that time and which no one has ever found. The two families have disliked each other ever since. The only things that have been added are the journals and the possibility of finding the treasure.''

"It is precisely that which strains credulity. Miss Verrere, I know you think I am a frightfully dull sort, but I have found that the simplest answers are usually the correct ones. Margaret Verrere did not hide the dowry and leave clues lying about for others to find it. She didn't write journals that coincidentally wound up in Verrere hands two hundred years later. The answer is that she took the dowry and used it to start a new life in the colonies. All these recent developments are merely a scheme to sell a few books at a greatly inflated price to a man who was well-known to be obsessed on the subject.'' He stopped, realizing that once again he had let his tongue run away with him and had stated the facts too baldly.

"Then you refuse to help me." Cassandra's face fell, and she stepped back. She had pinned all her hopes on this man, and he had turned her down. She was flooded with disappointment. "I am sorry that I wasted your time," she said stiffly and started to turn away from him.

Sir Philip reached out and grasped her arm, holding her back. "No, wait. Don't go yet."

Cassandra turned, fighting back the tears that threatened. She refused to let Sir Philip see how his refusal had hurt her. She lifted her eyebrows in silent inquiry, striving to look cool and disinterested.

"Miss Verrere, 'tis only the authenticity of these journals that I question. The coincidence of them falling into your hands after all these years is simply too much for me to accept.''

''I *explained* that to you. It isn't coincidence—it is a logical progression.'' She felt a tiny spurt of hope rise up in her again at his attempt to explain. ''Don't you see?''

''No, I don't,'' he said softly. ''I see a very lovely young woman whom a scoundrel has probably taken advantage of. A woman still sorrowing over her father's death, hopeful that his dream might become a reality.''

''Oh!'' Cassandra's gray eyes flashed. ''I am not some silly little girl who can't spot a deception that's right in front of her. My father was not a fool, and neither am I! Those journals are real, but you are simply too prosaic to see it.'' She tried in vain to jerk her arm away. ''I should have known that a Neville would find the whole thing too quixotic. Too romantic.''

''Miss Verrere, I assure you that I do not think you are a silly little girl. Indeed, I think you are a very intelligent, as well as beautiful, woman. I admire you greatly.'' He paused, smiling faintly. ''Nor am I unromantic.'' He leaned closer, looking down intently into her eyes. ''Indeed, I am having thoughts of quite a romantic nature at this very moment.''

Cassandra swallowed, unable to look away from his piercing golden brown gaze. Her throat was dry, and it seemed suddenly difficult to breathe. She tried to speak, but found she could not.

Philip slid his hand up her arm and around her back, pulling her gently and completely against him. ''Your story is the only thing I do not find appealing about you.''

''S-sir Philip...'' Cassandra managed to stammer, washed with a weakness and confusion that were foreign to her.

He bent and brushed his lips against hers lightly, then more forcefully. Cassandra could feel the pulse suddenly pounding in her head, and her breath caught in her throat. The memories of her lascivious dream of the night before came flooding back, turning her knees weak and melting her loins. She sagged against him. His arms went more tightly around her, pressing her up into his hard body, and his lips sank into hers.

For one long moment she gave herself up to the pleasure, not thinking of her disappointment, her plans, or anything, just feeling the liquid fire that sizzled through her veins.

"Cassandra..." he murmured, releasing her mouth long enough to trace her jawline with kisses.

Somehow the sound of his voice saying her name brought Cassandra back to reality. Through the haze of delightful physical sensation, she recalled where they were and how improper their conduct was—not to mention the fact that he had just dismissed her search for the Spanish dowry as a fraud and characterized her as a naive woman grasping for straws to relieve her sorrow over her father's death.

Cassandra jerked back and slapped his face. Neville's jaw tightened, and for a moment anger flared in his eyes, but then the usual cool, polite mask descended, hiding both the anger and the passion.

"I beg your pardon," he began stiffly.

But Cassandra cut in on him, in no mood for polite apologies. "I should have known! It is so typical that it is almost laughable. You have no interest in anything I said. All you care about is trying to steal a kiss while we are secluded in the maze. No wonder you were so willing to listen to what I had to say. You knew that it would give you an excuse to get me alone and try to seduce me. I should have known that any man who spends his nights sneaking into young women's bedchambers would only be interested in taking advantage of a woman. I suppose I am naive, as you said—not because I believe Margaret Verrere's journals are genuine, but because I did not realize that the only thing you were interested in is lust! Oh, I knew that a Neville would be difficult to persuade, but I did not realize that an even worse problem would be having to deal with a libertine!''

"I did not try to *lure* you out here," Neville protested, his own brows drawing together furiously. It occurred to him that Cassandra Verrere could be quite as annoying as she was attractive. "It was you who asked to speak to me, if you will remember, and it was also you who suggested that we talk privately in the maze."

"Oh! So you are going to use that against me! I merely wanted to be able to speak in private. I did not mean it as an invitation to kiss me!"

"No," he responded bitingly, "'twas your lips that provided that."

Cassandra gasped. "You are insulting."

"Only truthful. If you will think back on it, you returned my kiss quite willingly, at least until you remembered that you were supposed to react with maidenly outrage." Neville found it supremely annoying that even while he was irritated with Cassandra, his wayward body was still thrumming with desire for her. *Damn it! She had a most peculiar effect on him.*

Cassandra ground her teeth, letting out a low and most unladylike growl of frustration. "Blast you!" she snapped, her mild father's favorite oath, and wished she knew something worse to say. "I was a fool to think that a Neville would help me. I wish I had never talked to you. I wish I had never even *seen* you!"

With those bitter words, she whirled and ran away from him.

"Wait! No, Miss Verrere..."

Neville started after her, but Cassandra had a good head start, and she knew the map of the maze, so she quite easily made her way out ahead of him. Once or twice she heard him calling her name behind her, but she paid no attention. She burst out onto the smooth expanse of the lawn and stopped. Her aunt and cousin were walking along the path leading from the garden to the wide lawn. They looked at her in surprise, her aunt's eyebrows rising in disdain. Cassandra smoothed down her skirts and walked toward them at her usual brisk pace, hoping that her face would not give away her inner turmoil.

"Really, Cassandra, must you hurry about so?" Aunt Ardis complained as she drew near them. "You always are in such a rush. It is most ungenteel."

"I am sorry, Aunt," Cassandra responded automatically. "Good morning to you both."

She started to pass them, heading back toward the house, but at that moment, Sir Philip burst from the maze entrance, saying, "Damn it, Miss Verrere!"

Both Joanna and Aunt Ardis turned toward him, promptly forgetting all about their inelegant relative. Aunt Ardis's face underwent a miraculous change, becoming suddenly gracious and welcoming. Beside her, Joanna dimpled and smiled and began to fan herself coyly.

"Why, Sir Philip!" Aunt Ardis exclaimed warmly. "What a pleasant surprise to come upon you."

"Hardly an unlikely event," Sir Philip replied dryly, "since we are both staying here."

Joanna tittered as if he had said something unbearably amusing. Sir Philip turned toward her. "Miss Moulton." He gave her a sardonic look and continued, "I trust that you are feeling better this morning after your nightmare last night.''

Joanna's mouth dropped open, and she glanced from him to her mother and back. Aunt Ardis was of no help, appearing equally astounded. Sir Philip looked toward Cassandra. She met his eyes with a stony gaze, folding her arms across her chest. Sir Philip started to speak, then stopped. He nodded toward them in a general way.

"Good day, ladies.'' He turned and walked briskly away from them.

For a long moment Joanna and Aunt Ardis stared at his retreating form in stupefaction. Finally Joanna exclaimed, "He knew! Mama, he knew!"

"Nonsense. Just hush.'' Her mother frowned at Joanna and cast a significant glance toward Cassandra.

"Oh.''

"Please, don't bother trying to hide anything on *my* account,'' Cassandra told them. "I am quite aware of your scheme to entrap Sir Philip.'' She paused and added pointedly, "Obviously he is, too.''

"You told him!'' Joanna cried indignantly.

"Joanna!'' Aunt Ardis interrupted sharply.

"Well, she knows anyway.'' Joanna pouted. "She's probably been sneaking about listening at keyholes.''

"It is hardly necessary,'' Cassandra replied coolly. "Anyone who heard your mother banging on your door and shrieking last night would have had a fair idea what you two were up to. And given the way you were throwing yourself at Sir Philip yesterday afternoon, it was not hard to guess who you were trying to entrap.''

Mrs. Moulton let out a moan of mortification, but Joanna started toward her cousin furiously, shrieking, "Why, you jealous cat!''

Aunt Ardis had the sense to grab Joanna's wrist and

hold her back. "Joanna! Stop it! Right now. I will not have you creating a scene at Lady Arrabeck's house party. Things are bad enough already." She glanced around the lawn anxiously, as if she expected the other houseguests to be gathering around and whispering about her. "Do you really think they all believe that we—that Joanna—"

Seeing her aunt's look of humiliation, Cassandra almost took pity on her. However, she was in no mood to linger here, and she knew that if Aunt Ardis didn't fear the scorn of the other guests, she would remain at the country estate as long as she could, searching for another prey for her daughter or perhaps even convincing herself that Sir Philip was still interested in Joanna himself. Joanna was, as even Cassandra was forced to admit, an exceptionally handsome woman, and Aunt Ardis was of the opinion that every man swooned before Joanna's beauty. She never considered that anyone might be repelled by Joanna's shallow, selfish nature or her silly conversation. It would not take Aunt Ardis long before she began to tell herself that if only Sir Philip continued to see Joanna, he would fall in love with her despite the trick Joanna had tried to play on him.

So Cassandra said flatly, "I am sure that they found it quite as peculiar as I that you were shouting outside Joanna's room last night. It didn't help that Joanna opened the door and told you that 'he' was not there."

"You see?" Aunt Ardis exclaimed, rounding on her daughter. "I told you that you should not have said that. Anyone could have heard you. Why didn't you think?"

"I suspect that Sir Philip must have heard her, too," Cassandra added, hardening her heart to her aunt's piteous look. "He was probably coming down the hall when you enacted your tragedy in Joanna's doorway. No doubt he heard it all, and since he alone would have known for certain that it was *he* whom Joanna had invited to her room, he would have realized instantly what was going on.''

''I didn't invite him,'' Joanna protested, not very convincingly.

Cassandra did not reply. She merely cast her a look of patent disbelief that made Joanna screw up her face unattractively.

''Well, you needn't think he is interested in you,'' she huffed at Cassandra, ''just because you managed to get him to walk with you in the maze. He would never have any interest in such a bookworm.''

''No doubt you are right,'' Cassandra replied calmly. ''As it happens, we met by accident in the maze. He seemed unable to find his way out, and I had to tell him.''

Joanna sent her a smug gaze. ''You know nothing about men, Cassandra. No man likes to be told what to do.''

''How unfortunate, since so many of them seem in dire need of it.''

''Girls, please!'' Aunt Ardis snapped, drawing attention back to the truly important issue—her own discomfiture. ''This is not helping at all. We need to think what to do. I cannot bear to remain here with everyone staring at us and thinking that we—that you—''

''Engineered an incriminating rendezvous with Sir Philip Neville?'' Cassandra suggested crisply.

''Really, Cassandra, you have a most unladylike bluntness. It is very unappealing.''

''I'm sorry, Aunt Ardis,'' Cassandra said with a noticeable lack of regret. ''I am sure it must be a very trying situation for you. Perhaps we should leave.''

Aunt Ardis looked a little surprised, but a moment's consideration had her nodding. ''Yes, that's the thing. We shall go back to Dunsleigh, and soon everyone will have

forgotten this.'' She frowned. ''But what shall I say to
Lady Arrabeck? I must not offend her.''

''Blame it on me,'' Cassandra said cheerfully, knowing
that was the plan most likely to please her aunt. ''Say that
I have been taken ill. I will go straight back to my room
now, saying I feel poorly. This afternoon you can tell Lady
Arrabeck how wretched I am and that I insist on returning
home. Tell her you worry about me. Tell her I'm frail or
something.''

''You are as healthy as a horse,'' Joanna objected con-
temptuously.

''Lady Arrabeck doesn't know that.''

''You don't look sick. You look positively robust.''

''I shall do my best to look wan. Unless, of course, *you*
would rather act the invalid.''

Joanna considered the matter, thinking of the appealing
picture she would make, pale and fragile, leaning on her
cousin for support as she made her weak way out to the
carriage. Or she might even have to be carried out by one
of the footmen—that handsome one she had seen in the
hall yesterday, perhaps. Her lips curved up in a smile.
''Yes, I think that would be best. It would be much more
natural for Mama to be concerned about her daughter, anyway. Here, Cassandra, give me your arm.''

She put her hand through Cassandra's arm and drooped
against her. Cassandra stifled a sigh of irritation at her
cousin's dramatics, reminding herself that she would do
almost anything to get out of this place and away from the
odious Neville. She started slowly back toward the house
with Joanna. She refused to think about the way that Sir
Philip had ruined all her plans. All was not lost. She would
go home and continue her search for those letters, and
then...and then somehow she would figure out a way to
find the Spanish dowry on her own.

4

Joanna entered into her deception with such enthusiasm, applying white powder to her face for an interesting wanness and lying in her darkened room emitting effective groans and sighs, that it was all Cassandra could do not to slap her. Naturally, with Joanna "weak" in her bed, it fell to Cassandra to pack for both of them. She wondered darkly if her lazy cousin had taken that fact into consideration before she offered to play sick. It was the middle of the afternoon before Cassandra managed to get everything together and stowed away in their carriage, interrupted as she was by her aunt's often contradictory orders.

However, finally Joanna, wrapped in a blanket, was carried down the stairs and out to the carriage by a burly, graying footman and carefully bestowed within, and Cassandra and her aunt climbed in after her. Lady Arrabeck's daughter came out to graciously bid them farewell, and a few moments later they were wheeling at a smart pace down the drive and through the open iron gates of the estate.

"Whew!" Joanna pushed the carriage rug from her lap. "Get this thing off me. I'm sweating like a pig."

Cassandra noted that perspiration was, indeed, making

little rivulets through her cousin's white powder. However, she said pacifically, "You put on a wonderful performance, Cousin."

Joanna scowled. "Why did that awful old footman have to carry me down?" She was thoroughly disenchanted with the whole charade. "And no one was there to see us leave."

"Lady Patricia," her mother reminded her. "It was a very nice gesture, I thought."

Joanna snorted. "She's only the spinster daughter."

"And so will you turn out to be, if you make many more mistakes like yesterday's!" Aunt Ardis snapped.

"I! I made the mistake?" Joanna turned on her mother wrathfully. "It was you who came pounding on my door too early! You couldn't wait, and it chased him away!"

"I came when we had agreed I would! He didn't arrive on time, that's what happened."

"And that is my fault?"

"Yes. He wasn't eager. You didn't enchant him. He should have hurried to your room, and instead he dawdled."

"I did everything I could think of! I smiled and flirted and pretended I was interested in those silly old writers he kept talking about, when I had never heard of them. I even left the lace fichu out of my afternoon dress."

"Yes, and leaned over to pick up your fan several times," Cassandra put in dryly. "I noticed that."

"You see. Even Cassandra saw what an effort I made," Joanna said, oblivious to her cousin's sarcastic tone. "The man was stone. I finally had to kiss him in the conservatory before he became at all amorous."

"You were too fast and loose," Aunt Ardis decided. "You made him suspicious. That is why he was lurking around, listening."

Cassandra sighed and turned her face to look out the window, trying to ignore the bickering between her aunt and cousin and think about what she was going to do now. Despite her brave thoughts earlier, she was close to despair over Sir Philip's rejection of her proposal. She had had such high hopes for him, had built all her schemes around his agreeing. She had been prepared for him to be difficult to deal with—he was, after all, a Neville—but she had counted on the Neville taste for accruing money to make him see the sense of their cooperating to find the dowry. It had never entered her mind that he would reject the story altogether, that he would term it a fabrication and dismiss her as a naive fool. And never in her wildest dreams would she have foreseen that he would be more interested in kissing her than in finding a treasure!

Her cheeks warmed a little even now at the thought of his mouth on hers. She had never dreamed that such kisses existed, let alone that she could turn to hot wax inside because a man did such unthinkable, immodest things to her.

Sternly she pulled her mind away from such thoughts. She ought to be working on a way to get the Spanish dowry without his help, not mooning around about him. Cassandra felt uncharacteristically like crying. Normally she was a very equable person; she liked to think of herself as calm, decisive and strong. But the thought of not being able to recapture the treasure that the Verreres had lost so long ago was almost too much for her. From the moment she had started reading Margaret Verrere's diaries, she had realized that the dowry was the way out of her family's problems. She had been counting on it to take her brothers and sister and herself out of her aunt's house.

She had seen in Sir Philip's eyes that he knew of the decline of the Verrere fortunes, but she doubted that he knew the full extent of it. Their father had died virtually penniless. She had had to sell off much of the furniture in the house to pay off his debts. She had even, heart breaking inside her chest, had to sell many of his precious books. Worst of all, she and her siblings had had to move out of Chesilworth, their ancestral home. It was a noble hall, but very old, and the years had not been kind to it. Repairs had been neglected, not only by her father, but also by his father and his grandfather before that. The west wing had been closed off ever since she could remember, because they had no money for the extensive repairs needed there. Even in the central and east wings, there were several areas where the roof badly needed to be replaced. Air leaked in around windows; floorboards were loose or bowed; almost all of the draperies were moth-eaten. Only people who loved it as much as her family did would have remained there.

But after her father's death there was not enough money to pay even the skeleton crew of servants necessary to keep the great house running. Her family had had to leave Chesilworth and go to live with their aunt and uncle, only a few miles away in the village of Dunsleigh. The pain of leaving their home had been bad enough, but the humiliation of living on their aunt's charity was a constant thorn in Cassandra's side. Uncle Barlow, their mother's brother, was a pleasant man whom they all liked, but he was rarely at home, spending as much of his time as he could in the village or in London or off hunting with his cronies. Cassandra was sure it was his wife's shallow, venal nature that kept him away.

Aunt Ardis was a grasping woman who resented the presence of her husband's impecunious nieces and nephews almost as much as she enjoyed lording it over them. She had never liked her husband's sister, Delia, a vivacious butterfly of a woman who had outshone Ardis herself at every turn. Her aunt never ceased to complain about the extra expense and trouble Cassandra and her siblings entailed, just as she never hesitated to meddle in their affairs. She characterized Cassandra as a plain, mousy bluestocking of a girl, her sister Olivia as far too bold, and her brothers as young hellions badly in need of manners. She made sure that everyone, both inside and outside the home, was aware of the great sacrifice she had made in taking them in.

Joanna considered Cassandra's quiet plainness an excellent foil for her own beauty, and she did not mind her being there as long as her own comfort was not disturbed. Crispin and Hart, Cassandra's twelve-year-old brothers, however, were another matter. They were noisy, messy nuisances who teased her and disturbed her rest. But most of all she disliked Olivia, who at fourteen was already turning into a real beauty and a future threat to Joanna's dominance of the small social scene in which they moved.

More than anything else in the world, Cassandra wanted to get her family out of that household and return to Chesilworth. Her uncle was the boys' and Olivia's guardian, and she was sure that she could talk him into letting her raise them on her own if only she had a proper house in which to live and enough money to feed and clothe them. The Spanish dowry, she knew, would provide that money. The dowry represented freedom for all four of them—and now Sir Philip had carelessly trampled all over her hopes of attaining that freedom.

"—not that great a catch, anyway." Cassandra's mind came back from her gloomy thoughts at the sound of her aunt's voice mentioning Sir Philip Neville again. She looked at her aunt in some surprise.

"What do you mean? I thought you said he was one of

the best catches in England,'' she reminded her aunt innocently.

Aunt Ardis frowned, thinking that the girl had too good a memory. "Oh, he would be a feather in any girl's cap," she admitted. "But he doesn't have a title, you know. In that respect, even Lord Benbroke surpasses him.''

"Lord Benbroke is almost sixty years old and suffers from gout.''

"Yes, Mama," Joanna put in quickly. "Not Lord Benbroke. I just could not marry him.''

"I didn't mean that *you* should marry him, only that he had a title and Neville doesn't. And I am sure that there are those more wealthy than he.''

"I have heard that Richard Crettigan is quite the richest man in the country," Cassandra offered.

Aunt Ardis looked shocked. "Richard Crettigan is a…a merchant!''

"Yes, and from Yorkshire, too. Can you imagine listening to that accent all your life?" Joanna shook her head in dismay.

"But it must be comforting to know that at least there are other options for Joanna.'' Cassandra returned her aunt's and cousin's suspicious gazes blandly.

"I have heard," Aunt Ardis said loftily, ignoring Cassandra's comment, "that Sir Philip is a libertine.''

Cassandra's stomach tightened. "A libertine? Who said so?''

"I heard it from Daphne Wentworth, who told me it was common knowledge all over London. Of course, that whey-faced Teresa of hers had made no bones about setting her cap for him, and Daphne no doubt wanted no competition. Still, Mrs. Carruthers was sitting right there when she said so, and she agreed that he had a certain reputation.''

"A reputation for what?" Cassandra pressed. She wasn't sure why her aunt's words irritated her so, but she found herself wanting to deny them hotly.

Aunt Ardis lowered her voice conspiratorially and said, "For seduction."

"Oh, really, Aunt Ardis, how would they know?" But despite her words, Cassandra could not help thinking of Sir Philip's kisses and the way they had made her melt inside. She had to admit that he had seemed incredibly expert at what he was doing. Besides, there was the fact that he had made advances toward *her*. Cassandra did not fool herself that she was any great beauty. It followed then that Sir Philip must be interested in kissing any woman who happened to come across his path. She squirmed a little inside at the thought. "It is all rumors."

"It's more than rumors. I've heard things…" her aunt hinted darkly.

"What things?"

"The sort of things that young ladies like you and Joanna should not hear."

"Oh, Mama…" Joanna slumped back against her seat disgustedly. "You always say that."

Cassandra thought privately that as Joanna had set out to seduce Sir Philip into a compromising position in her bedroom, she was hardly an innocent creature whose ears should not be sullied, but she managed to keep from saying so. There was no point in getting into a wrangle with her aunt over something as unimportant as Sir Philip Neville and his reputation.

The truth was, she told herself sourly, that he was probably exactly the sort of creature that gossip had painted him. It was absurd that she should be standing up for the man who had dashed her hopes.

She turned her head to look out the window, and they continued the ride in silence.

Cassandra's head jerked up, and she blinked, looking around. She realized that she had been asleep, as were her aunt and cousin in the seat across from her. She pushed aside the window curtain and peered out. It had grown dark while she slept. Her stomach growled, giving her another reminder of how long they had been traveling.

She realized that what had awakened her must have been the carriage turning, for even in the pale moonlight she could recognize the narrow lane they traveled as the one branching off toward her aunt's house. They were almost home. Her spirits lifted in anticipation. Everything would seem better, she knew, when she was with her family.

The carriage pulled up in front of a Georgian mansion a moment later, and the front door opened. A footman hurried down to open the carriage door.

"Mrs. Moulton." He sketched a bow in the direction of Aunt Ardis and reached up to give her a hand down.

Aunt Ardis gave him a slight nod and swept on to the front door, Joanna trailing her. Cassandra came out of the carriage last, taking the footman's proffered hand and smiling. "Hello, John."

A smile broke the man's usually impassive countenance, and he said warmly, "Hello, miss. It's good to have you home."

"Thank you. How is your sister? Has she had the little one yet?"

"No, miss. We're all on pins and needles." Like most of the servants of Moulton Hall, John Sommers felt that the place had been much improved by the arrival of the Verrere family. Unlike his mistress and her daughter, the

Verrere children knew everyone's names and were always ready with a smile or a word of thanks. There had been many times when a vase broken by one of the running boys had been swept up and thrown away with never a mention made of it, and a secret supper had often been sent up to the nursery when Olivia or the twins were in disgrace about some misdeed or other.

"Cassie!" A pair of towheaded boys tore out the front door and bounded down the front steps two at a time, followed not much more sedately by a girl in blond braids.

Cassandra threw her arms wide and swept all of her siblings in. "Crispin! Hart—what happened to your hand? Olivia—oh, I think you've grown even prettier while I was away."

Olivia, whose braids and childishly shorter skirts could not hide the rapidly maturing body and face of a young woman, giggled at her sister's words. "Pooh—you haven't been gone but three days. What happened? Why are you home early?"

"Yeah!" Crispin added. "You should have seen Uncle Barlow's face when he heard John announce that the carriage was home. He looked like a hare that had heard the hounds."

Hart giggled. "He was looking all over like he thought there might be a hole he could bolt into."

"He's been home every night since Aunt Ardis left, and it's been ever so nice. He lets us eat dinner with him, and we talk about all sorts of things. It wasn't as good as being with Papa, but it reminded me of home, a little...." Olivia's voice trailed off wistfully.

Cassandra felt tears spring into her eyes. "I know, Olivia. I miss him, too."

"It was bang-up!" Hart, who had enjoyed his uncle's discussion of his hunting dogs far more than his father's scholarly ramblings, added, "He said he would take us hunting with him next time he went to Buckinghamshire, if Aunt Ardis will let him."

"Hah! Let us have fun? Not likely."

"Now, hush, Crispin. Aunt Ardis might be well pleased to have the two of you out of the house. I shall endeavor to point out the advantages in terms of dirt and noise of having two twelve-year-olds gone from here."

"Would you?" The twins' expressions brightened. In their experience, Cassandra was able to do anything she put her mind to. It had been she who had always made the household budget stretch to include entertaining outings or a pony to ride or a cricket bat to replace the broken one.

"Of course I will. I'm not promising, mind you...."

"I know." Crispin nodded gravely. A more serious boy than his twin, he realized better than Hart that Cassandra's ingenuity and intelligence were not always sufficient weapons against their aunt's power.

"Forget the silly hunting!" Olivia said impatiently. "Tell us what happened at the house party, Cassandra."

"Did you meet Sir Philip?" Hart stuck in eagerly. "Is he going to help us?"

"Just a minute. I shall tell you all about it later. Let's go in now and let me say hello to Uncle Barlow."

She did as she said, noticing with amusement that her poor uncle did indeed look like a trapped hare as he stood in the entryway listening to his wife's strictures on the excessive number of candles that had been lit throughout the house.

"Why, I could see from the carriage that the nursery was lit up like Christmas," Aunt Ardis was saying as the Verreres walked in. "There is no reason for that. The children ought to be in bed anyway."

"It didn't seem much light to me." Uncle Barlow tried

to defend himself. "There was Olivia trying to read by the light of one candle, and she mustn't strain those pretty eyes, you know." He smiled benignly at his niece, not realizing, even after years of living with Ardis, that he was saying exactly the wrong thing. "Those eyes will be her fortune."

"What nonsense! Olivia shouldn't be reading all those heathen books, anyway," Aunt Ardis sniffed, frowning toward her younger niece. "Olivia, straighten your skirts, you look like a hoyden. And your hair is all everywhere."

"Yes, Aunt Ardis," Olivia answered in a carefully colorless voice. Her high spirits had gotten her into trouble with her aunt more than once, but once she had realized how much her battles with Aunt Ardis caused Cassandra to suffer, she had learned to curb her ready tongue.

Cassandra gave her uncle a quick hug and a peck on the cheek, and whisked her brothers and sister upstairs to the bedroom shared by the two girls. The boys flopped down on the rug, and Olivia hopped onto the bed, curling her legs beneath her.

"All right," she told her older sister eagerly. "Now tell us all. Why did Aunt Ardis come home so early?"

"Who cares about that?" Crispin retorted scornfully. "I want to hear about Sir Philip and the treasure."

"Aunt Ardis and Joanna met with a little setback," Cassandra told her sister, eyes twinkling, and cast a significant look at her brothers. "I shall tell you about it later." She did not add that her younger sister would receive a carefully edited version of Joanna's escapade.

Olivia's eyes widened, but she made no demur as Cassandra started on the story that the brothers wanted to hear. "I am afraid the news is not good. Sir Philip refused to help us."

Crispin groaned, and Hart sneered. "I knew we couldn't

count on a Neville. Papa always said so. You shouldn't have asked him.''

"I don't know how else we're supposed to find it," Crispin reminded him. "The Nevilles have the rest of the clues or the map or whatever it is."

"We don't need it," Hart said stoutly. "Do we, Cassie? We can find it by ourselves."

"Of course we will." Cassandra plastered a heartening smile on her lips. "It will merely take us longer. I don't intend to give up."

"But how are you going to do it?" Olivia questioned. Though she had as much faith in her older sister as the twins did, she had a more practical bent of mind.

"The first thing is to find the old letters. I shall keep going over to Chesilworth every chance I get to search the attics. Once I actually have the letter in my hands, I can prove to Sir Philip that the treasure really was hidden and can be found. Then he will surely agree to help us look for it." It was the best plan that Cassandra had been able to come up with, and though it sounded rather flimsy to her ears, she hoped it would satisfy her siblings.

"You mean he didn't believe in the treasure?" Hart looked shocked at such heresy.

"No. He thought the diaries were something someone made up just to get Papa to buy them. He's a very stubborn, narrow-minded man. But once he sees the evidence with his own eyes, he will have to believe me."

"We shall help you look," Crispin told her gravely. Though he was as high-spirited as any lad his age, he was also aware that he was now Lord Chesilworth, and he took his responsibilities seriously. While Hart might look on the hunt for the dowry as a wonderful adventure, Crispin knew that it also meant the very future of Chesilworth.

"Of course," Olivia agreed. "Whenever that old battle-ax isn't looking, we'll sneak over."

"Olivia...manners," Cassandra reminded her absently. She smiled at her siblings, tears lurking at the corners of her eyes. "I knew I could count on you."

Olivia bounced off the bed to hug her, and even the boys followed suit. Cassandra hugged them tightly to her, promising herself that she would not let them down. Somehow, some way, she would find those letters, and she would make Sir Philip believe her.

Aunt Ardis did not approve of Cassandra and her siblings visiting their old home. In the time that Cassandra had been there, the older woman had become accustomed to Cassandra's taking from her shoulders many of the dreary tasks of running a household. As long as Cassandra stayed within her tight budget, Aunt Ardis was pleased to see the quality of their meals and the work of the servants improve. Though she told herself that of course she could have accomplished the same things had she spent the time and effort, she much preferred to spend her time on her toilette or gossiping with one of the two or three ladies in the area whom she considered of a social standing equal enough to hers.

As a result, it was most inconvenient when Cassandra took time off from her household duties to spend a whole day at Chesilworth. "I cannot imagine what you find to do there all day," she told her niece petulantly. "The place is falling into ruins."

Cassandra had carefully kept hidden from her aunt any hint of what they were really doing at Chesilworth. She wasn't sure how Aunt Ardis would feel about their hunting for treasure, but she was sure that the lady would at the very least dismiss the idea as nonsense and might even go so far as to forbid her nieces and nephews from going to Chesilworth. So she replied only, "I would like to stave off the ruin if I can. I clean up a little around the place, walk through it checking for leaks—things like that."

Her aunt looked at her as if she had taken leave of her senses. "I would think your time would be better spent here. This is your home now."

Cassandra curled her hands into her palms but forced her voice to remain even. "Of course, Aunt Ardis, but Chesilworth is still Crispin's inheritance. I must try to make sure that there is something left for him when he gets older. It would be too much to ask that you and Uncle Barlow continue to bear the burden of upkeep for all four of us, even when the boys are grown."

Aunt Ardis looked taken aback by this thought. "I—well—yes. I mean, if you must, I suppose you must. But this wanting to go every single day…"

"Only when you don't need me, of course, Aunt Ardis."

As it turned out, her aunt usually managed to find that she needed her three or four days a week, but the other times, Cassandra and her siblings hiked over to their old home and climbed up into the musty old attics, continuing their methodical exploration.

Cassandra did most of the work, for the boys, though eager, tended to become distracted by some odd object or other or fall into an argument over some prize they found, and Olivia, too, often grew tired and thirsty and decided to take a rest outside. Still, they did make progress, and as they worked, they found that they were moving into older and older periods of dress and furniture, which kept Cassandra's hopes up. While Olivia whooped over the elaborate tall wigs and wide, almost flat cages of hoops that had been worn under dresses in the 1700s, Cassandra continued doggedly to dig, thinking with determination that they were not that far away now.

She was particularly eager one morning to get over to the old mansion, but it seemed as if everything interfered with it. Her aunt wanted her to do first one thing, and then another until the morning was almost gone. Then there was a crisis belowstairs, which she was called upon to resolve. Finally, just as she was about to go upstairs and change into old clothes suitable for cleaning out the attics, the butler opened the door to the sitting room and announced that they had a visitor.

"Mr. David Miller, ma'am," he told Aunt Ardis in a frosty accent that usually indicated he did not entirely approve of the visitor, and handed her the man's card on a small salver.

"Who?" Aunt Ardis looked blank.

"An American, I believe, ma'am. He says—" his tone indicated his personal disbelief "—that he is related to Lord Chesilworth."

"Lord Ch—you mean Crispin?"

"Yes, ma'am."

Aunt Ardis and Joanna turned to stare at Cassandra, who shrugged, as puzzled as they. "I have never heard of him, Aunt Ardis."

"Well, hmm…I suppose we must see him, Soames."

As soon as Soames was out the door, Aunt Ardis turned toward Cassandra. "An imposter?" she suggested. "An American claiming to be a relative of yours?"

"I suppose someone in the Verrere family could have emigrated," Cassandra mused, frowning.

"No doubt he thinks that Chesilworth, just because he has a title, is a wealthy man. He's hoping to get money out of you, mark my words."

"He will be mightily disappointed, then," Cassandra remarked cheerfully.

A moment later Soames reentered the room, intoning, "Mr. David Miller."

A young man followed him into the room and paused, smiling tentatively at the three women who sat there. He was in his twenties, with sky blue eyes, a thick mop of blond hair and a rakish mustache, which Cassandra suspected he had cultivated to age his boyish countenance. He was dressed fashionably, but not glaringly so, and Cassandra judged him to be a respectably handsome man. Her opinion was confirmed by the sudden flare of interest in Joanna's eyes.

Mr. Miller bowed to them. "Please pardon my intrusion. I know I should have written to introduce myself, but when I found myself in London with unexpected time on my hands, I was seized by the urge to meet my British cousins. I hope you will not think me overly bold."

"Pray sit down. I am Miss Cassandra Verrere," Cassandra introduced herself. "My brother is Lord Chesilworth, but I am afraid he is still only a lad. This is my aunt, Mrs. Moulton, and her daughter, Miss Joanna Moulton."

The young man bowed over each of the ladies' hands politely before taking his seat. "It is the Verreres to whom I am related—quite distantly, of course," Mr. Miller explained eagerly. "One of my ancestors was a Verrere. She and her husband settled in Boston, oh, almost two hundred years ago."

"What?" Cassandra stared. "But what—what was your ancestress's name?"

"Margaret Verrere. Family legend has it that it was a most romantic affair—she eloped with a man of common birth, and they fled the wrath of her family to the colonies.''

"I cannot believe it.''

"Oh, 'tis true," David Miller assured her earnestly.

"No, I did not mean that I don't believe the story about Margaret Verrere. It is just that—well, it is so astonishing. You see, I have been reading her journals.''

He grinned. "Splendid. I hope you enjoyed them. I am the one who sold them to Mr. Simons. I am a merchant in Boston, and every once in a while I come to London to make purchases, see the latest things, you know. Last year I decided to bring Margaret Stone's journals—that was her married name, you know—to London and sell them. I sold them to a bookseller named Simons. This year, when I went by to see him, just to renew the acquaintance and see whether he had sold the journals, he told me that Lord Chesilworth, a Verrere himself, had bought them. I was most pleased to hear that they had found their way back to their proper family. Of course, I realized that we must be distantly related, and, well, when I had some free time on my hands, I felt that I must make your acquaintance.''

"I am so glad that you did.''

Joanna, who had lost most of her interest in the handsome young man when she learned that he was a mere merchant from Boston, was even more bored by this talk of books and ancestors. Properly, this young man, whatever his reasons for coming to Dunsleigh, should have been so captivated by her beauty that he talked of her, not musty old journals and dull relations. She stirred restively in her seat.

"Wonderful." Mr. Miller beamed. "I was afraid that you would find me too presumptuous. I find that the English often seem to find Americans so.''

"I am very glad to meet you. I find Margaret's story

fascinating, as did my Papa. It is he who was the Lord Chesilworth who bought them from Mr. Simons. But I am afraid that Papa passed away several months ago. He would have been so delighted to meet you. He would have had many questions about the journals.''

"Must we talk about books, Cassandra?" Joanna asked plaintively.

"I am sorry, Miss Moulton." Miller favored her with a smile. "Indeed, no doubt you found it boring, hearing two people talk about their relatives. I take it that you are not a descendant of Margaret's family."

"I haven't the faintest idea who Margaret is," Joanna said with a little giggle that more than one swain had assured her was delightful.

"No, my cousin and aunt are not Verreres," Cassandra explained. "We are related on my mother's side."

"I see."

"But tell me, Mr. Miller, pray, how did you come upon the journals and why did you decide to sell them?" Cassandra wished that Sir Philip Neville were here now to hear the full story of the journals. He had been so certain that poor Mr. Simons had played them false—perhaps Mr. Miller could put his mind to rest about the journals' authenticity.

"My mother died almost two years ago. It was through her that I was descended from Margaret Verrere Stone. My grandmother, her mother, had been very interested in the family history, and she had preserved many old family records—family Bibles, birth and death and wedding certificates. Anyway, she had several trunkfuls of such things, which my mother had merely stored in the attic. But then, when my mother departed this world, I was going through her things, and I came upon my grandmother's trunks. They were stuffed with old family relics, most of which I decided to get rid of. Among those things were Margaret's journals.''

Glassy-eyed by now, Joanna seized the opportunity of a pause in Mr. Miller's recital to say, "Perhaps you could show Mr. Miller the garden, Cassandra. Americans are always interested in English gardens, aren't they?"

"I am sorry, Miss Moulton. I fear I am boring you with such talk. It is just that I am so thrilled to be meeting a, well, a sort of cousin, I suppose."

"You are right, Cousin Joanna." For once, Cassandra thought, her cousin's wishes and her own coincided. It was always difficult to carry on a serious conversation with Joanna around, flirting and simpering and determined to keep the conversation on the one thing that truly interested her, herself. "I would be pleased to show Mr. Miller the garden. Would you care to continue our conversation there, sir?"

He agreed with alacrity, and Cassandra led him out into the formal garden behind the house. He courteously admired the various roses, delphiniums and daisies, and then he and Cassandra settled down on the bench in the grape arbor.

"Tell me the rest of it," Cassandra urged. "Did you read Margaret's journals? Why did you decide to sell them?"

Miller's blue eyes twinkled. "No doubt you will consider me a crass American, Miss Verrere, but the truth is, I have little interest in books or in searching out each twig of the family tree. I found it rather intriguing to learn that there were still Verreres here in England to whom I was distantly related, but as for studying the family history— well, I'm afraid I haven't either the time or the inclination." He gave her a small, self-deprecating smile.

"That is perfectly understandable. I don't expect everyone to share my interests. So you did not read the journals?''

He shook his head. "Not really. Oh, I glanced through them, but I read very little. I didn't know what to do with them at first. I hated to throw them away. I mean, they were so old, and I thought they must be valuable to someone. Finally one of my friends suggested that I sell them in England the next time I went. He pointed out that the English were, in general, more interested in history. He thought it would be a perfect market for old books, especially since Margaret came from here and doubtless left family behind. So I took his advice and brought them with me on my last trip to London. There, as I said, I sold them to Mr. Simons." He smiled and added, "Actually, I tried to sell them to several book dealers, but Mr. Simons was the only one who wanted them.''

"I am so glad you did," Cassandra told him warmly. She found herself liking Mr. Miller. He was open and direct in a way that most people never were. She wasn't sure if it was simply an American quality or an attribute of this man. Whatever it was, she found that she could not keep from smiling back at him whenever he smiled. He was also, she thought, quite handsome—better looking, in fact, than Sir Philip Neville.

"My father was thrilled to actually get to read Margaret Verrere's words," she continued. "Her history—the elopement—had been a particular interest of his.''

They continued to talk for some time. He was interested in Margaret Verrere's family, his relatives, and what had happened to them in the years since Margaret eloped. When Cassandra told him that the home in which Margaret had lived was still standing and had indeed been Cassandra's own home until her father's death, he was struck with awe and asked her if he might see it.

Cassandra was quite happy to show Chesilworth to him, and they went that afternoon, accompanied by the twins and Olivia, who always welcomed any excuse to get away from their aunt's house. The twins, of course, peppered David with questions about the United States as well as the ship on which he had come to England, but he answered them all with great patience.

"Are you going to hunt for the treasure with us?" Hart asked with excitement when they reached Chesilworth.

"The what?" He looked down at the boy, startled, then over at Cassandra.

"The dowry," Hart went on impatiently. "You know. Margaret's dowry."

"He's talking about something in the journals," Cassandra explained, adding to her brother, "Mr. Miller did not read the journals."

"There is a treasure mentioned in them?" The American looked intrigued.

"It tells how to find it," Crispin told him, and the two boys began to eagerly explain the existence of two maps. "One is in a letter. That's what we are looking for in the house. The other belongs to Sir Philip, but he refuses to help us, so we are going to have to figure out how to do it ourselves."

"A treasure hunt!" David Miller exclaimed. "How delightful. I am sorry that I cannot stay longer and help you with it."

"Yes, that would be bang-up," agreed Hart, who, along with Crispin had liked their American relation from the moment they met him.

"Why don't you stay?" Crispin suggested. "Couldn't he stay, Cassie?"

"He might not be able to, boys. Don't plague Mr. Miller.'' She turned to the man with a smile. "If you were able to stay, though, we would greatly enjoy it.''

"You tempt me." He sighed. "But I do have business in London that I must get back for. And my ship home sails in a week." He looked torn for a moment, then shrugged and said, "Well, perhaps I could stretch my stay to a second night.''

When they reached Chesilworth, Mr. Miller exclaimed aloud, impressed by its size and age, "Why, it's a castle!''

"Hardly.'' Cassandra laughed. "The Verreres were not great land barons during the Middle Ages, but the Elizabethan who built this tried his best to make it look like one.''

"You won't find anything like this in the United States," he told her, still in awe. "It's a grand place. You must have hated to leave it.''

Cassandra nodded, though it wasn't its grandeur that made her miss Chesilworth. It was its dear familiarity and its memories, the sense of family history that lived throughout it. They showed Mr. Miller through Chesilworth, even the damp and deteriorating west wing, and the next afternoon he returned to help them search the attics. In the end, he wound up stretching his visit to yet a third day, and it was with visible reluctance that he left them then.

After his departure, the days at Moulton House settled into their usual routine. Cassandra oversaw most of her aunt's housekeeping, and whenever she could, she sneaked away to Chesilworth, sometimes with her siblings and sometimes without.

One afternoon, about a week after Mr. Miller departed, all four of the Verreres were in the attic at Chesilworth, though only Cassandra was still looking through the trunks. The heat of the day and boredom had prompted the twins to engage in a pretend sword fight with two canes they had found against the attic wall, and Olivia stood by an open window, trying to find any stray bit of breeze.

Cassandra finished loading all the objects back into a trunk that she had just emptied and closed the lid, sending another shower of dust all over her. She coughed and sat back on her heels, drawing her hand across her forehead and sighing. Her back hurt, and she badly wanted a drink of water. She coughed again and thought about quitting the search for the day.

To her amazement, there was a sound in the hall below the attic stairs. Then her cousin's voice rang out cheerily, "Cassandra! Oh, Cassandra!"

Joanna? Whatever had possessed Joanna to come all the way over to Chesilworth? It was not like her cousin to move an inch out of her way, let alone visit their dilapidated house. There were footsteps on the stairs, and a man's head and shoulders appeared through the hole in the floor. Cassandra understood now why Joanna had gone to the trouble of coming to Chesilworth. She rose to her feet, staring in silence as the rest of the man came into view.

"Good day, Miss Verrere," said Sir Philip Neville cheerfully.

5

"Sir Philip!" Cassandra gaped at the man.

"Miss Verrere. It is a pleasure to see you again." A twinkle danced in Neville's brown eyes.

Cassandra was intensely, humiliatingly aware of the way she looked—sweating in a most unladylike manner, covered with dust, wearing one of her oldest and most ragtag dresses, and her hair no doubt sticking out every which way. She looked past Sir Philip to the attic opening, where Joanna now stood, a smug smile playing on her lips. Cassandra felt as if she could cheerfully have murdered her. *No wonder Joanna had gone to the trouble of coming over to Chesilworth. She had known the state in which she and Sir Philip would find Cassandra.*

Cassandra rose to her feet with all the dignity she could muster, trying vainly to brush the dust off her hands onto her skirts. "I—this is indeed a surprise, Sir Philip. I had not expected to see you again, least of all here."

"My visit to Lady Arrabeck's was over, and I was returning home, when it occurred to me that Dunsleigh would be a pleasant place at which to make a stop."

"How fortuitous that we lay on your way home," Cassandra replied, bringing up a mental map in her head and placing Lady Arrabeck's, Dunsleigh and Neville's Haverly House on it. It seemed to her that no one in his right mind would go through Dunsleigh to travel from Arrabeck Hall to Haverly House.

"Yes, isn't it?" Neville returned blandly.

He had to be here about the treasure. Cassandra was certain that his story about dropping in on his way home was utter folderol, even if Joanna was too poor at geography to realize it. She was grateful, though, that he had been smart enough not to tell her aunt or cousin the real reason for his visit.

He crossed the attic to where she stood, winding his way among the boxes and trunks, and bowed elegantly over her embarrassingly dusty hand.

"Please forgive my appearance," Cassandra murmured. "'Tis dusty work in the attics."

"I see." A flash of amusement crossed his face. "But there is no need to apologize. You look, as always, enchanting."

Cassandra felt a betraying heat rise in her cheeks and she glanced quickly away. "Uh—I—allow me to introduce you to my sister and brothers."

The twins had stopped their mock battle as soon as Neville had arrived, and they edged closer now, staring at him in fascination.

"My brother Crispin, Lord Chesilworth, and his twin Hart. And this is my sister, Olivia Verrere. Children, this is Sir Philip Neville."

Neville exchanged polite greetings with the other three, adding as he bowed over Olivia's hand, "Ah, another beauty in the family, I see."

Olivia's eyes grew even wider, and Cassandra knew that he had won her sister over. Behind them, still standing beside the attic stairway, Joanna shifted and sighed noisily.

She unfurled her fan and made a production of waving it in front of her.

"It is so dreadfully hot in here," she opined. "Cassandra, I don't see how you can stand it. I swear, I think I should faint."

"Oh, you know I am never subject to the vapors," Cassandra answered her pragmatically. "But perhaps you should go back downstairs, where it is less stifling."

"Yes, of course." Joanna gave her a cat-in-the-cream smile and went on in dulcet tones, "We ought to return to the house, Sir Philip. Cassandra and the other children could join us when they get through here."

"Thank you for your concern, Miss Moulton." Sir Philip sent her a brief, disinterested glance. "No doubt you should return to the house if you are feeling unwell. However, I shall remain here. Miss Verrere looks as if she could use some help."

Joanna stared at him. "You are going to help them clean the attic?"

"If that is what they are doing, yes." He gave her a perfunctory smile and turned back to Cassandra.

"But I—I can hardly go back to the house by myself," Joanna protested.

"Your groom was with us."

"Yes, of course, but that isn't the same. I mean, he is not a gentleman."

"You do not trust your servants to behave in a proper manner?" Neville asked, lifting his eyebrows in surprise.

"Of course—I didn't mean—that is—"

"If you are scared to go back with Jessup," Olivia suggested with great innocence, "then perhaps you had best wait downstairs. I am sure we will be through in a few hours. Won't we, Cassie?"

Cassandra had to bite her lip to keep from giggling at

Joanna's outraged expression. "Yes. Joanna, that sounds like an excellent idea."

Joanna cast a fulminating glance at Cassandra, then at the others, and finally stalked ungraciously to the nearest trunk, lifting her skirts from the dusty floor. She put on a show of dusting off the top of the trunk with her handkerchief, but it was lost on Sir Philip, who was once again looking down at Cassandra.

"Where shall I start, Miss Verrere?"

"Ah…" Cassandra glanced around vaguely, trying to pull her thoughts together. "Well, I had just finished this trunk, and I was going to move on to the one beside it. Perhaps you would like to go through that one." She pointed to the flat-topped, brass-bound trunk on the other side.

"Of course." He moved to the next trunk and opened it, sending dust cascading from its top.

Cassandra knelt in front of the trunk beside him and opened it. She glanced over at Sir Philip, still scarcely able to believe that he was there. Her initial embarassment over her appearance was subsiding. It didn't really matter how she looked; what was important was that he had come.

Quietly she asked, "You have decided that you believe me, sir?"

"I never disbelieved you, Miss Verrere. I was simply of the opinion that you had been duped."

"A vast improvement. You merely thought me a fool."

He looked at her, his eyes dancing. "Never that, dear lady."

"What made you change your mind?"

He shrugged. "I am not saying that I believe there is a treasure waiting for us, or that we can find these maps that will lead us to it. Let us simply say that for the moment I am willing to withhold my judgment.

The fact was—though he would not have dreamed of telling Miss Verrere this—that Sir Philip still found the idea of a hidden treasure and a secret map or two the stuff of gothic novels. He had merely found himself excessively bored at Lady Arrabeck's house party after Cassandra left. He had kept thinking about her and the offer she had made to him. Absurd as it was, it somehow intrigued him. But more than that, Cassandra herself intrigued him. He recalled the intelligence and clarity of her large gray eyes, the humor of her wide mouth and the slender femininity of her form. He had never gotten a good look at her pale hair in the daylight, he reminded himself; he would still like to see it. And their conversation, though bizarre, had made what everyone else said to him seem insipid. Most of all, he remembered the way Cassandra had felt in his arms, the taste of her mouth beneath his, and the memories made him feel most unsettled.

He was, he told himself, too old for treasure hunts, and, of course, he did not believe for a minute that Cassandra was going to find the clues she needed in some old letter to her ancestor. Still, he had begun wondering what it would hurt to go to visit her and see those precious diaries of hers. It would do nothing worse than waste his time, and, frankly, the idea of wasting a few hours' time in Cassandra Verrere's company had grown more and more appealing. Even the thought of having to spend time in the company of her aunt and cousin had not been enough to put him off.

"I am sure you will be convinced soon," Cassandra assured him, her eyes shining in a way that made his loins tighten. "Once you have read Margaret's diaries, I know you will realize that they are real. You can see how close we are growing in our search. We are already only fifty years or so away from Margaret's time, and we have all the way to the wall left to look." She waved her arm toward the end of the attic. "I am sure there are things left from her father."

"*If* he saved those letters."

Cassandra frowned. The possibility that Margaret's angry father had thrown away the letters from his wayward daughter was not something she liked to think about. She shook her head. "We will find them. We must."

They continued to unpack the trunks, searching through the stored articles for a packet of letters. Boxes were opened and clothes unwrapped to make sure that no letters were folded inside. Sir Philip was soon distracted by an intricately carved snuffbox so small that it fit into the palm of his hand, then again by a quaint old book on manners that made him chuckle and read choice excerpts aloud.

"Whatever are you doing?" Joanna asked snappishly. She did not understand Sir Philip at all. Her hopes had soared when the footman had announced him. She was certain that he had traveled to Dunsleigh because his desire for her had overcome his brief bitterness at the trick she had tried on him.

But then he had kept on asking about Cassandra and had actually insisted on riding over to Chesilworth to find her. Of course, he had expressed great consideration for Joanna and assured her that she needn't accompany him, but she had not been about to let such an opportunity to be alone with him get away from her. However, she could not understand why he refused to leave now, or why he was pawing through old trunks and chuckling with Cassandra over things in which Joanna could see no humor. She narrowed her eyes at Cassandra, who was smiling at Neville in a way that made her eyes positively luminous. She was almost pretty, Joanna thought in amazement, even with her hair covered in a powder of dust and a great streak of dirt across one cheek. Joanna found the revelation distinctly annoying. Did Cassandra actually think that Sir Philip Neville would have any interest in *her?*

"What are you doing, Cassandra?" she repeated when her cousin continued to ignore her. "Why are you looking through all these old trunks?"

"I thought there might be something of interest here," Cassandra replied vaguely.

Joanna quirked an eyebrow, but her cousin's interests were always so peculiar to her that Cassandra's answer did not seem out of the ordinary. "But you are making Sir Philip all dusty."

"I don't mind, Miss Moulton," Sir Philip replied cheerfully. "I am having a perfectly fine time."

A little to his amazement, he realized that he actually *was* enjoying himself. It was dusty and hot in the attic, but he was doing something that he had never done before, and it was rather fun exploring the old things in the trunk and sharing his amusement at the antiquated book with Cassandra. He could think of no other woman who would care as little about the fact that he had come upon her when she was dirty and disheveled, clothed in an obviously old, ill-fitting dress. Within minutes she was talking unselfconsciously with him and chuckling over the excerpts he read from the book.

He glanced over at Joanna, whose perfect looks were beginning to melt a little in the airless attic. She was dressed like a lady and acting as one should act; moreover, her coloring and features were such as any woman would envy. But, after ten minutes in Cassandra's company, Joanna struck him only as dull as ditch water, whereas he felt his eyes drawn over and over again to Cassandra's animated face.

Joanna frowned at him, annoyed at his cheerfulness. The

man was acting like a boor, she thought; any gentleman should have taken the hint and escorted her back to her home long ago. It was obvious to her that stronger action needed to be taken.

She rose to her feet. "I fear that the heat is too much for me. I must go back downstairs."

"Of course, Joanna," Cassandra replied in a pleasant voice. "Whatever you think best."

"Good day, Miss Moulton," Sir Philip said absently, distracted by a small stack of letters, yellowed with age and tied with a pink ribbon, that were fitted into the corner of the trunk.

He snatched them up and turned them over, aware of a surprising stab of excitement in his stomach. He did not even glance up to see the dagger look that Joanna directed toward him before she clattered down the stairs in a demonstration of ladylike rage.

"Cassandra—" he said in a low voice, not noticing that he called her by her first name, an unwarranted familiarity given the short time they had known each other.

Cassandra turned, as oblivious as he to his use of her given name. Her heart speeded up as she saw the pile of letters, even as she reminded herself that she had found dozens of other packets of letters already, and none of them had been the ones she was looking for.

She reached out for them, saying pragmatically, "I am sure these are too recent," even as her fingers closed around them with trembling eagerness.

Cassandra brought them closer, but as soon as she saw the spidery writing, she sighed. "Oh, no! This is Edna Verrere's writing. I would have thought I had discovered everything she ever wrote by now. She was a most faithful daughter, and she wrote her mother regularly after she married. Her mother was equally faithful about keeping her letters.''

She pulled the top letter from the pile and quickly skimmed it, just to make sure that it was indeed Edna Verrere who had written. ''Yes, she's talking about her son Reginald again—a most priggish-sounding fellow.''

''Oh, him!''

Both Cassandra and Philip looked up at the sound of one of the twins' voices. Both the boys had made their way over to them when they saw the packet of letters, but now Hart threw himself down in disgust atop one of the trunks.

''What a prosy bore,'' Crispin agreed, coming to stand beside his brother. ''Is it Edna again? We thought you had actually found something.''

''No. We are still in too recent an area, I'm afraid,'' Cassandra told them.

''Why don't you just move over a few trunks and start investigating further back in time?'' Neville suggested.

''Mm. We tried that. Unfortunately, they are not in perfect order. Sometimes you will find a box from a much earlier era in with the others—and sometimes items are even within the same trunk or box.''

''Besides,'' Olivia added, coming up to join them, her eyes glinting with amusement, ''it would not suit Cassandra's sense of order.''

Cassandra lifted her chin and gave her a lofty look. ''I merely try to bring some degree of order to all this chaos. If I left it up to you, in two days the contents of the trunks would be scattered all over the attic floor.''

''Yes, but we would have found the letters.''

''*If* you hadn't overlooked them among the rubble.''

Crispin, long used to Cassandra's and Olivia's running argument over Cassandra's tidiness and Olivia's lack of it, ignored his sisters and spoke to Sir Philip. "I say, sir, are you planning to help us look for the Spanish dowry now?"

Neville looked at the young boy's lit-up eyes and found that he could not bring himself to deflate his hopes. "Yes, if we are able to find the letters."

"Capital!" Crispin beamed. "I was hoping that you would turn out to be a right 'un, sir, even if Cassandra said you were not."

Philip looked at Cassandra, his eyes lit sardonically. "Is that what she said about me?"

"Crispin!" Olivia admonished, frowning at him. "Of course she didn't say that."

"She said you lacked imagination," revealed Hart, who was blessed with an infuriatingly accurate memory. "But you couldn't help it, 'cause you were a Neville."

"Miss Verrere, you wound me." Laughter shimmered in Philip's voice.

Cassandra rolled her eyes. "Don't be nonsensical. I told you that to your face, if you will remember." She bent a stern gaze on her younger brothers. "However, I think we've had about enough out of you two on the subject. It isn't always polite to quote one's elders."

"Especially if they've been maligning others," Crispin added, his eyes dancing.

"Oh, you!" Cassandra reached out to playfully swat at her brother, but he hastily jumped back out of her reach.

She returned the stack of letters to the pile of discards, saying, "Now, I suggest that you three get back to work—unless, of course, you prefer to join Joanna downstairs."

Hart made a choking noise at this suggestion, and the three children drifted back to their respective areas. Cassandra and Philip returned to their work, as well, and for the next two hours they worked steadily through the paraphernalia in the attic. They were interrupted twice by

Joanna's groom, coming up to relay Joanna's desire to leave, but they did not stop until the light slanting in through the small attic windows became too difficult to see by.

Then they rose and went down the narrow attic stairs, brushing—to little avail—at the dust that had settled on them. They found Joanna in the kitchen, where she sat at the huge, scarred oak table, the only piece of furniture in the house left unshrouded. She was drumming her fingers on the table impatiently, her face a study in discontent, and she jumped up when she saw them, her brows rushing together.

"There you are at last!" she snapped at her cousin. "Really, Cassandra, you have no consideration for anyone but yourself."

"*I* was not keeping you here," Cassandra stated reasonably. "You could have gone home any time you wished."

Joanna's eyes narrowed, and Cassandra thought that she was about to let fly with one of her temper tantrums, but at that point Joanna apparently realized the unattractiveness of her features in that expression and, with obvious effort, she smoothed her face out and forced a small approximation of a smile. "It would have been rude to have left our guest here." She directed a look of great sympathy in Sir Philip's direction. "I am so sorry that you have been subjected to such an afternoon, Sir Philip."

"Think nothing of it. I had a most…diverting time."

"You are too kind, Sir Philip." Joanna went to him, reaching out to tuck her hand companionably into his arm, but stopped, hand in midair, as she looked at the the state of his coat.

"Pray, Miss Moulton, you must not get too near me. I am afraid that I am something of a mess." Neville sketched a bow in her direction and started toward the door, taking Cassandra's arm.

Outside, the groom hurried toward them, leading Joanna's and Sir Philip's horses. Joanna mounted with the groom's help, but Sir Philip said cheerfully that he would walk and lead his horse, since the Verrere party were all on foot. Grinding her teeth, Joanna watched as Neville strolled along chatting with Cassandra and her sister, leading his bay gelding. Joanna, who had planned to cut Sir Philip from the group by riding with him while the others walked, instead found herself isolated by being the only one on horseback. Even though Cassandra and Neville politely addressed a few remarks to her, she still could not join in, for the two of them were discussing some boring book that Joanna had never heard of, let alone read. She would have been thoroughly disgruntled had she not been able to comfort herself with the reminder that gentlemen did not like ladies who were intellectual.

When they reached the Moulton house, they "happened" to meet Aunt Ardis, emerging from the door. She started toward them, smiling hugely, her hands extended toward Sir Philip, then stopped in some dismay as she saw his appearance.

"My goodness! Well, uh, won't you come in?" she continued gamely, trying not to think of the state of her silk damask chairs in the drawing room if Sir Philip sat upon one of them.

"No, no," Sir Philip said hastily. "I must return to the inn and change. I am not fit for company, I'm afraid."

"Then you will not be staying with us?" Aunt Ardis's face fell. "I thought you would be honoring us with a visit. Do not tell me you have come so far out of your way for only a day."

"No, I shall be happy to remain in Dunsleigh for a time,

madam, but I could not impose so as to stay with you unannouced.''

"But 'tis no trouble," Aunt Ardis assured him gaily, as if unexpected guests were a common occurrence at their home. "We at Moulton Hall are always ready for a guest or two."

They continued to argue politely over the matter, but Sir Philip won the day, steadfastly refusing to put Mrs. Moulton out with his presence. Cassandra knew, as did Sir Philip, that there was nothing Aunt Ardis would have loved as much as having one of the most eligible bachelors in England trapped in her house for several days, and she had to hide a smile as her aunt finally gave in to him with ill grace. After that there was another small skirmish over whether he would return that evening for supper, which ended with Sir Philip politely insisting on declining, with a promise to return to pay a call on them the following day.

When he had ridden out of sight, with Aunt Ardis and Joanna waving their kerchiefs to him to the very last, Aunt Ardis whirled around, clasping her hands together in front of her bosom in seeming ecstasy.

"Can you imagine?" she exclaimed. "Sir Philip Neville, here in Dunsleigh—and with no other purpose than to visit us! Oh, Lilah Davenport will have an apoplexy when she hears this." She seemed transported by the vision of her friend's jealousy. "Joanna, this is such a coup. He could not stay away from you."

Olivia let out an unladylike snort at these words. "I noticed how difficult he found it to stay away from her this afternoon."

Joanna rounded on her. "He was merely too polite to go over there to Chesilworth and then leave immediately. I am sure that it is all your fault, Cassandra, that he would not stay here or even come back for supper. He was probably afraid that you would trap him to work in the dirt and heat again.''

"I suspect it was a different sort of trap he feared," Cassandra commented coolly, sending her cousin a significant look.

Joanna's eyes shot sparks. "How dare you!"

"Dear cousin, I am afraid you left yourself open for that. It took little daring." Cassandra walked past her into the house.

Joanna followed, her face drawn up in a harsh mask of fury. "Why else would he come here, if not because he could not stay away from me? I certainly hope you don't entertain any delusions that he came to see *you!*"

"He did too come to see Cassandra," Crispin cried out in fury at the slight upon his sister.

Joanna cast him a withering glance. "What would you know about it? You're just a boy."

"I know plenty!"

"Crispin…" Cassandra said warningly. He shot her a mulish look, but closed his mouth and shoved his hands in his pockets.

"I have no delusions where Sir Philip Neville is concerned," Cassandra told her cousin blandly. "If you will excuse me now, as you can see, I must take a bath."

She walked off, leaving Joanna looking after her distrustfully.

Sir Philip came to call on them the following morning as early as it was polite to do so. Aunt Ardis did not bother to inform Cassandra of his presence, so she did not know he was there until Olivia came hurrying into her room with the news.

"That woman is such a witch!" Olivia exclaimed, her

cheeks high with angry color. "She is deliberately trying to conceal him from you. She knows that it isn't Joanna he is here to see."

Cassandra pressed her hand against her stomach, which had done unaccounted flip-flops at the news that Philip was in the house. She glanced in the mirror anxiously, then told herself not to be foolish. Neville did not care how she looked. It would not matter that she had worn her pale blue dress, the one that did so much for her eyes, or that she had arranged her hair this morning with greater care, creating a fuller frame for her face.

She strove to keep her voice light and calm as she replied, "I imagine Aunt Ardis thinks he is here because of Joanna. You know how highly she regards Joanna's ability to attract any and every male. If a person wears trousers, she thinks he is in love with Joanna."

"She does have a wonderful ability to delude herself," Olivia agreed. "But she didn't tell you he was here just for spite—to keep you from having any fun."

"Our aunt is not a woman who likes to share," Cassandra agreed. "However, I think that this time she is up against someone who is even more used than she to getting his way. And since, as we know, Sir Philip is not here out of desire for our dear cousin—" she smiled knowingly "—it might be interesting to see just what happens."

"That's true." Olivia's frown vanished at the thought of her aunt having to endure Sir Philip's insistence on seeing Cassandra. With a grin, she flopped down onto her bed and curled her legs up under her in her usual way. "He is a handsome man, isn't he?"

"Sir Philip?"

Olivia grimaced. "Of course Sir Philip. Who else would I be talking about? And don't try to act as if you did not notice. Who could not notice that dimple in his cheek?

When he doesn't smile, he looks quite stern, doesn't he? And then—when you made him grin yesterday, there was that dimple, and his eyes lit up, and, well, he looked like an entirely different person.''

"He is attractive when he smiles." Cassandra herself smiled at the memory of that boyish dimple.

"Oh, pooh, Miss Prunes-and-prisms," Olivia teased. "You are not an old spinster yet, no matter how you try to paint yourself one. And Sir Philip knows it, too."

"What?" Cassandra glanced sharply at her younger sister, heat rising in her cheeks. *How could Olivia have guessed that something far more than conversation had happened between her and Sir Philip?* "What do you mean?"

Olivia looked slightly taken aback by her sister's sharp response to her words. "I only mean that I think he is interested in you. Whatever is the matter?"

"Oh. I'm sorry, Liv, I should not have snapped at you. My nerves are a bit on edge this morning. The excitement of being so close to actually finding the treasure, I suppose."

There was a tap upon the door, and Cassandra and Olivia exchanged triumphant looks. The parlor maid, Janie, opened the door at Cassandra's bidding and stuck her head in.

"Mrs. Moulton requests your presence in the drawing room, Miss Verrere." She spoiled her formal announcement by grinning hugely and adding, "A certain gentleman's been asking for you, I hear."

"Thank you, Janie." Cassandra exchanged a glance with her sister and rose to go downstairs.

Sir Philip stood up with a look of relief on his face when Cassandra walked into the drawing room a few minutes later. "Miss Verrere. I am glad to see you looking well."

"Why, yes, why wouldn't I be?"

"Your aunt feared you were feeling ill this morning," he replied, his tone laced with irony, as he came forward and bowed over her hand.

Cassandra directed a sweet smile toward her aunt. "Why, no, Aunt Ardis, though it is most kind of you to be worried about me. But I have been feeling quite as well as I did at breakfast this morning."

"I was just telling your aunt and cousin how intriguing I found Chesilworth yesterday," Sir Philip continued as Cassandra sat down in a chair at some distance from him, the other two women having carefully planted themselves in the spots closest to his chair. "I should very much enjoy going to see it again."

"Would you? Then perhaps we should make another expedition this afternoon," Cassandra suggested.

"Nothing could be more delightful."

Joanna let out a forced twitter of laughter. "Oh, my, Sir Philip, I can assure you that there are any number of places much more interesting to visit than that musty old house. Why, as you could see, it is falling down."

"Yes. I admire antiquities," Sir Philip replied smoothly. "Nothing intrigues me more than things that are old."

"It has quite a history," Cassandra added. "Perhaps you would like to look at some of the books about it? The ones we were speaking of yesterday?"

"Yes, of course. I would be most appreciative."

"Cassandra…" Joanna tittered again, casting a dimpled smile toward Sir Philip. "I am sure Sir Philip is not interested in reading those silly old books of yours."

"On the contrary, Miss Moulton, I am indeed interested. Miss Verrere and I spoke about them at some length yesterday. We share a mutual interest in history, you see."

Joanna clenched her jaw and had to force herself to ease

her facial muscles into a smile. "I am sure that there are several excursions that you would find far more enlightening and pleasurable." She went on to list every possible attraction that she could think of in the area.

Sir Philip hung on to his polite smile grimly. "Indeed, Miss Moulton, you offer a veritable feast of options. I had not realized that Dunsleigh had so much for the visitor. However, this afternoon I am committed to going to Chesilworth with Miss Verrere."

Joanna's eyes flashed, and Cassandra thought that she was about to deliver a dressing down to the intractable Sir Philip, but Aunt Ardis jumped in before her daughter could speak. "If that is where you wish to go with Joanna and Cassandra, then that's where you shall go. We shall all go—you cannot be unchaperoned with two young ladies, you know—" She waggled a playful finger, at him as if he had suggested something naughty. "A picnic. That is just the thing. I shall have cook prepare us a hamper."

Now it was Sir Philip who looked as if he might lash out. Cassandra cut in hastily. "How wonderful! I would not have expected Cousin Joanna to want to explore with us. You shall have to wear something old and worn, you know, for it will be quite likely to ruin your dress."

"I don't want to explore those old ruins!"

"Then what will you do while Sir Philip and the children and I are exploring?"

"Yes, do think, dear ladies," Sir Philip had recovered his charm with some effort, and he smiled now at Joanna. "You would not want to get that beautiful hair of yours all covered with dust—and the thought of grime on your clothes, your porcelain skin, why, 'twould be a travesty."

Cassandra could barely keep herself from rolling her eyes at his blandishments, but the honeyed words seemed to work, for with a few more remarks about how wonder-

fully refreshing it would be to return to Moulton House
and find Joanna in her usual beauty, both she and her
mother agreed that the excursion was one more fit for children.

"Now, dear ladies, if you will excuse me..." Sir Philip
rose from his chair. "I have a few matters to attend to
before I go to work at Chesilworth this afternoon, though
I hate to cut our visit short."

Joanna and Aunt Ardis both urged him to stay, but he
smiled and persisted in bidding them adieu. Finally Joanna
made a coy little moue and said, "Well, all right, but only
if you will consent to come to our party tomorrow evening."

"Party? What party is that?"

Cassandra had to press her lips together hard to keep
from laughing at the faintly ill expression that crossed Sir
Philip's face as he said the word.

"Why, the one Mama and I are having tomorrow night.
We were just saying this morning how lucky it was that
you came to visit when we have a party in the offing."

Cassandra, to whom the news of a party was a surprise,
raised her eyebrows but refrained from saying anything.

"Of course, it is merely a small thing. We live so retired
in the country, you know—nothing like the season in London. But, still, we must have our little amusements now
and then," Aunt Ardis explained with a girlish smile.

"A small dinner with a few friends," Joanna added.
"Do say you will come, Sir Philip. Everyone will be so
disappointed if you do not."

"Of course." Sir Philip gave them a strained smile. "I
will be happy to attend. But for now, I am afraid I really
must go."

He bowed over each of their hands, politely going to

Aunt Ardis first, then to Joanna. Lastly he turned to Cassandra, taking her hand and bending over it.

In a low voice he murmured, "Ten minutes. The well we passed yesterday."

Cassandra blinked, surprised. Sir Philip straightened, looking questioningly into her eyes.

She smiled and nodded. "Good day, Sir Philip. I look forward to seeing you soon."

6

Satisfaction flickered briefly in Sir Philip's face and was gone, then he turned and strode out the door. As soon as he was gone, Joanna and her mother burst into an excited babble, trying at once to arrange the dinner party, crow over their good fortune and everyone else's envy at having such a prize as Sir Philip Neville at their dinner, and also speculate over the extent of Sir Philip's interest in Joanna, the amount of his wealth, and the size of Haverly House. They scarcely noticed when Cassandra slipped out of the room.

She dashed upstairs and grabbed a bonnet and the stack of Margaret's journals. Then she scurried down the servants' staircase and out the back door, flying across the garden and down the path toward the old well. She carried her bonnet by the ribbons, not taking the time to put it on, and so she arrived at the well bareheaded, with soft, wind-blown tendrils falling about her face.

Sir Philip, waiting for her, straightened, smiling at the sight of her. The sun glinted off her hair, as pale as moonlight, and he thought with a kind of fierce delight that her hair was every bit as lovely in the daylight as he had thought it would be.

"Miss Verrere. You are on time. I admire that in a woman."

"Indeed? Well, I am glad I pleased you," Cassandra replied tartly. "I take it you do not mind if men are late?"

He looked slightly startled by her words, then let out a laugh. "I stand corrected. I should say it is an admirable quality in *any*one." He reached out and took the journals from her. "Here, let me carry those. Would you like to sit?" He gestured toward the wooden bench running around the trunk of a large oak tree. "I noticed this seat yesterday when we were walking back from your home. Somehow I suspected we might have need of a clandestine meeting place."

"I am so sorry. I must apologize for my aunt and my cousin."

"It is only reasonable to assume that I have some interest in someone, to be calling here on such a flimsy pretext. It takes no great skill to see that Dunsleigh is hardly on the route to my estate."

"I know. And you must think me foolish to have hidden my plans from my relatives."

"Oh, no," he responded quickly, sitting down with her on the bench. "I understand perfectly, and I suspect that you are following the correct course. I would say that the fewer people who know what you are about, the better."

Her eyes glimmered with amusement. "To spare me embarrassment when it turns out to be a hoax?"

He shrugged. "Perhaps. Who knows what people might say or do? The talk of treasure seems to do extraordinary things to people." He quirked an eyebrow. "Look at me. I would have said I would never be chasing after old letters in an attic."

Cassandra smiled and pointed to the books he now carried. "After you look at these, perhaps you will feel better about what you are doing. I brought Margaret Verrere's journals.''

"Ah." He picked up the top volume from the stack, which he had set down on the bench beside him. He turned it over, examining the binding, then carefully thumbed through the yellowed pages. He looked through each book with the same care and said finally, "I must admit that they appear authentically old."

"You see?"

"Not that I am an expert, of course. Still, if this is a forgery, I must say it was skillfully done—and would have taken a great deal of time, as well as talent."

"I can assure you that my father did not pay enough for them to make it worth the effort. He was not a wealthy man." She paused, then added, with a triumphant smile, "Another argument against Mr. Simons's forging them—aside from his excellent reputation, of course—is that I have met the man who sold them to him."

"What?" Sir Philip, who had been languidly leaning back against the tree trunk, sat bolt upright.

Cassandra nodded, pleased at the effect her words had had. "He came here to visit. His name is David Miller, and he is a distant relative of mine."

Sir Philip's brows knitted into a black frown. "How do you know he is a relative?"

Cassandra rolled her eyes. "Honestly, Sir Philip, I thought you had decided not to be so mistrustful of everyone and everything. I did not ask him for a description of his family tree. He told me that he was a descendant of Margaret Verrere, and I saw no reason to disbelieve him."

"Perhaps Mr. Simons was the victim of a ruse, too. Perhaps it was your David Miller who forged the books, then sold them to Mr. Simons."

"That's absurd. It makes no sense—he would have

made even less selling them to a dealer than Mr. Simons made selling them to Papa. Only a fool would do so much for no more money than that.''

''You're probably right about that.'' He was silent for a moment—no doubt thinking up more objections, Cassandra thought wryly.

Then he asked, ''Why did he not sell them directly to your father?''

''Because he did not know that we were related then. He sold them to Mr. Simons last year. He is a merchant from Boston, and he travels to England every year. This time, when he came, he dropped by to see Mr. Simons, and Simons told him about selling the books to us. He was curious about us—wondered what his English cousins were like, you know.''

''Mm.''

''He sold the journals here because he thought they would fetch a better price. He found them among his mother's things when she died, and he has little interest in history or books. I think all your fears about the documents being forgeries are ungrounded.''

Sir Philip looked once again at the journal in his hand. It was hard for him to continue to believe that such a skilled and careful forgery would have been pulled off for no more reward that the sale of the journals had brought. ''And what other profit could there be?'' he mused aloud.

''What?''

''Nothing, just thinking to myself. You are right. It is difficult to believe that these journals are not genuinely old. And are they indeed the work of Margaret Verrere?''

''Oh, yes, you would have only to read the beginning, and you would have no question.'' She pulled out the first journal and opened it, handing it to him to read. ''It begins right after their elopement, during the ocean voyage. You can see all her worries and fears about her father, as well as her joy at escaping a loveless marriage.''

Sir Philip began to read, squinting down at the faded, spidery script. After a few moments he looked up. ''Yes. I can see that it is indeed work of a young girl, full of high drama and violent emotion.''

Cassandra quirked an eyebrow at him. ''Something you disapprove of, no doubt.'' She reached over and took the book, opening it to a place she had already marked with a scrap of paper. ''Look, here is her first mention of sending the letter to her father. See? And down here she explains about wanting the two families to have to join together to search for the dowry.''

She ran her finger down the page to the passage she sought. '''...for which reason I did leave part of the answer to the mystery in Neville's hands.'''

''Since he spent his whole life searching for it, I would scarcely say it was in his hands.''

''Perhaps she left him word where it was, and it was somehow lost. I don't know. She isn't very clear here about where it is. But, later on, when she was older and she mentioned it again...'' She put down the book and picked up a later journal, again going to a marked place. ''Here—'...along with the Neville map, the one I hid in the Queens Book.'''

''The Queens Book?'' Sir Philip repeated. ''What is that?''

''I was hoping that you knew, since it is something in your house.''

''Something that was in my house almost two hundred years ago,'' he corrected. ''It isn't a famous piece of family lore, if that is what you have been thinking. I have never heard of a Queens Book. Surely that is not the name of it.''

"I thought it must be a particular history of the queens of England. Or perhaps a specific one about a particular queen. It is difficult to tell with this writing. It is so fine, and the ink is faded. And the habit they had of capitalizing the oddest words—it makes it difficult to guess whether that is the title or what. But I presume that, being a book, it would be in your library."

"Probably. Unless it was sold or borrowed or given away. Or perhaps even tossed out—it has been several generations, you know. Who is to say that someone along the line would not have thrown the book out?"

"Don't say that!" Cassandra gazed at him in horror.

"It has been a great deal of time, Miss Verrere. Not all my ancestors were lovers of books—including my father."

"Yes, but surely this was an important book, a valuable one, maybe. It was one that Margaret knew of, so it must have had some significance."

"At the time."

"Yes, but if it had significance, one would think it would have been regarded as important enough to be saved by future generations."

"We do have a number of old books, especially on the higher shelves in the library. Certainly we can look for it at Haverly House."

"We?" Cassandra's breath caught in her throat. She had been half afraid that once she gave Sir Philip the clues to the location of the map, he would insist on looking for it by himself. Men were so often strange about things like that. Cassandra suspected that they disliked sharing the fun.

"Why, yes." He cast an amused look at her. "You don't think that I am going to slog through all those books on my own, do you? Oh, no, my dear Miss Verrere, if I search through the attics with you, then *you* have to help me search my library.''

Cassandra beamed. ''It will be my pleasure, I assure you.''

''However, it looks as if we shall have some difficulty searching *your* attic.''

''What do you mean?'' Cassandra glanced at him, startled.

''I mean, your aunt and cousin are difficult people to maneuver around.''

''Oh.'' Cassandra sighed. ''Yes. I am so sorry. Joanna seems to have set her cap for you in a most inflexible way.''

''Mm.''

''I am sure it is most improper, but I think that the best way to handle the situation is to do what we did today. We will have to continue our search in secrecy.''

''You are a woman of great intellect—not to mention kindness.''

''What, to not make you endure Joanna's and Aunt Ardis's company?''

He grinned. ''Did I mention that you are also exceedingly blunt?''

''No.'' She grinned back. ''You did not need to. It has been pointed out to me before.''

It was ludicrous, Philip knew, to be enjoying himself so much, to be sitting here and smiling over this woman's behavior, which was definitely not what one would expect or want in a lady. And yet he could not deny that just being with her lifted his spirits immeasurably. Somehow being here in the backwater of Dunsleigh, meeting Cassandra in secret and crawling about through an old musty attic with her and her siblings, made him much happier than any of the entertainments at the far grander and more sophisticated Arrabeck House. No doubt his friends, if they knew of his odd start, would think that he had run completely mad.

"Miss Verrere," he said, his face suddenly serious, and he reached out to take her hand. "I had another reason for coming here."

Cassandra's nerves began to race at his touch. She had not stopped to put on gloves in her mad dash from the house, and she could feel the warmth of his bare skin against hers. He did not release her hand, and she made no effort to pull it away.

"What is that, sir?" she asked a little breathlessly.

"I needed to apologize."

"Apologize?" She looked puzzled. "Oh. You mean for the way we met—indeed, sir, you have already done so, and it was not your fault. You need not speak of it."

"No. Not that, although it was scarcely behavior worthy of a gentleman. No, I am speaking of the way I acted the following morning, when we were in the maze."

"Wha—oh!" Her thoughts went to the end of their conversation and the way he had kissed her then.

"Yes," he replied grimly. "That. I behaved like a cad. I have no excuse, other than my own lack of control. You…seem to have a certain effect on me."

"I do?" Cassandra was astonished at the idea that her charms might have driven a man to lose control of himself.

Sir Philip had to chuckle at her expression. "My dear lady, that is scarcely the way to respond to a gentleman's apology. You make me want to prove all over again why I kissed you the other time."

"Oh!" Cassandra hadn't the slightest idea how to respond.

"I do not apologize for the feelings that I had, you understand. I— Well, looking at you now, I feel the same desire to kiss you." His voice dropped huskily on the words, and Cassandra went weak in the knees. She could remember no other man who had looked at her in quite the way Sir Philip did now.

"What I apologize for," he continued, "is that I put you in an uncomfortable situation. That I made you feel that I had not listened to your words, or that all I was interested in was a, well, a physical relationship of some sort. I wanted you to know that I do not and would not ever regard you as anything less than a perfect lady. I did not intend to demean you in any way."

"I, uh…" Cassandra could not continue to meet his eyes, for the look there affected her breathing in the most peculiar way. "I accept your apology."

"And I want you to know that I would never…push myself on you. I would not use this situation or our working together in the attics to—to take advantage of you."

"Please—you need not apologize. I would be less than honest if I pretended that the fault was all one-sided."

She glanced up and saw a look of intense male satisfaction cross his face. "Then I was not the only one who felt the attraction?"

He reached out to brush his knuckles across her cheek, and his touch scattered all her thoughts. Cassandra quickly moved away.

"Of course, the fact that there was blame on both sides does not mean that we should allow it to happen again." She hoped he did not hear the panic in her voice. She was not sure how she would respond if Philip were to kiss her again. Just the thought of it made her insides jump around as if she had swallowed live coals. "I—uh, we are going to be working together, and we should, I think, conduct ourselves in, uh, the manner of professional colleagues."

"Professional colleagues?" Humor rose in his eyes.

"What profession, may I ask? Treasure hunter? Aren't those usually pirates?"

"You know what I mean. We should act the way we would act if, say, you were doing this with another man."

He did not point out to her that with another man he would have dropped the whole thing at the beginning and left it that way. What had brought him back to Cassandra was Cassandra herself and not some long-lost dowry, but he was not about to tell her that.

"Otherwise," Cassandra concluded, "our work would suffer. And we would be uncomfortable working together."

"As I told you, I have no wish to make you uncomfortable." It was for that reason that he stood and stepped back from her now, letting out a little sigh of regret.

"Excellent. Shall we agree to meet at Chesilworth this afternoon?"

"No, you must allow me to escort you," he protested. "After all, there is no need for secrecy this afternoon."

"It is doubtless safer if you do not appear at Moulton House this afternoon. I don't know what scheme they might have cooked up to keep you there or to accompany us. Besides, I have no need of an escort; the children will be with me," Cassandra reminded him with a smile. "I know of no men of evil intent who would not be thwarted by the sight of twin twelve-year-old boys and a young girl, too. Besides, there is never need for escort here. Dunsleigh is the most peaceful of places. Olivia often complains that nothing ever happens here."

"With two rowdy young boys, I cannot imagine how that is possible."

"Oh, but whatever one's *brothers* do does not count as anything happening, you see."

"Of course. How silly of me not to realize that. Miss Olivia, I take it, longs for grand adventures."

"Yes. We are all, as you are aware, a family of dreamers." She cast him a significant look.

Sir Philip winced. "Ah, I can see that that statement will come back to haunt me often enough."

Cassandra chuckled. "I shall not mention it again. After all, you have joined us in dreaming now."

"Without your wholehearted enthusiasm, I fear."

"Don't worry. It will come."

Sir Philip watched the way her mouth curved up as she smiled, the inviting fullness of her lower lip and the appealing little dent in the middle that cut into its plump flesh. Oddly, her smile seemed to accentuate the narrow crease. He was aware of a strong desire to kiss the dent away. Though he had meant it when he told Cassandra that he would not want to offend her by making advances or try to take advantage of her, he was not sure how he was going to be around her for any length of time and continue to act like a gentleman.

He forced himself to step back and sketch a bow to her. "Then I will meet you this afternoon at Chesilworth. One o'clock?"

Cassandra nodded. She felt curiously reluctant to part from him. "Yes. One. We will be there."

As soon as Cassandra returned to the house, she was swept up in her aunt's frenzy over the party she had decided to give the following evening. Even though Aunt Ardis had pretended to have already arranged it, in fact there had been no thought of a party until this morning. It would, perforce, be small—if nothing else, there were few people in this rural spot whom Aunt Ardis considered worthy enough to be invited to witness her triumph in having

Sir Philip Neville as a guest. Still, there were invitations to be written and given to a footman to deliver, as well as a dinner to plan, not to mention a thorough cleaning of the formal rooms, flower arrangements and a number of other logistical chores to be taken care of. Such chores, of course, fell, in Aunt Ardis's opinion, into the realm of her efficient niece.

Cassandra managed to get everything set in motion so that she was able to slip away right after luncheon, and she and her brothers and sister went to Chesilworth, where they found Sir Philip waiting for them. They spent the afternoon working as they had the day before, the time livened by Sir Philip's occasional bursts of horseplay with the twins or his twinkling teasing of Olivia. They enjoyed themselves so much that they were late leaving Chesilworth and missed tea at Moulton Hall.

The next day Cassandra once again spent the morning working on her aunt's dinner party, scheduled for that evening. Then she and her siblings hiked the familiar path through meadow and woods to the grounds of Chesilworth.

When they crested the rise behind the house, they saw the figures of two men, and as they drew nearer, it became clear that one was holding a shotgun on the other. With a gasp of dismay, Cassandra recognized the man holding the gun as their former groundskeeper at Chesilworth, Jack Chumley, and the man he threatened as Sir Philip.

"Chumley!" Cassandra lifted her skirts and ran down the hill, her brothers and sister running along with her.

They came to a panting halt beside their former employee, and it was a moment before they could speak. Hart, typically, recovered his breath first.

"What are you doing to Sir Philip?"

"You mean you know this chap?" Chumley asked, his

bushy eyebrows lifting in surprise. "I caught him sneaking around the house just now."

"Sneaking! No, Chumley..."

"I reckoned he was trying to break in."

"He was not trying to break in," Cassandra assured him earnestly. "Pray, put down your gun. Sir Philip is our guest. We invited him to meet us here today."

She turned toward Sir Philip as the servant reluctantly lowered his gun. "I am so sorry, Sir Philip. I cannot think why Chumley would have accosted you."

"I'll tell 'ee why," Chumley volunteered loudly. He had been growing gradually more hard of hearing over the years, and the volume of his voice had grown with the decrease in his hearing. "'Cause of the strange happenings out here last night, that's why. I may not be working here no more, but it'll not be said that Jack Chumley allowed such goings on where he lived and worked his whole life."

"Dear Chumley, of course you would not. But what are you talking about? What happenings are you talking about? What goings on?"

"You mean nobody's told you? It was all over the village this morning. Ned Plumpton was the one told me. Folks are saying there're ghosts in the house." He jerked his thumb toward the castlelike structure behind him.

"Ghosts?" Cassandra repeated blankly.

"Aye," he said disgustedly. "Ghosts! 'Ye're mad,' says I. 'Weren't never any ghosts at Chesilworth.' Why, his lordship would'a gone on and on about it if there had been. He'd'a been tickled pink, he would, been talking on and on about 'em, tryin' to see 'em and all."

Cassandra smiled fondly. "You're right about that. But I still don't understand—"

"Well, it weren't just Plumpton, now, was it? Missus Brookman, she tells me she'd heard the rumors, too. From

Farmer Crawford. Now I know Farmer Crawford, and he's one with a good head on his shoulders. Missus Brookman, she says it were his son what seen it.''

"The ghost?"

"Yes'm. So I goes over to the Crawfords' place, and he says the story's true enough. His son—"

"Ben?"

"No, not that one. Beggin' your pardon, miss, but that one's got bats in his belfry, he does. No, Crawford wouldn't go 'cause Ben saw it. It were young Alf. Only the age of the young lordship here, but he's as sharp as the day is long. So when he come in talking about lights in the windows and such, Crawford knew he'd seen something, well, just like we would if it were Master Crispin or Master Hart.''

"He saw *lights* in Chesilworth?" Cassandra repeated, her gaze going to Sir Philip. She saw mirrored in his face the same sudden concern that stabbed her.

"Aye, miss, lights, and not just him, neither. When he told his pa about it, Farmer Crawford went back over with him to look. He knew Alf wasn't lying, but he figured he must have been mistaken about what it was. Well, Crawford saw the light, too. It were in the attic, he said. You can only see it from those little windows. But it were there, and it glowed.''

"I see." *Someone had been in the attic.* Cassandra could think of only one reason why anyone would go there at night—to search alone and undetected.

"'Course, I knew it weren't no ghosts. Intruder, more like. A tramp or something, I thought, who'd broken in for a place to stay. Though the attic seems a mighty uncomfortable place to choose, if you ask me. So, anyway, I decided I best come over here and check things out, see if there's sign of someone breaking in. And who do I find but this one—skulking about.''

''My good man, I was *not* skulking,'' Sir Philip protested. ''I was waiting for Miss Verrere and family.''

''And how was I to know that, sir? Ye're a stranger to these parts.''

''He was telling the truth, Chumley,'' Cassandra assured him. ''But it was very thoughtful of you to come to check on the place for us.''

''I reckon it were my duty to his lordship, God rest his soul.''

''Papa would have been very grateful. You may go on home now. I don't expect you to watch Chesilworth for us. We will check and see if there are any signs of an intruder.''

The old man looked doubtful. ''Mayhap I'd best come in with you. You might need a weapon.''

''I am sure that whoever it was is gone now.''

But the old man would not be satisfied until he had gone around to each of the downstairs doors and windows and found the broken pane where the intruder had reached in and opened the window. He nodded, vindicated, and said that he would board it up.

They made a cursory inspection of the upper floors with Chumley, but as all of them expected, they found no one, or even a sign of anyone. Even the attic floor, dusty as it was, had had too many people tramping through it to isolate an intruder's footprints.

After Chumley clumped down the attic stairs, the others stood for a moment, looking at one another. Finally Crispin cried, ''Well? Who is it? Is somebody looking for our treasure?''

''It could be simply an intruder, I suppose,'' Cassandra

said slowly. "Someone who needed a place to spend the night."

"In the attic? With all the beds downstairs?" Olivia said scornfully.

"Yes, I know. But it seems so absurd—I mean, who?" Cassandra carefully avoided looking at Sir Philip, for fear he would see the thought that had immediately sprung into her head as soon as she said the question. The most likely person to have been searching for the letters was Sir Philip himself.

He alone had access to the other half of the map. Now that she had told him where the map was located, he could steal her letter and have both halves. Perhaps he had only pretended to want her help and not to know what the Queens Book was. It might have been as familiar to him as the family Bible, so he had known instantly where he could find the other half. He wouldn't need her help to find it, and if he could steal the letters from Chesilworth, then he could have the whole dowry to himself.

"What about your American cousin?" Sir Philip suggested.

Cassandra was startled out of her thoughts. Her head snapped up and she stared at Neville. "What?"

"I am referring to Mr. Miller. Isn't that his name? The former owner of the journals."

"No!" Olivia's answer was swift and emphatic. She moved forward, crossing her arms pugnaciously over her chest. "He would never do such a thing. David, I mean, Mr. Miller, was a very nice man."

Cassandra narrowed her eyes thoughtfully at her sister. She had suspected that Olivia had developed something of a crush on the handsome American. *Perhaps it was worse than she had realized.*

She shrugged aside the thought. There was more to

worry about now than her little sister growing up and forming *tendres* for inappropriate men. "Honestly, Sir Philip, you take suspicion to new heights. I thought you envisioned Mr. Miller as the forger of the journals, swindling Mr. Simons out of a few pounds."

"Perhaps I am rethinking my position. Someone breaking into the attic here puts a new light on things."

"I am glad to find that *something* will make you examine your opinions a little more closely," Cassandra told him tartly.

"It makes more sense," he stated, ignoring her remark. "The quality of the forgery would have to be stupendous, and it would have been far too much work, as you said, for a relatively small amount of money. If the journals are real, then Mr. Miller, in reading them, would have realized that there was the possibility of finding a fortune here in England."

"I don't understand," Crispin interrupted. "What do you mean, if they are real? What else could they be?"

Cassandra gave him a pithy explanation of the possibility of forging such documents, adding, "But obviously there must be something to them, or there would not have been a person searching our attic for the letters Margaret wrote to her father." She turned back to Sir Philip. "But I see no reason for it to have been Mr. Miller. Why would he have sold the journals in the first place if he knew of the existence of the treasure? Why not come here and steal the letters, steal the book from your library...we would have had no idea why anyone had broken into either place, since we would have known nothing of the maps to the dowry. We would have written this episode off to a thief or a vagrant breaking into Chesilworth for a night."

"Yes, but you have to remember that Mr. Miller is an American several generations removed from the events.

The legend of the missing dowry probably was not handed down in his family from generation to generation, as it was in ours. When he read the journal, he would not have even known where to start. He wouldn't have known where the Neville and Verrere families lived or who might still have the maps in question. He wouldn't even know that the dowry was still lost. Our families could have joined together as Margaret requested and found the treasure long ago. The best thing he could do was bring the journals to England and try to sell them. He could wait and see who was interested in them, see if he could stir up the Verreres or the Nevilles. He could follow the leads and locate maps. He did, after all, follow the journals to you."

"He only wanted to meet us," Olivia interjected.

"And if I remember correctly," Sir Philip continued inexorably, "you told him how you were searching your attics for the letters in question. I suspect you even told him about the Nevilles' part of it. All he would have to know was that Haverly House was the Neville home seat and he could have figured out that he would need to search the library there to retrieve a book. After that, it would have been relatively simple. Search the attics, find the letters, then go on to Haverly House, cutting out all the pesky relatives."

"Why wait a year?" Cassandra queried. "He could have followed the journals here when Papa bought them, with exactly the same result. Why wait till now? It seems to me that that is the important thing—that it is only now that someone started searching for the letters. It would suggest that that someone just learned of it."

Sir Philip quirked an eyebrow, and his voice went ominously quiet. "Are you suggesting that *I* am the thief?"

7

Cassandra wavered a little at his icy demeanor, but she kept her voice calm. "There is a certain logic to it."

Neville pressed his lips together, and for a moment, Cassandra thought he was going to explode into a furious denial, but he said only, "Yes, I can see that it has logic— I am sure anyone would trust a man about whom they knew absolutely nothing, like David Miller, over a man whom you know is a peer of the realm, a scion of one of the oldest and most honorable families in England, and, moreover, a man of enough wealth that this Spanish dowry would hardly swell his coffers."

Cassandra's spine stiffened. She had felt a moment's discomfort over voicing her suspicion, but Neville's arrogant words drove the vague guilt completely away. "No doubt all rich men are exempt from seeking further wealth, as well as from being greedy villains. It is only we impoverished folk who have such low morals that we would stoop to look for money. It is only unknown *foreigners* who would break into houses."

Neville shifted uncomfortably. "I did not say that. I simply pointed out that logic would indicate the stranger rather than the man you know."

"But I know neither of you," Cassandra reminded him crisply. "Indeed, I have probably talked with you less than I have with Mr. Miller, since he visited with us for several days. But I do know that you are a Neville, and historically Nevilles have not been friends of Verreres. I also know that wealth is often obtained in dishonest ways, and that wealthy men often cannot get enough money to satisfy them. It is my intent not to blame you or Mr. Miller or some other person until I have more facts. I strive always to be fair."

Sir Philip ground his teeth. He was not sure why it made him furious that Cassandra should so coolly and reasonably suggest that he could be the intruder. But he did know that it galled him to the point where he would have liked to grab her by the shoulders and shake some sense into her.

"You are the one who dislikes coincidences," she continued calmly. "Wouldn't you say it was rather fortuitous that this break-in occurred the day after you arrived here? And that it occurred two weeks after you learned of the treasure—and a *year* after Mr. Miller did?"

Flame crackled to life in Philip's golden eyes, but he clenched his fists tightly at his sides and waited a moment before he spoke. "Fortuitous, too, that it happened only a week after Mr. Miller was here and you showed him where you were looking for the key to the treasure." He let out a noise of disgust. "You are determined to make me the villain, are you not?"

"No. I would far rather trust my partner," Cassandra admitted honestly. "But I also have difficulty believing that Mr. Miller is an evil man, and, besides, it makes no sense that he would wait a year."

"Ah, but it does if you consider that he might have sold the journals having no idea that there was any truth to the story of the treasure or that the families still existed. He may have thought he would be content with the money he made from selling the journals. But then this year, when he came back and visited your Mr. Simons, he learned of the Verreres' existence. Perhaps Mr. Simons even told him about the legend of the lost dowry and of your father's interest in trying to find it. Perhaps then he rethought the matter and saw that he could come here and trick you into telling him about it. That he could seize the whole treasure for himself.''

"That is all speculation."

"Indeed. So is everything else we have been saying for the past few minutes. We have absolutely no idea who was up here last night. We don't even know for sure that they were looking for the letters. We only presume that."

"It makes little sense otherwise."

"Unfortunately, I have found that things all too often do not make sense."

Cassandra cocked a disbelieving eyebrow. "Are you saying that you think it was coincidence that someone was in this attic last night?"

He sighed. "No. It is a possibility, but I cannot really believe it. Someone must have been looking for those letters. With any luck, they had as much trouble finding them as we had. Still, it makes it imperative that we find the letters as quickly as possible, wouldn't you say?"

"Absolutely. I am glad that there is something upon which we can agree. Shall we stop our guesswork and get down to business?"

"Immediately." He stripped off his coat and ascot, tossing them over a chair, and rolled up his shirtsleeves. "Where shall I start?"

They worked along quietly for some time, slowly moving through box after box and trunk after trunk, moving aside furniture and all sorts of the odd detritus left from occupying a house for hundreds of years. Then Olivia let out a gasp, and they all swung toward her.

"What is it?" Cassandra started toward her worriedly, afraid that she had hurt herself. She paused and wrinkled her nose. "Phew! What is that smell?"

"Camphor, I think. There are little bags of something in here with the clothes. Funny, isn't it, how it still stinks? But look." She reached with both hands into the trunk before her and stood up, pulling out a bodice with one hand and a skirt with the other. "It's faded over time, but isn't it magnificent?"

Cassandra came over to stand beside her. "Yes. It is. Beautiful." It was a heavy gown of green velvet, faded, but still rich with golden embroidery. It had a square neckline, and the stiff bodice laced up the back. The front of it was covered with a large pattern of flowers done in thread and braid, still richly golden despite the years, and a matching pattern ran around the ends of the full sleeves, puffed to the elbow and then slit open the rest of the way down over a cascade of lace, now tattered and yellowed with age. The hem of the skirt, too, was trimmed in the same pattern of embroidery and braiding.

"When is it from, Cassandra?" Olivia asked excitedly. "Do you think it was a court dress? Or a wedding gown?"

"It looks very special indeed." Cassandra reached out and grasped the skirt, holding it out on the sides. "It looks made to be worn hooped out to the side, but not nearly so wide as those dresses during the 1740s and later. I think it's older. Not as old as Elizabeth or even James I. There aren't any ruffs, the sleeves are attached, and the waist is more normal, not that long, waspy shape. I would say maybe the time of the Cavaliers—or maybe later, King Charles II."

"It's so romantic!" Olivia held the skirt up to herself, pulling one side of it out, and executed a twirl.

"Oh, my." Cassandra peered down into the trunk and pulled out a shoe, also of velvet, this time deep blue, and also richly embroidered. It had a thick, blocky heel and squared-off toe.

"Goodness! Imagine wearing that. It's so big!" Olivia marveled.

"Much too big to be a woman's, I think. My guess is that it belonged to some Lord Chesilworth," Cassandra told her.

"That!" Crispin stared in fascination at the ornate shoe. "You're jesting."

"Men wore much more colorful attire back then," Sir Philip answered, joining them around the trunk. He took the shoe in his hand. "There is a portrait of one of my ancestors in shoes much like these. He wore a very fancy coat and vest, as well, and rather baggy trousers and huge sleeves, slit like this dress's to show billowing lacy shirt-sleeves."

"Let's try it on!" Olivia cried. "Please, Cassandra…"

"I suppose. But be very careful. It's ancient." She went with her sister behind a stack of boxes large enough to conceal them and helped her sister into the old, formal clothes.

"Oh! It's too big!" Olivia wailed. The skirt, without hoop or petticoats beneath it, was far too long, and the bodice hung on her still-undeveloped body. "You put it on. It will fit you much better," she told Cassandra, perking up. "Please…I want to see how it looks."

Olivia helped Cassandra out of her own dress and into the other one. "Oh, Cassie…" she breathed. "It's beautiful."

Olivia pulled Cassandra out from behind the boxes to

where Sir Philip and the boys stood. "Look how beautiful it is on Cassie."

Sir Philip turned and gazed at her for a long moment. "It is indeed," he said quietly, and his eyes traveled down her body.

Cassandra was very aware of the way the stiff, undarted bodice pushed up her breasts so that their tops swelled above the neckline. She could feel the heat rising up her neck as he looked at her. She wet her lips unconsciously and turned away, going to the trunk.

"If I am having to play dress-up," she said, "then I refuse to be the only one." She bent over the trunk and shuffled through the other clothes that were there. "Aha!"

She pulled up a coat, also decorated with embroidery and boasting the sort of loose, full sleeves that Sir Philip had mentioned earlier. She turned, holding it out. "Here. You have to try on this coat."

Sir Philip looked at it doubtfully, but reached out to take it. Carefully he pulled it on and straightened it down the front. Cassandra caught her breath. He looked as if he should have a slender sword strapped to his side and an upturned hat with a plume.

She started to speak, but nothing came out, and she had to try again. "You look as if you are about to go out to fight the Roundheads."

"Mm. More likely tuck one of Charles's toy spaniels under my arm and mince about the court."

"You?" Cassandra smiled. "Never!"

"Why, thank you…I think."

"'Twas meant as a compliment. Come, we should see how we look."

Cassandra led him through the trunks and boxes to where a long cheval glass stood propped against the attic wall. She was not aware that she had taken his hand to lead him there until she saw their clasped hands reflected in the looking glass. She dropped his hand as if it had suddenly grown hot. Her eyes flew involuntarily to his in the mirror. There was none of the amusement she had expected, only a fierce flame, a fire that mirrored the sudden spark deep inside herself. She wished suddenly and intensely that Olivia and the twins were back at Moulton Hall instead of here with them.

It required a physical effort on her part to turn away from him. "This is not getting the letters found," she said stiffly, sounding priggish even to her own ears. "We should get back to work."

"You are right, of course."

"Cassie..." Olivia complained. "What about the other things in the trunk?"

"Check through them, of course. This trunk is most encouraging." She kept her voice carefully businesslike, not betraying that her pulse was running a trifle fast or that she could still feel the way Philip's hand had felt in hers as she had led him to the mirror. *It had been so hard and firm in contrast to hers, so warm, so...exciting.* She cleared her throat, jerking her mind back to the matters at hand. "It, ah, is the first thing we have found from the right century. However, it is a little *too* early, I think. Perhaps we *should* move our search closer to it. Except that the attic isn't completely neat and orderly."

"Why don't Olivia and the boys work from the wall in?" Neville suggested. Cassandra thought his voice was enviably, irritatingly, devoid of emotion or nerves. "You and I will come in from where we are, and perhaps it will lie between the two."

Cassandra agreed and retired behind the boxes to get rid of the Cavalier lady and return to the workaday woman who was committed to the search for Margaret Verrere's letters. She shrugged off the faint deflation she felt when she was once again in her own worst clothes and returned to the trunk she had been methodically unloading earlier.

They continued to work through the afternoon, but though they covered another large chunk of the attic, they did not find anything relating to Margaret Verrere or her father. Finally Cassandra sat back on her heels with a despondent sigh and wiped the sweat from her forehead with an unladylike swipe of her hand.

Sir Philip removed his watch from its pocket and opened it. ''I fear we must stop. I have to return to the inn to get ready for this evening's dinner.''

''Oh!'' Cassandra jumped to her feet. ''Sweet Lord, what time is it?'' When Sir Philip told her, she let out another moan. ''What was I thinking of? I have to get back to Moulton Hall to prepare for the party.''

She had left everything humming along, but one never knew what might have happened to derail her plans—contradictory commands from her aunt, or Joanna's meddling, or an obstacle she had not foreseen and which none of the servants were willing or able to take care of without the advice of someone in authority. She had meant to leave herself plenty of time to look over the house and the food preparations, and make sure that everything was in order, but she was, she realized now, much too tardy, and she would probably have to skimp on her own preparations for the dance.

Well, that was something that was of little importance, she told herself as she bade Sir Philip a short farewell and hurried with the children up the hill toward Moulton Hall. She had never been one to shine at parties, and she dimmed even more than normal around Joanna's beauty and vivacity. Why, she didn't even have a new gown to wear. The coffee-colored satin she planned to wear was at

least three years old, and the new lace and ribbons, and
the resewing she had done to the skirt, could not make it
appear new. Moreover, it had not been a good color for
her, and she had wished that she had not ordered it from
the dressmaker in Bath, but it had been too dear not to
wear it.

She did not like to admit it, but the truth was that she
coveted the dress her aunt was wearing tonight. Well, not
that actual dress, of course, for anything her aunt could
wear would have been so short that Cassandra's ankles
would have showed and so large around it would have
swamped her. What she envied was the material. It was a
lovely light gray satin, perhaps not the favored color for a
young woman, but Cassandra had been certain that its
color would complement her eyes, and, besides, the color
had a shimmer to it that lifted it above mere gray and
seemed to contain flashes of mauve and lavender and other
elusive pastel colors that enlivened Cassandra's pale skin.

Aunt Ardis had seen her staring at it in the shop window
one day in Fairbourne, and she had come over to see what
it was that had caught Cassandra's attention.

"Why, what lovely material!" Aunt Ardis had exclaimed, and for a brief moment Cassandra's heart had
leapt with hope that the woman would purchase it for her,
seeing what a perfect color it was for Cassandra.

Instead, she had said, "How lucky that you saw it, Cassandra. It would make a lovely dress for me. Edged with
black lace, perhaps. Come, let us go inside. Of course, the
dressmaker here in Dunsleigh is hopelessly behind the
times, but perhaps, just this once, she could whip up something acceptable."

So Cassandra had gone in with a heavy heart, biting her
tongue as her aunt ruined the material with rows of ruffles
and the addition of lace and ribbons and fichu until it was

girlish and overdecorated enough to suit Aunt Ardis's tastes. Cassandra did not think that her aunt had taken the material she had loved and made it her own out of sheer cruelty. It was, she thought, simply that her aunt was so uncomplicatedly, utterly selfish that it never occurred to her that she might give up something she liked to anyone else.

Of course, the dress was nothing Cassandra would want now. Still, when she was dressed in her old café-au-lait satin, her hair hastily twisted up into a simple knot, she could not help releasing a little sigh as she glanced over at her aunt and saw the shimmer of color in the pale, watery silk as the soft glow of the candles touched it.

But Cassandra was not one to bemoan circumstances that she could not change, and, besides, she had her hands full making sure that the dinner went off smoothly and that no one was left standing about with no one to talk to. She circulated through the room, signaling to a footman when refreshment was needed and stopping beside Squire Harrelson's chair to chat when she saw that he was sitting alone, pinned to his chair by the latest in a long string of hunting accidents. The squire's desire to hunt far outpaced his ability to ride, and over the years he had acquired an assortment of broken arms, sprained ankles and bruised hips that would have daunted a lesser man.

She sensed rather than saw when Sir Philip entered the room. She wasn't sure how she knew, for she had never felt anything quite like it before. But all of a sudden the skin on the back of her neck prickled, and she could not stop herself from glancing quickly behind her. She saw Sir Philip standing in the doorway, his eyes on her. He smiled when she spotted him and started across the room toward her.

Aunt Ardis quickly waylaid him, however, and dragged

him across the room to meet the vicar and his wife and daughter. It was not until after dinner that Cassandra actually talked to Sir Philip, though she saw him now and again across the room and smiled. Sir Philip was not a guest whom she needed to worry about being entertained; he would have to be fighting off everyone all evening, for he was the prize of the party. Nor did she have any desire to give either Joanna or Aunt Ardis the slightest reason to scold her for trying to "compete" with Joanna for Sir Philip's affections. Though she cherished none of the delusions the Moulton women did that Sir Philip had any regard for Joanna, life would be much easier as long as Joanna and Aunt Ardis thought he did. While Aunt Ardis and Joanna were hot in pursuit of a supremely eligible male, they cared little for what Cassandra was involved with.

However, sometime after dinner, as Cassandra was turning away from Mr. Winton's boring, braying sister, escaping at the first reasonable lull in the conversation, she almost ran right into Sir Philip, who was standing behind her. She gasped, then laughed.

"Sir Philip. I am sorry. I did not mean to run you over. I did not realize you were standing there."

He deftly drew her away from the loud Miss Winton, saying in a low voice, "I was hiding behind the curio cabinet. I did not wish to call attention to myself, as I feared I would have to join your circle. Having been ensnared by Miss Winton for ten interminable minutes earlier this evening, I was very cautious."

"Wise man," Cassandra murmured.

"I haven't spoken to you all evening. Every time I head in your direction, you disappear. Are you avoiding me, Miss Verrere?"

"Of course not." Cassandra preferred not to think how

pleasant it was to be talking to Sir Philip as they skirted another pocket of guests and eased into the hall. "But you are the honored guest. Everyone wants to talk to you."

"At tedious length," he acknowledged.

"I did not think I should take up your time, since I spent the entire afternoon in your company."

"Still, you could have had a pang of pity for me," he told her, his eyes glinting in the gentle light of the hall sconces. "It would have alleviated my boredom a great deal to hear a few minutes of intelligent conversation."

"Sir Philip, you flatter me."

"No flattery, Miss Verrere. The simple truth. A bit of your astringent wit would have worked wonders against the cloying sentiments of most of the guests. If I hear another description of a daughter's or niece's insipid watercolors or lifeless execution of sonatas, I fear I will strangle someone."

Laughter bubbled up from her throat. "How unkind of you, sir. You have not seen these works of art or heard the pieces."

"No, but I have heard of them, and I have met the young women in question, and if anything greater than mediocrity could issue from them, I would be most amazed."

"Dunsleigh is not a place of great accomplishments," Cassandra admitted, unaware of how her eyes sparkled as she smiled or of the creamy texture of her skin.

Sir Philip, on the other hand, was well aware of both things, as well as of the outmoded, ill-colored dress she wore. He was also aware of an urge to buy something lovely for her. He wanted to see her in some elegant dress the color of which played up her cool gray eyes and the style of which emphasized her delightful slender, high-breasted figure. Something, say, like the dress her aunt had worn tonight—not the awful frilly style, of course, but the material, a lovely shimmering silk that made him think of light summer rains and the rainbows afterward.

However, the offer of a top-notch modiste's gown was a present that no woman of good character could accept from a male other than her father or brother or other relative. Even a strand of milky pearls to circle her long, elegant throat would be unthinkable from any but a fiancé. For the first time that he could remember, Sir Philip chafed under such social restrictions. He thought how absurd it was that a man could lavish presents upon a woman of easy virtue, whereas even the poorest woman of gentility could accept nothing from a man. He would have liked very much at that moment to give Cassandra something lovely and see her eyes light up with pleasure.

"There you are!" came Aunt Ardis's ringing voice.

Cassandra and Philip glanced up, startled, to see her bearing down upon them from the drawing room doorway. Philip could not hold back a heartfelt groan.

"Whatever are you thinking, Cassandra?" her aunt scolded with heavy playfulness, wagging an admonitory finger at her. "Keeping Sir Philip talking out here in the hall!" She reached them and linked her hand through his arm. "You must excuse her, Sir Philip. I am afraid my niece has never been much in society."

"Yes," he responded coolly. "I find her most refreshing."

Aunt Ardis smiled at him archly. "Now, don't you be using that charm on us poor country girls, eh, Cassandra? You will leave a string of broken hearts behind you."

He made a polite demurral as Ardis led him away. Cassandra, watching them, sighed. All the glow seemed to have gone out of the evening. From then on, she felt as if she were merely marking time, waiting for the party to end.

Eventually it did, breaking up within minutes after Sir Philip's departure. As soon as the last guest left, Aunt Ardis collapsed into a chair, as if she had brought off the evening successfully with great effort on her part. However, she soon recovered enough to launch into a discussion with Joanna over the success of the evening, hashing and rehashing every movement Sir Philip had made and each attention that he had paid to Joanna.

Cassandra grimaced and went straight up to bed. The light was burning dimly in the room she shared with Olivia, and she could see that Olivia was already asleep. Olivia, deemed too young by her aunt to participate in the delights of the evening, had refused to even watch the festivities through the stair rail, as her brothers had, and Cassandra suspected that she had gone early to bed.

She undressed quietly, careful not to disturb her sister, and crawled into bed for a brief nap, leaving the lamp burning low. She could not sleep deeply with light in the room, and she awoke after a couple of hours, as she had known she would. Olivia was still sleeping soundly beside her. Cassandra crawled out of bed and dressed without making noise. She did not pull on the usual number of petticoats to fill out the skirt. She wanted to be as free and unhampered in her movements tonight as possible. Opening the lid of the chest at the foot of the bed, she pulled out a blanket, which she tucked under her arm. Then she picked up her sturdiest pair of boots, turned out the flame of the lamp and slipped out of her bedroom, closing the door softly behind her.

She stood for a moment, letting her eyes adjust to the darkness of the hallway, lit only by the long windows at one end. She moved like a wraith along the passage and down the stairs to her uncle's study. Once inside, with the door closed, she dared to light a candle to help her see. She crossed to a cabinet and pulled a wrapped object from inside it. Carefully she peeled back the cloth to reveal a revolver. From a drawer she took out a handful of bullets and loaded the gun, then slipped both the gun and extra bullets into the capacious pocket of her skirt. Cassandra had never used a gun except for target practice, but her father had been a believer in a complete education for his girls as well as his boys, and he had had their gamekeeper instruct her in the use of firearms. Always a quick student, Cassandra had proved to have a steady hand and a good eye, and she was confident that she could defend herself if the need arose.

A final stop in the kitchen got her a lantern, which she lit, then lowered the shields on all sides but one. She left the house and crossed the garden, taking the familiar path to Chesilworth.

It had taken her only a few minutes of thought after Jack Chumley's startling news to realize that the best thing to do would be to return tonight to the mansion and try to catch the intruder. Her plan was simple: she would make her way to the hill behind the house and there, beneath the cover of a clump of trees, she would settle down to watch for signs of a light in the house. When a light appeared, she would sneak closer and take a good look at who it was. She had brought the blanket to make sitting for some time on the ground more bearable, and she had brought the pistol for protection. She had thought at first about actually confronting the intruder, but even though she was armed, she thought it might be too dangerous. There was, after all, only one of her, and there was no telling what a cornered man might do. It would be better, she knew, to control her impulses and merely find out who was searching for the letters.

She could not bring herself to believe that it was either Sir Philip or Mr. Miller. Sir Philip could be a most aggravating man—but a thief? It hardly seemed possible. He was, as he had pointed out, a very wealthy man already. Would he risk being exposed as a thief—or at least a trespasser—to acquire what was to him a relatively small amount of money? He would get half of it anyway! And Mr. Miller had had the most honest of faces. Surely a man who laughed so easily and talked so openly could not be a villain inside. Still, she had nothing to go on except her instincts, and she wanted proof.

She reached the copse of trees behind Chesilworth and spread out the blanket to sit on. Turning off the lantern, she sat down to wait. She stared across at the dark hulk of Chesilworth. There was no sign of a light in the attic or anywhere else. After a while her back began to ache, and she shifted so that she was leaning against the tree trunk. More time passed. Her eyelids began to grow heavy as she watched, and she had to struggle to keep them open. Suddenly she came to with a jerk, and she realized that she had fallen asleep, her head lolling forward.

Cassandra rubbed her face with the heels of her hands and gave herself a bracing lecture on the value of staying awake. Yet, despite her best efforts, she soon felt herself nodding off again. It was just that the night was so velvety dark, the house so unchanging, the sounds of the night so soft and somnambulant.

She blinked, suddenly fully awake, and leaned forward. There it was, the flash of a light. The light appeared again, and she realized that its carrier had gone behind the side garden wall and then reemerged behind the house. A huge cold knot formed in Cassandra's chest. She wasn't sure whether she was more excited or terrified. She rose to her feet, reaching into her pocket to close her hand reassuringly around the pistol.

Leaving the cover of the trees, she started down the hill toward Chesilworth. She did not want to carry the lantern, for its light would make her as obvious to the intruder as his had made him obvious to her. But without the light the uneven ground was shrouded in shadow, and she had to go slowly for fear of stepping in a hole and twisting her ankle or slamming into a hillock of grass.

The intruder's light was gone. Either he had shut it off or he had disappeared around the corner of the house. No doubt he was looking for another entrance, since Chumley had blocked the broken windowpane. In retrospect, Cassandra wished that she had told Chumley not to. Seeing that piece of wood across the empty pane, he would be bound to realize that his break-in had been discovered. It might make him wary of going in. He might guess that someone was out in the dark lying in wait for him.

The thought hastened Cassandra's feet. Her eyes were intent on the ground. Suddenly she sensed something to her left, but before she could turn, a heavy weight rammed into her, knocking her flat on the ground.

Frantically Cassandra struggled, lashing out with her arms and legs. One of her elbows connected sharply with something hard. She heard her attacker gasp and mutter a low curse. His hold on her lessened involuntarily, and Cassandra seized the opportunity to try to crawl out from beneath him. But he was too quick for her, and he grabbed at her shoulders. One hand caught in the neckline of her dress, and as Cassandra tried to twist away, it tore, ripping straight down the front. His hand slid down across her bare chest and onto the top of her breast.

"Christ in heaven!"

Cassandra found her breath again and shrieked a half second before the sound of his voice registered in her ears. He turned her over roughly and pinned her arms to the ground. For a long moment they simply stared into each other's faces, barely visible in the dim light.

"Sir Philip!" Her chest felt as if someone had stabbed her. "It was *you*? *You* are the thief?"

8

"I should have known," Sir Philip said with weary bitterness. Letting out a muffled curse, he sat up, releasing her.

But Cassandra did not move. She felt too heavy, as if her heart weighed her down. "But why?" She could feel tears lurking embarrassingly close. "Why would you try to steal the letters from me?"

He stared at her, the import of her words only now sinking in on him. He let out a disgusted noise. "You think that I— You little fool! *I*'m not the intruder! I thought *you* were."

"Me? That's insane. Why would I break into my own house at night to look for the letters when I am already doing so every afternoon?"

"I didn't mean *you,* you."

Cassandra stared at him. "Exactly what me did you mean?"

He let out a low growl. "What I am trying to say is that I did not realize it was you when I jumped at you. I saw someone skulking down the hill. It is rather dark, you know, and I assumed it was the thief coming to break into the house again. So I ran at him—and took you down."

He touched his cheek gingerly. "Damn, but you wield a mean elbow!"

"Do you mean to tell me that you were hiding, trying to catch the intruder?" Cassandra asked in exasperation.

"Of course. As soon as your man told us about it this afternoon, I realized that I must come here tonight and lie in wait to see if I could catch the villain. But all I caught was you."

"That is what *I* was doing." She giggled, swept with relief. *Of course, it could not have been Philip she saw with the lantern. Surely he could not have doubled back and attacked her from behind so quickly—and how would he have even known she was coming down the hill?*

"But he was here!" she exclaimed, sitting up. "I saw a lantern moving behind the house. That is why I started down the hill."

"You were planning to confront him?" Neville almost shouted. "Really, Cassandra! The man is probably dangerous! What's to stop him bashing you over the head?"

"Don't worry. I have a gun." She reached into her pocket and pulled out the pistol.

"A gun!" His voice slid comically upward. "And you tell me not to worry? For God's sake, put that thing away. You are a menace to yourself and everyone around you!"

"Me!" she retorted indignantly. "I am not the one who goes about knocking people to the ground without even waiting to see who they are!" She pulled her legs under her and tried to stand, but Philip was still sitting on her skirts, and she could not budge. "What are we sitting here for? The intruder is—"

"Long gone by now," Neville interrupted wearily. "Do you honestly think he has been hanging about while we screamed and wrestled and shouted at one another?"

"Oh. I suppose not." She pulled at her skirts in irritation. "Would you get off me?"

He looked at her. Cassandra was suddenly aware of the sexual import of what she had said. Her words seemed to hang in the air between them, and she could not help but recall that only a moment before he had indeed been on top of her, his muscular body pressing into hers. Her heart began to hammer within her chest, and she could feel the betraying heat rising in her face.

"I didn't mean—that is—" She stumbled to a halt, realized that she could only make it worse by enlarging on her statement.

She stole a peek at Sir Philip and saw that his eyes were not on her face but had drifted downward. It wasn't until then that she remembered the ripping sound when he had grabbed her. She was aware suddenly of the caress of the night air on her bare chest, and she glanced down, horror-stricken. The bodice of her dress was torn at a slant from the neckline on one side almost to the waist on the other. It hung open, exposing her whole front, clad only in a thin white cotton chemise. The tops of her breasts swelled above the beribboned chemise, and her nipples pointed obviously beneath the material, aroused by the cool touch of the air.

Cassandra swallowed, her embarrassment so acute that she was past blushing. *How could she possibly manage to be caught again in such a compromising position with this man?* Looking at his face, however, she knew that there was another feeling inside her, something that was not embarrassment at all, but a dark, hungry sensation, titillating and almost proud as his eyes ate up her near-naked form.

Sir Philip's eyes were pools of darkness, his mouth heavy with desire. Looking at her made him hungry, she knew, and that thought aroused an answering heaviness in her own loins. His gaze dropped lower, going to her legs, clearly outlined beneath her skirts, with no concealing petticoats to hide the shape. Slowly, caressingly, his eyes moved upward again until he was gazing into her face.

"I want you," he said baldly. He felt suddenly so light-headed with desire that he could scarcely think. Cassandra's hair was hanging loose around her shoulders, pale and silky, inviting his touch, and her lush body was so close....

Cassandra wet her lips. She could think of nothing to say. She could feel her nipples tightening even more, just at his words. She thought of his lips on hers, his tongue in her mouth. She remembered his hands caressing her breasts, his mouth fastening on her nipple.

"That wasn't a dream, was it?" she asked huskily. "That night when we met...I wasn't dreaming. You were doing those things...."

"Yes." Blood was pounding in his loins. "I kissed you." Cassandra's hand went unconsciously to her breast. "I touched you."

He reached out, laying his hand over hers. She looked up, startled, and her eyes were caught by his. Mesmerized, she stared into the dark depths of desire glittering in his eyes, and her hand dropped away. His palm settled on her breast. His fingers curved around the soft orb, hot even through the cloth of her chemise. Heat flooded Cassandra's face, but she could not tear her gaze from his. She was too breathless to speak, and her brain could not find the words to protest, anyway. Her thoughts were too jumbled, too searing.

His hand moved up and then down beneath the light chemise, gliding over her naked breasts. He caressed her, finding the point of her nipple and taking it gently between his forefinger and thumb. Cassandra drew in her breath sharply at the sudden, intense pleasure as he manipulated the little bud of flesh. Heat flooded her abdomen, and there was suddenly moisture between her legs. A groan escaped her, and the soft noise almost catapulted his own desire past control.

"Cassandra..." He moved closer, swinging one leg behind her, the knee up so that his leg formed a support for her back, and moving the other across her lap, its weight pinning down her legs.

He pushed down the front of her chemise, exposing her pale breasts. He stared at her in the pale starlight, his eyes avidly taking in the smooth, plump orbs and the large dark circles of her nipples, the hardening buttons of flesh thrusting out from the centers. He swallowed, unable to speak, aware of little except the desire raging in him.

"You are so beautiful," he murmured, delicately tracing each nipple with a finger. Cassandra closed her eyes and leaned back against his leg as though drained of energy, the very picture of a woman surrendering to passion. Desire slammed through him like a giant fist, making him tremble.

Philip knew that despite all his good intentions, he was going to make love to her now. He was going to lay her back on the ground and feast on her lush breasts. He was going to kiss her until her lips were dark and swollen. And he was going to move her legs apart and thrust himself deep inside her, claiming her, ravishing her, making her his.

His arms went around her, and he pulled her up tightly against him, pressing the side of her hip into his pulsing desire, and he bent to sink his lips into hers.

"Who's there!" a man's voice bellowed, slicing through their passion like an icy knife. "Stand up, I say, and identify yourself before I let loose with this."

Philip froze, letting out a groan of frustration.

"Chumley!" Cassandra whispered in accents of horror.

"What?"

"You hear me?" the voice rang out again. "Stand up, I say!"

"It's Chumley!" Cassandra repeated. "The man who was here this afternoon—yesterday, I mean."

Philip began to curse in a low voice as he pulled away from her, raising his arms in the air and unfolding into a standing position. "Don't shoot. I assure you, we are quite peaceable."

"Chumley, it is I, Cassandra Verrere." Cassandra called, struggling to rise and at the same time pull her bodice together. Sir Philip reached down a helpful hand to pull her up.

"Miss Cassandra!" the groundskeeper repeated in shocked tones and hurried toward them. "Whatever are you doing out here? I nearly shot you, I did!"

Philip, seeing Cassandra's dilemma, quickly shrugged out of his jacket and draped it around Cassandra's shoulders to cover her. She pulled it closed gratefully and summoned up a smile to greet her former employee.

"I am sorry to have alarmed you, Chumley. I never dreamed that you might be out here."

"Why, of course. Somebody had to protect the house, now, didn't they?"

"Apparently the same thought occurred to all of us," Philip interjected dryly.

Chumley eyed him with suspicion. "You again! What are *you* doing here?"

"Sir Philip and I were here on the same errand as you," Cassandra explained quickly. "We all hoped to catch the intruder. It is unfortunate that none of us communicated that intent with the others." She turned and gave Neville a dark look. "I am afraid our culprit was here and got away—unless that was you I saw with the lantern a few minutes ago."

"No, miss, weren't me. I wouldn't come here hunting a thief with a light announcing me, now would I?"

"No." Cassandra sighed. "Well, there's no harm now in lighting one, I suppose." She turned back to where she had set down her own lantern, taking the opportunity to shrug her arms into Philip's coat and button it tightly up the front so that her ruined bodice did not show beneath. As for the heavy heat in her loins and the sizzling sensations still running along her nerves—hopefully no one would be able to detect those things, even in the light of the lanterns. She smoothed her hair down and tied it in a self knot behind her neck, hoping that at least she would not look quite so wild. Then, relighting her lantern, she rejoined the two men.

They had gotten their own lanterns lit and were standing eyeing each other disapprovingly.

"I am sure your father would not approve of your being out here at this time of night, Miss Cassandra—and with a strange man."

"Sir Philip is not a stranger, Chumley. He is a dear friend of the family. And, besides, I was not with him. I came alone. I happened to, ah, run into him after I arrived here. He thought I was the burglar, you see."

Chumley released a snort that clearly indicated his opinion of a man who could think that Miss Verrere was a thief. "Not much better, your running about in the middle of the night alone."

"I should think that *that* is a great deal worse," Philip stated heatedly, stung by the groundskeeper's contempt. "A young woman alone and defenseless in the middle of the night!"

"Depends on the young woman, now, don't it?" Chumley replied equably, stroking his chin. "If Miss Cassandra's carrying a gun, as I reckon she's smart enough to, then I would say the burglar's more likely the one needing the protection. Arly himself taught her to shoot."

"Why, thank you, Chumley." Cassandra could not resist casting a smug look at Philip. "I tried to explain that to Sir Philip, but he didn't understand. Now, are we going to stand around here all day arguing, or shall we go look for that intruder?"

Without waiting for an answer, she strode off toward the back of Chesilworth, where she had last seen the light, leaving Sir Philip and Chumley to follow her. Chumley did so without question. Sir Philip, after an exasperated sigh, hurried to catch up with them.

"Really, Cassandra, must you go charging in headfirst every time?" Sir Philip moved protectively in front of her. "You are going to get hurt one day."

"Don't be absurd. I am sure our quarry is long gone. Besides, I think we have already established that I am well able to take care of myself. Ah, there—" She pointed past him to a set of windows across the back of the house. "That is where I first saw him."

The three of them moved closer, holding up their lanterns to illuminate the ground in front of them. It was Chumley who first spotted the footprints.

"There!" He pointed to the earth beneath one of the windows. "See? Where the ground's a little damp."

"Yes, you're right. A definite footprint." Sir Philip moved carefully closer, with Cassandra at his side. All three of them bent down and peered more closely at the imprint in the ground.

"Definitely a man's," Cassandra said, looking at the large outline.

"I would guess a big man, too," Sir Philip offered.

"Aye, tall, maybe," Chumley spoke up, "but I'm thinking not too heavy. The ground here is pretty soft. A heavy sort would have sunk in deeper, you see. But no lightweight, either."

Tall, but not heavy, Cassandra thought. *A man of the size, say, of Sir Philip.* She could not keep from sneaking a glance toward his feet.

He caught her look, and his mouth twisted ironically. "Large enough, Miss Verrere," he said, "but not quite my style, don't you think?"

He made a show of sticking out his foot and twisting it this way and that so that she could see that his shoes did not fit the outline. Cassandra sent him a disdainful look and said, "Really, Sir Philip, if you could refrain from joking, perhaps we could find something useful."

She turned away, following Chumley, who was circling around the corner of the house, his lantern held low to the ground.

"Here's another, Miss," Chumley called out, stopping, and Cassandra and Philip hurried to his side. There, in the circle of his lantern's light, was another imprint, this time of the man's other shoe. It was obviously the same type of round-toed shoe, but this impression held something interesting, a small V in the imprint of one heel.

"What is that?" Cassandra asked, pointing.

"A mark on his shoe, I imagine," Sir Philip offered, and Chumley nodded.

"Yes, miss, looks to me like he's got a hole or at least a mark gouged out on the left heel there."

"So all we have to do is inspect everyone's shoes for an indentation like that on one heel," Sir Philip said sardonically.

"It's more of a clue than we have had so far," Cassandra stated.

"Yes, but it's only feasible if we have a suspect."

"I thought you had one," Cassandra retorted. "My American relative."

Chumley's eyebrows sailed upward at her words, and Cassandra regretted having said anything. The last thing she wanted was for the locals to be gossiping about treasures and hidden maps at Chesilworth.

"Believe me, he is still high on my list. But since we have no idea where your Mr. Miller is, it would be difficult to check his shoes."

"I was only joking," Cassandra said quickly, giving Philip a hard stare, which she hoped he would be able to interpret. "Just because you have taken an unreasonable dislike to David Miller does not mean that he is a thief. I saw nothing to indicate it. Besides, as Chumley will be happy to tell you, there is nothing in Chesilworth worth stealing."

"Oh, no, miss, the silver and such is all locked up...what's left of it."

"Exactly. Mr. Miller was here. He would have seen the state of the house on the inside." Cassandra hoped she had said enough to discourage any gossip about her American relative. She decided to turn Chumley's thoughts in a more helpful direction. "No. I think it was some outsider—"

"Yes, miss," Chumley agreed, nodding his head energetically. "Wouldn't nobody from around here steal from you or your family."

"A person who saw the big house and decided that it was empty and thought, given its size, that it must have something valuable in it," Cassandra added, wanting to set a reason firmly in Chumley's mind.

"I am sure you are right," Philip agreed with a face so

studiously bland that it was all Cassandra could do not to laugh.

"That would mean that he must have been staying around here," Cassandra continued. "He was, after all, here two nights in a row. Where was he in between?"

"Ah, you was always a canny one, Miss Cassandra," Chumley told her admiringly. "You're right. Surely someone's seen him—even if he's been camping out in the woods like a gypsy, people'd notice. I'll ask around Dunsleigh tomorrow, miss, see if anyone's seen a stranger around here."

"And I shall check the inn where I am staying," Philip promised. "Of course, he could have been staying at another small town nearby and riding over at night, to escape detection."

There were three or four footprints going away from the house, but after that the ground became harder and drier, and there were no more signs of the would-be intruder.

"The noise scared him off, no doubt." Sir Philip stood for a moment gazing into the darkness, as if considering plunging off in search of the man, but then he turned back to the others.

"I shall escort you home, Miss Verrere."

Cassandra realized that earlier he had been calling her Cassandra. Now they were back to Miss Verrere. But, then, earlier, they had been... *Well, better not to think of that.*

"I assure you that I am well able to find my way home by myself," she replied in as formal a tone as he had used.

"I am sure of that, but if you think that I am about to allow a young lady to set off in the dark, alone, with an intruder lurking about, you had best think again."

"The gentleman's right, Miss Cassandra," the former groundskeeper chimed in reluctantly. "If he don't, then I'm going to. It ain't fitting, not to mention safe."

Cassandra gazed at her old servant, who stared back at her truculently. She knew Chumley well enough to know that he would do as he said, and that even if she set off alone, he would trail along after her. Since her aunt's house lay in the opposite direction of Chumley's own cottage, she would be making the man walk a good distance out of his way.

"All right, Sir Philip," she accepted his offer rather ungraciously and strode off up the hill without waiting to see whether he came with her.

With a sigh, Philip caught up with Cassandra. They walked for the most part in silence. Cassandra was quite aware of Sir Philip's opinion regarding the intruder they had not caught, as well as of her sneaking over to the house tonight to try to catch him. Since he was equally well aware of her views on both matters, they each decided not to broach the subject. Cassandra's thoughts kept straying to the moment when Sir Philip had captured her—and what had followed. The incident crowded out even the thoughts of the intruder. But it was hardly a subject she wanted to bring up with him. She was in enough turmoil just walking along beside him, intensely aware of his heat, his scent, his masculine power. She could not deny that she had enjoyed his touch and his kisses, that everything within her had leapt up in response to him. *But what did he think of her for doing so? What did he want from her? How did he feel about her? And*—this was a first for her—*how did she feel about him?* Cassandra could not remember ever feeling so unsettled, so unlike herself, so…so…thoroughly confused.

Sir Philip, beside her, was in as great a state of confusion as Cassandra herself. He knew that he should apologize for what he had done earlier. He had let his passion completely take over, had lost control—and after he had sworn to her that it would never happen again. There seemed to be something about Cassandra Verrere that made him forget all the rules by which he normally lived, that blurred the once clear lines between behavior with a woman of easy virtue and behavior with a lady of quality. Sir Philip had never felt with any young woman of good family the overwhelming passion he experienced when he was with Cassandra. *Damn it, now that he thought of it, he could not remember when he had felt such loss of restraint with a member of the demimonde or a willing, experienced woman of society, either.* There was simply something about Cassandra that was like no other woman he had ever met, and his responses to her were equally foreign.

Perhaps it was the very innocence of her response, the natural passion, that aroused him so. Or perhaps it was the piquancy of the juxtaposition of her sweet kisses with her tart, quick remarks. Sir Philip was not sure. Indeed, he was sure of very little—beyond the fact that he wanted very much to continue to see Miss Verrere. And he wanted even more to kiss her again.

It was for this reason that he could not bring himself to beg her pardon for his behavior. To do so would mean that he would have to promise not to do it again, and he had the distinct feeling that he would not be able to honor that promise. Indeed, he was quite sure that he did not even *want* to honor it. All he wanted was to continue along this path until he found out where it led—and damn all the consequences.

Cassandra came to a halt, reaching out to touch Philip's arm and stop him. He looked down at her, his pulse suddenly speeding up, at once excited and wary of what she might say next.

But she only said prosaically, "There is my aunt's house. Among the trees—you see it?" She pointed.

"Yes."

"I should go the rest of the way myself. It would not do at all for even a servant to see me walking back to the house at this time of night with a man, especially you."

He nodded, stifling his disappointment that she had had no more personal comment to make. *What did he expect— that she was going to ask him to start up again where he had left off earlier?* "Of course. Go on. I shall watch from here to make sure that you are safe."

"I assure you that is unnecessary."

"Shall we meet at Chesilworth again tomorrow?" he asked, ignoring her comment.

"Yes. Tomorrow afternoon would be fine—say one o'clock?"

"I shall be there."

She nodded and without another word turned and walked away from him. Sir Philip watched her form as it grew smaller and smaller, until at last it disappeared into the house. With a sigh, he turned away and began the long walk back into the village.

The gentle tapping at the door finally brought Cassandra awake. She groaned and turned over, throwing an arm over her eyes to block out the sunshine streaming in through the crack between the draperies. She fervently wished now that she had not told the maid to wake her early so that they could get started on cleaning up after the party. However, she knew that the best way to deal with her aunt was to get the house in order while she and Joanna still slept. Then she would have the afternoon free to work at Chesilworth.

With a sigh, she threw off her covers and rolled out of

bed, going to the door to admit the maid. Bleary-eyed, she let the girl help her into a dress and gratefully downed the toast and coffee that the maid had brought with her. Then she went downstairs to direct the servants in their cleaning-up operations, joining in now and then to help.

Cassandra was both surprised and relieved when the house was back in order again well before eleven. She would have an extra couple of hours to work in the attic, and it would be very easy to slip away now, before her party-weary aunt had even ventured out of her room. So she wheedled a picnic lunch out of cook and set off two hours early for the walk to Chesilworth, leaving behind her envious sister and brothers, who had to remain for their weekly religious lesson with the curate.

The day was beautiful, and Cassandra hummed as she walked along, her lack of sleep forgotten in the enjoyment of the day. With each new day of searching, there was always the possibility that this would be the day on which she found the letters. She pushed aside the thought that the prospect of seeing Sir Philip added to her anticipation of the day ahead.

She stopped when she drew in sight of her home and stood for a moment looking at it. It loomed dark against the horizon, its windows unlit, and for the first time in her life, Cassandra felt a chill run down her spine at the sight of it. She could not keep from remembering that someone had broken into the house two nights ago and had tried again last night. *Who was to say that he had not come back after they left and succeeded in getting inside? What if there were someone up in the attic right now, looking for the letters?*

For a moment she wished that she had waited for the time when she had agreed to meet Sir Philip, or that she had made up some sort of excuse to get her siblings out of their religious lessons so they could come with her.

She shook her head, willing such thoughts away, and reminding herself that this was her beloved Chesilworth, not some frightening and remote castle from a novel. She knew every inch of it. *And even if the intruder had returned the night before, which seemed extremely unlikely, he would hardly have continued to hang about until noon the next day, knowing that someone was likely to come back.*

Cassandra refused to be weak and timid. Squaring her shoulders, she settled the small basket comfortably on her arm and marched into the house. There on the kitchen table sat the oil lamps that they used while they were in Chesilworth, and she quickly lit one and started upstairs.

The empty house seemed even quieter than usual today, and she had to force herself not to glance down the dim, dark recesses of the corridors as she passed them on her way up the stairs. On the upper floor, however, she had to walk along the corridor to the back of the house to reach the narrow attic stairs. Her spine prickled as she marched along, and it was all she could do not to whirl around and look behind her.

Cassandra knew that she was letting herself be frightened by nothing, that it was her own mind creating the ominous atmosphere around her, yet she could not seem to stop it. For a moment she even thought about going back downstairs and waiting under one of the trees until Sir Philip showed up, but she quickly dismissed that idea as far too cowardly. Once she was up in the attic working, she told herself, she would forget all this nonsense, and it would be absurd to waste a couple of hours waiting for Sir Philip.

She climbed the stairs to the attic briskly, pushed up the

hinged door and climbed inside. She held the lamp up and looked around the attic. The light from her lamp and the small attic windows left the huge room in shadow, but she could see nothing out of place. She started forward, then glanced back at the open attic door. After a moment's hesitation, she closed the door before she settled down to work where they had left off searching the afternoon before.

As she had predicted, she grew absorbed in her work and forgot the ghostly shadows and dark corners that lurked around her. Sometime later, however, a noise impinged on her consciousness. She raised her head, not quite sure what had gotten her attention. After a moment she heard another faint sound. She rose to her feet and started forward, not even realizing that she was tiptoeing to make no noise. Halfway across the attic, she heard more sounds, but these were clearly identifiable as footsteps along the hall below. Someone was passing right beneath her feet. She froze, her chest tight and her stomach icy.

The steps started up the attic stairs.

Cassandra whirled and ran silently to the side of the attic. She did not want to be trapped at the far end. She ducked behind an abandoned lacquered screen from some former occupant's chinoiserie period and wedged herself between an overstuffed chair and a tall, slender curio cabinet. Her stomach tightened as the steps came inexorably upward. The trapdoor in the floor opened upward. Cassandra leaned forward, her nails curling painfully into her palms.

The door landed flat on the floor, and a man stepped up into the room.

9

It was Sir Philip.

Cassandra sagged in relief. But before she could call out his name or even move from her hiding place, another realization struck her. Sir Philip had said he would meet her at one o'clock, as they had every day. *What was he doing here nearly two hours early?*

Suspicion, painful as a knife, pierced her. *What if he had come here early to look for the letters on his own?*

Cassandra did not consider why such treachery on Sir Philip's part should hurt so much. She only watched, numbly, her heart hammering inside her chest, as Sir Philip glanced around the attic.

"Miss Verrere?" he called, raising his lamp and turning around. "Cassandra, are you here?"

She waited, struggling to make not a sound, as he strode toward the back of the attic, calling her name.

"Damnation!" He returned to the center of the attic. "Where is the girl? Cassandra!"

There was a long moment of silence so profound that Cassandra was afraid he would hear her breathing. At last Sir Philip muttered an oath and started back down the stairs.

He was leaving without looking for the letters! Cassandra's chest, so tight the moment before, was suddenly filled to bursting, and she catapulted out of her hiding space, sending a child's snow sled tumbling over on its side.

Neville whirled around, his shoulders still above the floor of the attic. "Cassandra!" Exasperation tinged his voice, stilling whatever remaining doubts Cassandra had. "What the devil are you doing? Why didn't you answer me? Are you hiding back there?"

He came back up the stairs as he spoke, and Cassandra moved toward him. She felt foolish now, both for working herself up into a state of fright to begin with and then for suspecting Sir Philip of double-dealing.

"Yes," she admitted shamefacedly. "I was all alone, and I heard someone coming and I...was a little frightened."

"Well you should be," he retorted unsympathetically, but he took her hand in his and squeezed it in a way that made her feel better. "I don't know what you are thinking, coming to this empty house all by yourself—and after we nearly caught an intruder here last night. I could not believe it when your aunt's butler said you had come over here."

"You went to Aunt Ardis's house this morning?"

"Yes. I had to make a courtesy call to your aunt for the party last night, and I hoped that if I arrived this morning, the Moultons might still be abed," he replied honestly. "I had thought I might have an opportunity to sit and talk with you someplace other than a hot and dusty attic." He cast a wry glance about at their surroundings.

Cassandra had to smile. "You mean you do not find this room elegant enough?" She struck an arrogant pose, her arm outstretched toward the jumble of goods that filled the attic.

"Indeed, Miss Verrere." He put one hand theatrically to his heart. "Any room is elegant as long as you are there."

Cassandra giggled and started back toward the trunk where she had been working. It was amazing how light-hearted she felt now that her suspicions about Sir Philip had been proved false.

Sir Philip followed her, good-naturedly pitching in to help with a box just beyond Cassandra's trunk. They laughed and talked as they worked, making their way closer to the trunk in which Olivia had discovered the clothes the day before. Neville opened a trunk and pulled out a moth-eaten suit of men's clothing. Looking at the style, Cassandra's heart skipped a beat. It was the sort of attire worn by Richard Verrere, the Lord Chesilworth who was Margaret Verrere's father, in the painting of him in the ancestral gallery on the second floor.

Eagerly she came over to kneel beside Sir Philip as he dragged out piece after piece of clothing. Carefully he made his way down to the very bottom of the trunk, but there was no sign of anything other than clothing. Cassandra sat back on her heels with a groan.

"At least we are close," Philip reminded her. "Here, let's shift these things and get out that trunk."

He began to move a bedstead, and Cassandra went to help him. He pulled a chair out of the way, and there, in front of the other trunk, hidden beneath a small table, was a square metal box. Cassandra reached down and dragged it out by its handle. Philip moved around her and shifted a last piece of furniture so that he could open the trunk he had indicated.

Cassandra turned the box around to undo its clasp, but when she did, she found that it was fastened with a lock. She sighed. She had no idea where its key might be. For a moment she started to ignore it, but she couldn't put aside the niggling thought that it looked the sort of box in which one might store valuables and papers to protect them from the elements. She searched around her for something heavy and finally returned with a fireplace poker.

She began to beat on the lock with the poker, and after a few moments, Sir Philip took over. It took some time, even with his superior strength, and in the end, it was the clasp that came away in a shower of rust from the box, not the lock.

Cassandra lifted the ruined lid. Inside, on top, lay a ledger book. She lifted it out and opened the cover, her heart going into her throat when she saw the date at the top of the page—eleven years after Margaret eloped with her lover. Carefully, she set the old book aside and reached in for the papers below it. She found several bills of sale for various horses and other animals, as well as a few IOUs. All the dates were in the years following Margaret's aborted engagement.

She lifted a deed, and there, on top of another ledger book, lay a stack of letters, bound by a black ribbon and all addressed in a hand now familiar to Cassandra.

Her chest tightened, and she put in a shaky hand to take the stack and pull it out. "Philip..."

He turned, and when he saw the expression on her face, he moved quickly to her side. "My God. Are they hers?"

Cassandra nodded. Her voice trembled when she spoke, "It is her writing. I can scarcely believe it. These are Margaret Verrere's letters to her father!"

"It is all true." Sir Philip looked stunned. "I cannot believe it. The diaries, the letters, the map, everything—it's all true."

Cassandra narrowed her eyes at him. "You mean you still didn't believe it?"

They were sitting beneath the shade of a spreading oak tree in front of Chesilworth, the remains of Cassandra's picnic lunch spread out before them. The pile of letters, once again bound, lay on the ground next to Neville, and now and then he reached out and touched the top one, as if to convince himself of its reality.

They had unbound the letters and gone through them, breaking the seal of each unread letter. It was a heartrending series of a daughter's attempts to reconcile with an unyielding father. Cassandra thought that if Margaret's father had wanted to remain at odds with her, he had been wise not to read the letters. They would have melted any but a heart of stone. Just glancing through them for mention of the map, she had had tears in her eyes by the time she had found the letter she sought.

"No, I really did not believe it," Sir Philip admitted. "I think perhaps I *wanted* it to be true, and after your intruder tried to break into Chesilworth, I began to think that perhaps the diaries were real, but I could not believe that the letters would still be here after all this time, or that one of them would contain a treasure map."

"Somewhat of a treasure map," Cassandra corrected, pulling the document in question from the top of the pile and gently opening the yellowed, creased page. She laid it on the dark background of her skirt and studied it. Sir Philip moved closer and gazed over her shoulder.

"It still makes as little sense as when we first looked at it," he commented.

There were lines drawn here and there on the page and a block that Cassandra thought might indicate a building of some sort, with an arrow pointing away from it. In two places, there were numbers, and in another there was the word *Littlejohn*. The letter *N* was written on one side of the paper. By common consent Cassandra and Philip had designated the *N* to mean the direction north and had turned the paper so that it lay at the top.

"I know." Margaret sighed. "I had hoped that it would contain enough information that we could at least figure out the general area where the treasure might be hidden. But this... Margaret has done her job too well."

"I hope that when we get the other half—*if* we get the other half—it will all become clear, and we will not have two incomprehensible maps."

"The other map must carry the key to this one. I cannot believe that a woman who wrote as clearly and well as Margaret would have drawn a foolish map." She paused. "I think the important thing here is *Littlejohn*. Is there anything near your home named Littlejohn?"

He let out a snort. "Oh, yes, indeed. The problem is that there is a great deal too much named Littlejohn. It is a common name in the area. There are several families named Littlejohn, as well as a meadow and a creek—two creeks, actually, a greater and a lesser. And of course, the lane to where two or three of the Littlejohns live is called Littlejohn, too, for convenience."

Cassandra groaned. She cast a last look at the map, re-folded it with a sigh and slipped it back into the stack of letters. "We shall be able to figure it out, I'm sure, when we have the other map. I refuse to be discouraged." She smiled at Philip. "Not on this day, when we have found what I had almost given up hope of getting."

Philip leaned closer. Their heads were almost touching, their faces only inches apart. Cassandra looked into his eyes, golden in the sunlight. She wanted him to kiss her. Instead, she moved back.

"We had better go," she said, turning her face aside

and beginning to rise. "There are...things to do. I mean,
now that we have the map."

"Of course." Sir Philip rose reluctantly. "Let me walk
you home. I—we need to make arrangements for your
coming to Haverly House."

He untied his horse and led him as they started along
the path toward Moulton Hall.

Cassandra's heart rose in her chest at the thought of
traveling with Sir Philip to his home. She told herself it
was the excitement of looking for the rest of the map.
"Yes, of course. How—how soon do you think we can
go?"

"How soon can you get packed?"

Cassandra smiled. "That, sir, I can do this evening. I
do not need a multitude of trunks for my wardrobe."

Sir Philip looked at her with some disbelief. He had
never known his mother to be able to pack for a journey
to London or Bath in less than a week.

Cassandra raised her eyebrows. "Do you doubt me,
sir?"

He chuckled. "No, indeed. I am not foolish enough to
issue you that challenge. You would work through the
night just to prove me wrong."

Cassandra merely smiled for an answer.

When they arrived at Moulton House, they found Aunt
Ardis and Joanna in the sitting room. Aunt Ardis rose,
smiling broadly.

"Sir Philip! What a delightful surprise!" Aunt Ardis
gave him her hand and shot Cassandra a glare over his
shoulder as he bowed. Cassandra knew that Aunt Ardis
was miffed, not only that Sir Philip had been with Cassandra, but that Cassandra, by bringing him in unan-
nounced, had not given her and Joanna a chance to primp
before seeing him.

Joanna bared her teeth at Cassandra in something resembling a smile. "Why, Cousin, wherever did you find such a delightful escort?" she asked in a teasing voice, looking up at Sir Philip from beneath her lashes and dimpling.

"We met as I was returning from a walk," Cassandra said hastily. The last thing she wanted right now was to set Aunt Ardis against her by admitting that she had spent the past two hours with Sir Philip. She was already afraid that her aunt would find a way to block her going to Haverly House. "Sir Philip was coming up the lane from town."

"Yes. I came to call on you ladies to thank you for the delightful party yesterday evening," Philip continued smoothly and spent the next few minutes congratulating them on the excellence of the repast, guests and entertainment, until Aunt Ardis and Joanna quite forgot their irritation at his arrival with Cassandra.

When the women were done simpering over his compliments, he went on casually, "I also came because of a missive I received from my mother this morning."

"And how is your dear mother?" Aunt Ardis asked, as if she had known the woman all her life, when, in fact, they had never met.

"In excellent health, thank you. She wrote to say that she was delighted that I had decided to come by Dunsleigh on my way home. And she begged that you would allow me to escort Miss Verrere to Haverly House for a visit."

Aunt Ardis's beaming face went suddenly still. "Miss Verrere," she repeated blankly. "Cassandra? You mother is inviting Cassandra to visit her?"

"Yes. As you no doubt know, my grandmother and Miss Verrere's grandmother were friends."

Cassandra's brows rose at this whopper, but she said nothing, hoping that Aunt Ardis would be too unwilling to admit that she did not know something to call his statement into question.

"Indeed?" Aunt Ardis replied vaguely.

"Yes. Quite good friends, actually. My grandmother is very desirous of seeing her friend's granddaughter. So my mother urged me to bring Miss Verrere home for a visit."

"You can't take Cassandra!" Joanna burst out furiously. Cassandra glanced over at her cousin, whose features were drawn into a most unattractive scowl.

"Indeed?" Sir Philip looked at Joanna, his eyebrows rising disdainfully.

Aunt Ardis, catching his expression, hurried to say, "Poor Joanna. She would be quite bereft without her cousin. They are so close, you know. But I am sure that Lady Neville's invitation extends to us, as well, Joanna. After all, she would not expect a young lady to go jaunting off alone like that to a strange house without family to accompany her. Why, I would never consider allowing Cassandra to make a journey with a gentleman *unchaperoned*. Isn't that right, Sir Philip?"

She smiled blindingly at Neville, who understood the implied threat perfectly. Aunt Ardis would refuse to give her permission to Cassandra to travel to Haverly House unless she and Joanna went with them, and Sir Philip could hardly take her without her aunt's permission or it would create a scandal.

He returned Ardis's smile and replied blandly, "Of course, Mrs. Moulton. I expressed myself poorly. My mother invited the entire family. You and Miss Moulton and Lord Chesilworth, Master Hart and Miss Olivia, as well. My grandmother is eager to see all her friend's grandchildren."

"The children?" Aunt Ardis's voice rose uncontrollably. "Sir, you must be joking. The children are far too young."

"Twelve and fourteen, I believe. Just the right age to enjoy a journey. I believe I was about that age the first time my parents took me to London."

Cassandra's eyes danced with laughter at her aunt's outraged expression, and she had to press her lips together tightly to keep from chuckling.

"But, Sir Philip, you cannot have thought—I—well, there simply will not be enough room in the carriage for so many people," Aunt Ardis argued gamely. "Six of us, and children are so restless and noisy. My nerves could not bear it."

"Of course not," he replied soothingly. "I would not put you out for the world, madam. You and Miss Moulton shall have your carriage to yourselves. I have my carriage with me, and the Verreres may travel in it. I, of course, shall ride."

Aunt Ardis gazed at him, flummoxed.

"Very good, then. It is all arranged," he concluded breezily, taking her silence for consent. "When shall we leave, ladies? Tomorrow morning?"

"Tomorrow!" Aunt Ardis squawked. "We cannot possibly— Oh, I see. You are teasing us poor women." She tittered and coquettishly waggled her finger at him. "What a naughty thing to do. You know we cannot possibly be ready for three days at least."

Cassandra ground her teeth. It was bad enough that her aunt had wormed her way into coming with her on this trip and bringing Joanna, too, but to delay the trip when Cassandra was impatient to start was simply too much for her.

"Oh, no, aunt, it won't take so long. Not if I help you and Cousin Joanna." She knew that she would have to perform all the practical chores necessary to get the two women on the road anyway. Joanna and her aunt would do little but impede matters by changing their minds about what clothes and shoes to take. "I am sure that we can leave by day after tomorrow."

"Excellent!" Sir Philip beamed at her aunt. "I shall look forward to it. Now, ladies, if you will excuse me, I have preparations of my own to make." He did not add that his primary preparation would be to dash off a quick message to his mother to expect the imminent arrival of six complete strangers for an indefinite stay—and to inform his grandmother that she had acquired a past friend whose grandchildren she wished to meet.

Sir Philip was barely out the door before Joanna pounced on Cassandra. "Why did he invite *you!* What did you do? How did you make him invite you?"

"I didn't *make* him," Cassandra responded mildly. "It had nothing to do with me. As you heard, it is all because of my grandmother knowing his."

"I never heard that," Aunt Ardis mused suspiciously. "Whoever heard of a Neville being friends with a Verrere? Everyone knows they don't associate—why, I cannot imagine, except that the Verreres were always such odd ducks."

Cassandra, ignoring the slight to her family, said airily, "That was all so long ago that I am sure it does not matter any more. Besides, I believe my grandmother must have known Lady Neville before she married into the Verreres. That is probably why the woman is so eager to see us. She probably lost contact with Grandmama after the two of them married, and she wants to hear about her life."

Aunt Ardis narrowed her eyes, looking unconvinced. "Why did you never tell me about this friendship?"

"Truthfully, Aunt, I did not know about it until Sir

Philip told me this afternoon.'' And, Cassandra added to herself, she truly wished that Sir Philip had told her what lie he intended to tell before he did it. ''I had no idea that Grandmama was friends with a Neville—but then, of course, it is not something she would have talked about in our family.''

''It sounds very fishy to me.''

''Why would Sir Philip make up such a story?'' Cassandra asked innocently. ''I cannot imagine any other reason for him to invite my family to Haverly House.''

''That is true.'' However, her aunt's expression was still uneasy.

Cassandra decided to make her exit as quickly as she could before her aunt asked any more difficult questions. With a smile and a polite ''Excuse me,'' she left the room and hurried upstairs to break the news to her family.

Cassandra folded the last of her dresses and laid it in the trunk, closing the lid with a tired sigh. After talking to her siblings—who had been predictably excited about the discovery of the long-sought-after letter and almost equally thrilled at the prospect of taking a trip to Sir Philip's home—she had spent the rest of the day preparing like mad for the trip. As well as her own packing, she had had to supervise Olivia's and the twins' packing, especially the boys, for they were as likely as not to include cricket bats and butterfly collections and leave out such mundane things as underclothes. She also had to leave instructions regarding the household chores while they were gone and oversee the servants' packing of her aunt's and cousin's things, a task that was made extremely difficult by Joanna's tendency to change her mind every few minutes about which dresses she should take. Each change of gown, of course, necessitated a complete change of shoes and accessories, as well, and, as always, Joanna could not bear to leave any of her darling hats behind. It took subtlety, patience and a certain ruthlessness to cut the number of hatboxes down to three.

Even though Cassandra had now finished her own packing, she had a few other tasks to complete before she went to bed. First of all, she had to make copies of the old map they had found today. She was afraid not only of losing the precious document, but of the fragile paper falling apart at the creases, as it was already showing signs of doing. It would destroy the map to continue to fold and unfold it as she was sure they would do as they tried to make sense of it. So she intended to lay a thin sheet of paper over the ancient map and trace the information on it.

Just as she started across the room to lock her door, however, she was started by a sharp rap on it. The next moment the door was opened without waiting for her to respond, and her aunt strode in.

Aunt Ardis was an imposing sight. Wrapped around by a quilted satin robe, she looked even wider than usual, reminding Cassandra of a rather large blue pigeon. Her face was covered with a cream that gave it a greasy shine, and her hair was done up in curling rags all over, so that with every movement of her head, ragged ribbons danced all about her face. The crowning touch was a long cotton scarf, which she had run under her jaw and tied at the top of her head. It was a remedy for a double chin which she had heard about from one of her friends, and it had the result of making it difficult for her to move her jaw, so that she seemed to be talking through clenched teeth the whole time.

"Aunt Ardis." Cassandra was surprised to see her aunt up this late. "Can I help you?"

"No, my dear," Aunt Ardis replied, lockjawed and nasal. "I have come to help *you*."

"To help me?" Cassandra gazed at the older woman in some amazement. "In what way?"

"You are like a daughter to me, Cassandra. I am sure you realize that."

Cassandra gave a noncommittal murmur as she led her aunt toward the single chair in her room. Cassandra dragged the stool from her vanity table over beside the chair and sat down upon it.

"Now, I have only your best interests at heart, my dear," Aunt Ardis began.

Cassandra's heart sank. *Was her aunt going to forbid her to go to Haverly House after all?*

"I must warn you about Sir Philip."

Her statement was so unexpected that Cassandra could only stare at her. *Could Aunt Ardis somehow have found out about the maps? The treasure? Was she telling her that Sir Philip would betray her?* "What do you mean? Warn me about what?"

"You may not be young anymore, Cassandra, but I know that you are not experienced in the ways of the world. You don't realize what a man like Sir Philip is after."

It took another moment before Cassandra finally realized the import of her aunt's words. *She was not talking about the treasure at all!* "Are you telling me that Sir Philip is a libertine?"

Aunt Ardis nodded her head. "Exactly. I know that normally you are a most sensible girl, but a man like Sir Philip—handsome, charming, monied—well, he could turn anyone's head."

Cassandra could not keep a blush from rising into her face, and inwardly she cursed her fair skin that showed every flush. Her aunt would now be bound to think that she had feelings for Sir Philip. "I assure you, I do not consider him in any light other than a...a friend."

The older woman's eyes narrowed shrewdly, but she said only, "I hope that is true. Sir Philip has paid you some small attentions while he has been here, and I know how a young girl who is not used to such things can have her head turned by them."

"A wallflower like me, you mean." Cassandra set her jaw.

"Heavens, no, you are a lovely young girl, but you had only that one season, and your poor dear papa, God rest his soul, did raise you so oddly, well, it wasn't to be expected that you would take. All I am saying is that with your lack of experience, you may tend to make more out of the blandishments that Sir Philip may have said or exaggerate the meaning of a compliment from him."

"I have no illusions on that score," Cassandra replied flatly. "I do not believe that Sir Philip has any affection for me. You may rest secure in that knowledge."

"I was not speaking of affection." Aunt Ardis's eyes bored into Cassandra's. "Some men will pursue a woman not out of affection, but only in the hopes that he will receive certain favors from her. They will dally with her, trifle with her affections, when they have no intention of offering her anything honorable."

"And Sir Philip is that sort?"

"I have heard rumors...."

"Rumors? You know nothing for a fact?"

"When you hear the same rumor enough times from enough sources, I think that there can be little doubt of the truth behind it. People say that he keeps a mistress in town."

"Many men do that," Cassandra replied defensively. "He is not married, after all."

"True. But I have heard that he pursues women assiduously, that he is a man driven by his lower appetites. At Lady Arrabeck's, I even heard—" She lowered her voice portentously. "I heard he keeps a home for his by-blows right there by Haverly House."

"What!" Cassandra stared. "You cannot be serious."

Aunt Ardis nodded so vigorously that the strips of rags all over her head danced. "I am. I could not believe it, either. Too bold, I thought. Too flouting of convention. I said so, but Lady Arrabeck said not a word to deny it. Mrs. Livenham, who told me, swore that it was true. She says he has a whole houseful of illegitimate children, with a nurse to look after them. She said that there were at least six or seven of them."

"Seven!"

"Yes." Aunt Ardis looked smug, for she had obviously struck a nerve. "If a man has that many babes born on the wrong side of the blanket whom he acknowledges as his and even supports, then you know that there must be many others, too. And it is quite clear that the unfortunate mothers are not all actresses and such that he keeps as mistresses. Wicked women know how to keep those things from happening, I've heard, and as for the married women he sees, well, they would pass them off as their husbands' children. That means that most of those babes came from honest young girls like yourself, whom he seduced and ruined."

"I don't believe it," Cassandra said defiantly. "Perhaps you are right that he is a man who consorts with women of the night, but I cannot believe that he is a villain who sets out to ruin innocent young girls!"

"Ah…" Aunt Ardis shook her head with sorrow. "Many a devil has worn the face of an angel."

"He does not try particularly to please," Cassandra argued. "He is not all smooth words. Why, he and I quarrel half the time." But she could not help but think of the way he had kissed her, the way his hands had swept expertly over her body, arousing in her feelings that previously she had never even realized existed. *Was his touch so pleasurable, his kiss so heady, because he had perfected the art on so many other young women? The Lord knew that her aunt was right when she said that Cassandra had little experience in such things.*

Cassandra frowned. "I wonder, then, if he is such a rake and a libertine, that you encourage your own daughter to associate with him! Aren't you afraid that he will try to seduce her, too?"

Aunt Ardis let out a smug little laugh. "There is a world of difference between your situation and that of Joanna. Joanna is a young girl, quite marriageable, who stands to inherit a good portion. When a man like Sir Philip shows interest in her, he knows that the end result must be marriage. Even if he seduced her, her family would force him to marry her."

"As you tried to force him at Lady Arrabeck's party."

"I don't know where you get such absurd ideas. I would never put Joanna in a compromising position with any man. When a girl is, well, getting older, almost a spinster, one might say, as you are, and when, in addition, she has no particular beauty and no fortune at all, it must be clear that such a catch as Sir Philip Neville is not interested in *marrying* her. Especially when you consider the fact that you have two penniless brothers and a sister to raise—no man could want to take on that sort of burden. You are exactly the sort of girl upon which such men prey."

Cassandra jumped to her feet, drawing herself up to her full height. Her eyes flashed. "I am so glad to hear your opinion of me! It confirms everything I thought about you. You may rest assured that Sir Philip has no interest in me, for seduction or marriage or anything else! Nor have I any interest in him, except as one of the few intelligent conversationalists I have been around since we moved to this house. I refuse to believe that he callously ruins young women, but even if it were true, I would not be caught in that web! As for my brothers and sister, not everyone considers bright, entertaining children a burden. Sir Philip obviously likes them, since he invited them to visit his house, something which, I might add, he did *not* ask you or Joanna!"

"Well! I never heard of such a thing!" The older woman's face flushed a dull red, and she pushed herself to her feet. "After all that I have done for you, to have the gall to speak to me in that tone! When I was only trying to save you from disgrace."

"*I* was only speaking the truth."

"I'll tell you this—you will never catch a husband as long as you can control your tongue no better than this!"

"I have no wish to 'catch' a husband who cannot stand to hear the truth."

The two women glared at each other. Aunt Ardis marched past Cassandra and opened the door. "I shall expect an apology in the morning," she said, not looking back at her niece, and stalked out, slamming the door behind her.

"Hah!" Cassandra made a face at the blank door. She knew she would apologize, of course. However annoying and venal her aunt might be, she was still an older relative and therefore deserving of courtesy. But the apology would indeed have to wait until the next morning. Right now Cassandra was too seething with rage at her aunt's clumsy warning.

It wasn't true. Cassandra was certain that Sir Philip was not so base a man. She did not believe that he went about the country leaving a trail of poor seduced maidens in his wake. Perhaps he was a man of great appetite. Heat stabbed her abdomen at the memory of her own experience with that appetite. But he was not wicked. He would not take his pleasure at the considerable expense of another.

Would he?

She could not help but think of the other night, when he had kissed her. Sir Philip's actions certainly had not been those of a gentleman. What would have happened if Chumley had not happened along? There had been no indication that Sir Philip would have stopped.

And what about the other times? She had to admit that Sir Philip's interactions with her had been disturbingly sexual. *Did that mean he intended to seduce and abandon her?* Her aunt was right in saying that she knew little about men. Everything women said about men seemed to indicate that men pursued a woman for either honorable love or dishonorable sex, and there was a great chasm between the two. As lowering as her aunt's blunt assessment of her was, Cassandra was honest enough to admit that it, too, was true: a spinster possessed of neither fortune nor a beautiful face. It was not the description of a woman a man would pursue for marriage.

It followed then that if Sir Philip was interested in her personally, he was interested in her only for sex. *Was he that callous? That cruel? Was he the sort of man who would ruin a woman's reputation for his own pleasure?*

Cassandra sighed. She could not believe Sir Philip was uncaring and deceitful. He did not talk with her and laugh with her, acting as if he enjoyed her company, because he was trying to lure her into his bed.

Yet she could not still the small, insidious voice inside her head that kept asking: *Why else would he be interested in her?*

10

Cassandra leaned her head back against the richly stuffed leather squab of the carriage and sighed with pleasure. She had slept little the past two nights, and the entire day yesterday had been one long trial. But she had finally gotten through it, even apologizing dutifully to her aunt this morning for what she had said to her the night before. The atmosphere between them had remained stiff and unpleasant, but at least Aunt Ardis had been willing to start out on the journey to Haverly House.

Her aunt, of course, had tried every stratagem to get Sir Philip to ride in the Moulton carriage with her and Joanna, but he had politely and smilingly refused, saying that he preferred to ride his horse. It was only his riding outside either of the carriages that had made it at all acceptable to Aunt Ardis. Had he ridden in his own carriage with Cassandra and her family, Cassandra was sure that her aunt would have been red with apoplexy.

Cassandra, on the other hand, was well content with the arrangement. Sir Philip's carriage was both roomier and more luxurious than her aunt's, as well as being much better sprung. Of course, there had been the little problem of Hart's bit of travel sickness at the beginning, but once they had stopped and let him relieve himself of his breakfast by the side of the road, he felt much better, and they were able to continue in relative peace.

Sir Philip rode beside his carriage, and with the curtains rolled up both inside and out, it was possible to talk to him through the open window—not to carry on a full conversation, of course, for it was too noisy, but she could exchange a remark now and then or ask a question. Cassandra also noticed that it gave her a wonderful opportunity to look at him unobserved.

He sat his horse superbly, back straight, his strong thighs easily controlling the spirited animal he rode. He rode hatless, and his hair glinted black in the sunlight like a crow's wing. The breeze tousled his hair, giving it a faintly unkempt look that Cassandra found appealing. She studied the firm jut of his jaw, the strength of his mouth and chin. And she wondered, all over again, how much, if any, of what Aunt Ardis had said was true.

She watched idly as the familiar landscape of the Cotswolds passed by. They stopped to rest the horses at an inn in Chipping Norton. As soon as they jumped out of the carriage, Hart and Crispin began to pepper Sir Philip with questions about his carriage and the horses, a beautifully matched set of four that even Cassandra, no connoisseur of horseflesh, could tell were remarkable.

Philip, laughing, suggested that they ask the coachman himself. "Will!" he shouted in the direction of his driver, who was overseeing the hostlers unhitching the horses. "I have a couple of would-be coachmen here. Why don't you and Tommy take them in hand?"

"Of course, sir," the coachman answered affably, nodding to his assistant Tommy to take his place supervising the inn's hostlers and walking over to where Sir Philip stood with the boys. "Mayhap you'd like to climb up and see what the view is like from where I sit."

"Would I!" Crispin cried, while Hart was rendered speechless by such bounty.

"Could I, too?" Olivia asked.

The coachman turned toward her, surprised, but Philip with a smile said, "Of course, Miss Olivia—that is, if it is all right with your sister."

Cassandra nodded, smiling, pleased that he had not denied the pleasure to her sister. Olivia grinned and began to clamber up after the boys.

"Olivia swings back and forth between wanting to put her hair up and wear long skirts and dazzle every man in sight and wanting to climb trees with her brothers," Cassandra told him, amused, watching her siblings. "Thank you for letting her. I know many would think it an unfit thing for a girl, but Papa and I always believed in not restricting activities to certain sexes. Papa said it was stifling to the mind and weakening to the will."

"It is obvious that your father applied his principles to you, as well."

"Thank you. I will take that as a compliment."

"It was meant as such." Sir Philip grinned down at her, admiring the way the sunlight turned Cassandra's serious gray eyes almost silver.

"Olivia!" A shocked cry burst from their aunt as Ardis crossed the yard toward them. "Get down from there at once. Cassandra! What are you thinking, letting her scramble around like a hoyden? It's disgraceful!"

"It's all right, Aunt Ardis," Cassandra replied easily as Olivia ignored her aunt's command. "Sir Philip gave Olivia and the boys permission. His coachman is looking after them."

"But Olivia!" Aunt Ardis came to a stop beside them,

looking shocked. "It is bad enough that the Lord of Chesilworth is making a spectacle of himself, but for a girl—"

"Lord Chesilworth is only twelve years old," Cassandra reminded her aunt crisply. "One can hardly expect him not to act like a young boy, whatever his title."

"A young lady certainly cannot clamber about atop coaches."

"I am a very progressive thinker when it comes to children," Sir Philip interjected, his eyes twinkling. "I don't believe in stifling young minds, girls or boys."

Aunt Ardis looked as if she would like to argue, but with an effort she pressed her lips together and drew herself up a little taller. "Of course, Sir Philip. If it is your wish…" She tried to smile.

"Shall we go in, ladies?" Sir Philip continued, ushering the women toward the door of the inn. "I am sure that the innkeeper can find you a private room and some refreshments."

"That would be lovely. I find traveling so tiring." Joanna took Sir Philip's arm, leaning against him as if she had trekked the miles from Dunsleigh on foot rather than in a comfortable carriage.

Cassandra cast a jaundiced eye on her cousin and said, "You go ahead. I think that I shall walk around a bit first."

"An excellent idea," Sir Philip agreed. "Let me escort Mrs. Moulton and Miss Moulton into the inn to rest, and I shall join you."

Cassandra received a dagger glance from her cousin as Sir Philip turned and, deftly extricating his arm from Joanna's grasp, placed an impersonal, helping hand on one arm of both Joanna and her mother. He guided them into the inn while Cassandra walked idly around the yard. At first she kept an eye on her siblings, but a few moments of watching was enough to convince her that they were in expert hands with the coachman.

When Sir Philip returned, she had no qualms about leaving them and strolling with him along the broad main street of the quaint market town. She was sure that her aunt would scold her for her boldness, but Cassandra was enjoying herself too much to think about that. What her aunt had said about Sir Philip still niggled at her mind, and she wished that she could find out the truth of it, but she could think of no way to politely ask him about a houseful of illegitimate children, so she pushed that out of her mind, as well.

"Tell me about your home," she said instead.

"Haverly House? It is old and rambling, gray Norfolk stone."

"I have never been in Norfolk."

"It is more isolated than the Cotswolds. People have gone there for centuries to get away from things. The fens were a great barrier in the past. They say that's why there are so many churches in East Anglia. The religious moved there for the peace. Of course, now with the fens drained, it is more accessible, but still, very few people pass through it. There is nothing to go to on the other side, you see, just the ocean."

"I hate to think what your mother will say, having all of us descend on her."

"Mother is rather used to my eccentricities by now. As long as she is not put out, she is as placid as a clam. Since we have an excellent housekeeper, she is rarely put out. I sent my valet on with a message to her and the housekeeper that we were coming. Now Mrs. Benby may ring a peal over my head for giving *her* so little notice, but Mother will be quite unaffected. My sister, of course, will be in ecstasies at the idea of company."

"Your sister?" Cassandra felt a jolt of surprise. "I—I didn't realize that you had one."

"Did you think me incapable of it?" He cast her an amused glance. "Anyone can have brothers and sisters, you know, even rigid and unimaginative sorts like us Nevilles."

"I didn't mean that. I just—I don't know, you seemed to me to be an only child."

He shrugged. "She is much younger than I, fifteen years, so most of my life I was raised alone. I was off at school when she was born, so we were not close in the way of siblings, at least not when she was young."

"What is her name?"

"Georgette." He smiled down at Cassandra. "You will like her. She is a young lady of great spunk and curiosity."

"I am sure I will." Cassandra hoped that Georgette would like her, although she told herself that there was no reason for it to matter.

"Sir!" a young boy called, and they turned to find one of the hostlers pelting down the street after them. "The lady sent me to fetch you." He bobbed a bow toward them and paused to catch his breath. "She says the young miss must be careful of getting too much sun."

"Too much sun!" Cassandra repeated in astonishment and glanced up at the mild June sky.

"Yes'm. She said to tell you to come back."

Cassandra sighed. She knew that her aunt was not concerned about her health but about the amount of time she was keeping Sir Philip away from Joanna's presence. "Tell them that we will come straight back."

Her aunt's poor temper was evident from the moment they stepped inside the private room where she and Joanna sat, sipping at drinks while Crispin, Hart and Olivia talked, laughed and hopped about in an excess of energy.

"Sir Philip!" Hart greeted Cassandra's companion as an old friend. "It was capital. They let us help them water and feed the horses, and Will Coachman even let me hold the whip!"

"Did he, now? He must have been impressed with you indeed."

"He let us all hold the whip," Olivia said, giving her younger brother a scornful glance.

"He said we could take turns riding on the seat with them, if it was all right with you," Crispin told them eagerly. "Is it, sir? Could we?"

"Will said that?"

"Yes." Olivia nodded vigorously. "He said we asked clever questions, and he had never heard the like of us. That's good, don't you think?"

"Definitely." Neville's lips curved up into a smile. "If Will is willing to take you on, it is all right with me."

"Who gets to go first?" Hart pursued the subject with his usual tenacity.

"First?" Sir Philip looked unprepared for this controversy, and he cast a beseeching glance toward Cassandra.

"Me, silly," Crispin demanded, giving his twin a shove on the shoulder. "I am Lord Chesilworth."

"Hah! You think that gives you the right to do everything first!"

"*I*'m the oldest," Olivia stated. "Besides, if you were gentlemen, you would let a lady go first."

"A lady! You?" Hart snorted.

"A flimsy reason, if you want to be allowed to do the things that the boys are," Cassandra reminded her. "Hart could make arguments that he should go first because he is the youngest or because, since he will not be receiving the title and lands, he should at least get the compensation of things like riding atop the carriage. My suggestion is that you draw straws to see who will go first.''

''And a very sensible suggestion it is, too,'' Sir Philip said gratefully.

In the end, it was Hart who got the first chance to ride atop the carriage, followed by Olivia, then Crispin. Crispin put on a look of noblesse oblige, as if he had allowed them to go before him because he was too noble to do otherwise.

With the children rotating their turns in the high driver's seat, there was plenty of room within the spacious carriage, and Sir Philip took advantage of it by tying his horse to the back of the carriage and riding inside. Cassandra was sure that her cousin and aunt were furious, but there was nothing they could do about it, riding in a separate carriage.

It was scarcely as if they shared a private moment, for there were two of Cassandra's siblings with them the entire time, but at least they were able to chat about whatever took their fancy, cudgeling their brains all over again about the incomplete map, the possible location of the other map and the likelihood of finding the treasure even with both maps.

The carriage stopped for a late luncheon in Banbury. Cassandra watched with some amusement as Joanna and her mother maneuvered to sit at the table on either side of Sir Philip, excluding her. Joanna proceeded to monopolize him with teasing, girlish chatter, and her mother took up the slack whenever she paused to draw a breath. Cassandra, sitting across the table, watched Sir Philip's eyes glaze over with boredom and thought with a glee that she was sure was unworthy and not at all ladylike that Joanna was probably doing the worst thing she possibly could to snag Philip Neville's heart. Cassandra wasn't about to enlighten her—not that Joanna would have listened to anything a bookish spinster such as Cassandra would have to say.

As soon as they finished eating, Sir Philip bobbed up, relief all over his face, and announced that they must press on if they hoped to reach their destination by nightfall.

It turned out that they missed that goal, for they were delayed by a broken wheel on the Moultons' carriage. Leaving the carriage to be mended and brought on to them, they continued their journey with Joanna and Mrs. Moulton riding in Sir Philip's carriage. If she could have thought of any way for her to have done it, Cassandra would almost have believed that Aunt Ardis had caused the wheel to break so that they could ride in Sir Philip's carriage. Their happiness was short-lived, however, for Sir Philip, noting that the carriage would be too crowded if he were to continue to ride in it, with gentlemanly courtesy resumed riding his horse.

"Coward," Cassandra murmured as he moved past her on his way out the door, and he flashed her a conspiratorial grin.

They arrived after dark at a stately manor house not far from Northampton, the home of Sir Philip's aunt and uncle, Lord and Lady Philby. Lady Philby was a woman of great rectitude and snobbery, and so boring about it that even Aunt Ardis could barely hide her yawns. His Lordship, on the other hand, was a benign, avuncular sort who managed through the course of the evening to pinch the bottoms of all three of the young women present. It was a great relief when it was late enough that they could excuse themselves, citing travel weariness, and bolt for their rooms.

Sir Philip, escorting them, bowed over Cassandra's hand in front of the room she would share with her sister and

said, with a wink, "Every family tree has a few branches
they would like to lop off, wouldn't you say?"

Cassandra, even tired as she was, had to laugh.

The tower of Ely Cathedral thrust heavenward in the
distance, commanding the attention of all who saw it. Built
on a knoll, it dominated the flat land around it. Cassandra,
her head stuck shamelessly out the window to get a better
view, let out a long, heartfelt sigh.

"Ohh..." She breathed. "It is even more awe-inspiring
than I had imagined."

Eyes sparkling, she turned to Sir Philip. It was the afternoon of the third day of their journey, but whatever
tiredness she had felt from their travel had been swept
away by the sight of the cathedral, bathed in the glow of
the afternoon sun.

"The best time to see it is in the autumn at twilight.
Then, rising up out of the mists, the dying sun touching it
with gold, it looks...well, as it must have looked hundreds
of years ago, a sanctuary for the hunted."

"Eely," Crispin drew out the word, making a face. He
was hanging out the window across from Cassandra, with
Olivia right behind him, maneuvering to see. He turned to
Olivia and made a snaky movement with his hand. "Better
watch out, Livvy, or the eels'll get you."

"Not anymore," Sir Philip commented with a smile.
"But you are right, Crispin, the name did come from the
word *eels*. Ely used to be an island rising up out of the
fens all around, and the eels in the water were the staple
of the local people's diet."

"It's where Hereward the Wake hid out for years, fighting the Normans," Cassandra told her brothers.

"Yes, until some of the monks got tired of hiding him

and showed the conquerors the way in through the fens,''
Philip added.

"Can we go inside?" Olivia asked.

"It is reputed to be beautiful," Cassandra commented.

"It is. And I promise that one day soon we will make
a trip here. It isn't too far from Haverly House. But today
I think we should continue."

"Yes, you are probably right," Cassandra agreed.

Crispin nodded. The excitement of their journey had
worn off somewhat over the past couple of days, even for
the boys.

After they passed through the small cathedral town, Cassandra continued to gaze out the window, fascinated by
the new landscape. "It is so unusual here. So flat. And
what is that odd, long mound over there on the left? It
seems to have been running on for miles."

"It has. It is a river."

"What?"

"The banks of the rivers are higher than the land around
them. You see, this all used to be marshland, but when
they drained the marshes in the seventeenth century, it left
the land much lower than the banks of the rivers. They
had to build up the banks of the rivers to keep them from
overflowing."

"But why did they drain them?" Crispin asked, disappointed. "I would have liked to see the swamps."

"So you shall. There is still a fen left on our lands. The
Neville of that time—the father of Sir Edric, the one who
was affianced to your Margaret—did not approve of draining the fens. When the Earl of Bedford brought
Vermuyden in to drain the land, my ancestor held out. Of
course, eventually he died, and his son, the much despised
would-be groom, hired another Dutchman to drain our
lands, too. Out of respect for his father, however, he did

leave a small portion of the fens intact. I shall take you there while you are at Haverly House."

"But why?" asked Crispin. "I don't understand why they wanted to get rid of the fens."

"Economics, dear boy. As your sister will tell you, we Nevilles have an eye toward money. The land left when the marshes were drained is very rich black, arable soil. Instead of acres and acres of unproductive fens, we now have acres and acres of farmland, all leased or sold and making profits."

"I wish I could have seen it the way it used to look."

"You know, Crispin, I wish I could have, too." Sir Philip looked a trifle wistful. "I always enjoyed the time I spent on Blackley Fen."

"What are all these windmills?" Olivia asked. "Why are they here and why are there so many of them?"

"To pump the water out of the fens. They are no longer used, of course. Now they use steam engines for the pumps, but in the seventeenth century they were all over, driving the huge pumps that kept the fens from reclaiming the soil. Many of them were torn down after they went out of use, but there are many of them still standing."

"It's fascinating," Cassandra breathed. "It looks... almost foreign."

"There are those who say that fen country is a world unto itself."

In a little more than two hours, they turned off the road and started up the lane leading to Haverly House. The lane was shaded by a row of stately silver birches on either side, and among them grew masses of rhododendrons, delighting the eye with great splashes of red, purple and blue. Cassandra drew in her breath with astonished pleasure, and Sir Philip smiled, pleased by her reaction.

"This is beautiful!" she exclaimed, craning her neck this way and that to take in all the color.

In the distance the trees ended before a magnificent gray stone house, its stately walls softened with ivy. Cassandra felt a stab of pleasure at the beauty of the estate, but mingled with it was regret that their journey was over. The three days had been tiring, but they had been wonderful, too—spent largely in Sir Philip's company and largely *out* of her aunt's and Joanna's. She knew that it could not be the same once they were inside his house.

The massive double doors were opened by liveried footmen before the carriage came to a halt, and by the time the vehicle had stopped, a footman was there to fold down the steps and open the door. A tall man with a yellow, cadaverous face and a wealth of thick white hair descended the steps of the house with great dignity.

"Good day, Sir Philip. Welcome home," he said gravely, bowing.

"Good day, Shivers. These are my guests, Lady Cassandra Verrere, Lady Olivia, Lord Chesilworth, and there, in the driver's seat, is Master Hart. No doubt you will think you are seeing double. His lordship and Master Hart are twins."

"Of course, sir." The butler bowed gravely toward the two young boys. Even Hart seemed subdued by his dignity.

The second carriage pulled in behind them and stopped, and Sir Philip turned to introducing Mrs. Moulton and Joanna. At that moment a blur shot out the front door and vaulted down the steps.

"Philip!" The girl leapt from the last step into his arms, trusting Philip to catch her, which he did with the ease of long practice.

"Georgette!" He hugged his sister and gave her a buss

on the cheek, chiding playfully, "Are you never going to start behaving like a lady? My guests will think you are a hoyden."

Georgette turned toward the others, grinning infectiously. She was beautiful, Cassandra thought, and much resembled her brother, with thick dark locks and the same golden brown eyes, now sparkling with interest as she surveyed the new arrivals.

"I'm so happy to see you! It has been ages since Philip brought anyone home to visit, and it is deadly dull here." She stopped, looking a bit embarrassed. "No. I said that wrong, didn't I? I mean, I would have been happy to see you even if it were not dull here. But since it is," she added irrepressibly, grinning, "I can tell you that I am twice as happy to see you."

Before Philip could introduce her around, an older woman emerged from the house and advanced on them, smiling, her hands outstretched. "Philip! My love!"

"Mother." He smiled and greeted the woman with a kiss on the cheek. "You are looking lovely, as always."

She patted his cheek. "Darling boy. Now introduce me to everyone."

"Yes, Philip, please do." Joanna said, coming up beside him and linking her arm with his in a possessive way. "I am so looking forward to meeting your family."

Philip glanced down at her in some surprise. At that moment, another woman appeared on the front steps. She looked to be in her twenties, not unattractive, but dressed in the plainest of ways, her hair pulled back tightly into a bun. She carried an equally plain straw bonnet and was pulling on her gloves.

"Sarah!" Lady Neville turned to the young woman with a smile. "Do come here and see Philip. He has just returned with his guests."

"Yes. I see. That is why I—I do not wish to intrude...."

"Nonsense," Lady Neville said calmly. "You are not intruding. Why, you are practically one of the family. Isn't she, Philip?"

The woman colored a little with pleasure at Lady Neville's words and came forward.

"Miss Yorke was paying us a social call when you arrived," Lady Neville explained. "She is in charge at Silverwood, and a very dear friend of the family."

Silverwood? Cassandra wondered what Silverwood might be and what she was in charge of there.

Her question was all too quickly answered, for Georgette went on bouncily, "Yes, she takes care of Philip's children—and a daunting task it is, too."

Philip smiled, disengaging his arm from Joanna and taking Miss Yorke's hand in greeting, saying, "Good day, Miss Yorke. How are the children?"

"Doing well, Sir Philip. Of course, they have been asking about you frequently."

"I shall be sure to visit them first thing tomorrow. But pardon me, I am forgetting my manners. I was about to introduce everyone."

Through this exchange, Cassandra stood, stunned. Her heart seemed to have dropped clear down to her toes, and her stomach was twisting into knots. She could not think, hearing over and over again Georgette's words: *Philip's children.*

It was true! Sir Philip was so promiscuous that he had a whole houseful of illegitimate children, and he had set them up in a house that was obviously near here. Cassandra had not believed that what her aunt told her was true; it had seemed too preposterous. Her gaze turned involuntarily toward Aunt Ardis. The woman nodded at her with grim significance, and Cassandra's stomach felt even sicker.

Philip was going through the long introductions now, and Cassandra tried to smile and greet everyone. His mother greeted her placidly. *How could she speak of this Silverwood place so calmly?* Planting a whole household of one's illegitimate children practically on one's mother's doorstep seemed to Cassandra a slap in her face. Cassandra could not imagine treating it with such equanimity.

Lady Neville suggested that they go back inside, but Miss Yorke demurred. "I am sure that you wish to visit with your guests. I will come again another time." She smiled in the general direction of the visitors. "I hope you will come to visit Silverwood while you are here."

Aunt Ardis's jaw dropped, but Cassandra managed to reply with a faint, "Yes, of course. Thank you."

Miss Yorke started off, and Lady Neville repeated, "Do let's go inside, where we can be comfortable. I am sure that you must be exhausted after your journey."

"Not I," Joanna said gaily, flashing the woman a dimpling grin. "Sir Philip is so considerate that it made the trip quite easy." She turned toward Philip's sister. "I myself am looking forward to a long coze with Georgette. May I call you Georgette? Philip has spoken of you so often that I feel as if I know you already." She gave her the same dazzling smile, slipped her arm through the girl's and steered her toward the front door. "I am quite sure that we are going to be the closest of friends."

Georgette looked a trifle taken aback but went along with Joanna, and the others followed. Aunt Ardis grabbed Cassandra's arm and held her back behind the others.

"You see?" she hissed into Cassandra's ears. "Did I not tell you?"

"Yes, Aunt. You did."

"I hope you have taken my warning to heart," Aunt Ardis continued.

"Yes." Cassandra tried to ignore the sick feeling in her stomach. "Don't worry. There is nothing between Sir Philip and me, and there never will be."

11

Cassandra dressed for dinner in her best gown, but even so, she felt dowdy sitting at the elegant long table in Haverly House. The seemingly endless expanse was made of teak and polished to a mirror gleam. A silver epergne of fruit graced the center, so tall that Cassandra was grateful their small group did not go down so far, for it would have made conversation across the table impossible. All the dishes, silverware and crystal were of the finest, and from overhead in the enormous wainscotted room, crystal chandeliers showered them with soft light.

Chesilworth had once been such an elegant house, Cassandra knew, but it had not been so in her lifetime—or even that of her father. The best pieces of silver had all been sold, most of them long ago, and the ceiling of the Chesilworth dining room had become so stained from water leakage that they had given up eating there and taken their meals in a much smaller room nearer the kitchen. Even Moulton Hall, which her aunt liked to think of as being furnished in the best of style, could not compete with Haverly House's ageless elegance.

Cassandra's best dress, other than the ballgown she had worn the night of her aunt's party, was a dark brown silk that she had made over from one of her mother's dresses and had brightened up with new trimmings of beige lace. It was a nice material, of course, and she and Olivia had managed to make it look rather up to date in style. But it was not the best color for her pale skin and light blond hair, and nothing she had been able to do could make the neckline and shoulders of the dress fit right. Besides, she thought, it was the sort of color old ladies wore, a feeling which was confirmed when Sir Philip's grandmother entered the drawing room wearing a gown of very similar color.

On Lady Neville, of course, it looked exactly right, especially given the blaze of topazes that encircled her throat and winked in her ears. It helped, of course, that the tobacco-colored gown had obviously been designed and sewn by a master modiste rather than created by a seamstress in Dunsleigh and altered by two less-than-accomplished girls.

Cassandra looked across the table at the formidable old Lady Neville. It had come a little as a surprise to find herself seated at Sir Philip's right, with his grandmother on the other side, and his mother, Aunt Ardis and Joanna down the sides of the table. Then she had realized that in terms of nobility she outranked not only her aunt and cousin, but even Sir Philip's mother and grandmother.

"Well, my gel," the elder Lady Neville drawled in an aristocratic tone, fixing Cassandra with a bright eye. "So you are the one I wanted to see."

"Yes, ma'am," Cassandra answered dutifully, grateful that Sir Philip had filled his grandmother and mother in on the details of his lie—and, apparently, that they were willing to go along with it.

"Yes," Aunt Ardis interjected. "I had forgotten—you

were friends with Cassandra's grandmother, weren't you?''

"Yes." The old lady sighed, looking out blankly across the room as if seeing across time. She was, Cassandra decided, something of a ham. "Dear Caroline."

"Caroline?" Aunt Ardis asked, looking confused. "I thought your grandmother's name was Emma, Cassandra."

Cassandra gathered breath to explain away the discrepancy, but she need not have bothered. Lady Neville the elder obviously was quite capable on her own. She turned a cool stare in Aunt Ardis's direction, one eyebrow slightly raised. It was a look she had used a few minutes earlier, when she had heard Joanna addressing her grandson familiarly as "Philip." Joanna had turned pale and subsided, not speaking since.

"No doubt you are mistaken," Lady Neville told Aunt Ardis, with a just a hint of gracious forgiveness in her voice.

"I believe Grandmama went by a different name when she was older," Cassandra hastened to tell her aunt. "She, ah, came out with a cousin, I believe, whose name was also Caroline, and so she started using Emma, her second name, and of course that was the name by which Grandpapa knew her, so it hung on for the rest of her life."

"Oh, yes, that's right," Lady Neville agreed. "I remember the cousin now. Not nearly as pretty as Caroline." She turned her regard back to Cassandra. "It's something I never thought I would live to see—a Verrere in Haverly House."

"It was hardly a blood feud, Grandmother," Philip commented with some amusement.

His grandmother glanced at him coolly. "Of course not, Philip. We are English, after all."

"Yes, Grandmother." Philip looked chastened, except for the twinkle in his eyes.

His grandmother obviously saw the wicked light in his eyes, for she added, "Don't you laugh at me, young man," and smiled in an affectionate way that took the sting out of her words.

"Me?" Philip managed to look indignant. "Never."

"Don't try to distract me, either. I was talking to Miss Verrere."

She studied Cassandra for a moment, and Cassandra tried not to squirm under her regard. Finally she said, "You look like a very sensible young woman, Miss Verrere. I approve."

"I, uh, thank you." Cassandra was not sure exactly what Lady Neville was judging or approving her for, but she was grateful that she had not been found wanting.

"Did you tell Philip about the intruder, Violet?" the old woman went on, changing course once again.

"What?" Philip barked, sitting up straighter, and Cassandra leaned forward intently.

"I forgot," the younger Lady Neville admitted. "It happened several days ago."

"Three days. Scarcely a lifetime, Violet," Lady Neville remarked acidly.

"Mother! Why didn't you tell me? What happened? Someone entered the house?"

"Actually, very little happened. No doubt that is why it slipped my mind." Lady Violet, quite lovely in a watered silk gown much the shade of her name, looked as if things frequently slipped her mind. "I didn't hear it, of course. Shivers told me about it the next day. He said that someone broke into the house in the middle of the night. Fortunately one of the servants heard the noise and went to investigate.

He found the man in the library. They tussled, and the intruder ran away. Nothing was taken.''

"The library?" Philip repeated flatly, and his eyes went involuntarily to Cassandra.

"Yes. Odd, isn't it? He didn't try to get the silverware or anything valuable. There is nothing in the library but all those books. I suppose he must have thought there was a safe hidden there.''

"Yes, most likely." Sir Philip drummed his fingertips on the table a time or two. "Are you sure that nothing was removed from the library?"

His mother looked faintly surprised. "I did not check it myself, dear. I wouldn't know if something was missing in there, anyway. That is what Shivers related to me. I believe the footman who caught him was Michael. You might ask him if the burglar was carrying anything when he found him."

"Yes. Perhaps I shall."

Cassandra would have liked to pursue this highly interesting development further, but from then on the two Lady Nevilles kept the dinner conversation on a firmly trivial ground. After dinner Cassandra spent an interminable time in the drawing room with the other women. Lady Violet politely suggested that Joanna might play something for them on the piano, and Joanna, not a good pianist at the best of times, had been so unnerved by Philip's grandmother that she stumbled through a sonata that was as painful for her listeners as for herself.

Lady Neville decreed that there had been enough piano for the evening, and so they passed some time in stilted conversation. It was a relief when Sir Philip returned to the room, but Cassandra still could not talk to him alone. It wasn't until Lady Neville retired to her room and Lady

Violet kindheartedly let Joanna attempt another piece on the piano that Cassandra got any chance to speak to him.

Cassandra was sure that Joanna expected Philip to come stand behind her and turn the pages for her, but he sat down beside Cassandra and murmured under cover of the noise, "Well? What do you think?"

"That someone was searching the library for something other than what one would normally consider theftworthy property," Cassandra replied promptly. "The Queens Book, for instance."

"It seems highly suspicious. It also would seem unlikely that it was anyone other than the same man who broke into Chesilworth."

Cassandra nodded, then added, "However, we are basing this on nothing but speculation. Nothing was taken either time—or, at least, nothing that we know of."

"I am fairly certain that he did not get anything here. I took the opportunity to slip out to the entry hall, where Michael is on duty this evening, and I spoke to him about his little adventure. He said that he caught the man only moments after he entered the library. Michael had not yet gone to bed. He said he was making a last-minute check around the house before retiring, but I have my suspicions that he had been paying a visit to one of the maids' rooms on the fourth floor. Whatever the reason, he heard glass breaking in the conservatory and went to investigate immediately. He doesn't believe that the intruder had the time to seize anything, and he is certain that the man had nothing in his hands, for he swung at Michael, and they struggled for a few minutes. I asked him what the intruder looked like, but he said that it was too dark for him to see."

Joanna made a great show of slowing down her playing and fumbling to turn the page, casting a beseeching look over her shoulder toward Philip, but he did not even look up. At the end of the next page, Joanna managed to send several sheets tumbling from the stand when she turned the page, and she stopped abruptly.

"I am so sorry." Looking aghast, Joanna hopped off the stool to pick them up.

Philip's mother, with a sigh, said, "Philip, do come help Miss Moulton by turning the pages of her composition."

"What?" Philip looked up distractedly. "Oh." He grimaced, but rose to his feet and did as his mother bade.

Cassandra excused herself as soon as Lady Violet retired, hard-heartedly leaving Sir Philip to squirm out of the Moulton women's clutches by himself.

Upstairs in her room, she was not surprised to find her sister and brothers waiting for her. She was, however, a little taken aback to see Georgette Neville casually sitting cross-legged on the bed with Olivia, playing a game of checkers.

"Cassandra!"

"Miss Verrere!" Georgette scrambled off the bed, as did Olivia, coming around to meet Cassandra. "I hope you will not think me too bold, coming here like this."

"I told her it was perfectly all right," Olivia said.

"Of course it is," Cassandra agreed. "I am delighted to have a chance to visit with you."

Georgette smiled. "Good. I wanted to talk to you earlier—it was so strange and mysterious getting that note from Philip saying to expect you and telling Mama to lie about Grandmama knowing your grandmother. We could not imagine what was going on. Mama was sure that Philip must be in love. Grandmama kept saying that it was 'decidedly peculiar,' his inviting a Verrere that way. Except, of course, that it was four Verreres, as well as these Moulton people, whom Mama and Grandmama did not know at all. It was odder than any of Philip's starts.''

Cassandra reserved her own judgment on that. It seemed to her that a young gentleman installing his bastard children in a nearby house was a bit more peculiar than bringing home a few strangers, but she certainly was not about to bring *that* up.

''But then I couldn't talk to you because Miss Moulton stayed with me the whole afternoon, chattering about this and that. I don't want to say anything against your cousin, ma'am, but is she always this friendly?''

Cassandra chuckled, and Olivia let out a short of disgust.

''No. She's just trying to get on your good side, hoping you'll have some influence with your brother,'' Olivia told her bluntly. ''Or perhaps she thinks that Sir Philip will be so impressed by how sweet she is to you that he will immediately offer marriage.''

''I wondered if that was it,'' Georgette admitted. ''Philip's first note sounded as if it was only *you* he was bringing.'' She nodded toward Cassandra. ''I couldn't understand why he would do that if it was Miss Moulton he was interested in.''

''He's not interested in her.'' Olivia rolled her eyes. ''Cousin Joanna is the only one who thinks he is.''

''And Aunt Ardis,'' Cassandra added.

''Who cares about that?'' Hart put in scornfully. ''The only thing that's important is the treasure.''

''Yes! The Spanish dowry!'' Georgette exclaimed, obviously quoting, and clasped her hands together ecstatically. ''Thank heavens I decided not to go down to dinner. Mama had told me that I could, as it was a special occasion, but after spending all that time with Miss Moulton, I thought I simply could not bear it any longer. So I told Miss Pritchard that I would rather eat with Miss Olivia and the twins, and I told Miss Moulton that I had to eat supper in the nursery with the other children.'' She grinned irrepressibly. ''I was so glad I did. Olivia and Hart and Crispin told me all about Margaret Verrere and the Spanish dowry and how you are searching for it. I want to help. May I?''

''Certainly. If it's all right with your brother.''

''Oh, Philip won't mind. He's a wonderful brother!'' Her eyes shone. ''Whenever Grandmama and Uncle Robert get all prissy about how Mama allows me too much freedom, Philip always tells Mama to ignore them. I know he would let me.''

''Wonderful. The more minds on this, the better, I say. Did Olivia show you the map we found?''

''No, I couldn't get in your case!'' Olivia cried, looking wounded.

''That's right, I locked it.'' Cassandra reached inside her bodice and carefully unpinned the key which she had attached to her chemise when she dressed for dinner. ''Perhaps I am too careful, but after what I heard tonight...''

''About the burglary?'' Crispin cried. ''Isn't it capital? Georgette told us all about it—how someone was searching the library for that book we need.''

''We don't know that he was searching for that book. We only know that he went to the library.''

''What else could he want there?'' Crispin asked reasonably. ''This is turning into a slam-bang adventure.''

''Personally, I thinking finding the treasure would be ample excitement for me,'' Cassandra told him, ''without throwing in a thief, as well.''

The other four seemed to think this attitude poor-spirited, but Olivia reminded her brothers that Cassandra was, after all, old, and everyone found this reason enough to excuse her behavior. Cassandra opened the box and showed Georgette the map. She wrinkled her brow over it just as they had, saying that it looked like nothing familiar to her. She pored over the pages in the diary where the Neville portion of the map was mentioned, but, fascinated as she was, she, too, had no idea what the "Queens Book" might be.

Cassandra soon shooed the children out of her room so that she could go to sleep. She was feeling quite weary, but she knew it was as much from a malaise of the spirit as from the long journey they had made. Hearing that Philip did indeed have a house for his illegitimate children, as rumor had said he did, had made her feel quite low, confirming everything her aunt had said about his libertine ways. The kisses they had shared, the caresses, had meant no more to him than an opportunity to snare another female, to add another heart to his collection—although obviously one's heart was not what he was interested in.

Occupied with such blue thoughts, Cassandra's mind drifted for a long time between sleep and wakefulness, and when she did at last go to sleep, she was bothered by fitful, restless dreams. She awoke the next morning feeling little more rested than when she had gone to bed the night before.

Downstairs, she found only Georgette and Olivia at the breakfast table, starting on their second helpings. Georgette and Olivia had by now become fast friends, apparently, and Georgette greeted her with the happy news that her governess, Miss Pritchard, had agreed to take the girls on an outing for the rest of the day.

"We are to have the carriage and go to Downham Market. Life is so much more interesting when one has guests."

"Where are the twins? Are they going, too?"

Olivia looked horrified at the notion. "No! It is a shopping expedition. They would be a nuisance. Besides, Sir

Philip promised them that the head groom would give them a tour of the stables when they get back.''

"Get back?"

"Yes. They've gone with Philip to see the boys at Silverwood."

"Indeed?" Cassandra still felt shock at the way Georgette and her mother spoke so casually about Philip's blatant indiscretions.

Georgette nodded, then looked a little anxious. "You don't mind, do you?"

"What? That he take Crispin and Hart with him? No, I am grateful to him for that. I am sure they are ecstatic."

"There are some who would not like their brothers playing with children like that. They would find it improper." Georgette made a face. "Mrs. Carter in the village says that it's a disgrace to even have those children living here, that they are a bad influence."

Cassandra's dislike of injustice came welling up. She had worried about the impropriety of Sir Philip taking the boys to his mistress's house, but she would not think of condemning the children as unfit playmates simply because of the circumstances of their birth. "That's a horrid thing to say, as if it were those poor children's fault."

"That's what I think. Mama says that she is quite proud of Philip, for most men ignore poor children of that sort, and they wouldn't have had a chance in life if Philip had not taken them in."

"I'm sure that is true." Cassandra had to admit that Philip had done the decent thing to acknowledge the children as his and to take care of their upbringing. Many men denied their bastard children, leaving the woman and child to fend for themselves. Still, Cassandra could not quite understand Lady Neville's seeming pride in having her son flaunt the numerous products of his licentious ways. Surely she could not be indifferent to the fact that her son was a lecher.

There were footsteps in the hall behind Cassandra, and she knew from the grimace that touched her sister's face who the new arrival was.

"Georgette!" Joanna cried enthusiastically. "How wonderful to see you again. And where is your dear Mama?"

She came bustling into the room, a vision in a cherry-and-white striped dress of polished cotton.

"Miss Moulton." Georgette returned Joanna's greeting with something less than pleasure.

However, Joanna seemed not to notice as she sat down on the other side of Georgette. "I am so looking forward to visiting with you again today."

"I cannot. I, uh…my governess is, I mean, I have to spend the day with my governess."

"I am sure that this once you could be excused from your studies," Aunt Ardis said with heavy joviality as she followed her daughter into the room. "After all, it isn't every day that you have visitors."

"Philip is quite strict about my studies," Georgette countered. "I do not think he would be pleased to find that I had ignored them."

"Oh, well, of course, if that is what *Philip* wants…" Unconsciously Joanna's shoulders relaxed.

"In fact, I had better go up there now." Georgette jumped from her seat, leaving the rest of her eggs, and Olivia followed suit.

"But where is Olivia going?" Aunt Ardis asked.

"I believe Miss Neville's governess has kindly offered to allow Olivia to participate in, um, their studies, as well," Cassandra replied.

"And Olivia wants to?" Joanna asked, obviously

amazed at the idea of voluntarily setting out to learn something.

"Mm."

"I always said that your father raised his children in an odd way." Aunt Ardis dismissed the subject.

"Where is Sir Philip?" Joanna asked eagerly. "Has he come down to breakfast yet?"

"I am sure he will arrive soon, now that you are here," her mother told her smugly. "I do think that Sir Philip is showing a decided interest in you, my dear."

It was all Cassandra could do not to roll her eyes at her aunt's self-deception. *The woman had had to twist Sir Philip's arm even to get Joanna invited to Haverly House, and now she saw in that some interest on Sir Philip's part?*

She had to endure her aunt's and cousin's company for the rest of the morning. Her misery was alleviated only slightly by the fact that Lady Violet joined them later in the sitting room. Sir Philip's mother was a nice woman, but so easygoing that she did nothing to stem Joanna's almost nonstop dialogue on the beauties of Haverly House, interspersed with lengthy descriptions of her own wardrobe. Violet also placidly agreed when Joanna suggested an outing, saying that she would arrange a picnic beside Linning Broad for the following afternoon.

"The children will quite enjoy it," Violet said, smiling.

"You mean Crispin and Hart?" Joanna asked, and it was all Cassandra could do not to laugh at her fallen expression.

"Yes, and Olivia and Georgette."

"Well, of course, Georgette." Joanna's smile was turned on again. "I quite delight in dear Georgette. But I do not think of her as a child."

"No? She is only sixteen." Violet sighed. "But you are right. I fear she is growing up too fast. In only two more years it will be time for her debut.'' She sighed again. ''I do so hate having to attend the season. I much prefer my quiet life here in Norfolk.''

''That's quite understandable,'' Cassandra murmured. ''This is such a lovely place.''

''Perhaps by that time your son will have married, and his wife can take care of Georgette's season,'' Joanna suggested with a coy smile.

''Do you think so?'' Violet looked faintly surprised. She glanced toward Cassandra, as if for confirmation.

''I would not be at all surprised,'' Joanna continued, dimpling and trying to conjure up a blush in her cheeks.

Her efforts were wasted, for Lady Neville was not looking at her but at Cassandra. Cassandra smiled back at her weakly. She could hardly say bluntly right in front of Joanna that she thought Sir Philip had as much interest in Joanna as he did in yesterday's fish.

Finally she said lamely, ''I don't know. Sir Philip seems a dedicated bachelor.''

''All men are until they meet the right woman,'' Joanna replied archly.

''Indeed. You know, I believe that I shall send an invitation to Miss Yorke to join us tomorrow,'' Violet said. ''Such a sweet young woman, and she hasn't much entertainment in her life, I'm afraid.''

''Miss Yorke?'' Joanna looked as if a bad odor had crossed under her nose. ''The...housekeeper?''

''Mm. I suppose one could call her that, but she is primarily in charge of the children's education. Mrs. Watson does the housekeeping.'' She rose to her feet. ''Now, if you ladies will excuse me, I must tend to that, and, of course, I must tell Henri about the picnic lunch.'' She looked a bit daunted by this idea. ''I don't know how I shall get across to him what I want. I don't believe the man speaks a word of English. I cannot imagine why Philip brought him here—except, of course, that his sauces are really quite delicious. And his desserts! Lady Neville loves them, you know, so I suppose it is a good thing.'' She sighed. ''But I find him so intimidating. I try to tell him what I want, and he starts babbling in French, and I cannot understand a thing he says. He waves his arms about and gets all red in the face. So generally, of course, I just let him do as he pleases, and that seems to work well enough. But I'm not sure he would quite understand a 'picnic.'''

"I am sure Cassandra could talk to him," Joanna volunteered. ''She knows French.''

Cassandra glanced at her cousin, surprised. Joanna was not in the habit of pointing out anyone else's accomplishments. Then she realized that Joanna was probably hoping to relegate Cassandra to the level of the staff, to embroil her in running the household and keep her out of the drawing room, giving Joanna free access to Philip's company.

"Do you really?" Violet turned to Cassandra, her eyes wide with admiration.

"Yes, I do, and I would be happy to talk to him, if you'd like."

"That would be wonderful!" Violet beamed. "I do hate to impose on you, but..."

"It's no bother at all," Cassandra assured her, rising.

"Wonderful! Come along, then." She started toward the door, motioning to Cassandra. "Let us go right now, and you can translate everything I say for him. This will be marvelous! You are a jewel to do this for me."

Cassandra suspected from the look on Joanna's face that she had not intended for Lady Neville to go with Cassandra to the kitchen. She had probably envisioned Cassandra making her way like one of the staff to the kitchen while

Violet remained in the sitting room with them, grateful to Joanna for suggesting it.

They found Henri in the kitchen, overseeing the preparations for luncheon. He looked none too happy to see them, but bowed humbly and released a spate of French. Violet looked immediately unhappy and worried. Cassandra quickly returned the chef's effusive greeting, and his eyes lit up.

"Mademoiselle!" he cried, as if she had just offered him a chest of gold, and launched into an even longer speech.

It took her only a few minutes to sympathize with the man's frustration and homesickness and to assure him as to Lady Neville's delight with his food. He perked up a good bit at Cassandra's fulsome words of praise, and when she then conveyed the special request for the noon meal the next day, he answered with a careless wave of his hand that it would be no trouble at all, merely another challenge for his culinary skills.

They had just left the vast kitchen and were making their way toward the front of the house when a side door opened and Sir Philip stepped in.

"Mother! Miss Verrere. Just who I wanted to see."

"How sweet of you, dear." Lady Neville presented her cheek to him to kiss. "We have been talking to your chef. Miss Verrere knows French. Isn't that clever?"

He grinned at Cassandra. "Miss Verrere is a very clever girl, I find."

"Hardly a girl," Cassandra corrected, striving to keep her voice cool. Her heart had leapt in her chest at the sight of him, and she had to struggle not to return his grin. But she was determined not to let him charm her into being another one of his victims. She was not some man-crazy thing like Joanna nor deluded enough to think that she alone would be the one woman whom he married rather than abandoned.

Philip raised a brow at her tone, but said only, "If you are not in need of Miss Verrere's services any longer, Mother, I had promised to show her the library today."

"Of course not, dear, go right ahead. I must send Miss Yorke an invitation, anyway."

"Invitation to what?"

"You explain it to him, dear," Violet told Cassandra, already walking away from them.

"Explain what to me?" Philip turned to Cassandra.

"We are picnicking tomorrow at something called Linning Broad."

"Egad. All of us?"

"Yes, including your Miss Yorke." Cassandra kept her voice and face aloof.

Philip groaned. "I should have known that Mother would think she needed to entertain us. Ah, well, we had better get to work, if we are going to waste tomorrow. Are you ready?"

"Of course."

He glanced at her oddly, but guided her along the hallway to where it branched and then on to the library. Cassandra gasped when she stepped inside. It was an enormous room, rising to the height of two floors, with a small balcony on the second floor. A winding metal staircase rose up to the balcony. One wall was a line of windows on both floors, flooding the room with light, which was augmented by sconces on the walls and shaded reading lamps on a desk and two small tables. There were several comfortable chairs near the lamps, creating small, cozy areas in which to read. But most of all, there were books, rows and rows of books. Wooden bookcases were built from floor to ceiling on both levels, filling almost three entire walls of the room.

"Oh! How beautiful!" Cassandra turned, looking all around her. "I have never seen a lovelier room!"

Sir Philip chuckled. "I thought you would like it." He paused, gazing down at her face, now softened with pleasure. "I am glad that it pleases you."

Cassandra could not keep from smiling back at him. His smile had a way of warming her through and through. She felt an urge to move closer to him. Instead, she drew herself up and stepped back. He was, she reminded herself, quite practiced in his charms. She could not let herself trust him.

"Well," she said coolly, "with such a task, we had better get to work."

"Of course." Disappointment flashed across Philip's face, but he quickly masked it. "Where shall we start?"

Cassandra glanced around the room. "I'm not sure. It is so massive."

"I suggest the second level. The books that are more recent and more read are usually on this floor. The older things tend to be up the stairs."

"All right." Cassandra started purposefully up the twisting staircase, saying, "Why don't I start at one end and you at the other? We can work our way toward the middle."

Philip stopped at the top of the steps, watching her walk to the other end of the loft. *This was not the way he had envisioned their working together.* "Cassandra? Is something the matter?"

She turned back, her expression carefully bland. "I don't know what you mean."

"You are acting a little strange today."

"In what way?"

"You know what way," he retorted, frustrated by her cool responses. "As if you were angry with me, and I haven't a clue what I might have done."

"I'm sorry. I wasn't aware of it. I merely want to get on with our search. Don't you?"

His eyes narrowed, but he did not dispute her words. "Yes," he said shortly. "Of course I do. Let's get started."

He walked to the opposite side of the loft. Cassandra turned to her task, telling herself to forget about Philip's presence on the other side of the room. She squatted down and began at the bottom shelf, moving along the row of books. Whenever she came upon a title that seemed even remotely something that could be a book about queens, she pulled it out and looked through it.

The work was dusty, physically tiring and soon boring. Cassandra, too, had imagined working side by side with Philip, talking about the books they found and whatever else struck them, laughing and enjoying the search as they had in the attics of Chesilworth. But there could be no laughter or sharing with him on the other side of the room; it was what she had intended when she suggested it. However, getting what she wanted left her feeling dissatisfied and lonely.

She reminded herself that what was important was finding the dowry, not spending time with Sir Philip, and she forged ahead. They worked steadily through the afternoon, keeping the door closed and not answering anyone's knock. Sir Philip had a tray brought for lunch, which they ate at the large desk, their conversation stilted and uncomfortable. Cassandra could feel Philip's confusion and frustration, and she wished that she could return to the ease that had marked their relationship earlier. But she could no longer feel comfortable with him. The thought of his illegitimate children kept intruding.

As soon as they finished eating, Cassandra suggested that they get back to work. It was physically tiring work, involving stooping, bending and squatting. Her feet and legs began to ache, but it was her shoulders and neck that really felt the strain. As tea time approached, her neck grew stiff, her shoulders cramping from holding her awkward position so long, head bent to the side. She straightened, letting out a tired sigh, and rolled her head, pressing against the hard knot at the base of her neck.

"Tired?" Philip asked from behind her as he reached out and began to knead her shoulders.

Cassandra jumped, startled to find him so near to her. She had not heard him approach. His touch was much too intimate, too; it aroused a fluttering sensation in her stomach. She knew she should tell him to stop, but at that moment his thumbs found the hardest spot of her stiffened muscles, and instead she let out a low groan of relief.

"Got it, huh?" He bore down a little harder, and the result was somewhere between ecstasy and pain.

Cassandra sagged, letting her head fall forward. He worked his way up the taut muscles of her neck, his thumbs massaging away the tension. Cassandra thought she might melt into a puddle on the floor. The release of the tension was delight enough, but there was another, insistent sensation, a tingling that sizzled straight down to her womb and had nothing to do with the muscles of her neck. Limply she let the feelings wash through her, aware of the heat filling her loins, her nipples prickling, the sudden moisture between her legs.

Philip bent and placed a gentle kiss on the side of her neck. It was the merest breath, a brush of sensation that sent passion gushing through Cassandra. She drew in her breath sharply, her legs suddenly trembling. She wanted him. She wanted to turn and move into his arms. She wanted to taste his mouth on hers, feel his hands on her body.

"Cassandra," he murmured. "So sweet..."

His hands slid down from her shoulders, moving slowly along her arms, and her skin turned to fire beneath his touch. His hands glided back up, and he took her by the shoulders, turning her to his kiss.

12

"No!" Cassandra wrenched herself away from Philip. She faced him, trembling, frightened by the torrent of emotions that he could so easily awaken in her. "I will not be another of your conquests!"

"My conquests!" He stared back at her in disbelief, his face still slack with desire. "What are you——"

"No!" Cassandra stepped back quickly from his outstretched hands. Whirling, she ran across the loft and down the staircase, her shoes ringing on the metal steps.

He did not follow her, for which she was grateful. If he had caught up with her and tried to persuade her with kisses and caresses, she did not know what she would have done. She was afraid it would have been something foolish. The fact of the matter was that she seemed to have no self-control around Philip. Her vaunted will vanished when he began to kiss her.

Cassandra closed herself in her bedroom until teatime, pulling the curtains closed and lying on her bed in the dark, trying to bring her rampant emotions back to some sort of rational order. It was absurd that he should have so much power over her. It frightened her. She had always been so completely in charge—of herself, her family, whatever situation she had to deal with. She prided herself on it; everyone looked to her. *But Philip Neville had blown that pretty picture sky-high.* She felt like the silliest rustic maiden, a vacant-headed ninny ruled by her desires.

But even as she reprimanded herself, something inside her cried that it was unfair. Her body thrummed with passion—*and what was so wrong with that? Would it be so terrible to give in to her feelings for Philip? Men gave way to their passions all the time, and no one despised them. No harm came from it—except for those poor children like the ones at Silverwood.*

She pointed out to herself that she didn't know that Philip was interested in seducing, then dropping, her. She had only her aunt's word for that, and Aunt Ardis had a vested interest in keeping Cassandra and Philip apart. *But what about his children at Silverwood?* Aunt Ardis had been right about that; the rumor mill had been right. Only a hardened libertine could have so many illegitimate children that they filled a home.

Cassandra groaned. It was so hard to believe that he was a roué, a rake. The truth was that she did not want to believe it. Her feelings for Philip were clouding her usually clear mind. *But that notion was in itself absurd! She did not have feelings for Sir Philip. She could not.*

It was a relief when she went down for tea and found that Philip was not there. He was at the table at supper, however, and she had to endure sitting beside him. His face was stony, and he spoke as little as possible to her. She was sure that he hated her, and even though she told herself that he had no reason to, she felt even more unhappy.

After supper, in the drawing room, Joanna flirted wildly with Philip, hanging on his arm, bending over strategically so he could get a full view of her swelling breasts above the low neckline of her dress, plying her fan coquettishly. She asked his opinion and hung breathless on his reply. She called him Philip, as if she had the right to address him familiarly and favored him with arch smiles.

The worst of it was, Cassandra thought, that Philip did not seem terribly annoyed at having to endure Joanna's flirting. Cassandra wished that she had pleaded sickness and had a tray brought to her room instead of coming down for dinner. Or she could have eaten in the nursery with the twins, Olivia and Georgette. That would have been infinitely more enjoyable.

As soon as Philip's grandmother decided to retire for the night, Cassandra jumped up and left for her bedroom, also. She simply could not bear any longer to sit and watch Joanna fawn over Philip.

Having little else to do, she changed clothes and went to bed early, but she quickly discovered that that was a mistake. She was wide awake, and, lying there in the dark, all she could do was think about Philip and the many problems surrounding him. It was almost enough, she thought, to make her wish that she had never come to Haverly House.

The picnic the next day interfered with any work they might have done in the library. Cassandra chafed at the delay in their search, although she was also relieved that she was not going to have to spend the day in close quarters with Sir Philip.

The picnic was a huge production. Even the elder Lady Neville went. Miss Yorke walked over from Silverwood, and they set out: the older ladies and Miss Yorke in an open carriage, parasols up to ward off the sun, and Sir Philip, Georgette and the children on horseback. Joanna, upon learning that her quarry planned to ride, decided that she would ride, also, even though it meant being in the company of the twins and Olivia. Cassandra, thinking of having to watch Joanna flirt with Sir Philip the whole time, opted to ride with the older women in the carriage, even though it made it a rather tight squeeze. Several servants followed them in a wagon with the food and other necessities.

They made their way to a large, shallow pond, known locally as a "broad." The broads, Lady Neville explained, were areas where the locals had once "mined" peat, leaving wide holes in the ground that soon filled with water. The ride along tree-dappled lanes, often bordered by masses of rhododendron, would have been pleasant had it not been for the fact that Aunt Ardis talked most of the time, usually about her daughter's attributes and virtues. By the time Cassandra had heard four times how much Joanna valued her new fast friend, Georgette, and how admired Joanna was by her many suitors, not to mention how sweet she found Duchess, the elder Lady Neville's foul-tempered Persian, and how utterly lovely she thought the furnishings of Haverly House were, Cassandra was almost ready to walk the rest of the way. Having to watch Joanna and Philip now seemed like a petty price to pay for being able to ride in the open air, far away from Aunt Ardis's babble.

She glanced across the carriage and saw mirrored in Sarah Yorke's eyes the same fervent wish. She smiled and looked hastily away for fear that she might burst out laughing. Miss Yorke, she thought, might be someone with whom she could be friends.

When they finally arrived at the wide-spreading oak tree where they would have their picnic, Cassandra climbed nimbly down, followed immediately by Miss Yorke. Both of them were several feet away before the other women began to move. Cassandra cut her eyes toward Miss Yorke and smiled conspiratorially. Miss Yorke returned her smile shyly.

The riders were dismounting and handing their horses over to the grooms who had accompanied the party. Cassandra saw Philip walking purposefully in their direction, so she turned quickly to Miss Yorke and suggested that they take a stroll beside the pleasant broad.

As they walked, Miss Yorke pointed out some of the local vegetation and birds, seemingly most comfortable in her governess role. "You see the swallowtails?" she asked, pointing toward several beautiful butterflies floating over a patch of green plants. "This is one of the few places where they visit. They feed on the milk parsley, you see."

"Ah. Lovely. Have you lived in this area all your life?" Cassandra asked.

"No. But I find it very beautiful." She flushed a little. "I am always intrigued by the flora and fauna of an area. My father, you see, was a naturalist, and I often accompanied him on his explorations of nature. It is one of the things I most enjoy about teaching the children. They still have a joy in learning about nature."

"I am sure that you are an excellent teacher."

"It was very kind of Sir Philip to hire me," Miss Yorke continued, her voice warm. "He knew my father, and he realized in what position I must have been left when Father died. Father was a wonderful man, but his love of nature barely produced a living. I tried to write the same sort of articles he had for some of the books and magazines—I had helped him write many of the ones he sold—but they were reluctant to accept an article written by a woman."

Cassandra made a noise of disgust. "I know exactly how you feel."

"I didn't know what I was going to do. My skills were

deficient in a number of areas that people think are essential for being a governess to young ladies. I cannot paint or sing or even play the piano. My handwriting is no more than adequate. Father never thought such things were important. He trained me very well in mathematics and the sciences, which, I found, is not highly valued for a teacher of girls. The only thing left to me was to become a companion, but I had trouble finding a position even as that. I was at my wits' end—then Sir Philip rescued me.'' A smile lit her face. ''I shall be forever grateful to him. He says that he thought of me because he knew that I would be perfect for the task, but I know that it was his kindness and compassion that made him write to me. There are many others he could have found who are equally qualified and just as good with children.''

''Yes, he can be kind.'' Cassandra had to admit that he had been very good to her brothers and sister. He had talked to them, invited them here, even put them up on his carriage and let them ride his horses. Nothing could have pleased them more. Many men would not have been so considerate. It made her heart warm to him, as so many things about him did—yet she could not get around the fact that he also callously seduced women, leaving them pregnant and unmarried.

Hastily she changed the subject, pointing across to a clump of reeds at the edge of the broad. ''What a lovely bird! What kind is that?''

Miss Yorke returned to the subject of flora and fauna, and they began to retrace their steps, returning to the group under the spreading oak.

By the time they got back, the servants had spread out blankets on the grass beneath the tree and set up stools for Philip's mother and grandmother and Aunt Ardis. Georgette and Olivia were huddled together as far from the older women as they could get, talking and giggling. The boys were playing catch with Sir Philip, and Joanna stood watching them. She had taken off her riding jacket in the heat, and she made a pretty picture standing there in the velvet skirt and white shirtwaist, a parasol on her shoulder to protect her fair skin from the sun.

Cassandra and Miss Yorke sat down with the other women, but Miss Yorke soon left to get a glass of lemonade for Philip's grandmother. Violet shook her head in exasperation. "That girl simply cannot sit still and enjoy herself. I told her that a servant would bring Mother's drink soon."

The elder Lady Neville, fanning herself desultorily, said, "It's all right, Violet. It won't do her any harm."

"No, but she will find something else she thinks she must do in order to justify her being here. I intended for her to enjoy the party."

"I am sure she will, Violet. *Some* people like to be busy." Lady Neville cast a pointed look in her daughter-in-law's direction.

Violet did not even notice Lady Neville's barb, either too unaware or too used to her mother-in-law's remarks to let it ruffle her composure. Cassandra had yet to see anything that did.

"Such a sad story," Violet went on, shaking her head. "Her father died penniless."

Beside her, Aunt Ardis sighed lugubriously. "She will never marry, then." She did not have to look at her niece to see if her shaft had gone home. "A girl without face or fortune..."

"Miss Yorke is not unattractive," Lady Neville said flatly. Cassandra had the feeling that the older woman had taken a thorough dislike to Aunt Ardis.

"But not a beauty, either. It takes a beauty to snare a man if one has no fortune."

"Surely men fall in love for more than a pretty face," Violet protested mildly. "Some do, anyway."

"I am not speaking of falling in love, dear Lady Neville. I am speaking of marriage. Men's fancy often wanders far afield from what they would consider for marriage."

"She is right," Lady Neville agreed grudgingly. "The younger generation makes too much of love. As if we could all choose as indiscriminately as peasants. Family, position, and wealth, those are what family alliances are based upon."

"A good family alliance is not necessarily a good marriage, though," Cassandra felt compelled to say.

"Good in what sense?" Lady Neville's eyes sparkled. There was nothing she loved so much as a rousing discussion, and she could rarely goad the placid Violet into arguing.

"In the sense of happiness, my lady. My own parents were very happy."

"But poor as church mice," Aunt Ardis added tartly.

"What good would it have been for them to have married wealth and been miserable all their lives?"

They passed the rest of the time until the luncheon was served in a lively discussion. Sir Philip returned, Joanna hanging on his arm, with the twins trailing behind them, tired, their trousers smeared with grass stains, and quite happy.

"What are you ladies talking about?" Sir Philip asked, smiling. "It sounded as if you were quite impassioned about the subject."

His grandmother smiled at him. "Why, Miss Verrere was telling us her views upon love and marriage."

"Indeed?" He turned to Cassandra, his brows rising lazily and a slow smile curving his lips. "I should be very interested indeed to hear them."

Cassandra felt herself blushing annoyingly under his scrutiny. "I fear 'tis a subject we have hashed out enough, sir. Besides, I am sure that you would find it quite boring."

"On the contrary. I am all ears."

"I shall tell you in a nutshell," Violet spoke up unexpectedly. "Miss Verrere and I believe in love and in a man's ability to love a woman for more than just her looks. Lady Neville and Mrs. Moulton do not."

Cassandra was grateful to Philip's mother for aligning herself with Cassandra, although she suspected that a touch of an enduring rivalry between the lady and her mother-in-law had also inspired Violet. The elder Lady Neville looked a little miffed at being lumped with Aunt Ardis.

"Indeed." Philip's smiled deepened, and Cassandra felt her heart speed up in response. "I am grateful to you and Miss Verrere for believing that we males are able to think and feel on a higher plane."

"Come now, Sir Philip," Joanna said with a playful pout, "do not tell me that you do not value a pretty face."

"Of course I value beauty," he responded easily, "whether in a painting or music or a woman."

He disengaged Joanna's fingers from his arm and guided her to a seat on the grass. She arranged her skirts attractively around her, expecting him to sit down beside her, but he stepped nimbly away and sat between his mother and grandmother. Cassandra had to smother a smile at Joanna's startled and decidedly irritated expression.

"However," Philip continued, his gaze returning to Cassandra, "I believe that there is far more to a woman's beauty than a nice arrangement of facial features."

"Hah! I won't argue that," Lady Neville said, reaching down to poke his arm with her fan. "But do you intend

to marry for love? That is the real question. Whether you
fall in love for beauty or a clever mind, would you marry
her if she hadn't a cent? Or couldn't trace her lineage past
her grandparents? What then?''

"You are bound to get me in trouble with someone,
aren't you? I cannot speak for other men, but I can say
that I do not believe that I could marry where I did not
love. But what are we doing, talking of such serious
things? We are here, are we not, for amusement?''

Joanna was quick to agree with him and proceeded to
launch into a silly story that Cassandra had heard many
times before. Cassandra ignored her burbling voice, her
mind going back to Philip's words. He had said he could
not marry without love, but that was not exactly the same
as marrying for love. He had not said that he would marry
a woman he loved even if she had no money. Not that it
mattered, anyway, she reminded herself, for she had no
reason to think that Philip loved her or would ever con-
template marrying her. Firmly, she turned her attention to
her food.

When the luncheon was over, Lady Neville retired to
the carriage for a discreet nap, and the twins, Olivia and
Georgette began a lively game of tag. Joanna, dimpling,
begged Sir Philip to escort her on a walk. Cassandra
watched them set off, Joanna's skirts swishing in the grass.
She felt a sudden, intense hunger for a beautiful dress,
something that was not made over or out of style, something in a rich material sewn up by a fashionable modiste.

Cassandra turned and strode away from the party, not
much caring where she went, only wanting to distance herself from the others. She struck off down a narrow path,
finding, to her surprise, that it led to a pleasant stream. She
sat down on a large rock beside the stream, watching the
water burble soothingly over mossy stones. She reminded

herself of all the reasons why it did not matter that Joanna was pursuing Sir Philip so avidly—or even that she might catch him. *All she herself needed from the man was his help in finding the Spanish dowry.*

She tried to concentrate on the treasure, imagining how it would feel to find the missing map, how they would search for the treasure and find it. It would be so wonderful to pull out the old strongbox and know that they had located the treasure. She could picture herself touching the golden leopard, trying on a ring or a bracelet. *Philip's eyes would glow, his smile curving in pleasure. She would turn to him, and a look would pass between them. And he would...*

"Woolgathering?" Philip's actual voice intruded on her daydream, and Cassandra jumped.

She whipped around and glared at him. "What are you doing here?"

"Looking for you," he admitted easily, strolling over to sit down on the large rock beside her. "Sorry I startled you. I thought you heard me coming. You must have been very deep in thought."

"I was thinking about finding the dowry." Cassandra hoped a blush would not betray where her thoughts had led.

"It appears we have quite a task before us. I hadn't realized what slow going it would be, looking through the library."

"It will take some time."

"Hopefully we shall not have many more outings like this to delay us."

Cassandra smiled faintly. "I am surprised to see you here. I thought you were walking with Joanna."

"I was. Thank God she got tired, so I whisked her back to the blanket with Mother."

A giggle escaped Cassandra's lips. She could well imagine her cousin's outrage when Philip had done that. Cassandra had no doubt that Joanna had timed her "tiredness" to coincide with a cozy spot where she and Philip could be alone.

Philip allowed himself a smile. "Yes. Miss Moulton was not too pleased, I'm afraid. How can you be related to her?"

"I didn't notice you running very hard from her last night in the drawing room."

He shrugged. "I was feeling out of sorts."

Cassandra stopped. She did not want to pursue that subject, for it led straight back to what had happened in the library yesterday. She pressed her lips tightly together and turned her attention back to the stream.

"What have I done?" Philip asked after a long moment. "How have I offended you? When we were traveling here, you... Well, it was entirely different. What has happened since then? Is it your cousin's flirting? Surely you must know that I had nothing to do with—"

"It is not Joanna." Cassandra turned away from him, speaking toward the water rather than him. "I— Well, we need to concentrate on finding the map. That is what is important."

"It is not the only thing in our lives."

"Perhaps not. But disgracing myself is nothing I want in my life, either."

"Disgracing— Cassandra, what *are* you talking about?"

"I think you know."

"I would never do anything to harm you! Surely you know that. Do you still distrust me? Think I am trying to steal your treasure from you? I assure you that it is the farthest thing from my mind. I don't care if—"

"It's not that! I am not worried about losing the

dowry.'' Cassandra got agitatedly to her feet. "Please, could we go back to the others?''

He rose, too, taking a firm grip on her arm. "Not until you tell me what is wrong.''

"Nothing is wrong!'' She pulled her elbow from his and began walking away.

"Do you take me for a fool? Suddenly you hate me, and you say that nothing is wrong?''

"I do not hate you.''

"Then why are you running from me?''

"I am not!'' Cassandra stopped, planting her hands on her hips and facing him.

"My mistake,'' Philip said dryly. "I seem to be making any number of wrong assumptions these days. You are not running away. You do not hate me. Nothing is wrong.''

Cassandra let out an exasperated noise. "All right. If you must know, it is not anything you did. I mean, nothing you did to me, specifically. It is your attitude in general. It is your smug, male—'' She sputtered to a stop, unable to think of a way to express herself decently. "Oh, damn and blast!'' She let out one of her father's favorite oaths. "How could you put that home here?''

His jaw dropped. Whatever he had expected her to say, it was not this. "What? What are you talking about?''

"Silverwood, of course. How could you have set it here, not a stone's throw from Haverly House?''

"You are upset because of where I put the boys?''

"Yes. It's bad enough that everyone knows about them, that it's common knowledge that you— But to insult your mother in such a way! And your grandmother, too.''

His face changed, settling into lines that, to Cassandra's amazement, looked very much like disappointment. "That is why you have been avoiding me? Why you turned from me yesterday? Because I gave those children a home?''

"No. Not that you house and feed them. It is certainly decent of you."

"Thank you. Your enthusiasm overwhelms me."

"Surely you cannot expect me to praise you for doing your duty!" Cassandra flared. "But the *way* that you do it! Plopping them down right here, practically on your mother's doorstep. She must be mortified."

"Not all women are like you. Believe it or not, Mother is rather proud of me. She bruits it about far more than I care to have it known."

"I am sure that is true," Cassandra retorted sarcastically, stung by the contempt in his voice. *How dare he act as if she were in the wrong?*

"I would never have thought that you, of all people, would object to Silverwood. There are those who do, of course—straitlaced, arrogant snobs who think that children like that should be hidden away somewhere—but I would never have counted you in their number. Obviously I was mistaken."

"Obviously you were, if you thought that I would countenance your setting up a house for your by-blows right in front of your family! Did you think me that loose, that I would not care that you have a score of—of—"

He stared at her, understanding dawning on his face. "Bastards? Is that what you were going to say?"

"Not exactly. But it will do. I agree that there are men who would have denied their obligation, but I cannot find it noble on your part not to deny them. It is, I think, basic decency."

"I see." His jaw tightened. "So I am a decent man to house and feed them, but a cur to do so near to my home."

"No," Cassandra flared. "Merely disrespectful to do that to your mother and grandmother. What makes you a cur is callously bringing them into the world to begin with.''

''I see. Pray tell, how did you find out all this?''

'''Tis a common rumor. Aunt Ardis told me.''

''And you, of course, believed her.''

''It is obvious, isn't it? You have made no effort to hide it!''

''No. I am not ashamed of Silverwood.''

Cassandra felt hot tears starting in her eyes, and she turned and began to walk away again. She refused to let him see that she was crying because of him. *How could he be so cold? So unfeeling?*

After a long moment Philip began to walk after her. He stayed at a distance, not trying to catch up. Cassandra wished miserably that he would stop and let her get far ahead of him. It was a struggle to hold back her tears. She had been hoping that somehow Philip would explain away Silverwood, that there would be another explanation for it. But he had not said a word to deny it. He had not even seemed embarrassed. Indeed, he apparently thought that it was somehow reprehensible of her not to be in awe at his kindness in taking care of his own children!

She continued walking briskly, trying to ignore his silent presence behind her. It was a relief to see the small rise that lay this side of the broad and know that they were almost there. Cassandra picked up her pace.

At that moment a scream pierced the air.

13

Cassandra began to run, lifting her skirts to keep from stumbling. The piercing shriek came again and again. Philip tore by her as she crested the rise and raced down toward the water's edge. Someone was floundering in the water, not far from the shore. As Cassandra drew closer, she saw that it was Joanna. At the edge of the broad, everything was chaos. Miss Yorke, the twins and the two young girls were darting about, calling to the person in the lake. One of the maids was having hysterics, and the other one was hitching up her skirts to go into the water. The footmen were running, carrying something, followed by the grooms. Closer to Cassandra, beneath the tree, Violet and Aunt Ardis were standing, looking down at the pond in horror. Even old Lady Neville, in the carriage, had awakened and was looking about.

Cassandra hurried down the hill after Philip. Beneath the tree, Aunt Ardis was shrieking in concert with her daughter. By the time Philip reached the broad, the two footmen had already waded out into the pond, extending a long branch to Joanna. She flailed uselessly around, managing to both knock the branch out of everyone's hands into the water and also to propel herself farther from shore.

"Stand up!" Crispin yelled, cupping his hands around his mouth. "It isn't deep!"

But Joanna went under, splashing. Philip, who had been pulling off his boots, now shrugged out of his coat and walked into the broad. He moved to where Joanna struggled and reached down to pick her up in his arms. The water, Cassandra noted, did not even reach his waist.

Joanna was limp in Philip's arms, her head resting against his shoulder, her eyes closed. Her velvet riding skirt was soaked with water, and the white cotton shirt-waist, Cassandra noticed, was almost transparent in its wet condition, clinging to her curves like a second skin. Her hair was down and wet, flowing about her shoulders like a mermaid's.

"I told you it wasn't deep," Crispin commented disgustedly.

Philip set Joanna down on the grass and would have stood up, but Joanna clung to him convulsively. "Oh, thank you, Philip!" she cried. "You saved my life!" She looked up at him with melting blue eyes. "I am so lucky you were here."

He shook his head. "No need to thank me."

"I owe my life to you."

This was too much for Crispin, who exclaimed, "Joanna, you goose! It wasn't deep enough to drown in. I kept yelling at you to stand up. Didn't you hear me?"

"Mort the groom says the whole broad is shallow enough to walk across," Hart chimed in. "It's just a pit where they used to cut peat, not a real lake."

Joanna glared at the boys. "I almost drowned!" Her eyes narrowed. "It was probably you two who pushed me in!"

"What!"

"Joanna, don't be such a goose," Olivia said flatly. "You slipped and fell."

"No. I distinctly felt a push on my back. I couldn't see them, but it is just like one of their loathsome pranks."

"We didn't!" Crispin and Hart cried in unison.

"That's not fair," Crispin went on reasonably. "If you didn't see, how can you say it was us?"

"Who else would do it?" Joanna countered.

"You don't want to admit that you did something as stupid as fall into a pond," Hart said scornfully.

"I am sure it was no one's fault," Cassandra said firmly. "It was just one of those things that happen."

"Yes, yes, I am sure that is it," Miss Yorke agreed, obviously distressed by the conflict. "No one's fault."

One of the servants brought a blanket to drape around Joanna's scantily clad body. Cassandra was sure she saw a flash of irritation in her cousin's face as the maid wrapped it around her tightly.

Cassandra had her own ideas about exactly how Joanna had wound up in the water. She felt quite sure that her cousin had staged the whole thing in order to get Sir Philip to rush to her rescue. She had doubtless seen him go off in the direction Cassandra had taken, and she had decided to bring him back. With the water as shallow as it was, she would have had ample time to scream and thrash about without any fear of hurting herself until Philip came running back. When the servants had tried to pull her out, she had managed to thwart them and wait for Philip's rescue. It was exactly the sort of thing that Joanna would do, but, of course, she could not prove it.

"Oh, Joanna! My darling! My baby!" Everyone had been vaguely aware of a low keening sound behind them, growing in intensity, and now Aunt Ardis burst into words as she rushed the last few yards to her daughter and threw herself down on the ground beside her. "Are you all right?" She clasped the girl to her bosom dramatically. "Oh, my baby!"

"I'm fine, Mama, really." Joanna pulled away from her, turning back toward Philip, whom she had been clutching earlier. But Sir Philip had taken advantage of her mother's embrace to rise to his feet and step back.

"Why don't we move back and give her some air?" Sir Philip suggested.

"You are right, Sir Philip," Miss Yorke was quick to agree.

Everyone stepped back a few paces, looking down at Joanna as if she were an exhibit in a museum. It occurred to Cassandra that with her heavy riding skirt soaked and her boots filled with water, the blanket wrapped around her, and her hair streaming down every which way, Joanna looked more sodden and unkempt than fragile and alluring.

Joanna obviously realized, too, that her moment was slipping away, for she turned her face up piteously to Sir Philip, saying, "Please, Philip, could you carry me to the carriage? I do not think that I can walk so far, and I must go back. I can stay here no longer."

He did not look overly eager, but there was little he could say. Kneeling beside her, he lifted her up into his arms again and started toward the carriage. Joanna once again leaned against his shoulder trustingly, and her arms curled around his neck.

Cassandra watched them go. It had, she thought, been a thoroughly miserable day. Now it would be capped off by being squeezed into the carriage with Joanna, soaking wet.

She trailed along with the others toward the carriage. She arrived just as Philip was finishing tucking Joanna's blanket around her to ward off all possible chills. Suddenly an imp seized her, and she turned toward Miss Yorke.

"Oh, dear! Miss Yorke, now there are too many for the carriage, I'm afraid."

"Oh. You're right." The other woman looked disappointed, but said only, "I shall ride in the wagon."

"Nonsense!" Cassandra protested. "My cousin's horse is now without a rider. Why don't you ride Joanna's horse instead of going in the carriage?"

Cassandra was doubly rewarded by the way Miss Yorke's face lit up, as well as by Joanna's scowl. She knew that Joanna selfishly would not like any woman riding with Sir Philip, even the quiet and retiring Miss Yorke.

"I doubt that I am a good enough rider for it...." She began to demure reluctantly.

"Don't worry about that," Cassandra assured her breezily. "Joanna only rides very gentle horses. Besides, you will have Sir Philip with you in case you need help."

"But I haven't my riding habit."

"Your skirts are amply full. I'm sure no one here will mind."

"That would be lovely—if you are sure it would be all right...?" Miss Yorke turned toward her employer.

Sir Philip smiled at her. "Of course it would. Miss Verrere has thought of the perfect solution, as always. Come, Miss Yorke, ride with me."

The woman went off happily with Sir Philip, and Cassandra climbed into the carriage beside her cousin. Joanna scowled at her blackly.

"Now, isn't that nice for Miss Yorke?" Violet said happily. "She deserves a treat."

"Yes," Cassandra agreed pleasantly and smiled at her cousin. "Everything worked out perfectly, didn't it?"

The next morning, as Cassandra was leaving the breakfast table, Philip asked her curtly if she wished to work in

the library again. She replied as briefly, and they walked
down to the library and started to work. Later the twins
offered to help, as did Georgette and Olivia, and for a
while the library was enlivened by their young voices.
However, the work was far too dull for them to last long
at it, and when Philip and Cassandra came back that afternoon after their meal, the youngsters decided that they
would rather go for a ride. Philip and Cassandra reverted
to silence, working in stiff courtesy at opposite ends of the
room.

Cassandra was dismayed at how long it was taking to
search the library. She had not counted on its being such
a massive room. It was slower going, too, than she had
realized, twisting and turning to read the titles and having
to pull out books and look through them when she wasn't
sure what sort of book it was. As the day passed, she found
two books that seemed to be real possibilities. One was
written by a man whose last name was Queen, and the
other was a biography of Mary, Queen of Scots. Each time
her heart leapt within her chest, but after going through
them page by page, she found no evidence of a map.
Philip, too, discovered a few books that might be the one
they wanted, but all of them turned out to be disappoint-
ments, as well.

It could take days, even weeks, Cassandra realized before they found the correct book—and every minute that
she spent with Philip was painful. She thought with longing of the days when they had talked together easily, when
they had laughed…when he had looked at her in a way
that made her insides melt. Now they said almost nothing,
and there was no laughter. When Philip looked at her, it
was with a carefully cool, blank face.

That evening Cassandra excused herself from supper
and ate instead with the younger set in the nursery. She

did not think she could stand to sit through another evening of watching Joanna throw herself at Philip.

She went to her room soon after they finished, not feeling up to the rousing game of charades the children were planning, but not wanting to spoil their fun with her gloom. She was wandering aimlessly around her bedroom, trying to find something to occupy the rest of her evening, when there was a tap on her door.

"Come in." Cassandra turned and was surprised to see Philip's mother open the door and walk in. "Lady Neville!"

She glanced a little curiously at the cloth that Lady Neville carried draped over one arm, but Violet made no mention of it. "Hello, dear. I wanted to make sure you were feeling all right, since you didn't come down to supper."

"I'm sorry. I didn't mean to make you worry. I didn't explain it well in my note. It wasn't that I was ill, I just...felt I ought to eat with my brothers and sister. It is what they're used to at home, you see, and I..."

"No need to explain," Violet assured her airily. "I understand. That wasn't the only reason I came. May I lay this down on your bed?"

"Yes, of course."

Lady Neville put the cloth down on the bed and unfolded it. Cassandra could see now that it was a dress. Made of the palest lavender silk, it was a simple but lovely gown sewn in the latest style with the newer, narrow skirts drawn back over an underskirt of the same shade of satin. The bodice had a low, rounded neckline, with a soft cowl draping, and short, puffed sleeves.

"What a beautiful dress!" Cassandra exclaimed softly.

"Do you like it? I'm so glad." Violet smiled at her. "You see, I ordered it a few weeks ago, and it just arrived today. I found when I tried it on that, well, it simply did not look the same on me as it had in the drawing. Of course, it is far too old for Georgette, but I thought perhaps you might be able to wear it.''

"Me?" Cassandra looked at her, startled.

"Why, yes. We are much the same height, you know, and while you are slenderer than I, that is one of the problems with it. It is too tight, I'm afraid to say. I must have gained some weight recently.''

"Well, I…'' Cassandra looked back at the dress. It was so pretty that her fingers itched to pick it up and try it on, but she felt vaguely that it would be wrong of her to take it. "Surely you don't want to just give it away.''

"What else can I do? I shan't wear it, I know. Lady Neville would say something, I'm sure, and I would regret it.''

"But there must be something else you could do with it, someone else you could give it to.…''

"Who? You were the only one I could think of. Of course, if you don't like it, I will understand. I would never—''

"No! It isn't that! I love it. It's just—'' She couldn't quite explain her dread of wearing someone else's clothes; it was too much like accepting charity for her to feel comfortable. But of course Lady Neville could not understand that feeling; she was too wealthy and had always lived so.

"Why don't you just try it on and see if it fits?" Violet suggested.

"All right.'' Cassandra could not resist. With Lady Neville acting as her lady's maid, she took off the dress she was wearing and slipped into the one Lady Neville had brought.

Even before Violet had finished buttoning up the tiny pearl buttons in back, Cassandra was in love with the gown. It fit her as if it had been made for her, and the lavender was a perfect complement to her coloring. It was exactly the sort of dress she had been longing for yesterday. She thought of wearing it to supper tomorrow night and wondered if Philip's face would change when he saw her in it.

"It's beautiful on you!" Lady Neville exclaimed. "My dear, you simply have to wear this dress. It looks far better on you than it ever would on me. Please, tell me you'll take it."

"All right." Cassandra smiled at her reflection in the mirror, smoothing down the front of her skirt. Whatever her feelings about accepting charity, she knew that she could not bear to give up this dress. "Thank you, Lady Neville."

"It's a pleasure, my dear," Violet replied, beaming.

The next morning, when Cassandra went down to eat, Philip was no longer at the breakfast table, so after eating, she went to the library to see if he was already at work. He was there, but seated in one of the chairs, reading a newspaper. He stood up when she entered and took a step forward, then stopped and gave her a polite nod.

"Good morning, Miss Verrere."

"Sir Philip."

"I noticed you were not at supper last night. I hope you were not feeling ill."

"No. I ate with the children. I have been neglecting them of late."

"I see." They stood for another awkward moment, then he turned toward the circular staircase. "Well…shall we get to work?"

They climbed the staircase and went to their usual places. Cassandra began to work her way through another shelf. She had never guessed that looking for treasure could be so boring. After a few minutes she began to get a vague, uneasy feeling, the sort of twitching between her shoulder blades that she got when someone was watching her. She turned quickly. Philip was indeed looking at her.

"Yes?" she asked, raising her brows in cool inquiry.

He started to say something, stopped, then closed the book in his hands with a snap and shoved it back into place. "Damn it! This is enough!"

He turned and clattered down the stairs. He went to the bell pull on the wall and yanked it. When a footman appeared moments later at the door, he said something to him in quiet tones, then closed the door and returned to the loft. Cassandra watched the whole performance in silent mystification. He strode across the loft to her and seized her wrist.

"Come," he said peremptorily. "I think it's about time you saw something."

"Saw what?" Her flesh tingled where his hand curved around her wrist, and his nearness made her tremble inside. She told herself she was an idiot. There was no reason to feel like swooning just because an attractive man was standing only inches away from her. But she could not shut off her heightened senses, could not keep from being inordinately aware of his size and strength, of his familiar, masculine smell. She swallowed, trying to pull together some semblance of self-assurance.

He did not reply, merely pulled her toward the staircase. She went with him, unable to stop herself. She would have liked to think that it was only because his greater strength compelled her, but she knew that she went willingly. She could not bring herself to break away from his touch.

Philip led her down the stairs and out of the library to a side door. "What are you doing?" Cassandra asked. "Where are we going?"

"You'll see." He headed toward the stables. "We are going to pay a call this morning."

"A call?" Cassandra was even more puzzled. "Whatever are you talking about? We have work to do."

"And I cannot do it. Not until we have settled this."

Cassandra's stomach coiled uneasily. "Settled what?"

He shot her a brief, irritated glance. "Must you ask so many questions?"

"Hardly a strange thing to do when you refuse to tell me why you dragged me out of the library or where we are going, or, indeed, anything."

One of the grooms was leading a horse and light trap out of the stable yard, and Philip handed her up into it, then climbed in and took the reins. They started off at a brisk pace. Cassandra grabbed the seat to keep from sliding into Philip as they turned smartly out of the yard.

"I haven't even a hat and gloves!" she protested. "I cannot call on anyone like this. Why, my dress isn't fit to go calling in."

"Don't worry. They are very informal there. No one will care."

"*I* will." Cassandra grimaced in exasperation. "If that isn't like a man. You say no one will care, but everyone will think I am utterly without manners."

"Not where we are going. If they do, you have my permission to tell one and all that I abducted you and would not allow you to wear either hat or gloves."

Cassandra smiled reluctantly. "I shall."

She could get nothing else out of him, and it was too pleasant to be out driving with him through the sparkling summer day for her to brood about it. Even with the current stiffness between them, Cassandra could not help but enjoy being beside Philip—the warmth and strength of his body only inches from her on the seat, the sun lighting the planes and angles of his face and turning his brown eyes the color of whiskey. She wished it didn't feel so good to look at him. It simply made it hurt all the more to think of his turning his looks and charm on all those other girls, those unfortunate mothers of his children.

The trip was short, as he had promised. Before long they were turning into a driveway leading up to a warm red-brick house. A stand of silver beeches shaded it on one side, and as they drove up, a group of boys came tearing around the corner in hot pursuit of another boy. All of them skidded to a halt at the sight of Cassandra and Philip. They waved enthusiastically, jumping up and down.

Cassandra's stomach began to churn. "Where are we? Is this Silverwood?"

"Yes." He pulled back on the reins, stopping the horse, and looked down at her. "Will it taint you to visit them?"

Cassandra's cheeks flushed with anger. For an answer, she whipped around and climbed out of the trap without waiting for his assistance.

"Philip! Philip!" cried the smallest of the boys, running around the vehicle and throwing himself against Philip's leg as soon as he stepped out. He wrapped his arms tightly around Philip's legs, and Philip had to unwind him, chuckling.

"Harry...Harry. You will topple me over."

The other four boys had come to a halt and were gazing at Cassandra with interest. One of the boys, she saw, had a withered arm. Another's face was marred by a large reddish stain over one cheek. The oldest one, though not large, looked to be about fifteen or sixteen, the others ranged in age down to the smallest one who had wrapped himself around Philip. Sixteen, Cassandra thought, astonished. *Philip had obviously started when he was young.*

She did not think that he could be more than thirty-four now.

Philip came around the end of the trap, leading his small admirer by the hand. "Good morning, boys."

"Good morning, Sir Philip." They came eagerly forward, though with less exuberance than Harry.

"I want you to meet someone." He introduced the young men to Cassandra, and they answered politely, bowing.

They moved inside, the boys following them, and just as they stepped into the entryway, Sarah Yorke swept out of a room down the hall and advanced toward them, patting nervously at her hair and smoothing down her skirts.

"Sir Philip! What a pleasant surprise. And Miss Verrere."

"Miss Yorke."

"I thought I would bring Miss Verrere to see your excellent work, Sarah."

"I am sorry if we are intruding," Cassandra added hastily.

"Heavens, no, Sir Philip is always welcome here. This is, after all, his home."

"Why don't you show Miss Verrere around, Sarah? Explain everything to her. I apparently promised the boys last time that I would play cricket with them next time I came."

"Of course." Miss Yorke smiled shyly at him. "Please, go on. They will love it, I am sure."

She ushered Cassandra into the first room, where three boys of varying ages were working at their books. Two of them jumped to their feet politely when she came in. The third stayed in his chair; Cassandra saw that his legs were both missing from the middle of the thighs down.

"We are working on math in this room," Sarah explained. "Boys, Sir Philip is here and is getting up a game of cricket. You may go if you like."

Two of them pelted out. Only the crippled boy remained.

"Wouldn't you like to go outside to watch, Dennis?" Miss Yorke asked.

"Why?" he retorted sullenly. Miss Yorke patted him on the shoulders. "Well, you may continue with your studies then, or do something else if you prefer, since the other boys are off now."

She led Cassandra down the hall, saying in a low voice once they were out of earshot, "Dennis is still a very angry young boy. Understandable, of course. His legs were run over by a milk wagon. He fell from it trying to cadge a ride." She shook her head and smiled. "But he will get better. They always do after they have been here a while. He will realize how much good life he has left ahead of him."

They entered another room, this one floored in stone, where three children were up to their elbows in clay, laughing and squealing while they formed images under the watchful eye of a strong-armed woman. It was clear that two of them were blind. The third made strange guttural noises. Miss Yorke explained that he had been deaf from birth.

Cassandra had a sinking sensation in her stomach. *How could so many of Philip's illegitimate children have physical problems?* Blind, deaf, crippled, branded with a lurid birthmark...and she had not even seen them all yet.

Miss Yorke was going on about the belief that she and Sir Philip shared of how much children could learn and grow with artistic expression, such as modeling in clay and drawing or music. "We make sure that all of the arts, even dance, are included in our curriculum. It is amazing what can be accomplished if one gives children the chance. Thank God that Sir Philip was willing to give these children a chance.''

Miss Yorke's eyes glowed. Cassandra suspected that the governess might have a *tendre* for her handsome employer.

''Sir Philip has done a great deal for his children,'' Cassandra said carefully.

''My, yes. Most people pay no attention to such children, just hurry past them on the street—if they even notice them. But Sir Philip is the soul of kindness. Not only does he clothe and feed them, and even give them an education, he takes the time to come and visit them. To talk and play with them. That is most uncommon. Most charity, if given at all, is limited to money. But Sir Philip gives of himself. He is genuinely interested in their progress.''

Cassandra's uneasy feeling was growing by leaps and bound. *Why were there only boys?*

Miss Yorke showed her through the spacious kitchen, where a woman was busily cooking a pot of stew, and they stopped to look out the back door into the yard, where Sir Philip was engaged in a game of cricket with several boys. Quite a few more sat by, watching the game. Cassandra noticed a young boy with a horribly contorted spine and two boys on crutches.

''There are so many of them,'' she murmured.

''Yes.'' Miss Yorke seemed pleased, though she frowned. ''We are bursting at the seams. Lionel will be leaving soon. He is so talented that Sir Philip was able to get him apprenticed at the Wedgwood factory. But even then, we will have over twenty boys. I don't know what we are going to do. We have already converted the attic into a dormitory room for the younger boys.''

As Miss Yorke led her back down the hallway into the

small room that served as her office, Cassandra asked bluntly, "Where do the boys come from?"

"All over." Sarah gestured her toward a chair. "Would you like some tea?"

Cassandra shook her head. "No, thank you. You were saying…"

"Oh, yes, where the boys come from. I believe Sir Philip caught John trying to pick his pocket in London."

"Pick his pocket!"

Miss Yorke nodded. "You see how good Sir Philip is? He could have had him thrown in jail. Instead he took him into his household, had the servants take care of him and feed him. But he could tell that it was not the best solution. And he could see how many more boys like John there were in London and, indeed, all over the countryside. That is when he came up with the idea for Silverwood. He knew that the owner of this house had died, and that the heirs wanted to sell it. He thought it would be a perfect place to raise boys. So he bought it and hired me—saving my life, as I told you, in the process of saving the boys, too. We started out with four boys, but Sir Philip continues to bring back unwanted children. Dennis, whom you met, is the most recent. Sir Philip found him begging on the streets of Manchester. He found several of the others doing the same thing, or stealing so they could eat."

Cassandra felt numb. "But I—I had been told that Silverwood housed Sir Philip's illegitimate children."

"Oh! That vicious rumor!" Miss Yorke's eyes flashed. "It still persists. People seem to prefer to believe the worst about people rather than the best. Of course they are not Sir Philip's illegitimate children. They are simply poor orphans whom everyone else has abandoned."

Tears pricked at Cassandra's eyelids. Sir Philip had done a tremendously kind and humane thing, and she had accused him of being a vile seducer, of insulting his mother by placing his by-blows in a home so near to Haverly House. Cassandra wanted to sink through the floor. *How could she have been so hasty in her judgment, so ready to believe the worst of him? He must despise her now for the things she had said to him.*

She stayed on, listening to Sarah talk about the boys and Sir Philip's philosophy of education and the various subjects they taught them. She contributed very little to the conversation, for she was too stunned to think very clearly. Her mind hummed with regrets and painful memories of the things she had said and the way she had acted toward Philip. She felt sunk in guilt, and when Philip finally came back into the house, she could not even look him in the face.

They stayed for luncheon with the boys who, because it was summer, ate beneath the trees on two long trestle tables. Cassandra watched them pack away an incredible amount of food with an air of being seriously at work. Only toward the end of the meal did they begin to talk and laugh and jostle each other.

She was amazed at the happy spirit among them, children of the most unfortunate circumstances. She was also struck by the ease with which Sir Philip mingled with them, tousling one's hair, patting another on the shoulder, making fish faces for the youngest, Harry. Something warm and sweet swelled within her as she watched him, mixing with the bitter rue that had plagued her since the moment she had realized how much she had wronged him. Tears sprang into her eyes, and she had to turn away so that no one would see them.

After the meal, they left. Cassandra bade Miss Yorke and the children goodbye and walked out to the trap beside Philip, still silent and unable to look at him. He gave her a hand up into the vehicle, and they drove down the drive away from the house, giving a final wave as they turned out into the lane.

Cassandra gazed out at the scenery, her hands clenched in her lap. She swallowed, then said tightly, "Obviously I owe you an apology."

He glanced at her. "I didn't take you there for an apology."

"Nevertheless, I have to give one. I was wrong, terribly wrong. I insulted you, blamed you for—for—seducing young women when all the time you were doing something magnanimous and kind. No wonder your mother and sister seemed so proud of you! I should have known when I heard the way they talked about Silverwood and you." She turned and glared at him. "Why didn't you tell me? You knew what I thought! Why didn't you explain it the other day? Why did you allow me to go on thinking that— that—"

"I find that people usually believe what they want to," Philip said in a world-weary voice. "It is a constant source of amazement to me that what people want to believe is always the worst."

"I didn't want to!" Cassandra cried. "I tried not to."

He pulled off onto the side of the road and stopped beneath a stand of trees. He turned to face her.

"Then why did you? Why did you trust the rumors over what you knew of me?"

"It was what Aunt Ardis told me. She said that everyone said you were a rake, a libertine. That you had even set up a house for your illegitimate children. I told her that it was absurd, but then, when we got to Haverly House, you and Lady Neville started talking about Silverwood, and I realized that there really was a house of children. And— and your mother called them 'your children.'"

Philip groaned. "She didn't mean that they were *really* my children. It was just an expression."

"I realize that now. But I didn't then. All I could think was that Aunt Ardis was right—that you really did have a house filled with your by-blows."

"And that I had the audacity to set them up a few miles down the road from my mother and grandmother. How could you believe I would do that? How could you think that I have been spending my adult life procreating? Spreading my seed throughout England like a rutting bull, with no regard to consequences!"

"I didn't see how not to believe it!" Cassandra retorted. "The evidence was there right under my nose. The house that Aunt Ardis had told me about. Your mother and Georgette calling them your children. What else was I supposed to think?"

"You could have come to me." Anger burned brightly in his eyes. "You could have asked me if it was true."

"I still wouldn't have known the truth. If you were the sort of man who went about seducing and abandoning young ladies, why would you have hesitated to lie about it?"

"Why do you insist on my seducing young ladies? Even bastard children don't necessarily mean I callously picked young innocents to dally with."

"But that is what the rumors said. That is what Aunt Ardis told me—and if they were right about the house for bastard children, then it would imply that they were right about everything else. Aunt Ardis pointed out that it is more likely the young and innocent who get trapped with a baby. She said an older woman, an experienced, *professional* sort of woman, would know how to avoid it." Cassandra blushed, but she looked up squarely into his eyes. "Besides, I knew, you see, how expert you were at the art of seduction. I—you—well, I had experienced your kisses.'' Her voice faltered, but she pressed on. "I knew that you were a man of great passion, that you knew how to make a woman, uh…'' She cleared her throat, her face aflame with embarrassment. "I knew that you had been seducing me.''

"I wasn't!'' he exclaimed. "I mean— Well, it wasn't purposeful. It wasn't calculated.'' His voice dropped huskily. "I simply wanted you.''

Heat flooded Cassandra at his words, so raw and simple. She let out a shaky breath.

"I didn't try to lure you into anything. I simply could not keep my hands off you.'' His gaze flickered down over her body; then he looked back up at her face, eyes bright with lust. "I still can't, God help me.''

He leaned forward then, his hand coming up to the back of her neck, and bent to kiss her.

14

Her mouth opened naturally to him, and her hands came up to cup his face. The very feel of his skin beneath her fingertips made her tremble: the warmth, the texture, the underlying hardness of his cheekbones and jaw. There was nothing else except this moment, this kiss, his arms around her. Their lips clung together, tongues intertwining fervently.

He broke off their kiss only to pick her up and lift her onto his lap, his arm going around her back to support her, and then his mouth found hers again. His free hand roamed her body, caressing her breasts through her clothes and moving down her stomach and over her hips and legs, then gliding back up to cup her breast. Cassandra's skin was fiery everywhere he touched her, and she arched up against his hand, moaning, as he repeated the caresses. He groaned deep in his throat at her unconscious gesture of passion, and his lips dug harder into hers. Cassandra felt as though he might swallow her whole, as if her body were no longer her own but a wild thing that responded only to him. Strangely, the feeling was not frightening, but exciting, as if she were entering a world she had never known.

He unbuttoned her bodice, his fingers clumsy with haste

and desire, and slipped his hand beneath the cloth, delving down beneath bodice and chemise to caress the soft orb of her breast. He pulled his mouth away, raining kisses across her face to her ear. Gently he took her earlobe between his teeth and began to worry it, and at the same moment his finger and thumb teased at her nipple. Desire slammed down through Cassandra and exploded in her abdomen. He continued to play with her nipple, rubbing and gently squeezing and pulling, until it was a hard, tight bud, and with every movement, moisture pooled hotly between her legs. Cassandra moved her hips unconsciously; she could hear her own panting breath, fast and loud.

"Cassandra..." he breathed, kissing his way down her soft white throat. His lips were searing, and his breath tickled her flesh, setting still more sensations spinning through her. She could feel the hardness of his masculinity pressing against her bottom, pulsing with desire. A hot ache grew between her legs, threatening to overwhelm her, and she squeezed her legs tightly together to try to ease it.

In answer, his hand went beneath her skirts and up her leg, gliding over her thigh, nothing between their flesh but the thin cotton of her undergarments. Then, shockingly, his hand was between her legs, pressing against the hot center of her ache. She knew he could feel the wetness and the heat of her, and it embarrassed her, but the shame was swept away under the intense pleasure of his touch. It was exactly what she had been inchoately longing for, and she whimpered at the fiery sensation.

His mouth continued its journey down her chest, and he nuzzled aside the bodice and chemise. His mouth fastened on her nipple. Cassandra drew a startled breath, amazed that the pleasure she was feeling could intensify. He suckled her nipple, surrounding it with heat and wetness, every pull of his mouth sizzling as if along a cord straight down into her abdomen. At the same time his hand pressed against the gate of her femininity, stroking in time to the pull of his mouth, and Cassandra trembled under the double force of delight. She was adrift and confused, wanting him to go on forever, yet feeling as if she might explode and fly apart as the pleasure escalated.

Her hands caressed his back and shoulders, and she realized that she wanted very much to feel his bare flesh beneath her hands, to touch him as he had touched her, to explore his neck and chest with her mouth. Her hand went to the nape of his neck, caressing the skin there, and he jerked and groaned at her touch. She breathed his name.

The horse whinnied and stamped its feet, moving restively, and Philip and Cassandra froze, the world around them suddenly intruding on their passion.

"Oh, God," Philip groaned, laying his head against her chest and drawing in deep breaths. Reluctantly he drew his hand away from her legs and straightened. His eyes were ferally blazing, his face flushed and slack with desire. "Anyone could see us."

He glanced around them at the road and the meadow beyond. "Christ, what was I thinking?" He let out a short laugh. "Obviously I was not thinking at all."

Cassandra sat up shakily, sliding off his lap and back onto the seat beside him. Her face flamed with embarrassment as she thought of how exposed they had been to the passing world, and she began to button up her bodice with trembling fingers. "I'm sorry. I shouldn't have…"

"No," he answered hoarsely. "'Twas not your fault. It was mine. Here I was, taking you to task for thinking me a seducer, and then I fall on you like a ravening animal." He sighed and ran his hands over his face, hard, as if he could wipe out the passion still raging within him. "I seem to have no control around you."

"I am the same with you," Cassandra admitted honestly, and her words sent a fresh wave of heat through Philip.

"Lord, Cassandra." He let out a shaky little laugh. "How do you expect a man to exercise willpower when you say things like that?"

"Philip...is what we did so very wrong?" Cassandra asked, her eyes fixed on her fingers as they pleated and repleated a piece of her skirt.

"Wrong? No! I do not think it is wrong. Only a very inconvenient place and time. I think what I want to do with you is very right. But the world," he noted, "does not look upon it quite so tolerantly, I'm afraid."

"No. That is very true."

Cassandra continued to frown down at her lap. Philip took her chin in his hand and turned her face up to his. "Cassandra, I would never want to hurt you in any way, to make you feel unhappy or to damage you in the eyes of the world. I will not lie to you. I want you more than I have ever wanted any woman. But the decision must be yours. I refuse to persuade or seduce you. I will not take advantage of you."

She smiled at him, a golden glow of a smile that pierced his heart. "I was so wrong to think what I did of you. You are a good man."

He smiled back crookedly. "There are many who would dispute that. But I am well satisfied if you think so." He kissed her lightly on the lips, then released her chin and turned away, gathering up the reins. "Now, let us talk of other things, so that we can arrive home with some semblance of dignity."

Cassandra wore the new gown that Lady Neville had given her yesterday to supper that evening, and she reveled

in the way Philip's eyes lit up when he saw her. Olivia
and Georgette had helped her with her hair, styling it in a
softer way so that it framed her face beautifully. Violet
beamed when she saw her, and Lady Neville gave her a
short nod of approval. Cassandra even had the satisfaction
of seeing her cousin and aunt staring at her as if they could
not believe she was the person they knew.

Later, as they sat in the drawing room after supper,
Philip leaned over and murmured, "You test a man's control sorely in that dress, Miss Verrere."

Cassandra chuckled throatily and threw him a sparkling
glance. "Indeed, sir, I believe that is the idea."

She realized with some astonishment that she was actually flirting with a man.

During the next few days Cassandra and Philip worked
steadily in the library, explaining to their rather curious
relatives that Cassandra was helping Sir Philip catalogue
the Neville books. To Cassandra's amazement, the search
was no longer dull or tedious. With the strain of her doubts
about Philip gone, they worked side by side, talking as
they went. Sometimes the children helped them, but more
often not the lure of future treasure was not enough to
prevail over the pleasures of the outdoors, of games and
horseback riding.

In the afternoon Cassandra and Philip usually broke off
their work for a ride. Though Cassandra protested at first
at the time lost, she had to admit that a brisk ride blew
away many of the cobwebs that accumulated in her brain
during the slow, methodical search. Joanna often managed
to find a way to insinuate herself into their riding party,
but Cassandra soon found that Sir Philip grew quite adept
at avoiding her annoying cousin.

They rode sometimes beside the Ouse and sometimes
along twisting, tree-shaded country lanes, through mead-

ows and woods. But their most frequent journeys took them to the ruins of an old abbey.

Cassandra gasped with delight the first time that Philip took her there. It lay beside a twisting, tree-lined brook, a romantic ruin of gray stone, only one small part of it still standing, the rest of the walls in varying stages of decay. Grass had started growing between the paving stones, and vines had taken over some of the tumbled-down walls. It looked mysterious and ancient, a place of secrecy, yet of peace and beauty, as well.

"If I were hiding a treasure," Philip said, dismounting and coming around to help her down, "this is the spot I would choose."

"Oh, yes," Cassandra breathed, enchanted by the place. She looked up at him with wide eyes. "Do you think this is where Margaret chose?"

He shrugged. "It wouldn't surprise me. It was well-known, a landmark that she would certainly have been shown, even though she wasn't here long. If she went further afield than the estate grounds, this would be the most likely place."

Cassandra looked around, her eyes glowing. "Oh, Philip—don't you just itch to go looking for it?"

He chuckled. "Yes, but I cannot think how we would have a chance of finding it. We can't just start digging up the ground everywhere around the abbey. Besides, we don't have a clue that it is buried here—or even that it is buried at all. It could be in a room somewhere."

"Behind a wall?" Cassandra suggested. "A hidden room, perhaps. Do you suppose the abbey has any false walls?"

"I am discovering more and more what a romantic you are, Miss Verrere." He smiled and pulled her to him, wrapping his arms around her and squeezing. When he looked into her shining face like this, it was all he could do not to begin kissing her as he had the other day coming back from Silverwood. But he had promised himself after that torrid moment in the trap that he would not try to pressure or seduce her.

For the first time in his life, Sir Philip was not sure what he felt or what he wanted. He wanted to make love to Cassandra, he was certain of that much. When he had first gone to visit her and her family, he had to admit that an affair with her had been the uppermost intention in his mind. She had aroused his interest and his desire, and though it was usually his policy to avoid unmarried young ladies of quality, she was so different from the others that he had broken his rules.

Now, however, as much as he wanted her, he could not help thinking about the ruin that would face her if their affair were discovered or if she became pregnant. He had never worried about such things before, for the ladies he pursued had been experienced, as Cassandra had pointed out, and he had assumed that they would take care that such a thing did not happen. *But Cassandra was different...in so many ways.*

He was stuck, he thought, between Scylla and Charybdis, not wanting to ruin her reputation yet feeling sure that he could not bear not to have her in his bed. There was only one way out, of course, and that was marriage. There was something oddly intriguing about the thought of being married to Cassandra. God knows, life would never be dull if she was his constant companion. There would be passion, too, at least at first, and if it burned out, as all his passions for other women had, well, she would still be a witty, engaging friend. He supposed he had to marry sometime to ensure the succession of the line; it was one of the duties that a Neville simply did. And Cassandra came from a good family, however odd the Verreres sometimes were.

Of course, she had no money, but wealth was not really a consideration; he had plenty of that. She was not, he supposed, the sort of beauty others would expect him to marry—but to Philip she was far more beautiful, with her pale hair and intelligent gray eyes, than someone like Joanna. And the children she would bear him—his loins tightened at the thought of Cassandra pregnant with his child. They would be bright, laughing, wonderful children if Cassandra was their mother—pert little minxes like Olivia, if they were girls, or daring, engaging rascals like the twins, if they were boys. *Would she give him twins?*

He paused, amazed that he was even thinking of marriage. He had never done so before, not even in the throes of passion or when presented with a most suitable mate. He had always thought that he would prefer not to marry. His father had been a cold, unfeeling man, and his parents' marriage had been unhappy. Philip had come of age determined that he would never allow himself to be in that sad state—tied in a loveless marriage to a suitable person, bored or miserable or furious. He had no real belief in love; it had never been part of his life, except for his mother's fond, vague affection and Georgette's childish doting on her big brother. It had never occurred to him to think that he could love a woman or be happy in a marriage. *Until Cassandra...*

Not, of course, that he was *in love* with Cassandra, he reminded himself hastily. But she was the first woman that he had ever thought he might marry without finding his life a trial afterward. It amazed him—and perhaps alarmed him a little—that he was thinking of marriage. It was, he thought, an indication of the depths of his turmoil over Cassandra.

Torn as he was, he was determined not to do anything until his mind was clearer as to what he *should* do. Much as he wanted her, and as difficult as it was to keep from touching and kissing her, he made himself refrain. He knew that if he began to kiss her and caress her, he might not be able to stop. Ever since that day after the visit to Silverwood, he had been careful not to give in to his impulses.

So today, as on other occasions, he released Cassandra without giving in to the desire to bend down and kiss her inviting mouth. He turned away, saying in a falsely light tone, "Well, we'd best be getting back for tea."

"Oh, yes," Cassandra said with a teasing smile, walking with him toward their horses, a little relieved that he had gone no further. She, too, was in turmoil over her feelings and desire. "I know that you must be most anxious for your afternoon tête-à-tête with Cousin Joanna."

Philip groaned in response. Joanna had countered their frequent absences by practically pouncing on Philip every afternoon at tea and during the evening. He could not sit without her sitting next to him or move without her following, and any conversation with anyone else among their guests was always interrupted by Joanna after no more than two or three sentences.

"You minx," Philip retorted feelingly. "You never do the slightest thing to help me, either, I've noticed." They had reached their horses, and he untied them, handing Cassandra her reins.

"Why, you're a grown man," Cassandra responded with a laugh as Philip helped her back up into her saddle. "I am sure that you can handle a five foot, two inch woman." She gave him a look of bland innocence.

Philip snorted inelegantly. "She may not be tall, but

she's got the damnedest long reach I've ever seen in a woman.''

With a laugh, Cassandra dug in her heels, and they started back toward the house.

As the days passed, though, they grew more and more disheartened by their inability to find the "Queens Book." They had come across a few biographies of Queen Elizabeth, as well as one about Queen Anne, but since Anne had not even been on the throne yet when Margaret fled England, and the two about Elizabeth had been written in the last hundred years, it obviously was none of those three. They had even looked through every history of England written before Margaret's time, although Cassandra could not see why any of them would have been called a "Queens Book." They had worked their way through the loft of the library and started on the bottom floor, but Cassandra was beginning to worry. The books on the lower level were all much more recent. Few of them had been written before Margaret's elopement. The loft was the place where they should have found it.

Still, they kept on looking until finally one day they reached the end of the shelves of the lower level. Discouraged, they sat down and looked at each other.

"It's not here." Philip stated the obvious.

Cassandra sighed. "Is there anywhere else your family might have put any books?"

"My father and grandfather were not really readers. I suppose they could have taken out some of the old books and stored them in the attic. Ones that didn't look as nice as the others. Their interest in the library was purely aesthetic. Father used it primarily as a cigar-and-brandy room."

Cassandra groaned at the thought of digging through another huge attic.

"Worse, I am afraid that it might have been thrown away," he added discouragingly.

"But we cannot find the treasure without the second map!" Cassandra wailed. "I have looked at the other map till my eyes crossed, and I can't make sense of it."

"I know. Neither can I. I cannot connect that drawing to any place around here. I shall ask my mother if she remembers Father getting rid of some of the old books or storing them in the attic."

It was galling to think that they had done so much work and gotten so close, only to be thwarted in the end by the sheer passage of time. Philip hated to admit defeat at any time, and it was frustrating to think that their mystery might never be solved. But worst of all, he realized, was that if they had to give up on finding the treasure, Cassandra would return home.

Desperate, he cast about in his mind for some solution. Suddenly he sat up straight, light dawning in his eyes. "Of course! Why didn't we think of it earlier? The nursery!"

"What? What about the nursery?"

"The schoolroom. There are lots of old books there. Father would never have bothered to do anything about them. And where would you be likelier to find a book about queens than the schoolroom?"

Revived, they launched an all-out search of the schoolroom bookshelves and closets, accompanied by all four of the younger set. But, again, at the end they had to admit defeat. Though the schoolroom had contained many more books concerning various queens, as well as quite a few remarkably old books, none of them had proved to have any sort of map inside them.

Cassandra sat back with a sigh. "Well, I guess there's nothing for it but to search the attics, then."

Philip nodded. "I'll ask Mother and Grandmother if they know of any other place where there might be old books stored."

That evening before supper he went to his mother's bedroom. He found her in her dressing gown, sitting in front of the vanity. Her maid was repinning her hair. Violet turned, delighted, when he came in.

"Philip! Darling!" She held out both her hands to him. "How nice. Do you remember when you were little how you used to come see me when I was getting ready for supper?"

"Of course. It is one of my fondest memories."

"Come, sit down." She gestured toward a chair close to the vanity, then turned to her maid. "Finish pinning it up, Mary, and then you may leave. I shall ring you when I'm ready to finish dressing."

They chatted of commonplace things for a few minutes while the maid deftly pinned the remainder of the curls. When she was done, she left the room, and Violet leaned forward, smiling, and patted her son on the knee. "Now, what brought you here tonight?"

"Can't a son come visit his mother?"

"Yes. You visit me often—in my sitting room or the drawing room or any of a number of rooms in the house. But since this is the one room in which you are assured that no one might unexpectedly come in on us, I assumed you wanted privacy."

Philip smiled faintly. "You are very perceptive, Mother."

"You know I am only vague about some things. Now, tell me, what is this about? Miss Verrere?"

"Cassandra!" He stared at her. "Whatever made you say that?"

Violet's eyebrows lifted. "I'm not blind, Philip. Everyone in this house can see that you have a particular interest in the young woman. Even Sarah Yorke commented on it to me the last time she came to call. Of course, I told her you were only friends. I could hardly say anything else, since you have told me nothing about your intentions toward Miss Verrere."

Philip's jaw hardened. "I hardly see that it is anyone's business other than mine."

"Perhaps. But you must see, my love, that the way you have been in her company every day—in the library, out riding, seeking her out every evening after supper—those actions are enough to encourage any young woman to believe that your intentions toward her are serious. And you asked me to have that dress made for her and then pass it off as something I had bought—though, of course, no one knows about that. You were right—she does look lovely in it. But that is neither here nor there. What I am saying is that you must not lead her on, or you will break her heart *and* make her an object of pity or ridicule."

"I would never do that to Cassandra!"

"Then what do you intend to do? Surely you are not planning to marry her?"

He scowled. "Why do you say it like that? Is the idea so preposterous? You have been after me for years to marry."

"Well, of course you must do so, for the sake of the succession. I would not like to see Haverly House go to that weedy little Chauncey Trent. I have never been able to stand him or his mother. However, I would not have thought that..." Her voice trailed off as she met her son's steely gaze. "Philip, really, you needn't glare at me so. I have nothing against your Miss Verrere. She is a very nice girl, though sometimes, I admit, when she is talking about Shakespeare and things like that, I am really not sure what she is saying. She is a good woman, quite kind, and she seems most efficient. And, of course, her breeding is irreproachable. I never could understand why your father disliked the Verreres so much. But..."

"But what?" Philip crossed his arms over his chest and waited.

"She is not the most eligible female. You must see that. I have heard that her family is in utter financial ruin. And that aunt of hers!" Violet rolled her eyes. "An encroaching sort of female, and that daughter is even worse. 'Fast' is the only way to describe her."

"We have some relatives that are rather odd fishes, as well," Philip said. "And money is not my first requirement in a wife."

"But, Philip, she has been out for years and, well, she did not take."

"Other people's tastes are not my concern, either, Mother. I find Miss Verrere most...unique. Intriguing." His face softened as he spoke of her. "I find her...beautiful. She is not the common sort, I'll grant you, but then, as you know, I have never been attracted to anything common."

Violet stared. She felt as if the wind had been knocked out of her. "Philip...are you serious? Do you plan to marry Miss Verrere? I thought you were merely dallying—"

"I am not dallying with her. I—I don't know what I'm going to do!" he said crossly. "I find Cassandra entertaining and refreshing, and I enjoy spending time with her. But I am not leading her on. She knows that. We are working on a project together. That is why we spend so much time together. Believe me, she would not build her hopes on marriage.''

''A project?'' Violet looked confused. ''Whatever are you talking about?''

''It is…something about our ancestors. It concerns the animosity that has existed between our families for years and the reasons for it.''

''Oh. A historical thing.''

''Yes.''

''I never understood why you found history interesting.''

''You are not alone. But that is one reason why Miss Verrere and I are friends. We can talk about things like that.''

''I see.'' Her tone expressed anything but the meaning of her words.

''This project is why I came here this evening. I need your help.''

Her expression of confusion deepened. ''You need *my* help about history?''

''No, no.'' He smiled. ''I had a question about this house. Cassandra and I have been looking for a certain book. Did you ever hear of a book in the house known as the 'Queens Book'?''

Violet's forehead wrinkled. ''No, dear, but you know I know very little about books. Is that why you two have been spending so much time in the library?''

''Yes, but we could not find it. We searched the schoolroom in the nursery, too. Is there anywhere else in the house that books are stored?''

''Umm, I'm not sure, dear. The attic, perhaps? Was it an old book?''

''Yes, very old.''

''I suppose there could be some books packed away up

there.'' She stared off into space for a long moment, then shook her head. ''Not since I've lived here, though. At least, I don't think I ever stored any books there. Let me think about it. Perhaps I will remember something.''

He thanked his mother and left her with a kiss on the cheek and went down the hall to his grandmother's room. His grandmother, as he had expected, was already dressed for the evening meal and was sitting in a chair by a lamp, doing needlepoint until it was time to go down for supper. She looked up questioningly as he came in.

''Philip. Well, this is unexpected.'' She held out her hand for him to make a bow. The elder Lady Neville was one who insisted on the courtesies. ''What brings you up here, you young jackanapes? Have you decided to offer for that girl yet?''

''What girl?''

She grimaced. ''Don't play the fool with me, young man. You know good and well what girl. The same girl whose company you have been monopolizing ever since you got here. The Verrere chit.''

''Is this all anyone ever talks about?'' Philip wondered out loud.

''One takes what gossip one can in the country. But only a cake would think you could dance attendance on a woman all day long for two weeks and not be suspected of being in love.''

''I am not in love.''

''In a marrying frame of mind?''

''If I decide to marry, I promise that you will be the first to know. Well, perhaps the second.''

''Third, more like. Well, then, what brought you up here if it wasn't to ask my advice about offering for a Verrere?''

''Cassandra and I are trying to locate an old book. A

book about a queen or queens. It is at least two hundred years old.''

She gave him the full blast of her aristocratically cold face. ''I hope you are not suggesting that I am old enough to know anything about that.''

He smiled. ''Not about when it came to the house. Only whether you ever heard anything about it in the time you have lived here.''

''I've been here fifty-five years now. But I must say that we never did much talking about books. Sir Richard didn't care for books much, and he seemed to pass that feeling on to our son.'' She leaned her head back, thinking, but finally shook it and shrugged. ''I cannot recall ever hearing of a book about queens. What queens, anyway?''

''I don't know, ma'am. That is why it is so difficult to find. It is merely a passing reference in a family history.''

''Two hundred years ago?''

''Yes.''

''You expect a book to hang about for a rather long time.''

''I was hoping that it would be important enough that it would not have been thrown away.''

''I don't think it was important to *my* husband. Perhaps to his father. That was why Sir Richard hated books so much. His father rammed them down his throat from the time he was a boy. He used to say he decided that when he was grown he would never read a book. I believe he kept his word.'' She paused, looking much struck. ''You know, I just thought of who might know. Aunt Liliane!''

''Grandfather's aunt? But, Grandmother, the last time I went to see her, she didn't know who *I* was. I can't think she would remember a book from her childhood.''

''I don't know. People keep the oddest things in their heads. Particularly when they get old.'' Lady Neville's ramrod-straight back and disapproving face indicated that she herself would not reach that state for some years, if ever. "Sometimes they remember what happened far in the past better than what happened this morning. My father was like that. The reason I thought of Liliane was that she was bookish, like Sir Richard's father. She would be much more likely to know if such a book existed."

"Thank you, Grandmother. I should have known you would come up with something." He stood and bent over her hand again politely.

"Of course you should have, my boy," she agreed, with a twinkle in her eye.

He left the room whistling, his spirits much improved. Aunt Liliane might not be much of a hope, but she was better than what they had at the moment, which was nothing. And visiting her also meant that he and Cassandra could spend a pleasant day away from the house.

"She is your great-aunt?" Cassandra asked as the open carriage spun along the lane at a fast clip.

"No, my great-great-aunt. She was my grandfather's aunt."

"Oh, my. She must be very old, then."

"Around ninety, I think."

"Goodness. Perhaps she will know something about the 'Queens Book,' then." Cassandra began to feel more hopeful. When Philip had suggested the day trip to see Aunt Liliane, she had been pleased to go along, as it meant almost an entire day alone in Philip's company, since he had firmly turned down Joanna's suggestion this morning that they all go to see the old lady, saying that Aunt Liliane was too frail to have more than one or two visitors. But now she felt a spark of hope that the old woman might provide a useful clue to their search.

It was a lovely ride to Aunt Liliane's house. It took a little over three hours, and they followed the Ouse almost the entire way. Cassandra, parasol tilted to keep the sun off, drank in the scenery and tried not to think about the fact that they were getting perilously close to a dead end with the Neville map.

Aunt Liliane lived in a very old house built in the distinctive style of the Tudors. The front door was so low that Philip had to stoop to enter it. He had to stoop again as they went up the stairs to Aunt Liliane's bedroom, for the ceiling at the landing slanted down to a height that Cassandra could barely pass under standing straight.

"When I was young, I thought of this as a witch's house," Philip said to Cassandra in an undertone. "It is full of strange nooks and crannies."

"It's charming."

"Aunt Liliane moved here after she was widowed. She couldn't stand her son's wife, and she refused to live with them. This house, she said, was big enough for her and a companion and their servants. Of course, she was getting on in years even then, and everyone worried about her. But she was an independent old soul. I used to visit her for a week or so now and then. I loved it. She had all sorts of books and a...a more carefree way of doing things than we had at Haverly House. We had meals at all sorts of odd times, and she didn't care if I wanted to take things apart to see how they worked or anything like that."

"You sound as if you love her very much."

"I do." He sighed. "But it's sad. She was so bright, but now she rarely even knows who I am."

The maid led them into a bedroom. The windows were open, flooding the room with light, and a wizened old crone sat in a wicker chair in front of one of the windows. She looked to be about four and half feet tall, but the effect was heightened by the fact that she was bent over at the shoulders to such an extent that she had to twist her head to look up at them, giving her an odd, birdlike appearance. The dark eyes that watched them alertly added to the illusion. White hair stuck out in tufts from beneath a dark cap. Gnarled, large-jointed hands were clasped in her lap.

Aunt Liliane looked at them brightly for a long moment, then gestured toward a chair. Philip escorted Cassandra to the chair and brought another over for himself.

"Rosemary?" the old woman barked, startling Cassandra.

"Uh, no, ma'am. My name is Cassandra."

"Do I know you?" Her voice again boomed out, at odds with her fragile appearance.

"No, ma'am."

"Aunt Liliane, let me introduce you to Cassandra Verrere."

"Verrere!" The old lady's eyes widened, and she shot Philip a sharp look. "A faithless Verrere? In my house?"

"No," he replied hastily, realizing his mistake. "Ferrars. Cassandra Ferrars is what I said."

She nodded, easily accepting the excuse of her poor hearing. "Don't know any Ferrars." She gaze at Philip for a long moment, then said, "It's been an awfully long time since you have been to see me, Edward."

"No, Aunt Liliane. I'm not Edward. I am Philip, Thomas's son." The names seemed to mean nothing to her, so he pressed on. "Sir Richard's grandson."

"Richard?" She frowned at him suspiciously. "You don't look like Richard."

"No, ma'am. I'm not Richard. I am his grandson."

"Richard's not old enough to have a grandson." She stared at him some more, then crowed delightedly, "Hah!

You're that boy Cecily married, aren't you? That is just like you—always playing tricks.''

She smiled, apparently fond of the boy Cecily married, despite his tricky ways. Philip sighed and let the matter drop.

"We came to ask you about a book, Aunt Liliane," he began.

"A book? What book?'' She glanced around, looking confused. "I don't have any books in here anymore. Can't see worth anything now. That silly chit of a parson's wife comes in and reads to me. She skips all the hard parts and thinks I don't know. Hah!'' She sighed, her face falling into sad lines. "Ah, well, one has to make do with what one can.''

"Yes, ma'am.'' Philip hesitated and turned to Cassandra helplessly.

"Do you remember the library at Haverly House?'' Cassandra asked.

The old lady swiveled toward her. "Of course I do! What a silly thing to ask.''

"I'm sorry. But you see, I don't know you very well.''

Aunt Liliane nodded. "True. You never came to visit as much as your sister.''

"No,'' Cassandra said hesitantly. *Did the vague Aunt Liliane think she was someone else?* "But...my sister once told me about a book you had told her about. A book about queens.''

"Queens?'' Aunt Liliane wrinkled her forehead. "Which ones?''

"I'm not sure. It—it was in the library at Haverly House. An old book.''

"There were many old books there, young lady,'' Aunt Liliane told her crisply. "Are you talking about a biography? A history?''

"I'm not sure. My, uh, sister just called it the Queens Book."

The wrinkled old face cleared, and she let out a chuckle. "Oh, of course! Why didn't you say so? You want to know about the Queen's Book! Oh, yes, I can tell you all about that."

15

A frisson of excitement ran down Cassandra's back like an icy finger. *Could it be that this forgetful old woman actually knew about the book?* For a moment she could not speak, could not move, could only stare at Aunt Liliane.

Fortunately Philip was not so handicapped. "You know of it?"

"Of course I do. Everyone does. It is the most valuable book in Papa's collection."

"Is—is that the title? *The Queens Book?*"

"Title?" Aunt Liliane looked at him oddly. "Young man, what are you talking about? You are the one who sounds as if he doesn't know it."

"I don't," Philip answered rather desperately. "You see, we are trying to find it."

The old woman's face filled with suspicion. "Now, see here, young man, what do you think you are about? You say you are a Neville, but you don't know about the Queen's Book?"

"No. I don't. That is why I came to you. You see, the family has lost it, and we are trying to find it again."

"Lost it! Lost Queen Elizabeth's prayer book?" Aunt Liliane gazed at him in horror.

Suddenly everything she had said made sense. "Of course!" Cassandra exclaimed. "It all makes sense now! The word Queen was capitalized, and that smudgy thing must have been an apostrophe. I thought it was a spot of mildew. The Queen's Book. It was so well-known to the Nevilles at that time that they would have known immediately what it referred to. And if it had belonged to Queen Elizabeth, it would have been far too valuable for them to get rid of. Margaret would have been sure that it would remain there and that no one would go browsing through it, looking for something to read. What a clever idea!"

"Indeed. Except it did not remain there," Philip stated.

"What are you talking about?" Aunt Liliane asked querulously. "I don't understand a word of it."

"Aunt Liliane, it has been some time since you lived at Haverly House. You married and left there almost seventy years ago. In the time since then, the Queen's Book has been misplaced. Sir Richard, your nephew, do you remember him?"

"Of course," she retorted impatiently. "What does he have to do with the Book?"

"Well, he did not love books as you and his father did. As your father did."

"Yes. I remember. It made my brother so sad."

"He paid little attention to any of the books. His son Thomas was the same way. Somehow, during their lifetimes, the Book disappeared. No one today knows anything about it."

"That is absurd!" Her ancient face was shocked. "It could not have been misplaced."

"When was the last time you remember seeing it? Since you were a grown woman?"

She frowned. "I can't remember. A long time ago, I suppose. I remember it from my childhood. After that...no, I can't remember."

"Did your father keep it in the library at Haverly House?"

"Heavens, no! It was much too valuable. He kept it in a metal lockbox for safekeeping. In the storeroom in his bedroom."

Philip thought for a moment. "The little locked room inside the dressing room?"

"Yes." She nodded, pleased at his understanding. "He would get it out and show it to me sometimes. I was fascinated by the jewels, of course."

"The jewels?" Cassandra's words came out as a squeak. *Was it possible that some Neville had already found the dowry?*

"On the cover," Aunt Liliane explained. She shook her head. "You have really never seen it?"

"No," Cassandra responded.

"Could you tell us what it looked like? So we could recognize it if we saw it?" Philip asked.

"It was a prayer book, not large. Leatherbound, with gilt writing and gilt-edged leaves. There were three gems set into the spine. A ruby and two topazes, I believe. And little pearls bordering the cover. About this big." She held up her hands a few inches apart to show its size. "'The Book of Common Prayer,' it said on the outside. On the inside, it read 'For Sir Everard, my loyal knight.' And it was signed 'Elizabeth R.' It was a gift from her, you see. She stayed at Sir Everard's, and she gave him that when she left."

"Do you have any idea what could have happened to it?" Cassandra asked.

"No," the old lady answered, looking worried. "It should still be there."

"Do you think it is?" Cassandra asked as they drove back toward Haverly House. "Still there, I mean. It sounded as if you knew the storeroom she was talking about."

"Yes. It is a small closet in my dressing room. I suppose they used it to put valuables in it once, but Father installed a safe in his office, and that is where the jewels and bonds and things of that sort are."

"Is there a lockbox in this room?"

"Yes. I don't know if it's the same one, but I am certain that there is no jeweled prayer book in it. That is where Father kept his legal papers—deeds and such. I have been through everything in there, more than once, and there is no book of any sort."

"At least now we know what we are looking for." Excitement tinged Cassandra's voice. "Surely we will be able to find it."

"Yes. Mother or Grandmother may remember what happened to it. It sounds distinctive enough."

Cassandra was on pins and needles all the rest of the drive home. Yesterday she had been close to despairing of ever finding the second map. All her visions of a new future for Chesilworth had seemed about to turn to dust. And though she disliked herself for the petty selfishness, she admitted to herself that not the least of her unhappiness had been that if they could not find the map, she would have no reason to remain in Sir Philip's house any longer. But now...now all sorts of possibilities seemed open again.

When they arrived at Haverly House, they had the misfortune to run into Joanna, who must have been sitting and watching out the window for their arrival.

"Sir Philip," she cried, hurrying toward them in the entry, all smiles and dimples and coquettish pouts. "It's been such a long day here without you! You wicked fellow, to leave me to the company of children all day!" She laid her hand upon his arm, smiling warmly up at him.

"Ah, but I thought you were such particular friends with my sister," Philip countered, smoothly moving his arm out from underneath her hand.

Joanna looked momentarily nonplussed, but she recovered quickly. "Oh, well, of course I did not mean darling Georgette...."

"Have you seen my mother?"

Joanna blinked at the abrupt change of subject, clearly disgruntled at the conversation turning away from her. "I'm sure I don't know."

"Then we shall have to talk later, Miss Moulton, for I must speak with mother right now. I am sure you will excuse us." He steered Cassandra around Joanna.

"But we've hardly had a chance to speak," Joanna protested, a scowl forming on her smooth face.

"This evening, my dear Miss Moulton. We shall have plenty of time to talk this evening." Philip nodded toward her and hustled Cassandra off down the hall.

"I'll look forward to it," Joanna trilled behind them.

Philip led Cassandra to his mother's sitting room, where they found both Lady Violet and Philip's grandmother. The women turned toward them with smiles.

"Hello, darling, how was Aunt Liliane?" his mother greeted them, turning her cheek to be kissed.

"She looks as if she might blow away in a strong breeze," Philip said bluntly, "but her nurse says that she is actually in good health."

"We must go see her, Violet," Lady Neville said decisively. "I never did get along with her well, but I suppose that at that age one welcomes the visit of anyone she knows.''

"She didn't have any idea who I was," Philip went on.

"Oh dear, that is too bad. Did she not know anything about this book, then?"

Philip grinned. "No, that she seemed to have no problem with. She knew almost immediately what we were talking about. We have been chasing the wrong thing all this time. It wasn't an ordinary book. Did either of you ever hear of a prayer book that was given to Sir Everard Neville by Queen Elizabeth?"

Both of them gazed at him blankly. Lady Neville frowned. "You know," she said slowly, "I do remember something about a prayer book. Sir Richard's father was rather proud of it."

"Apparently it was a family treasure. It belonged to Queen Elizabeth, and she inscribed it to Sir Everard herself, which would make it valuable enough. But apparently it was also richly bound, with three jewels on the spine and pearls around the cover."

"Oh!" Violet sat forward. "But I've seen that!"

Lady Neville nodded in agreement. "Yes, there was some sort of bejeweled little book. Sir Richard kept it stored in a strongbox."

"It isn't there any longer. I have looked through that box many times."

"Of course not, dear," Violet told him. "We don't have it anymore. It was in that trunk load of things—don't you remember, Lady Neville? That year that Thomas wanted to buy the matched set of bays, but he was short of cash, and old Staley was so against him selling any of the bonds or anything. So he sold some of the old things around the house. The silver salt cellar, remember? And that broken old statuary that used to be in the conservatory—though why anyone would want that, even if it was Greek or Roman or whatever, I don't know. That little jeweled book was one of the things he sold." She looked at her son sympathetically. "I'm sorry, dear, but I'm afraid that book is gone."

For a long moment, Cassandra simply stared at Lady Neville, unable to take in the sudden drop from giddy hope to cruel reality. She plopped down in a chair, her legs feeling as if they could no longer support her, and let out a small moan.

"My dear, are you all right?" Violet asked with concern. "Is the book so important?"

"Yes, it is," her son answered crisply. He saw his mother's look of puzzlement, and he went on, "You know, the Verreres are very scholarly, Mother. And this book...well, it's part of the Verrere family history, also."

"It is? Oh." Violet looked only a little less confused.

Philip sighed and ran a hand through his hair. He walked across the room and back, stopping in front of Cassandra. He squatted down and took her hand in his, covering it with his other hand. He smiled up reassuringly into her face. "Don't worry. We will get it back. A well-known book like that—it can't have disappeared. There will be records. Mother..." He stood and turned back to Violet.

Violet, who with the older Lady Neville had been watching Philip's actions with great interest, gazed up at him limpidly. "Yes, dear?"

"Was there a book dealer whom Father used?"

Violet looked blank, and Lady Neville let out a most unladylike snort. "Don't be absurd, Philip," his grandmother told him bluntly. "My son Thomas could abide books no more than his father. He would not have traded with a book dealer often enough to have a particular one."

"Then Staley must have handled the sale. It was a precious item."

"I suppose so. If Staley were still alive, he might even remember it, but he's been dead these many years."

"There would be records, surely. His son still handles all our business, and I would think he's bound to have a record of the sale somewhere. I shall write to him immediately." Philip resumed his pacing. "Even if he does not, I am sure we will be able to find out something about the book. We shall go around and ask about it at all the book dealers in London, see if any one of them bought it."

"Of course!" Cassandra surged to her feet, smiling. "Mr. Simons will help us. Why didn't I think of it before? We shall go to London and see him. If he knows nothing about it, I am sure he can direct us to someone who deals in that sort of thing. When can we set out?"

"You are going to London?" Violet asked. "Just like that?"

Philip smiled at Cassandra. "Miss Verrere is a woman of action, Mother."

"But, Philip, Miss Verrere, think..." Lady Neville looked shocked. "Surely you cannot mean that the two of you are going to London together?"

"Yes, of course," Philip replied. "I am afraid that Miss Verrere would have my head if I insisted on going by myself."

"I certainly would. I'm not about to let you have all the fun."

"But it is impossible," Lady Neville said firmly.

"Your grandmother is right," Violet agreed. "The two of you cannot travel to London by yourselves. Or stay in Neville House without a chaperon. I suppose Miss Verrere could stay in an inn. There are a few where it is quite respectable for a single lady to stay by herself, but even so, there would still be the journey alone."

"No," Philip replied quickly, a little surprised at how much he disliked the idea of Cassandra residing under a different roof. "Of course she will stay at Neville House." He sighed. "We will have to take a chaperon."

He looked at his mother, but she quickly shook her head. "Oh, no, Philip, not I. I am not going to London. The season is in full swing, and the Haverlin girl is making her debut. I would have to give a party for her, and besides that, Cousin Amanda is there, and I would have to dance attendance on her. Besides," she added triumphantly, "I cannot leave Haverly House. We have a number of guests."

"Don't look at me," Lady Neville said, forestalling him even as he turned toward her. "I do *not* travel to London anymore. I am far too old."

Philip ground his teeth. "Oh, all right, then I suppose we will have to take Cassandra's aunt."

Violet brightened appreciably. "Why, Philip, what a splendid idea! That would be just the thing."

"Hmph. For you, maybe." He thought about being stuck inside the carriage with the Moultons for the trip to London, and suddenly the trip seemed far less enjoyable. But one look at Cassandra's shining face was enough to make him forget the annoyance. He would have done far more than that to have her look at him that way.

Aunt Ardis's delight at being the guest of Sir Philip Neville in London at the height of the season knew no bounds. They were all forced to listen to her effusive thanks and sly hints that Sir Philip's affections for "a certain young lady" were the reason for the invitation. Violet smiled vaguely and murmured something noncommittal. In truth, she found herself agreeing with the Moulton woman, though, of course, she was not foolish enough to believe that it was Joanna who had caught Philip's interest.

Lady Neville seemed to have arrived at the same conclusion, for she surprised her daughter-in-law by saying in a low voice as they walked together up the stairs later that evening, "I wouldn't be at all surprised if there are wedding bells in the future for Philip. Odd that it should be a Verrere, though."

"She seems a very nice girl."

"Intelligent. Philip has always had a strange bent in that direction himself." She frowned a little as she considered this oddity in her otherwise perfect grandson. "No money, of course. The Verreres never did have two pennies to rub together. My father-in-law must be spinning in his grave at the idea. No money and a Verrere to boot. But she does dress up well."

"That will be nice. The shopping for a trousseau, I mean." Violet brightened at the thought of several lengthy visits to fashionable modistes and millinery shops.

Lady Neville nodded. "I do hope that we shan't have the frightful Moulton woman staying with us all the time."

The woman in question was at this moment bending Cassandra's ear in the drawing room, enlarging on her theme of Sir Philip's infatuation with Joanna. Cassandra noticed with irritation that Joanna was preening under her mother's words. She wondered how the two of them could be so blind to Philip's obvious avoidance of Joanna's company. He had bolted to the library as soon as his mother and grandmother had decided to retire to their bedrooms.

"Aunt Ardis," she said at last, interrupting her aunt's flow of chatter, unable to endure any more, "are you quite sure that Sir Philip is interested in Joanna?"

Her aunt looked shocked. "But of course. Why else would he have invited us to London?"

She could hardly tell her that Philip had been forced to bring them as chaperons in order that she herself could go. Aunt Ardis would probably refuse to go just to spite her. Cassandra took another tack. "Has he actually spoken to you about his regard for Joanna?"

"No," the woman admitted, then added with a simper, "but it is too early for that. You are not as familiar as Joanna and I with the signs of a smitten male. Sir Philip exhibits them."

"He does?"

"Oh, yes. Did you not see the way he picked up Joanna's fan this evening?"

"She dropped it right in front of him. He could scarcely do anything else."

"And he spends every evening by her side."

"How can he help it?" Cassandra snapped. "Joanna attaches herself to him like a limpet the moment he walks in the door."

"You're jealous!" Joanna cried. "You have developed a *tendre* for him, haven't you? I can tell. It wounds your pride that he prefers me. Look at how he sat by me tonight."

"You sat by him," Cassandra corrected. "You were on the sofa when he came in, and you changed to the blue chair next to him."

Joanna glared at her. "I hope you don't think that he has any interest in you, just because you spend all day closed up in the library working on that silly family history. No man is interested in a woman who knows so much about books."

Cassandra pressed her lips together. She would not allow her irritating cousin to goad her into saying anything she would regret later. It was obvious that there was no hope of making her aunt and cousin see reality. They seemed determined to go galloping headlong toward the disappointment that awaited them.

"There is little point in continuing this," she said tersely. "I believe I shall go up to bed, also."

She left the room, ignoring Joanna's triumphant smirk at having vanquished the enemy. She started toward the stairs, but paused at the bottom of them. It wasn't late yet, and she really was not sleepy. She was too keyed up at the thought of going to London and finding the Queen's Book. A moonlit walk around the garden sounded quite pleasant, and perhaps it would help her to sleep. So Cassandra turned left instead, walking to the conservatory and through it to the rose garden.

She strolled along, thinking of all the things she would have liked to say to Joanna and had not. Some deep feminine instinct longed to throw it in her cousin's face that it was *she* Philip was interested in, not her beautiful cousin. But gradually, the soft evening breeze and the sweet scent of the roses worked to banish the tumult inside her, and her thoughts turned instead to the more pleasant prospect of finding the book they sought.

When she reached the steps leading down to the lower garden and lawn, she stopped, gazing across the moon-washed landscape toward the distant summerhouse, sitting on the edge of a small, man-made pond.

"Have you been inside it?"

Cassandra jumped and whirled to find Philip standing behind her, smiling. "You scared me! How do you manage to sneak up on a person like that?"

"One of my few talents. I took the shortcut across the grass so I could intercept you. I was looking out the library window and saw you walking."

"Yes. I hoped a stroll might calm me. I can't stop thinking about going to London."

"Mm. I am afraid that that will have to wait for a couple of days."

"What? Why?"

"My estate manager came to see me again tonight. He has been badgering me to look into some problems ever since we returned, but I have been putting him off. He is very insistent that I do something before I leave again."

"Oh."

"I am sorry. I shall get through it as quickly as I can. But I feel guilty. I should have stopped in to see him several days ago. I just—didn't want to take the time."

Cassandra smiled. "I understand. I can hardly expect you to spend all your time on me and my concerns."

"They are my concerns, as well," he reminded her. "Besides, I find spending time with you much more enjoyable."

They stood for a moment looking at each other. Cassandra felt a little weak in the knees, and she knew that it was not a smart idea to be out here with Philip in the garden, the moon lighting everything romantically and the air heady with the perfume of the roses.

"I—I should go back in."

"I should, too."

Yet neither of them moved.

"You are so beautiful," Philip said softly.

Cassandra smiled shakily. "I fear the moon must have affected your reason. I have never been considered more than passable."

"Passable!" He reached up and brushed his thumb lightly across her forehead. "You have a high, smooth brow." He drew a finger down the straight line of her nose. "A patrician nose." He brought up his other hand and traced her brows and cheekbones. "The loveliest, most intelligent, *laughing* eyes I have ever seen. How could this be accounted merely passable?"

Cassandra could scarcely breathe, the light touch of his fingers on her face affected her so. "You are a minority, sir."

"Indeed?" He arched a brow sardonically. "Ah, but I am arrogant enough to believe that *my* opinion is the only one that matters."

Cassandra's lips curved up into a smile.

"And your mouth…" he said huskily, continuing his inventory. Cupping her face in his hands, he traced the line of her lips with his thumbs. Heat stirred in her abdomen at his touch. His eyes darkened with desire.

"You have the most kissable lips." He bent and touched his lips to hers, matching his words with action. It was the merest whisper of a kiss, a breath, no more, yet fire flared inside Cassandra.

She went up on her tiptoes, her arms curling around his neck, and pressed her lips more firmly against his. Philip let out a groan, and his arms wrapped around her like iron, pulling her up and into him as he kissed her thoroughly.

Heat surged through them like a wild spark igniting dry timber, consuming all thoughts of caution or temperance. They strained together, their bodies aching for the union their mouths shared. Cassandra's fingers twined through Philip's hair. His hands stroked up and down her back and pressed her hips hard against his swelling manhood, rubbing her against him.

Finally he broke their kiss and stared down into her face. Every thought in his brain, every fiber in his body, was focused on making love to Cassandra. It took every shred of reason left in him to keep from pulling her down to the ground right there and taking her. He glanced around and his gaze fell on the gazebo at the end of the lower garden beside the pond.

"Come." He wrapped his hand around her wrist and started down the steps toward it, pulling Cassandra along with him.

16

Cassandra knew that she should protest, hold back—at least *hesitate*. But she did not. The desire that ran wild in Philip was thrumming through her, as well, and she had no interest in being responsible or proper. The past few days of working with him, being close to him almost every minute of every day had kept the flames of her desire high. She knew that the iron control Philip had maintained around her had been a sign of his respect for her, an indication of how little he was like the rumors she had heard of him. She was pleased that he had felt that way and exhibited such behavior, but she could not really say that she had *enjoyed* it. Every accidental touch of their fingers, every glance, had reminded her of the delightful passion that his kisses had awakened in her, and she wanted to feel that passion again.

They rushed down the garden path and across the wooden walkway to the gazebo, which sat a few feet out into the pond. Philip turned and pulled her to him, kissing her passionately. Her senses were all sizzlingly alive, and the taste and heat of him mingled with the faint sounds of the water lapping around the piers of the gazebo and the night birds calling, and with the caress of the breeze on her overheated skin.

His fingers went to the buttons of her dress, undoing them as they kissed. He parted from her only long enough to peel down the bodice, exposing her chest, covered only by a thin white chemise. Slowly, almost reverently, Philip slipped down the straps of the chemise until they dangled loosely around her elbows. He tugged at the ties of the ribbon threaded through the neck, undoing the bow, and the material sagged open. Hooking his fingers in the top of the undergarment, he dragged it down over her breasts, brushing her sensitive nipples with the backs of his fingers.

Her lush breasts were exposed to his gaze, her nipples large and dark, pebbling with desire. He gazed at her for a long moment, his breath coming faster in his throat. Then he cupped her breasts in his hands, gently squeezing, and stroked his thumbs across the hard buds. They tightened eagerly as desire darted straight down through her and blossomed into heat between her legs.

"I've wanted this for weeks. Since I first met you." His voice was low and roughened by desire. As he talked, he continued to caress her nipples, watching their response with delight. "The past few days have been sheer hell, wanting you and trying so damn hard not to kiss you, touch you. Cassandra, you don't know what you do to me."

"I know what you do to me," she replied, reaching out and beginning methodically on the buttons of his shirt, as he had with her. He drew in his breath and moved closer to give her free access.

His eyes drifted closed as she unbuttoned his shirt, his face stark with hunger. He stiffened when she slid her hands beneath the material, spreading them flat on his chest. Cassandra moved her hands apart, shoving the two sides of the shirt away, caressing his heated skin. The hair of his chest was prickly beneath her palms, his flesh smooth and hard. She found the flat buds of his nipples, and he let out a soft groan. She explored his chest thoroughly, caressing the ridges of bone and muscle, twining through the hairs, and gently tweaking the flat masculine nipples until his chest was rising and falling in rapid pants.

He tore off his shirt and threw it to the floor, then pulled her against him for a long, thorough kiss. Her breasts were flattened against his chest, the eager buds pressing titillatingly into his flesh, and the hard ridge of his desire pulsed against her abdomen. It seemed as if she were melting into a throbbing, aching mass of desire. She wanted to feel him against her, naked, all the way up and down. She wanted to feel him inside her.

The thought startled her, but she knew that that was exactly what the raw, hot, liquefying sensation between her legs meant—she ached to have him in her. She pulled away from Philip, and he gaped at her blankly for a moment before he realized that she was unbuttoning her skirt. He watched hungrily as she slipped out of her skirt and began to work on her voluminous petticoats.

Philip began to remove the rest of his clothes, an easier task than Cassandra's, all the while watching as she revealed more and more of her shapely hips and legs. Finally, with a grunt of frustration, she shoved down the cotton pantalets that were her last garment, and they joined the frothy pool of petticoats at her feet.

Cassandra glanced up at him for the first time then, embarrassment at her nakedness mingling with an unexpected pride and pleasure at having him look at her this way. The reality of his own nakedness was a jolt. He looked so powerful and male that it was almost frightening, yet at the same time the sight of his naked body started an intense heat in the very center of her. Her heart knocked against her ribs as she stood there, watching him and waiting.

The heat in his eyes almost melted her. He put his hands on her shoulders, and slowly, almost methodically, he moved down her body, sliding over her breasts and onto her stomach. His hands parted to glide down her hips to her thighs and back up, then over her abdomen until his fingers touched the pale thatch of curls between her legs. Everywhere his hands explored, his eyes followed, his arousal heightened by the sight of his hands upon her body. He moved behind her and caressed her back and buttocks in the same way, gently and thoroughly.

He dropped a kiss upon her shoulder, then made his way along her collarbone and up the side of her neck, his warm velvety lips sending shivers throughout her body. His hands stole around her and caressed her breasts and stomach as he nuzzled her neck and shoulders. One hand slid downward, crossing her navel and skimming over the flat plane of her abdomen. But this time he did not stop at the thatch of hair, but continued, delving into the damp heat between her legs.

Cassandra's knees trembled, and she was afraid they might give way beneath her. It made her blush to have him touch her there. At the same time, the excitement was so intense that she wasn't sure how she could stand it. He slid over the slick folds of flesh, his questing fingers separating and stroking. She gasped as he found the hot bud of flesh between her nether lips and gently began to tease it. She tensed automatically, moving back a little and going up on her toes, but he simply wrapped one arm around her waist, holding her up and hard against him, so that she felt the insistent pulsing of his manhood against her bottom while the other hand moved with her, continuing to caress her intimately.

Cassandra let out a little choked sigh, and her head lolled back against his chest. The way he held her, she could reach nothing of him except his thighs and the sides of his hips and waist, but she made do with that, stroking the outer sides of his thighs and reaching back around to the firm rounded cheeks of his buttocks. She heard his muffled groan, and his hand stilled on her for an instant. He began to kiss her ear, his tongue and teeth teasing her earlobe while his hand stroked her rhythmically.

Her heart was pounding, her breath rasping in her throat. She could hear whimpering noises arising from her which she was powerless to stop. She felt caught in a maelstrom of sensation, unable to distinguish among the wild, whirling pleasures that stormed her body.

Philip moved to her other ear, then began nipping little heated kisses down her back. His hand left her, and she almost sobbed at the loss, but he curved it over her buttocks, squeezing and caressing her, then once more sliding between her legs, but from the back this time, startling a little squeak of pleasure from her. Something hot and foreign to her seemed to be building in her. It was so powerful it almost frightened her, yet she wanted to rush straight into it. She moved her hips unconsciously.

Her untutored response almost unmanned him. Philip groaned and paused for a moment, leaning his head against hers and fighting for control. Then he turned her around almost roughly, pulling her to him, and began to kiss her mouth hungrily. Cassandra kissed him back with equal fervor, running her hands over his back and sides, discovering how exciting it was to feel the textures of his flesh. She moved her hands between their heated bodies and slid them tentatively down his ridged chest and stomach onto the softer flesh of his abdomen. With a boldness that surprised her, her fingers inched down until they closed upon the satin hardness of his manhood.

Philip jerked and made a noise deep in his throat, and Cassandra hesitated, pulling her hand away, thinking that perhaps she had done something wrong. But his hand went to hers, nudging it back to the stiff shaft. Her fingers closed gently around him, exploring.

At last he raised his head and bent, picking her up in his arms. He carried her to one of the long cushioned seats that ran along either side of the gazebo and laid her down on it. He hesitated for an instant, looking down at her.

"Are you sure you want this?" he rasped.

For an answer, Cassandra opened up her arms to him. A look of satisfaction crossed his features, and he lay down, positioning himself between her legs. It was not a wide seat, but there was room enough for them, and they did not notice any discomfort. His manhood probed the gate of her femininity, and Cassandra stiffened a little, but he kissed her until she relaxed. Slowly, he began to push up into her. Cassandra was aware of pressure, then pain, and she thought that somehow this was not working right, but then, with a single slash of pain, he thrust into her.

She gasped, but she was not sure if it was at the brief discomfort or at the new and delicious feeling of his filling her. He was sinking deep into her, stretching her past anything she would ever have thought possible, but it did not hurt. Rather, it was intensely satisfying, as if something missing all her life had been replaced. She wrapped her arms around him, luxuriating in the sensation. He began to stroke within her, pulling back and thrusting in again, moving with a slow rhythm, and with every stroke he built the fires of their passion. Finally he began to move more quickly, and the excitement that had been growing and spiraling inside Cassandra whirled ever faster. Suddenly the desire exploded within her like a fiery sun, shaking her to her core. She cried out, lost in the storm of pleasure. She felt Philip surging against her, then heard his hoarse cry as he shuddered and collapsed upon her.

Slowly the world came back together, and Cassandra was aware once again of who and where she was. Philip released a soft sigh and rolled over onto his back, pulling her up on top of him. He cradled her in his arms, and she rested her head on his chest, listening to the loud and furious thump of his heart, gradually slowing down to a strong, steady beat.

She had never felt such peace, such lassitude. Here, in his arms, she felt as if she were home.

Cassandra awakened reluctantly, pulled from her sleep by a shaft of sunlight that poured in through the crack in the curtains and fell directly across her face. Groaning, she rolled away from it, burying her head in her pillow, but sleep eluded her. With a sigh, she turned onto her back and lay staring up at the tester above her head, her mind filled with memories of the night before.

They had not lain together in the summerhouse long. Philip had shaken them from their dreamy, languorous state, saying that they had to get back to the house soon. It would never do for her aunt or someone else to find her missing from her room and go looking for her. For her part, Cassandra was too wrapped up in contentment to feel much concern for her reputation, but she did as Philip asked, dressing with as much speed as she could muster and walking back up to the gardens with him. She had gone into the house first, slipping through the conservatory and up the back stairs to her room, thankfully meeting no one on the way. She had fallen into bed and gone immediately to sleep. Now was the first time that she had really reflected on what had happened.

Her lips curved up into an involuntary smile as she remembered their lovemaking in the gazebo. She loved Philip. She had known that for sure last night as they had hurried off down to the summerhouse. She had been fully aware of what she was doing and of the consequences. Had she been uncertain of her feelings for Philip, she would have held back. But her heart had been as sure of what she wanted as her body.

She knew that marriage would not be the result of their tryst. Her aunt was no doubt right about that: men like Sir Philip Neville did not marry penniless girls. But that had not mattered. All that had mattered was the fact that she loved him and wanted to be with him.

She was, she supposed, a fallen woman now. If anyone found out about last night, her reputation would be in tatters. A virtuous woman, she reflected, would probably be consumed by remorse this morning. Cassandra realized that she felt none, only a wonderful joy that made her feel light as air.

She arose and rang for the maid, taking her time about bathing and dressing. By the time she went downstairs, the breakfast dishes had long been cleared from the sideboard in the dining room, and she made do with a cup of tea and a piece of toast brought from the kitchen by one of the footmen. He also informed her that Sir Philip had left earlier this morning for a meeting with the estate agent and had said that he probably would not return until supper that night.

The day seemed much bleaker after Cassandra heard that news. She was glad that she had already slept through much of the day. She idled through the afternoon, packing for the trip to London in a dreamy, desultory way that was not like her. She spent some time in the nursery, half listening to the twins' and Olivia's chatter.

Cassandra did not see Philip until supper that evening. As soon as she walked into the room, his eyes went to her, and there was a gleam in them, quickly shuttered, as he gave her his usual polite bow. They said little to each other directly, joining the general conversation both during the meal and afterward in the drawing room as they listened to Joanna butcher an etude. However, Cassandra noticed that time and again she would find Philip watching her. There was a look in his eye, a glint of warmth and familiarity that, brief as it was, Cassandra still found stirring.

She wondered what would happen later tonight, if he would risk coming to her room. Her room lay almost at the opposite end of the hall from his. He would have to move unnoticed and unheard past his own mother and grandmother, as well as her aunt and cousin. It would be dangerous for him to do so—dangerous for her reputation, at least—but Cassandra couldn't keep from hoping that he would. Later, when she went up the stairs to the bedroom floor in a group with her aunt and Joanna, Philip stayed downstairs after escorting the ladies to the foot of the spacious stairway. He bowed over each of their hands, and it seemed to Cassandra that his lips lingered a fraction too long on the back of her hand and that as he straightened up there was a meaningful gleam in his eyes. She wasn't sure if it was real or if she was simply indulging in wishful thinking.

But she prepared for bed with greater care than usual, taking a perfumed bath and brushing out her hair so that it hung in a shiny fall across her shoulders and back, instead of putting it up into a neat braid, as she often did. She had little to choose from among her nightgowns, for all of them were practical white cotton, without even any frills or ruffles to dress them up. She wound up deciding to sleep in a simple shift that she often wore beneath her petticoats. It was sleeveless, with a round scooped neck, a very plain thing but a little less concealing than her high-necked, long-sleeved nightgowns.

Cassandra crawled into bed, turned the lamp down low and lay waiting for the sound of Philip's footsteps in the hall. They did not come, however, and after a long while she fell asleep, curled up on her side, her pale hair spreading out over her pillow.

She was awakened by the feeling of the deep feather mattress shifting a little beneath her. Before she could come fully awake, a hand slid around her waist and Philip's voice whispered in her ear, "It is I. Don't scream."

"Philip!" She turned, smiling.

"Sorry to awaken you." He was lying on his side, propped up on one elbow, and he did not look the least bit sorry to her. "I wanted to make sure everyone was asleep. Grandmother has ears like a hawk when it suits her."

"I am glad you came."

"Are you?" He bent and brushed a kiss upon her lips. "I wasn't sure, but I did not think you looked at me forbiddingly tonight."

A giggled bubbled up inside her. "No. Indeed I did not." She thought about asking him about the work he had been doing today or about their upcoming trip to London, but she found that she really was not interested in talking about that or anything else.

"We have to talk," he said, gazing down into her eyes, his hand caressing her cheek. "I am sorry I was closeted all day with Simpson. And tomorrow will probably be the same." His hand drifted downward onto her throat. "Then we will have the Moultons with us on the way to London. We should do it now.''

His eyes followed his fingertips as they trailed down over the white expanse of her chest and onto the luscious upswelling of her breasts, and he seemed to lose track of what he was saying. Cassandra didn't care. She had no desire to talk; she suspected that he was wanting to make clear the parameters of their affair, and that was something she did not want to hear.

"There will be time enough later," she murmured, reaching up to run her hand through his hair.

"What? Oh, yes…later…" He bent to kiss her, and there was little talking after that.

Cassandra was alone when she awoke. She had not expected it to be otherwise. When she had snuggled back against Philip, spoon-fashion, last night, she had known that very soon he would slip away back to his room. She was grateful, of course, that he was concerned for her reputation, but she found herself thinking how nice it would be to wake up with him by her side. To look into his face first thing each morning. Then she gave herself a mental shake. *That* was never to be, and she must get used to it.

There was as little to do today with Philip gone as there had been yesterday, and by the end of the morning, she was completely packed except for a few last-minute things. She had even got most of her aunt's and cousin's things organized. Joanna looked quite pleased with herself, and Cassandra could only think that the reason was because Philip was not hanging around Cassandra as he had been ever since they arrived at Haverly House. It afforded her some inner amusement to think how utterly wrong her cousin was about the status of Philip's feelings for her, but even that was not quite enough to make up for the irritation of watching Joanna smirk.

Shortly after their luncheon, one of the maids knocked on Cassandra's door and handed her a folded note. Cassandra pounced on it and read it. Her lips curved up in a smile. It was from Philip, as she had hoped. It said that he intended to finish with the estate manager this morning and suggested that she meet him at the old abbey for a ride around two o'clock.

Cassandra wasted no time getting on her riding habit, an old one of Violet's, which she had kindly had refitted for Cassandra, and going down to the stables. The head groom wanted to send a groom with her, but she declined, reasoning that in a few minutes she would be joining Philip, anyway. When they had still been able to afford to keep a stable, she had always ridden without the services of a groom, and she felt rather foolish riding along with the groom trailing her at a respectful distance.

It was still a trifle early when she set off, but Cassandra didn't mind waiting at the abbey. It was one of her favorite spots. When she arrived, she was not surprised to find that Philip was not there yet. She tied her horse beneath the shade of a tree and strolled around, peering into the various ruined rooms of the old monastery.

She heard the scrape of something on stone, and she turned, thinking that Philip had probably arrived. However, she could see nothing but another wall beyond the tumbled-down wall of this room, so she walked back out of the room and turned down the remains of a long, narrow corridor. She passed another doorway, and a flicker of something caught her attention. But before she could stop or turn back to see what it was, something slammed into her from behind, knocking her to the floor. A sharp pain split her head. Then there was nothing....

* * *

Cassandra came to consciousness slowly. Her head was throbbing, and she felt sick to her stomach. She opened her eyes, which she quickly discovered was a mistake, and closed them again until the world stopped spinning. She let out a groan and lay there for a moment, collecting her thoughts.

She was lying on something hard—it felt like a wooden floor to her—and the smell of dust tickled her nostrils. The air was dead and still. Slowly her mind cleared, and she remembered being at the abbey, walking along the corridor…then being hit hard, the ground suddenly in her face, and pain exploding in her head.

The memory seemed to stir up the pounding in her head, but it did not clear up her confusion at all. *Where was she? What had hit her?* Her first thought was that a stone must have fallen from the wall and struck her, knocking her down. But even in her still-dazed state, it didn't take long to realize that that theory made no sense. If a stone had hit her, she would still be lying in the abbey, with the sun pouring light over everything, not in a dimly lit room.

Slowly, using great care to keep her head from spinning again, she raised her head, then pushed herself up onto her elbow. Thankfully, though her stomach lurched a little, she did not lose her lunch, and after a moment she felt better. Gradually she continued until she was sitting up, and she looked around her.

This was no place that she recognized. She was in a large round room that rose straight up about two stories tall. The walls were brick, and there were four windows higher up. Rickety stairs, in many places missing steps, ran up the wall to the wooden ceiling above. The last stretch was not stairs but a ladder that went through a square hole in the ceiling. In the center of the room stood a large pole going all the way up and through the ceiling. At the bottom the pole was some sort of machinery with gears. All of it looked quite old and long unused. A coating of thick dust lay over everything.

There was a trail through the dust on the floor, leading from where Cassandra sat to a short wooden door in the wall not far away. It was the mark, Cassandra supposed, of where someone had dragged her through the door and across the floor. There was no sign of any other person about.

Whatever last hopes Cassandra had that the knock on her head had been accidental were banished by the sight of the drag marks. Someone had intentionally hurt her, then hidden her in this odd place.

Cautiously she levered herself to her feet, groaning at the increased pounding in her skull. But after a moment everything settled down again, and she walked toward the door. She had little hope of it being unlocked, but she had to try.

As she expected, when she reached the stout wooden door and tried to push it open, it did not budge. With a sigh, she sat down, leaned back against the door and contemplated her surroundings once more. *Where in the world was she?* This place was so strange looking that she felt as if she could have been transported to another world.

She simply sat in a kind of stupor for a long time, the pain in her head gradually receding to a dull ache. After a time it came to her what this building must be—one of the round windmills she had seen here and there around Haverly House. None of them were in use now; Philip had said that they had been used to pump water out of the fens long ago.

The knowledge, however, helped her little. It only confirmed her suspicion that she had been stashed in a place where people rarely, if ever, went. She wondered if anyone would think to look for her here and, if so, when. She decided that she would be better off finding a way out of the place than sitting around waiting for the people at Haverly House to realize that she was gone and come searching for her.

She got up and examined the door again, going over the old-fashioned iron latch. It was quite sturdy, although it seemed to her that the latch was merely fastened and not actually locked. That meant that the door must be jammed shut from the outside, which took away the hope of setting herself free by somehow picking the lock. Since the door opened outward, there were no hinges on the inside that she could try to unfasten. She could think of no way to get out other than to batter down the thick wooden door, and that did not seem likely. She tried banging her hands against it and shouting, but that brought no response. The old door was so thick that she was not sure how much of the noise she was making even penetrated it.

After a time she stopped shouting and began to prowl about the room, considering her options and trying to ignore the hunger that began to gnaw at her stomach. She had doubtless missed tea. The light in the room was fading fast. She knew she would have to move quickly if she were to do anything at all. The windows were all too high for her to see out of, and she could find no way to climb up to any of them. She went to the dilapidated staircase, but after looking up at the treads, so many of them broken, missing or sagging, she knew that climbing up to the top of the windmill and trying to signal was out of the question.

Next she crisscrossed the floor, taking stock of the objects in the room. There were not many. She found a broom, which she supposed might be somewhat useful as a weapon if her attacker decided to return. There was also a length of coiled rope. She tried to figure out some way that she could use it to climb up to the lowest window, but there were no handy timbers or hooks to throw it across so she could climb. She found a broken chair, a few screws, a gear lying on the floor, and a small square of metal that she thought might have fallen from the machinery. She decided that either the chair or the piece of metal would be a better weapon than the broom.

She brought her finds over to the door and tried banging on it with each of them, hoping that someone might hear the sound, but after several minutes of fruitless effort, she gave up on that activity. She thought of tossing something through one of the windows. If there was anyone around, it might attract attention. It seemed unlikely that there would be anyone there, especially with night approaching, but at least it was something to do, instead of just sitting here. At least someone might notice the object lying there on the grass tomorrow and come to investigate.

For a while she tried hurling the few things she had at one of the windows. The gear was too heavy; she could not chuck it high enough to reach the window. So were the chair and the metal plate. She searched all over the defunct machinery for a smaller part that she might be able to use, but though she pulled and twisted, nothing came off. Finally she picked up the chair and began to bang it against the machine. After a good deal of smashing, one of the legs snapped off. She picked it up and hurled it at the window. Perversely, it sailed above the window. She retrieved it and tried again. On the fourth try the chair leg struck the paned window and bounced off harmlessly. But on the second try after that, it hit one of the panes just right and crashed through it.

Cassandra let out a shriek of exultation and jumped up

and down. After a few minutes, however, she sank back down again beside the door. *She had managed the feat, but what good had it done?*

Her stomach growled, reminding her of how long it had been since she had eaten. The room was growing darker by the minute. The dirty windows made it seem even dimmer than it was. The machinery in the center was only a hulking shadow now, and shadows seemed to gather all around the room, wherever wall and floor met. Cassandra did not like the idea of being inside this building when it was completely dark.

She got up and went over to the chair, now even more broken than before. She whacked it against the machinery a few more times and managed to break off another leg. It, she thought, would make the best weapon. Taking it and the metal plate, she returned to the door and tried banging the metal plate against it a few more times. Finally she sat down beside the door and leaned back against the wall. She could think of nothing else she could do to call attention to her plight or to protect herself. At least she had a weapon in case her attacker decided to pay her a visit.

There was no reason for him to return, of course, but, then, there was no reason for anyone to have attacked her and thrown her in here in the first place. *What good would it do?* She could not imagine that anyone would personally dislike her enough to abduct her. The only person she could think of who did was Joanna, who was growing more peevish every day about the amount of time that Cassandra and Sir Philip spent together. But Joanna was far too lazy to carry out something like this. And how could she, small and pampered as she was, have managed to move Cassandra's unconscious body from the abbey to this windmill?

No. It was patently absurd.

It had to have something to do with the treasure they were seeking, Cassandra surmised, and it was probably done by the same person who had broken into Chesilworth and tried to break into the library at Haverly House. The only problem was, she could not imagine what good it would do anyone to abduct her and lock her up. She and Philip did not have the Neville map yet, so they could not be hoping to steal that from her. There was, of course, the map they had found at Chesilworth. Obviously whoever had broken in there wanted it. But if that was what the attacker was after, why had he bothered to lure her out to the abbey and knock her over the head? It would have been easier, she would have thought, to try to steal it out of her room.

The only thing she could think of that would be accomplished by hiding her here was to delay their trip to London. *But what good would it do to keep them from going there? It would give the thief a chance, perhaps, to find the book in London himself, but how would he know what to look for?* She and Philip had found out the book's identity only days ago, and they had told no one but their immediate families. It simply did not make sense.

The only way it made sense… Her mind skittered away from the thought. She looked around her. The darkness had completely overtaken the room now. She could make out nothing in the velvety blackness except the squares of the windows on the walls, slightly lighter patches in the dark. She heard a creak, and she jumped, her heart pounding.

Cassandra told herself that she was being silly to jump at noises. There was no one and nothing in the room beside herself. She had seen it all clearly enough earlier, and she was sitting beside the only entrance into the building. The mill was old, and it was bound to have a few noises: the creaks and groans of old wood, the settling of the walls. Perhaps the blades of the windmill even moved a little, setting off some noise inside. There was nothing to be scared of.

But her sage words could not completely eliminate the vague fear inside her, the instinctive uneasiness brought about by being alone in the dark in a strange place. And there was something to be scared of, she knew, even if it was not inside the building right now. Someone had put her here, and she had no idea when or how she was going to get out—if ever. *Did her attacker mean to leave her here until she died from starvation?*

But, no, thirst would do her in first. She had been uncomfortably aware for some time of a dryness in her mouth and throat, exacerbated by the heavy dust in the room. She willed herself not to think about that…or the emptiness in her stomach…or the strange noises in the dark. It was like trying not to think about an elephant sitting right in front of her.

She returned again to the problem of who had done this and why. Perhaps Philip was right about David Miller. It was rather suspicious that he had turned up right when she was searching for the map to the dowry. *So what if he looked trustworthy and seemed nice?* A coldhearted villain could wear a mask of normalcy. Philip's argument made sense; David could have found the diaries but had no idea how to get the maps to the treasure and so had sold the journals in England, hoping that someone more knowledgeable would read them and lead him to the treasure. Or perhaps he had given up on being able to find the treasure until Mr. Simons had told him that Margaret Verrere's descendants had bought the diaries, and then he had realized the possibilities.

Still, she could not keep from coming back to the same
stumbling block: how could it help David Miller to lock
her up in the old windmill? It made no sense. *The only
person who would benefit—* She stopped, then made her
mind return to the thought. She had to face it. The only
person who would benefit from her being abducted—or
dead—was Sir Philip.

17

It was ridiculous! Anger brought Cassandra surging to her feet, but there was nowhere to go in the dark, and after a moment she drew a calming breath and sat down. She rejected the idea out of hand. *Philip would never hurt her.* However, she reminded herself that it was dangerously foolish not to look at all the possibilities, particularly one as obvious as this.

Philip had seen the Chesilworth map many times; he could easily have made a copy. Now he knew what they were looking for in London. He would be able to find the book without her help. He could return home and search for the treasure. With her gone, he would have sole possession of the dowry.

Cassandra shuddered. *No!* She could not believe that. *Philip could not have kissed and caressed her as he had, could not have made love to her so tenderly and then coldbloodedly throw her in some old abandoned building to starve to death!*

But she could not stop the coldly logical voice within her that pointed out that perhaps he had not been able to kill her when it came down to it, that he had thrown her in here, thinking that as long as he did not actually kill her himself, he would be able to ignore what he had done.

"No." Cassandra shook her head fiercely, as if there were another person in the room arguing with her. Philip was not a coward; if he decided to kill, he would do it outright. And she would not, could not, believe that he would kill her. She did not try to fool herself that he loved her, but she was certain that he was not the sort of man who could make love to a woman, then kill her.

But he would not have to kill her. He would only have to delay her. Philip did not have to go to London himself to find the book. He had written to his man of business, asking him to find the records of his father's sale of the book. He could also have instructed him to buy back the book when he found out who it now belonged to. All he needed to do was give his agent time to search for it. After all, he had already delayed them two days because of this "business" he had had to conduct with his estate manager. *What if there had not really been any urgent business? What if it was merely a stalling tactic?*

He could only use estate business as an excuse for so long. *But if she were kidnapped... Well, he could buy some more time, at least a couple of days, while they searched for her, and maybe a few more days for her to recover.* The agent could find the book; then Philip and Cassandra could go to London as they had planned. He could go through the motions of looking for the book, and they could return in defeat. Except that Philip would actually have the book and the map.

Cassandra felt sick. It made awful, slimy sense. Indeed, it made sense no other way. If there were someone else— David Miller or an unknown person—looking for the book, it would not help them to lock her up. They needed the map she held and the map in the book, neither of which kidnapping her would gain them. It would help only Philip. And it *was* a note from him that had sent her to the abbey.

She leaned back against the wall, hot tears leaking from her eyes. *It could not be Philip!* No matter how much sense it made, she refused to believe it. She loved him. Surely she could not have been so mistaken in him. She could not love a man so deceitful and greedy. And why, she thought, grasping at straws, had he made love to her if he felt so little for her that he did not care if she stayed in an abandoned building for a couple of days, scared, hungry and thirsty? Making love to her would not have furthered his plans.

She remembered how suspicious she had been of him about Silverwood, and how terribly wrong she had been. This was the same sort of thing. She was leaping to conclusions without enough evidence. Her mistake about Silverwood had made sense logically, but the truth had not been in it. It was the same this time. She would not condemn him on the basis of a few suppositions.

But, despite her resolution, the doubts returned again and again throughout the night. Alone in the dark, she found it hard to believe in anything, harder still to curb her fears. Every noise made her jump. No matter how tired and sleepy she was, she could not bring herself to close her eyes. It would leave her too vulnerable. Eventually her eyelids grew heavy, and she had to force them open. She nodded off, discovering it only when she was jerked awake by another noise or a bad dream. Heart pounding, she would sit there in the dark, struggling not to give in to the frantic urge to scream that clawed at her throat.

It seemed years before the windows of the windmill began to show as paler squares. Even then, it took Cassandra a moment to realize that the dawn was coming. Gradually the forms in the room grew more distinct. Her fear lessened. She knew that she was in exactly the same position that she had been in all night, but somehow now it seemed more bearable. She leaned her head back against the wall, letting her eyes drift closed and, finally, she fell into a real sleep.

She awakened to find herself curled up on the dusty floor beside the door. She blinked and sat up slowly, adjusting to the bizarre reality in which she found herself. It was quite light in the room now, and much warmer. She realized that the morning had advanced. She wondered exactly what time it was. She also wondered what had awakened her.

Slowly she stood up, stretching her aching muscles. She was sore and stiff all over, and felt uncomfortably sticky and dirty. Her mouth tasted awful and was so dry she could hardly even work up any saliva. She thought that she would kill for a sip of water. Hunger was next on her list of discomforts.

Since it was morning, she decided to try banging on the door again. It had seemed pointless during the night, but now there might possibly be someone passing by the windmill who would hear her. She picked up the metal plate and tried banging it against the door until her ears hurt from the noise. Then she walked around the room a little, trying to ease her sore muscles. It was on her second lap around the large room that she heard the sound.

She stopped dead still and waited, trying to identify what the noise had been. Then it came again. It wasn't from inside the building with her. The faint sound came from outside and it sounded like...voices. Cassandra stiffened, disbelieving. There it was again. The sound of a boyish call.

"Help! Somebody! Help me!" she shrieked, looking up at the window high above her. It was the one in which she had broken a hole last night. Perhaps now her voice had a better chance of carrying. She continued to yell.

When she paused for a breath, she heard the distinct sound of voices again. It was much closer this time, and it sounded like boys yelling. Then, blessedly, came a familiar adolescent voice. "Cassandra! Halloo! Cassandra!"

"Crispin!" she screamed joyously. "Hart! Crispin! It's me!"

"I hear it!" she heard one of the twins cry, and a moment later the voice was much closer. "It's over here! The windmill!"

Cassandra was jumping up and down, yelling herself hoarse, and now she rushed back to the heavy door and began to bang the plate upon it again. There were more excited voices, and she heard Hart say plainly, "Why, look! The door is blocked. Richie, go fetch Sir Philip!"

There were more noises, and suddenly the door creaked open. Both boys were pulling on it, but they could open it no more than a foot. However, that was plenty for Cassandra to rush through.

"Crispin! Hart!" She threw her arms around both of them. "Oh, I've never in my life been so glad to see anyone!"

The two boys babbled out questions while Cassandra held them, alternately laughing and crying.

"Whatever were you doing in there?"

"I say, did you know that you're covered with dirt?"

"We've been searching and searching ever since teatime yesterday, when you didn't come back!"

"Yes, and Sir Philip and the servants kept at it all night, with lanterns, looking through the fields and woods and everywhere!"

"He wouldn't let us," Crispin added in an aggrieved

voice. "He said we had to sleep. But we could hardly sleep a wink, could we, Hart?"

"No, and this morning, we set out as soon as cook gave us some bacon and bread. Sir Philip made us bring one of the grooms, but that's good, isn't it, because now he's gone to get Sir Philip."

"*He* went back to the abbey again. I don't know why he thinks you are there."

"Aunt Ardis keeps moaning and crying and saying for sure you're in the river, but I don't know how she could think you would be so stupid as to fall in a river. Joanna wanted to help Sir Philip search, but he snapped at her that he couldn't have her slowing him down. He told her to either go on her own or go back to the house."

"She didn't look half-mad," Crispin mused gleefully, and both boys chuckled at the pleasant memory of their cousin's frustration.

"Look!" Hart turned away, pointing toward the horizon. "There he comes now."

A horse and rider were tearing along the road, and as they watched, the graceful animal slowed a fraction, gathered itself and soared over the stone fence. It thundered straight toward them. The rider was distinguishable now as Sir Philip, and he pulled up at the last moment and flung himself out of the saddle, running across the last few remaining feet toward them.

"Cassandra!" His face was etched with lines of worry, and he held out his arms to her.

Without a second thought Cassandra flung herself into them. "Oh, Philip!"

She burst into tears. He held her for a long time, his arms so tightly around her that Cassandra could scarcely breathe, but she did not mind. It felt too wonderful, too warm and safe, in the circle of his arms. The twins bounced around, excitedly telling their story of hearing something odd and then recognizing it as Cassandra's voice and finally finding the door to the windmill wedged shut by boards. Philip nodded, scarcely hearing them, concentrating only on holding Cassandra and letting the knowledge sink in on him that she was safe, was actually there with him.

He had spent the most frightful night of his life frantically searching for her, with no clue as to where she had gone or why. He had been haunted by the fear that she had run away because of him, that she had been too shamed by their illicit passion or so overcome with guilt that she had had to get away from him. Logically he had known that the idea was foolish, that Cassandra was too levelheaded to run off like that without telling anyone or at least leaving a note.

But logic had not been able to stand up against his raging fear and guilt, and he had cursed himself for giving in to his desires last night and not taking the time to talk to her as he had meant to. He had wanted to explain that they would be married at the earliest possible time, that his decision to make love to her had been at the same time a decision to marry her. He had thought that surely she realized that, that she knew he would not have compromised her, that even in the midst of his raging passion he would not have taken her if he had not known that she was the only woman he could want as his wife.

He had said nothing, though. He was not the sort to bandy about words of love, and an offer of marriage was not easy for him to make. His family had never been demonstrative. One did not speak of emotions; indeed, one did one's best not to express them in any way. It had been much easier and more pleasant to express his feelings for her with his hands and lips. As his desire surged in him last night, he had shoved aside the matter of talking. When she disappeared, he had been racked with guilt that she had vanished because she thought he wanted only to make her his mistress.

Now he held her as if he would never let her go again, stroking her back and murmuring soothingly, "It's all right. It's all right. You don't need to be scared any longer."

"Oh, Philip! It was so dark, and I didn't know if anyone would ever find me...."

"I know. But it's all over now." He kissed her hair, murmuring something she could not quite hear. "I'm going to take you home."

She nodded, all her doubts vanquished in the warmth of Philip's arms. He put her up on his horse in front of him, and she leaned against his chest. They rode slowly back to the house, the gentle rocking movement of the horse and Cassandra's own weariness pulling her down into sleep.

When Cassandra next opened her eyes, she was lying in her bed in Haverly House, the drapes drawn against the light. For an instant she was stabbed with the fear she had known the night before, but in the next moment she realized where she was, and she drew a shaky sigh of relief.

"You're awake!" Olivia bounced up from the chair in which she had been sitting, watching her sister, and plopped down onto the bed beside her. "Thank heavens! I was beginning to think that you would never wake up!"

Cassandra licked her dry lips. She was still parched, she realized. She had slept straight through, not awakening to eat or drink anything. "Water?" she croaked.

Olivia flew to fulfill her request, and Cassandra drank down two glasses, one right after another, then flopped back down on the bed. "Oh, Lord, I'm a mess." She ran a hand over her filthy dress and touched her equally dusty hair and face. "I'm ruining the sheets."

"I know. You should have seen the housekeeper's face when Sir Philip insisted on putting you in between her pristine sheets, just as you are. But she knew better than to argue with him. He looked like he wanted an excuse to strangle somebody." Olivia giggled. "Aunt Ardis was babbling about how he should not be in your room, him being a man and all, and he gave her this look. I wish you could have seen it. Aunt Ardis shut her mouth like a clam." Olivia demonstrated, snapping her fingers. "But his mother did make him leave after he got you settled. He wanted to stay here until you awoke, but Lady Neville persuaded him that he would only scare you, the way he looked, and that he would be better to sleep and shave before he saw you again."

Cassandra shoved aside the sheets and started to stand up, but Olivia ran to her side worriedly. "What are you doing? Are you sure you're all right?"

"I'm not sick. I only spent the night in a most uncomfortable place. What I need right now is something to eat and a bath—in that order. Olivia, be a love and ring for a maid."

Olivia did so, then helped her sister undress and comb out her tangled, matted hair, all the while asking questions about Cassandra's ordeal. The maids drew a hot bath, and another one carried up a tray with a cold supper, and Cassandra eagerly partook of both.

She had just finished pulling on her dressing gown and was combing out her wet hair when there was a peremptory knock on her bedroom door and Sir Philip strode in without waiting for an answer.

"The maid said you were up. How are you?"

"Quite well, thank you." Cassandra felt strangely reserved with him. When he had found her, the doubts of the dark night had vanished, and she had felt instinctively safe in his arms. But, now, rested and refreshed, her primitive instincts had receded, and the logical doubts had come crowding back in.

"Olivia, leave us alone," Philip ordered. "I have to talk to your sister."

Olivia didn't stay to argue, even though her aunt had clearly impressed on her that her duty was to keep Sir Philip out of Cassandra's bedroom, where a gentleman did *not* belong.

Philip strode over to where Cassandra sat, a frown stamping his face. "I sent my gamekeeper to search the windmill and look for tracks. He could find nothing. The ground is utterly dry. This is completely inexplicable. The boys say that the door to the windmill was jammed. They insist that someone must have done it on purpose. Is that true? How did you get there?"

Cassandra stiffened. Except for his initial abrupt question, he had not shown a bit of concern about how she was doing after her ordeal. "My, aren't we the lord of the manor this afternoon?"

He cast her a glance of exasperation, born of a night of sleepless anxiety compounded by a frustrating inability to discover who had done this to Cassandra and a thoroughly annoying and concerted effort on everyone's part to keep him away from her. "Come, Cassandra, don't quibble. Just tell me how you got there."

"I don't know!" Cassandra snapped back. "Believe me, if I knew who had abducted me, I would be happy to tell you. But I was knocked out at the abbey, and the next thing I knew, I was waking up inside that windmill with a terrible headache and no idea what I was doing there."

"I knew you must have gone to the abbey," he said with a sense of vindication.

"Of course I did, since your note told me to meet you there," Cassandra responded with some asperity. She watched him levelly, trying to gauge his reaction.

He stared at her blankly. "I beg your pardon?"

"I said—"

"No, I heard what you said. It just doesn't make sense. I didn't send you a note."

"I received one, signed by you."

"Where is it? Let me see it."

"I don't have it. I put it in my pocket, and when I awoke, it was no longer there."

"Damn!"

Cassandra lifted her brows. "Do you think I'm making it up?"

"No, of course not. But I—it could not have been my handwriting."

"I am not very familiar with your hand," Cassandra admitted.

"Someone obviously lured you out there to abduct you."

"But why, Philip? That's what I want to know. What good could it possibly do anyone to kidnap me and stick me in an abandoned windmill?"

"It has to be connected with the map." He frowned. "It would delay our trip to London. I mean, if you were hidden away somewhere for a few days, and I was out looking for you, we could not have left when we planned. If someone—your American cousin, for instance—wanted to get to the Queen's prayer book before us—"

"First of all, David Miller is not even in England. He had to return home."

"So far as you know."

She grimaced. "All right. As far as I know. But how would he know about the Queen's prayer book? We found out only two days ago. Do you think your mother told him? Or your great-great aunt?"

"I don't know!" he snapped. "Perhaps one of the servants overheard us. Perhaps Mother or one of the children said something about it in front of a servant, and he told the others. If Miller had bribed one of them..."

"Then you think that David has been hanging about Haverly House, talking to the servants and bribing them, and no one has seen him? That he has been here, yet there has been no gossip about a stranger in the village?"

He shrugged. "It does seem unlikely. But who else would you suggest, then? Do you think one of the servants did it? One of our families?"

"Besides," Cassandra went on inexorably, bringing out the final, most damning detail, the thing that she had tried her utmost to ignore, but could not, "how would David Miller, or, indeed, anyone, know to tell me to meet you at the abbey? How would they know that it was our favorite place to ride?"

He stopped, frowning. "I don't know...." Suddenly understanding dawned on his face. "My God! You think that *I* did it, don't you? You think that I lured you out there and whacked you over the head and stashed you in the mill! In the name of all that's holy, why would I— Oh, but of course, with you out of the way, I would have the treasure all to myself, wouldn't I?"

He swung around. "Bloody hell!" He shoved aside a chair, sending it crashing to the floor. "After we—you can think that I—"

"I don't want to believe it!" Cassandra cried, springing to her feet. "I've tried every way I could think of to disprove it! I don't think that you—it is just that it is so suspicious.''

He turned back to her, his face blazing with a fury so fierce that Cassandra shrank back. "Damn your devious Verrere mind! Have you so little trust, so little *regard* for me? I'll tell you this truth." He jabbed his forefinger at her. "We are going to London, and we are going to find that benighted book and the map inside it. Then I am going to get that bloody dowry and dump every last jewel and coin and statue in your lap. You can have the Spanish dowry, every last penny of it. I want none of it."

His words struck Cassandra like blows, and she paled, feeling sick to her stomach. "Philip, please…"

"Please what? Please prove to you that I am not the one who hurt and frightened you, who left you thirsty and starving in that mill? You have no faith in me, no trust, and without that, there is no way that I can make you believe I am not a villain. How can I prove I did not write you a note that you don't have? How can I prove that I would never harm a hair on your head if our lovemaking did not tell you that already? I could tell you that I was with the estate agent until four o'clock that afternoon, but that would not be enough for you. After all, I might have hired someone to go out and knock you over the head. Perhaps the same fellow I hired to ransack Chesilworth that night?" he suggested with awful sarcasm.

Cassandra began to cry quietly. She felt as if his words were tearing her apart inside.

"Oh, Cassandra, please, at least spare me your tears." He turned on his heel and strode out the door, closing it with a quiet finality behind him.

Cassandra crumpled to the floor and wept.

18

The journey to London was not pleasant. They left the following day, for Cassandra had insisted that she did not need to rest from her ordeal. She did indeed feel sick, but she knew that it was not from the night she had spent locked in the windmill, but from the fact that she felt as if her heart had been torn from her chest. She wanted only to get everything over with and return to Chesilworth, where she could curl up and lick her emotional wounds in peace.

Cassandra rode in the carriage with her aunt and cousin, while Philip rode his horse. The times when they stopped to rest or eat, she and Philip ignored each other, speaking only whatever was absolutely necessary. Joanna, predictably, was elated by the obvious chill between Cassandra and Philip, and she spent much of the trip trying to pry out of Cassandra what had happened to make Philip look so coldly furious. When she could get no gossip out of Cassandra, she spent her time speculating on her gauche cousin's various odd ways, which would naturally offend most men.

Joanna seized the opportunity of the silence between Philip and Cassandra to fill the air at their meals with her own conversation, flirting madly with Philip all the while. Cassandra was too miserable to care about her cousin's bold coquettishness. She ached for the old companionship she and Philip had shared, for the laughter and good talk and even hearty disagreements. She ached as well for the pleasures that had more recently been theirs. She would not have thought she could so miss something that she had known for such a short time. She wished that the night in the windmill had never happened; she wished she could toss aside her doubts and tell Philip that she trusted him absolutely. But she could not lie to him, and she could not keep the doubts from intruding. Her heart did not believe him capable of wrongdoing, but her head could not dismiss the insistent logic of her reasoning, either.

At any other time she would have admired the spacious symmetry of the Neville's town house, a graceful white building on a secluded crescent in Mayfair. It was smaller than Haverly House, of course, its bedrooms closer together, but the elegance of its decoration more than made up for that. Cassandra's bedroom looked out over the small garden in back, and at night the scent of massed roses drifted up alluringly to her open windows, reminding her of that night in the rose garden when Philip had kissed her and led her down to the gazebo. She found herself wishing that her room faced the street instead.

The morning after they arrived in London, Philip took her to the offices of his business manager, one Mr. Staley, a prosperous-looking man of forty-odd years. He pointed out to them that he had no personal knowledge of the transaction, as it had been his father, unfortunately now deceased, who had handled the Neville business at that time. He had, however, immediately started looking through the company's records for any mention of the sale of books for Sir Philip's father. As yet he had found nothing. It was difficult, he explained, because Lady Neville had been unable to remember the exact year of the sale, only a vague period of three or four years.

Sir Philip nodded. "I expected as much. But keep looking, will you, Staley?"

"Of course, sir, of course."

"I don't suppose that there was a particular bookseller that my father used?" he queried.

The other man's look of amazement was almost comical, but he quickly wiped it from his face. "No, Sir Philip. I am sorry. But I do not believe that your father dealt much in books."

Their next stop was the shop of Perryman Simons, the bookseller with whom Cassandra's father had dealt. He came bustling forward from the back of the store to greet Cassandra, a huge smile splitting his face.

"Miss Verrere! How wonderful to see you. Aren't you looking lovely today?" Simons was a short, rotund man with a balding head, spectacles and a perpetually jolly expression. He bowed to each of them in a funny, jerky motion. "It's been so many months. I was afraid that I would not see you again." His gaze slid curiously to Sir Philip. "I was so sorry to hear about your father. A good man. A true scholar."

"Yes, he was. Thank you."

"Could I interest you in a book today?" he asked, gesturing around him at the store. "You know that you are always free to browse." Again his eyes went to Sir Philip.

"Actually, we are looking for a particular book, Mr. Simons." She introduced Sir Philip to Simons, satisfying the man's curiosity. "Sir Philip is looking for a book that once belonged to his family. It was sold during his father's lifetime, but it was a valuable book. We were hoping that perhaps you had heard about it."

"Why, certainly. I will help you if I can. Come back to my office." He led the way through the narrow walkway, lined on both sides with shelves, and into a small cubicle at the end of the store. He spent some time fussing over the chairs, clearing one of books and flicking invisible dust from the other before he judged that they were in good enough condition for such important visitors to sit in. "There, now. Could I get you some tea, perhaps?"

"No, we're fine, thank you. We only wanted to know about the book."

"Yes, yes, indeed." The chubby proprietor adjusted his round spectacles and beamed at her encouragingly. "What is it you are looking for?"

"It is a prayer book that once belonged to Queen Elizabeth. It has been in the Neville family for generations," Philip told him and proceeded to describe the jeweled cover.

The book dealer's eyes started to glow. "My, what a treasure! Oh, indeed, I wish I did have a book like that. Unfortunately, it has never crossed my path. I would remember it. Yes, indeed, I would." He nodded his head so vigorously that his cheeks wobbled like a baby's. "Let me see, let me see…Samuel Arrington might have knowledge of such a book. He quite often deals in rare books. Then, of course, there is Cohn and Sons."

They left his store a few minutes later with the addresses of three other dealers in old or rare books clutched in Cassandra's hand. They spent the rest of the day going to the booksellers, all with the same disappointing results. None of them had ever heard of a book such as Philip described. Cassandra felt rather depressed as they returned to Neville House, and it did not lighten her spirits any to sit through another gloomy dinner with Philip. She went to bed feeling that the situation was, indeed, hopeless.

The following morning she was in the sitting room, waiting to set out to see another round of book dealers, when a footman entered and told her that Sir Philip requested her presence in his study. "A Mr. Staley is with him," the footman added.

"Really?" Suddenly Cassandra's spirits lightened.

She rushed down the hallway and into Philip's study. Philip looked up and smiled, and for an instant it was as if the past few days had never happened. A warmth bloomed in Cassandra's chest, and she smiled back without a second's hesitation. Something flickered in Philip's eyes, and the smile dropped away.

He stood up, saying formally, "Miss Verrere. Staley came to me this morning with some news, and I thought you would like to hear it."

"Of course," Cassandra replied politely, though all the joy had spilled out of her as Philip's face changed.

"Go ahead, Staley. Tell us what you found."

"There was a ledger book going back twenty years. In it, I found records of selling a number of items for your father. Most of them were described as simply valuables, but a few were more specifically detailed, a certain statue, a Queen Anne table, and so forth. And a jeweled book. It did not give the name, but I remembered that you had said the prayer book you were looking for had jewels on the spine."

"Yes. Excellent! But did it say who the buyer was?"

"A bookseller by the name of Harrington Jones. He deals, I believe, primarily in rare and antique books, and his shop is still in operation."

"Staley, you deserve a reward for this. You have saved us fruitless days at bookshops. Now, if you will excuse us, I think we need to find this Mr. Jones. Cassandra?"

With their shared excitement, the walk over to the bookstore seemed almost like old times. The stiff constraint that had lain between them for the past few days was largely gone, and though they did not talk much, the silence did not feel forced.

H. Jones, Book Dealer, was tucked into a small corner of an aging brick building, the color of which had faded into a nondescript mellowness over the years. A bell tinkled over the door as they entered the long, narrow room, made darker by towering shelves of books. A clerk bustled forward, smiling in anticipation, recognizing well-heeled customers.

"May I interest you in a book?"

"Actually, we are trying to find a book which Mr. Jones purchased some twenty years ago. It was my father who sold it, and I would like to get it back into the family. Would it be possible to talk to Mr. Jones himself? I am Sir Philip Neville."

The clerk, after a closer look at Sir Philip, moved him up even higher in his estimation of wealth and influence. The mention of a title clinched it for him. "Of course. I am sure Mr. Jones would be most honored to talk to you. Let me announce you."

He led them through the maze of shelves to an office in the rear. Just outside the office, rows of glass-fronted, locked shelves held many old-looking books. The clerk gestured for Philip and Cassandra to wait there while he went into the office. A moment later an old man came out, frowning at them. He was thin and had probably once been tall, but age and a stoop-shouldered posture had shortened him. His hair was thick and white, much like his eyebrows, and the combination of the two gave him a slightly wild look. His dark eyes, however, were sharp and not the least bit wild. There was at the moment a speculative look in them; Cassandra suspected he was trying to figure out how he could make a profit out of the situation.

"Harrington Jones," he introduced himself shortly, giving both of them a perfunctory bow, and ushered them into his office.

That room was even tinier than Mr. Simons's office had been, and what space there was was entirely covered by books in all states of disrepair. The old man waved a dismissive hand at the stacks. "Junk, most of it. Here, miss, please sit down."

He showed her to his chair behind the desk, and he and Philip stood. There was no room to bring in more chairs for his guests.

"How is it that I may help you, sir?"

Philip once again explained that he was looking for a book sold twenty years earlier, describing the book in detail. The old man nodded, saying nothing. There was a knowing look on his face that raised Cassandra's hopes.

"Of course, there would be a finder's fee for you if you could help me locate it," Sir Philip added smoothly.

A gleam in the book dealer's eye showed his appreciation of Philip's perspicacity. "Most generous of you, sir."

After a few minutes' negotiation, they settled on an appropriate fee, and Harrington Jones began to talk. "I remember the book of which you speak quite well." He gestured toward the stack of ledgers on the table behind his desk. "I keep records, but the best books I usually store up here." He tapped his temple with his forefinger. "I don't recall the initial transaction, but about five years ago the family of the man who bought it brought it to me again. The man had died, and they were liquidating his collection. The Elizabeth prayer book was the gem of the lot. I sold it and one other book to one of my best customers, an avid collector of old and rare books."

He paused and glanced at Sir Philip. "I have to warn you, sir, in all honesty, that I do not believe that he will want to sell you the book. He is a very wealthy man. His father made a fortune in manufacturing, and it is said that he has doubled it. He is a true connoisseur."

Sir Philip nodded. "I understand. We would very much like to talk to him, however."

"His name is Ernest Bigby. I can give you his address, if you would like."

"Thank you."

They left the shop a few minutes later, having made Mr. Jones a happier man with a healthy finder's fee.

"Oh, Philip!" Cassandra exclaimed, barely able to keep from dancing in her excitement. "We're almost there! I can hardly believe it. But what if he will not sell the book?"

He smiled down at her, unable to resist the glow of enthusiasm on her face. "Then we shall strive to at least get a look at it. I have found that men who collect things usually can't help showing them off. If we can look at it, perhaps we can find the map and slip it out—provided that it is still there, of course."

Cassandra's face fell. "Oh. Do you think it will be gone?"

"I don't know. I'm sorry. I don't mean to make you unhappy. But after all these years, and with it passing through two buyers, as well as Mr. Jones's store twice, it seems unlikely that anything would have gone undetected."

"I refuse to think that way. Surely we cannot have traveled all this way and done all this, only to have the map gone forever."

"If willing it can make it be there, then I am sure it will be."

Cassandra looked up, catching an expression in Philip's eyes that took her breath away. He glanced away quickly, and when he turned back to her, his face was shuttered once more, all thoughts and feelings locked away. Cassandra was suddenly cold, the excitement of their find draining away from her.

They returned to Neville House, where Philip sat down and wrote a note to Ernest Bigby, explaining his desire to purchase the Elizabeth prayer book that had once belonged to his family. He sent a footman off with it at once, but after that, there was little to do but wait for Bigby's reply.

The next few hours passed in an excruciating fashion. Cassandra sat in the drawing room, trying to concentrate on a piece of needlework, which was hardly her favorite occupation to begin with, while Joanna and Aunt Ardis chattered inanely, and Philip sat, arms crossed, silent as the grave. By the time Joanna gaily suggested a shopping expedition, Cassandra jumped on the idea, feeling that anything would be more enjoyable than sitting there.

Much to her amazement, however, Sir Philip insisted on accompanying them. Joanna went upstairs to fetch a bonnet, casting a smirk over her shoulder at Cassandra as she went out the door. Cassandra knew that Joanna would interpret Philip's presence on the trip as a clear indication that he could not live without Joanna's company. Cassandra sighed. The shopping expedition would be as bad as the rest of the afternoon had been.

"Why are *you* going with us?" she snapped at Philip, irritated.

He raised an eyebrow. "You object to my company? In my own carriage?"

"We can walk or take a hack," Cassandra stated. "We do not need your carriage."

"Ah, but doubtless you need a man to carry all the packages Miss Moulton will purchase."

"We can always take a footman for that."

Philip grimaced. "Dislikable as you find my presence, Miss Verrere, I intend to go. If you will remember, someone tried rather successfully to harm you only a few days ago. I am aware that you would prefer to think that *I* am the villain of this piece, but since I know that I am not, I also know that there is someone out there who may try to hurt you. Therefore, I do not plan to let you leave this house unless I am with you. Is that clear?"

"Perfectly." Cassandra threw her needlepoint down and surged to her feet. "I find that I have a headache. I believe that I shan't go after all. I am going up to my room to lie down."

She stalked off to her bedroom, hoping that Sir Philip would not be able to wriggle out of taking Joanna and her mother shopping. It would serve him right for being so utterly odious.

She threw herself down in the armchair and stared moodily out the window at the small garden below. Her chest was stuffed with hot and conflicting emotions, and she wanted, quite badly, to cry. *How could everything have turned out so horribly?*

She almost wished that she had never read Margaret Verrere's diaries, had never known about the maps to the lost dowry—except, of course, that then she would never have met Sir Philip. And even as miserable as she felt right now, she could not wish for that.

Cassandra stayed in her room the rest of the day and, claiming sickness, even had a tray brought up to her room at supper and begged off the trip to the opera that the others had planned. She listened to Joanna's excited voice in the hall as she left her room, no doubt dressed in the most elegant of clothes and looking utterly beautiful. She was sure that Joanna would make the most of this evening alone with Sir Philip. By the end of it, she would be certain that he meant to offer marriage to her. Even knowing how little Philip liked Joanna, the thought of their spending the evening together at the opera made Cassandra's heart hurt. *It should be* her *with him.* She *was the one who loved him.*

She began to get ready for bed. But even after she had put on her nightgown, brushed out her hair and crawled into bed, she could not go to sleep. Even after she heard Joanna and Aunt Ardis come upstairs and go into their bedrooms, she lay wide awake, staring up at the ceiling. She could not keep from remembering the way Philip had come into her room late at night a few days before, slipping into her bed and making love to her. She could not stop wishing that he would do so this night.

Tears gathered in her eyes and slid down her cheeks. She told herself that she was insane, that she could not want to be made love to by a man whom she suspected of trying to harm her.

It was then that the knowledge came to her in a jolt: *She did not believe that Philip had tried to harm her.*

Cassandra sat up in bed, startled by her insight. She reminded herself of all the reasons she had to doubt him. They were still there, the logical explanation of *who* had locked her in the windmill and *why.* But she saw that while the doubts had been there in her head, she had not really believed them, not deep down inside her. Her heart had always known that he would not harm her. Had she really believed that he might harm her, she would have been afraid to travel to London with him, with only the dubious protection of Aunt Ardis and Joanna. She would have been afraid to go out into London alone with him. She would at least have experienced some trepidation and doubt. However, she had felt not the slightest hesitation in traveling to the city with him or in going about London alone with him. Never for a moment had she felt afraid in his presence. And the reason had been because in her heart and soul, in the very essence of her being, she had known that Philip would not hurt her.

Cassandra flung off her covers and began to pace the room, amazed by this epiphany. *Why had she not realized it before?* It was, she thought, because she had become so accustomed to letting her head rule her life. When logical doubts had intervened, she had given them heed, as she always gave her thoughts heed. But the doubts had not in any way changed her feelings for Philip or made her feel uneasy in his presence. Instinctively, she had believed him; it was obvious in her actions.

She let out a little sob, compounded of relief, regret and a great upsurge of love, and hurried out the door. She almost ran down the hall to the other end, where Philip's room lay, her bare feet making no noise on the runner. She did not even glance around, not caring whether anyone saw her. At Philip's door, she did not pause to knock, but pulled it open boldly and stepped inside, closing it behind her.

He was in the midst of undressing for bed, standing in front of his dresser in only trousers and his dress shirt, opened down the front. He whirled at her entrance and stared at her, dumbfounded.

Cassandra stared back, suddenly unable to think of anything to say.

Finally he broke the tableau, starting toward her, frowning in concern. "Cassandra? What's the matter? Did something happen?"

She shook her head. "No. Nothing happened." She paused, then added honestly, "Except inside me."

He stopped, looking puzzled. "I don't understand."

"I'm not sure I do, either." She let out a shaky laugh. "I don't know how to say this. I am so scared that you hate me now, that you won't accept my— Oh, God. I'm not making any sense, am I?"

"Not really," he agreed, not unkindly. "But I do not hate you, Cassandra, whatever you might think. I could not. Ever."

Cassandra drew a deep breath. "Thank you." Tears shone in her eyes. "I—I came to apologize. I know that I was very wrong, and I'm sorry. All those things, those reasons, I realized tonight that they didn't matter. All that mattered was whether I believed that you had tried to harm me. And I don't. I see how you could have, why you could have wanted to…but my heart refuses to believe that you did."

He gazed at her in some astonishment. "But what made you change your mind?"

"I didn't. I mean, I realized that it wasn't my mind that mattered. Even though I couldn't decide, up here—" she tapped her temple "—whether you locked me in the windmill, I realized that it made no difference. What was important was that in my heart, in here, I knew that you had not. It makes sense that it was you who locked me away, but when I look at you, I can't believe that you would have hurt me."

"Of course I wouldn't. Oh, Cassandra…" He took a long stride toward her.

"I'm sorry that I doubted you."

He shook his head. "No. I was wrong to expect you to not have doubts. You are far too rational not to see the obvious conclusions. I was merely hurt. I wanted you to have blind faith in me."

"I do have faith in you. Complete faith." She smiled up at him, and he crossed the remaining stretch of floor between them in two quick strides.

"Cassandra!" He swept her into his arms, and his mouth found hers.

With a little sigh of pleasure, Cassandra melted in his arms. *This was where she had been longing to be, where she belonged.* They clung together, kissing fervently. Cassandra's hands slid beneath the open sides of his shirt, caressing the flat, hard muscles of his chest and stomach. His flesh quivered under her touch, suddenly on fire.

This time it was she who took the initiative, undressing him, exploring his body with her hands and mouth, backing him up until he tumbled backward onto the bed. Boldly, she straddled him, peeling off her own nightgown and tossing it aside. Philip watched her, his eyes gleaming, struggling to hold back his raging need. She moved slowly, enticing him, tracing intricate patterns across his chest with her tongue, and stroking his thighs and abdomen, moving ever close to the hot, throbbing center of his passion until he was groaning, sure that he would burst if she continued much longer.

At last she touched his manhood, caressing it and kissing it, playing with him until he was arching up off the bed, his fingers clenched in the bedcovers and his face contorted with the effort of holding back. She positioned herself above him and sank down upon him, taking his shaft deep inside her. Cassandra groaned at the delightful sensation. She moved up and down with steady deliberation, teasing them both with long, tormenting strokes, until finally she could stand it no longer and began to pump harder and faster, the passion in her building and building until at last it exploded, sending them both hurtling into a dark void of utter pleasure.

They lay in the dark for a long time, idly caressing each other and murmuring, saying nothing particularly meaningful, yet expressing everything important. Finally, with a sigh, Philip reminded her that she must get back to her room or else when the servants came in early the next morning, there would a firestorm of gossip. Reluctantly, Cassandra agreed. She put back on her nightgown, and Philip pulled on his heavy brocade dressing gown, knotting the sash around his waist.

He opened the door to peer out. Satisfied that there was no one around to see them, he took Cassandra's hand and led her out. They started quietly down the hall, but halfway there, Philip swept her up in his arms, grinning, and carried her the rest of the way. Cassandra curled her arm around his neck and leaned against him, blissfully happy with his silliness.

When they reached Cassandra's room, he set her down and opened the door. The hall sconces cast a faint light into the dark room—enough to reveal the figure of a man bent over one of the drawers in Cassandra's dresser.

19

Cassandra cried out in surprise, and Philip rushed forward into the room. The figure raised his arm and something flew across the room, striking Philip in the head. Philip staggered, then started forward again, but the thief had bought himself enough time to run across the room and leap out the window.

Philip ran to the window and peered down. "Damn! He went down the tree. The man's like a monkey! He's already on the ground." He peered out at the tree. "I don't think the thing would hold me." He slammed his fist into the wall beside the window. "Bloody hell! I had him within reach!"

"It's not your fault." Cassandra went to him and laid her hand on his arm comfortingly.

"I suppose. But it's so frustrating." He sighed. "Well, let's see what damage he's done."

At that moment Aunt Ardis appeared in the doorway, a lamp in her hand. Joanna was right behind her, peering over her shoulder. They both stared at the room in shock.

Cassandra, seeing her room for the first time in the light, also stared in dismay. All the drawers of her dresser had been pulled open and most of the contents dumped on the floor. One drawer had even been pulled out completely and lay on the floor, her chemises spilling from it. The bottles and jars on her dresser had been pushed aside, some of them overturned.

"What happened?" Aunt Ardis gasped.

"Someone broke into Cassandra's room," Philip replied grimly.

"But whatever for? Cassandra has nothing worth stealing."

Joanna let out a moan and pushed past her mother into the room, her hand flying dramatically to her throat. "The thief must have gotten the wrong bedchamber. He must have meant to break into our rooms, Mother. To steal our jewels." She tottered shakily forward, one hand going to her forehead, the other hand stretching out toward Philip. "Oh! I feel faint at the thought! Philip...help me."

"Sit down and put your head between your knees," Philip told her callously, jerking forward a straight chair and shoving it under her, knocking it against the backs of her knees so that her legs gave way and Joanna sat down abruptly.

Joanna glared up at him, but he had already turned back to Cassandra.

"Perhaps you had better move in with your aunt for the rest of the night."

Cassandra shook her head. "There's no need. I am sure he won't be back tonight."

Aunt Ardis had turned her gaze from the wrecked room back to her niece and Sir Philip. She noticed that Cassandra was clad in nothing but her nightgown, and Philip was wearing his dressing gown and apparently nothing else, for a large swath of his bare chest was visible between the two sides of the robe. Her brows rushed together.

"What is going on here?" she demanded in stentorian

tones. "What are you doing in my niece's bedchamber at this time of night, anyway, Sir Philip? It isn't at all proper."

"It's all right, Aunt Ardis," Cassandra said quickly. "He, uh, just came because I shrieked when I discovered that a thief had been in my room."

Aunt Ardis looked doubtful. "*I* heard you shriek and came immediately to your aid. And he was already in here." She turned a hard gaze on the nobleman. "I think you had best leave, sir."

"Aunt Ardis! Please...I assure you that there is no need—"

Philip interrupted calmly, "Don't worry, Mrs. Moulton."

"Don't worry!" Aunt Ardis was in full dramatic steam now. "If word of this got out, it would mean the ruin of Cassandra's reputation."

Philip's eyes narrowed. "Ah, but it will not get out, now, will it, ma'am? Besides, there will be no damage to Cassandra's reputation. She is going to be my wife."

"What!" Cassandra turned as stunned an expression on him as her aunt.

Aunt Ardis began to splutter, seeing the tactical error she had made in the excitement of the moment. "Oh, no...I...Sir Philip, I am sure that is not necessary. The servants have not seen you here, and you can rest assured that Joanna and I will not breathe a word of this. It is, after all, my niece's reputation."

"I am sure you would not tell anyone," Philip agreed. "Nevertheless, Miss Verrere is my fiancée now."

"But you can't! I mean, that's absurd!"

Philip raised an insufferably aristocratic eyebrow, looking at Aunt Ardis as if she were some sort of strange specimen he had just recently uncovered. "I, too, was most surprised that Cassandra accepted my proposal. It is quite obvious that I am not worthy of her. But, there you are, she is always a kind and generous lady."

"No! Wait!" Joanna cried, springing to her feet. She turned toward her mother desperately. "Mother! Do something! He can't marry Cassandra!"

"I assure you, Miss Moulton, I *can*. And I will."

"But...but..." She turned back to him, opening her eyes wide in a wounded expression. "But what about me?"

"I am sure Miss Verrere will ask you to be an attendant at our wedding. Won't you, Cassandra, dear?"

Cassandra could not stifle a giggle at her cousin's horrified expression. "Of course, Joanna," she told her sweetly. "You must be my bridesmaid. After all, it was you and Aunt Ardis who brought Sir Philip and me together."

Aunt Ardis made a choking noise. "Cassandra, wait...consider...you cannot. Sir Philip, you cannot have thought! Cassandra is penniless."

"I have no need of a wealthy wife," Philip responded blandly. "I am sure you will be happy to know that Cassandra's love is more than enough treasure for me."

Cassandra had to clap a hand over her mouth to keep down a hoot of laughter at his syrupy words. Philip shot her a most unloverlike look.

"But there are her brothers and sister, too. Have you thought about the burden of raising them?"

"I am quite fond of children."

"But you can't!" Joanna shrieked at Cassandra, stamping her foot. "You can't marry him! You can't—you can't get married before *me!*"

This last thought was apparently too much for her beleaguered nerves, for Joanna turned and ran from the room.

An instant later they heard her door slam shut. Aunt Ardis gaped at them for a moment, her mouth opening and closing like that of a landed fish. Then she turned and hurried after her daughter.

Cassandra gazed after her aunt for a moment, laughter bubbling up from her throat. She was, she thought, filled with a most unworthy sense of triumph. Behind her, Philip lit a lamp to survey the damage.

Cassandra turned around and gasped. She was looking not at the mess on the floor but at Philip. For the first time she saw his face in full lamplight. "Philip! You are injured!"

She went to him quickly, pushing back the hair that had fallen down over his forehead and exposing the large red spot, already beginning to show a bruise, centered by a jagged cut. A line of blood had oozed down the side of his face from the cut.

"Yes," Philip responded almost casually. "He hit me full force with that little box." He grimaced. "I feel like a fool, letting him get away like that."

"It wasn't your fault. We were unprepared to find a thief in the room, after all. And while your head may be hard, I fear it is not impervious to flying objects."

He mustered a small smile at her comment, and she continued, "Here. Sit down on the bed and let me tend to that."

"It's nothing. What is important is the map. I am sure that is what he was after. Why else enter this particular room?"

Cassandra glanced over at the armoire. "Oh, it's fine."

She walked to the large cabinet and opened it, sifting rapidly through her dresses until she found the right one. She dug down into a pocket and pulled out the map, which she waved at Philip, then returned to its hiding place.

"Odd place for safekeeping."

"It's easy and always at hand, and not the first place anyone would think to look, as you can see." She gestured toward the ransacked room. "Had I thought anyone was going to try to steal it, I suppose I might have been more careful and put it for safekeeping in that very box he threw at you." She shrugged. "Anyway, it is only a copy. I have another one at Haverly House, and the original is at home."

"Still, I am very glad that our thief didn't get his hands on it."

Cassandra went about the business of pouring water into the wash basin and wetting a rag. She came back to Philip and began to clean his wound. "Did you get a look at him?"

He shook his head regretfully. "No. It was too dark, and then he knocked me silly with that box. He was tall, but slight, that's about all I could see of him."

Cassandra nodded. "I couldn't see him, either. I wish the light had been better."

"My money is still on it being your American cousin— or a burglar hired by him to get the map."

Cassandra sighed. "Except that he went back to the United States."

"Or so he told you."

"You always say that."

"Well, you have only his word for it," he argued mildly, then winced. "Ow! I don't think you are the future Florence Nightingale."

"What? Oh. Sorry. My mind was elsewhere. There. It looks clean enough. I am afraid that is all I can do for it. You really need a plaster."

He shrugged. "If it's not your Mr. Miller, my dear, then

who is it? I have always thought your aunt would fit well in the role of villainess.''

Cassandra smiled.

"Let's see, who else? Your Mr. Simons, perhaps?''

Cassandra chuckled at the thought of the chubby, avuncular book dealer engaging in such shenanigans. "Well, I'm certain he wasn't the one climbing in and out my window.''

"Thank God you were not in here when he did,'' Philip said in a heartfelt voice. "Promise me that from now on you will close *and* lock your window at night. Engaged we may be, but I think it would be too shocking for me to camp out in your room every night to make sure you are safe.''

"Philip...'' Cassandra turned toward him, distracted from the subject of their burglar's identity. "I want to talk to you about that.''

"Dates and clothes and such? I leave all that sort of thing up to you, my dear. Mother and Grandmother no doubt will want to have a say, but—''

"That's not what I meant. There really is no need for you to say we are engaged. It was very kind of you to try to protect me, but I can assure you that Aunt Ardis will not speak of this.''

"Cassandra!'' Philip opened his eyes wide, looking shocked. "I do believe you are trying to jilt me. And here we are, engaged for scarcely an hour.'' He tsk-tsked. "Oh, the callousness of it.''

"Philip! You know what I meant. There is no need for us to be married. My reputation will be perfectly all right.''

"Then your intention is to use me and toss me aside?'' he asked with mock indignation.

Cassandra ground her teeth in irritation. "Would you please be serious?''

"Ah, but I am serious. You are the one who is thinking frivolously. We are now engaged, and there is nothing to be done about it."

"Don't I have anything to say in the matter?"

"Knowing you, I am quite certain that you will have a great deal to say," Philip responded with a gleam of humor in his eyes. "However, it does not change the fact that marriage is the only option. If you will not think of your own reputation, my dear, consider mine."

Cassandra fought down a desire to hit him. Philip's lighthearted quips were blocking her attempts to do the right thing far better than a straightforward argument would. She was certain he knew that. It was most frustrating, especially given the fact that her own heart was not in her offer. The idea of marrying Philip had set up a warm glow in her chest; she realized that it was what she wanted more than anything else, the Spanish dowry included. It made it quite difficult to be noble and excuse Philip from his impetuous offer to save her reputation. However, she did not want to marry him merely because he felt a sense of responsibility. She wanted love from Philip, not duty.

With a sigh, she gave up for the moment. She would try again tomorrow to make him see reason. Perhaps after a few hours' consideration he would see what he was throwing away by tying himself to her.

"Oh, go to bed." She gestured toward the door.

"An excellent suggestion. One that I trust you will follow, also." He strode to the window and pulled it down, locking it with an emphatic click. He did the same to her other window, then turned back to her. "Are you certain that you don't want to sleep in your aunt's or Joanna's room tonight?"

"Don't be absurd. Here I'd have only a thief to contend

with. If I slept with either one of them tonight, I would probably be murdered in my bed.''

He chuckled and left the room, after a lengthy kiss that left Cassandra breathless and wondering why she had been so foolish as to protest their marriage. She cleaned up her room, folding her clothes and putting them back into the drawers, then crawled into her bed, where she fell promptly asleep and dreamed not of thieves and ransacked rooms but of wedding veils and rings.

''I cannot believe that you would do this to me!'' Aunt Ardis moaned. ''Your own flesh and blood. After all I have done for you! I have nourished a snake in my bosom.''

''Exactly what have I done to you?'' Cassandra asked pragmatically. Her aunt had been carrying on for ten minutes like this, from the moment she and Joanna had walked into the sitting room this morning. This was the first time that Cassandra had been able to get a word in.

''What have you done!'' Joanna almost screeched, bouncing up from her chair. ''You stole Sir Philip from me!''

''Stole him? Joanna, you talk as if Sir Philip were some knickknack or a piece of furniture. You do not *own* him.''

''He was interested in me first!''

''For a day or so,'' Cassandra replied agreeably. ''Until he found out your plans to capture him.''

''Hah! Miss High-and-Mighty! As if you didn't do exactly the same thing!''

Her cousin's words stung. Cassandra could think of nothing to say.

''There!'' Joanna crowed. ''You see! I'm right.''

''It is a far different situation,'' Cassandra said fiercely. ''Besides, it is none of your business.''

"None of my business? When he was mine to begin with?"

"He was never *yours!*"

"I took you into my house." Aunt Ardis shook her head mournfully. "I fed you and clothed you. I even took you with us to Lady Arrabeck's house party—all because I felt sorry for you. And look how you repaid me."

Cassandra slammed her fist down onto the arm of the chair and jumped to her feet. "Enough! I have had enough of this! First of all, you did not take us into your house and clothe and feed us. My uncle, my mother's brother, did that. I am sure if it had been left up to you, my brothers and sister and I would all be in the workhouse by now. Secondly, you showed no kindness taking me to that party. You only wanted another chaperon for Joanna and a foil for her beauty. And last, but not least, I did not steal Sir Philip from Joanna. No one could do that, because he did not have the slightest interest in her. He can barely stand to be in the same room with her, and anyone with even the slightest bit of intelligence would have realized that. How could either of you possibly think he was interested in her when he avoided her presence at every opportunity?"

The other two women gaped at Cassandra, dumbfounded.

"Sir Philip asked me to marry him," Cassandra continued, gliding over the exact truth, "and that is what I intend to do. There is nothing you can say or do that will change that. The only thing you can do, what you are doing right now, is to infuriate Sir Philip and me so much that you will never receive another invitation to Haverly House. You have the prospect of being related to Lady Neville, and that means entrée into circles full of eligible bachelors. If you have any sense, you will seize the opportunity that offers instead of griping over the loss of something you never had to begin with!''

"Bravo, my dear!"

Cassandra whirled to find Sir Philip standing in the doorway, lightly clapping his hands as if at a play, a sardonic grin on his face. She colored to the roots of her hair.

"Oh. I'm sorry."

"Don't be sorry. You are quite accurate." He nodded toward Aunt Ardis and Joanna. "Now, if you ladies will excuse me, I have something I wish to discuss with my future wife. My dear?"

He offered his arm to her, and Cassandra took it gladly, letting him escort her from the room and down the hall to his study.

"Please forgive me for creating a scene back there," Cassandra apologized. "I am not usually so—"

"How disappointing." Sir Philip grinned. "I was hoping to see you vanquish your foes in similar manner many more times during our life. It was vastly entertaining."

Cassandra made a face at him. "I am more interested in what you wanted to discuss with me. What is it?"

"This." They had reached his office, and as they stepped inside, he pulled a folded sheet of paper from his pocket and handed it to her. "Mr. Bigby replied to my note."

"Oh." Cassandra sighed. "I can tell from your face that the news isn't good."

"He refuses to sell the prayer book."

Cassandra began to read the note. "'It is with regret, blah, blah… But I would account it a great honor if you would visit my home this afternoon to see the Queen Elizabeth prayer book. I would be more than happy to show it to you, as well as my entire collection of books.'" She looked up excitedly. "Philip!"

"Yes, I have already sent back a gracious acceptance of his invitation for both me and my fiancée." He sighed. "But I'm not sure exactly how we will be able get the map."

"Perhaps you could manage to slip the book into your pocket while he isn't looking."

Philip feigned shock. "I had not realized what a larcenous girl I was marrying."

"We would return it as soon as we got the map out of it," Cassandra protested. "But it isn't workable. He would be bound to notice if you didn't return the book to him. However, we don't have to have the whole book. You can look through it and find the map. I shall distract him and give you plenty of time to examine it. I know enough from Papa about old books to keep him talking for quite a while."

"Cassandra…" Philip's face was tinged with concern.

"What? Why are you looking at me like that?" She had the sudden, horrible notion that he was going to tell her that he had reconsidered the engagement, and she realized how very much she did not want him to.

"It's just…well, I am afraid that the map may not be there."

"Oh." Cassandra felt almost giddy with relief at his words.

"It has been a very long time, and the book has passed through two owners since my father, as well as the book dealer, twice. Father's agent…God knows how many Nevilles have opened it and looked through it. I am afraid that the map was found long ago and simply tossed away. No one would have known what it was."

"But Margaret would not have simply stuck it into the book among the pages. I am sure she would have been more subtle than that. She would have wanted to make sure that it couldn't fall out. Perhaps she somehow tucked it inside the cover or attached it to a page or something."

"Perhaps. I hope so. I just don't want you to be too disappointed if this turns out to be a dead end."

"I won't be," Cassandra promised, faintly surprised to find that she was telling the truth. She was beginning to discover that her love for Philip overshadowed everything else.

They drove to Mr. Bigby's residence a few hours later, where they were shown immediately to his drawing room.

Mr. Bigby popped up out of his chair and bustled over to them. He was a balding, stocky man, bluff and energetic. "Sir Philip!" he cried and shook Philip's hand enthusiastically. No matter what the size of his fortune, he was obviously impressed to be hobnobbing with a baronet. "It is an honor to meet you. An honor, indeed. And Miss Verrere. I once read an article by your father—it was about an illuminated manuscript. Most erudite. Most erudite, indeed."

He paused for a breath, and they murmured polite words of greeting.

"I am sure you are eager to see that book, now, aren't you?" Bigby told his butler, hovering outside the door, to bring them refreshments in the library. Then he hustled Cassandra and Philip off down the hall.

It was an impressive place, almost as large as the library at Haverly House. Several of the bookcases were fronted with glass, which locked to keep out intrusive hands. "These are my old books, the rare ones."

He went to the center locked cabinet. In the middle, on the second shelf by itself, facing out, was a small, old leather-bound book. A row of small pearls, a few of them missing, lined the front cover.

Bigby unlocked the front of the cabinet and raised it,

indicating to Cassandra, who was standing nearest, to take the book. Gingerly, Cassandra picked it up and took it out of the case.

"Oh, it's lovely," she breathed, appreciation of the antique volume overcoming even her desire for the map for the moment.

The spine of the book held three large jewels. The edges of the pages were gilt and the paper tissue thin. Cassandra opened the cover with great care and read the faded, spidery writing inside. "'For Sir Everard, my loyal knight. Elizabeth R.' Oh, my. I can hardly believe I am holding this in my hands—something Queen Elizabeth once held."

She lifted her face and looked at Mr. Bigby. Perfect understanding gleamed in his eyes. "It takes your breath away, doesn't it?"

Cassandra nodded. She remembered herself enough to glance through the book a little, discreetly checking on the insides of the covers and flipping through the thin pages. Nothing fell out of it or made itself immediately apparent. She handed the book to Philip. "Look at this. Isn't it wonderful?"

He nodded, taking it, a similar awe on his features. Cassandra turned away, taking Mr. Bigby's arm. "Would you mind showing me some more of your collection? It is vast. What are these books over here?" She gently tugged him away from Philip.

It was not hard to get Mr. Bigby talking about what was obviously his favorite subject. He showed her around the library, opening several of the glass shelves and taking out books for her to inspect. Cassandra oohed and aahed over them and fortunately had enough knowledge from her father to ask intelligent questions. Bigby beamed, expounding on each book. Cassandra was sure she could have kept him talking even longer, but finally a servant knocked on the door and entered with their refreshments.

Philip, smiling politely, handed back the prayer book to Bigby, thanking him for allowing him to look at it. "If ever you want to sell it, please let me know."

"Of course, of course. But I doubt that day will come— at least until I'm dead." He stroked a loving hand across the cover and set the book reverently back in its place of honor, closing the shelf and relocking it.

Cassandra looked at Sir Philip, trying to determine from his face whether he had found the map, but he wore a maddeningly wooden expression. She was forced to wait through a polite consumption of tea and several more pleasantries before they took their leave and she was able to question him.

"Well?" she asked eagerly as soon as she had taken a seat in the carriage, while Philip was still closing the door.

He looked across at her and smiled. Her hopes rose. "Well...I looked all through it and couldn't find a thing. I peered down the spine and felt all around the cover for a slit cut into it or a bump beneath it. Nothing."

Cassandra slumped. "Oh, no..."

"But, then," Philip continued, "I slid a fingernail down the paper on the inside of the cover, right beside the spine, and, lo and behold, it lifted a fraction. I managed to slip in the ends of my fingers, and I felt something. I tugged, very carefully, and this came out."

He held up a thin sheet of paper, folded many times.

Cassandra stopped breathing for a second. "The map?"

He nodded. "The map."

20

Cassandra was across the carriage in an instant, sitting beside him and peering over his shoulder as he carefully unfolded the aging paper.

It was difficult to make out the faded ink on the yellowed paper in the closed carriage, but it was obviously the work of the same person who had drawn the map they had found at Chesilworth. There were little stick drawings indicating various landmarks, as well as writing, none of it close to the drawings. Just looking at it was enough to make Cassandra's insides shake. *They had done it! They had actually done it!* Much as she had believed in the treasure, as badly as she had wanted to find it, there had always been a part of her that feared she would never locate both parts of the map, never find the dowry.

"It makes no better sense than the other one," Philip said in exasperation. "But perhaps when we get home and put it together with the other map, it will all be clear."

Their plan to put the maps together was interrupted, however, by Aunt Ardis greeting them from the drawing room. "Ah, Cassandra. Sir Philip, there you are. We have a visitor. You must come in here and meet him. I am sure you will be delighted."

Cassandra frowned. She was nearly dancing with impatience to get to the maps, but there was no way to politely avoid the invitation since her aunt had spoken right in front of whoever their visitor was. Forcing her face into a pleasant expression, she stepped into the drawing room, Philip on her heels.

She stopped so quickly that Philip nearly bumped into her. She stared at the man rising from his seat on the sofa beside Joanna. He was grinning broadly.

"Look who came to call on us!" Joanna cried, her eyes gleaming with mischief. "Your American cousin."

"Mr. Miller," Cassandra managed to recover enough to say. She stepped forward to give him her hand. "What a surprise. I thought you were long since in America."

"This is Miller?" Philip asked a trifle rudely and cast a meaningful glance at Cassandra. He fixed the young man with a hard stare.

Miller looked a trifle taken aback, but replied, "Yes. David Miller, sir, at your service."

Cassandra introduced Philip, and he nodded politely, shaking Miller's hand, but he kept his eyes fixed on the young man in a way that Miller obviously found disconcerting, for he kept glancing over at Philip the entire time he was there.

"I, too, thought I would be home by now, Miss Verrere," Miller said, replying to Cassandra's earlier statement. "But when I returned to London after my visit to you, I found out that there had been quite a delay in one of the products I most particularly wanted to ship home. It took a great deal of time and trouble to straighten it all out. It is finally done, however, and I am hoping to leave next week."

"I am sorry you had so much trouble," Cassandra commiserated. "What have you been doing to keep yourself busy?"

She ignored Philip's snort, hastily turned into a cough when Miller looked at him oddly. David began to describe his visits to various museums and such.

"Haven't gotten out of London and seen the countryside any?" Philip asked.

"Not much, except for my trip to see the Verreres," he admitted. "Of course, I had to travel to Manchester to speak directly to the manufacturer once." He smiled a little self-deprecatingly. "Frankly, I was running out of things to do. That is why I went back to the bookstore yesterday. When Mr. Simons told me that Miss Verrere was staying here in London, I was thrilled."

"Yes, poor Mr. Miller was afraid that he had missed you," Joanna interrupted, cutting a look over at Philip to see how he reacted to her words. "Your cousin is *so* devoted to you."

Cassandra knew Joanna was hopeful that David Miller's presence would cause some sort of conflict between Philip and Cassandra, but she knew that her cousin was not aware of exactly how great a bombshell she was blithely dropping in their laps. It looked more and more as though Philip was right: David Miller must be the man who had broken into their houses, looking for the maps. It was hard to reconcile his boyish, eager manner with the soul of a criminal.

David blushed a little at Joanna's words.

Joanna plowed on. "When I told him that you had gone to that Bigby fellow's to look at books, he said he would wait for you. Isn't that sweet?"

"It was very kind of you," Cassandra told David politely.

He stayed for some time, idly chatting, until it was difficult for Cassandra to keep a smile fixed on her face. She wanted only to get rid of him so that they could examine their maps. Besides, it was difficult to be polite and friendly with someone when the whole time she was busy trying to determine if he was the same height and build as their thief of the night before.

Finally he took his leave. Cassandra scurried up to her room to retrieve the map they had found at Chesilworth and brought it back down to Philip's study. He set a lamp in the middle of his desk and spread out the two maps side by side in the lamp's full glow. They leaned over the desk and gazed down at the papers.

They looked like two confusing maps. There seemed no connection between them. Nothing jumped into crystal clarity. Cassandra and Philip glanced at each other. He moved the maps around, trying them against each other on different sides and at different angles. It still made no sense.

"This is mad," Philip said in disgust. "Only a bunch of disjointed names and symbols, nothing matching. There is nothing the same on both maps, no meeting place."

Cassandra studied them. Tears threatened at the backs of her eyes. *It was too awful—to have come so far and done so much, and still the location remained a complete mystery!*

She reached down and touched the tissue-thin paper Philip had taken from the book today. "I wonder why this one is a different kind of paper. The one we found at Chesilworth was on good, thick bond. This is so easily torn—why would she have used it?"

"Made it easy to fold it and slide it beneath the back cover," Philip answered pragmatically. "Anyone would have noticed a bulge there."

"Yes. I suppose. Still, it isn't a large piece of paper."

She looked at the map copy she had made. It, too, was on thin paper because she had used it to trace from the original map. Suddenly her heart began to pound. "Oh, my God!"

"What?" Philip glanced at her, startled, then down at the maps at which she was staring so fixedly. "What is it? Did you think of something?"

"I'm not sure. It's just this thin paper...it's like what I put over the map to trace on...." With trembling fingers, she picked up the tissue map and laid it gently on top of the other. The symbols and names from the other map showed through, but it was an even bigger jumble.

Carefully she turned the top page around, and suddenly everything clicked into place. The word *creek* on the new map lay beside the word *Littlejohn* on the first, and above them both was a squiggly line. Now the rows of lollipop shapes said *copse of trees,* and the square building held a steeple and the legend *Saint Swithin.*

"I'll be damned!" Philip stared at the map, stunned. "I know where this is. This church is no more than a mile from Haverly House, and this road leading from it past the creek... I know this place."

"What about this hut, the peat-cutter's hut? And the stone wall?" She pointed toward the small square, her fingernail tracing the words *fifteen paces* to a mark stating *stone wall.* On the other side of the wall, an arrow pointed five paces to a spot where a small round-topped chest was drawn, along with the simple word, "Dowry."

"They're not familiar to me. But you have to remember that this was drawn almost two hundred years ago. The hut has probably fallen to pieces by now. The remains of it might still be there, though. And the wall." He looked at Cassandra, excitement glowing in his eyes. "We can find it now, Cassandra. That treasure is in our hands."

* * *

They set out for Haverly House the following morning. Aunt Ardis grumbled about racing down to London to spend only three or four days, then racing back, but she allowed the maids to pack her trunks with only a minimum of fuss. She had apparently taken to heart Cassandra's warning of the day before and was afraid of losing the valuable connection to the Neville family. Cassandra had heard her assuring Joanna during one of her pouts that there were "other fish in the sea."

The servants had finished piling their cases atop the carriage and strapping them down, and they were just about to walk out to the carriage when there was a loud rapping on the front door. One of the footmen opened it and was nearly bowled over by a well-dressed man, who barreled into the hallway. He stopped, ignoring the agitated footman, and swung his head around. His gaze fell on Sir Philip, standing with Cassandra and the Moultons, and he charged forward, shaking off the footman's hand when he grabbed for his arm.

"Sir Philip! By God, I won't stand for this!"

"Mr. Bigby?" Cassandra stared at the man in astonishment. His suave demeanor of the day before was gone. He was red in the face, his eyes flashed, and he had not even worn a hat to cover his head.

"You appear upset," Philip said in a classic understatement. "Perhaps we should go to my office and talk."

"I'll talk right here and now!" the man thundered back. "You may be all high and mighty, but if you think that I'll just let you take my—my jewel—my precious—" He spluttered to a stop, looking as if he might burst a blood vessel.

"Calm down, man," Philip said in a tone of aristocratic

command, and, amazingly enough, it seemed to decrease Mr. Bigby's agitation somewhat.

"That's better. Now, kindly tell me what on earth you are talking about."

"The Queen's prayer book, of course!" Bigby snapped. "What else?"

"What about it?"

Bigby let out a snort. "You know good and well what about it! Don't try to cozen me with your elegant ways. It's gone!"

Cassandra gasped, and Bigby glanced at her, nodding vehemently.

"That's right! Gone. Stolen. Right out from under my nose."

"And you think that *I* did it?" Philip asked in tones of amazement.

"Who else? You were the one wanting to buy it, and I wouldn't sell it to you. I know you aristocrats—not used to not getting your way. When I wouldn't sell, you decided to snatch it back. That's why you came over yesterday, to see if it was worth stealing. To see where I kept it."

"Oh, no, Mr. Bigby," Cassandra assured him earnestly. "I promise you. Sir Philip did not steal your book."

"Not with his own hands, no doubt. He wouldn't want to get them dirty. No, he just hired a burglar to come in and get it, told him where it was and what it looked like."

The man continued in this vein for some time, with Aunt Ardis and Joanna looking on in avid interest, but finally Cassandra's and Philip's assurances that they had had nothing to do with stealing the book began to sink in on him.

"I assure you, Mr. Bigby, I would never steal that or any other book. We, too, have been the victim of bizarre break-ins, both here and at our homes in the country. Three of them.''

"Three of them! What did they take?''

"Nothing. But we think that they were looking for that selfsame book at Haverly House. The thief was discovered in the library. That was when we first became interested in the Queen's book. I don't know who the thief is, although I have my suspicions, and I promise you that if, in the course of investigating him, I find your book in his possession, I will make sure that it is returned to you promptly.''

"Investigating him?'' Cassandra repeated. "Do you mean to tell me that you have hired someone to investigate David?''

"Yes, this morning,'' he replied calmly. "I hired a man to follow him. Obviously I should have done it yesterday evening, and then he would have been caught trying to steal the Queen's Book.''

"What is so special about this book?'' Aunt Ardis asked, puzzled.

"Are you saying that David Miller stole it?'' Joanna added, her eyes getting bigger and rounder.

"That is my suspicion.''

"And nothing more,'' Cassandra stressed.

"My fiancée has a soft spot for Mr. Miller,'' Philip said in a sardonic aside toward Mr. Bigby.

Cassandra made a face at him. "That's not true. I am simply pointing out that David Miller wouldn't have known to break into Mr. Bigby's house to get the book. We are the only ones who knew it was there.''

"If you will remember, my dear, when he came to call yesterday, Miss Moulton told him that we were at Mr. Bigby's, *looking at books*. I don't imagine it would have been hard for him to put two and two together.''

Cassandra's eyes widened. "Oh, my, you're right." She sighed. "I guess there's no escaping it. Mr. Miller must be the thief."

"I'm afraid so, my dear. I know you hate to think it, but it is rather clear."

Aunt Ardis and Joanna continued to exclaim over the likelihood of David Miller's being a thief all the rest of the morning as the carriage left London. Mr. Bigby had finally left, mostly appeased, and they had been able to depart, only somewhat delayed.

Cassandra found the return journey to Haverly House much less tedious than the one coming to London. Philip rode inside the carriage most of the time, suffering the presence of Aunt Ardis and Joanna in order to be with Cassandra. It was a kind of exquisite torture for Cassandra to be so close to him and yet have to maintain a proper decorum in front of her aunt and cousin. She was supremely aware of his body beside her, of his broad shoulders and muscled thigh almost touching her, of his heat and masculine scent. She found herself gazing at the way his black hair curled forward just behind his ear and, moreover, finding it strangely endearing. She studied the firm bones of his jaw and cheek, the dark sweep of his lashes, and was tempted to trace the lines of his face with her forefinger.

He had not come again to her bedroom, telling her that he wanted no more risk to her reputation, particularly the night they spent in the public inn on the way home to Haverly House. Cassandra had difficulty going to sleep for thinking about him and his lovemaking. She was beginning to decide that she must be a rather wanton person to think such thoughts so much of the time. As the time passed, it seemed that she was thinking them more and more. She hoped that soon Philip would overcome his noble impulses and return to her bed.

They reached Haverly House in the afternoon. The children, who had spotted them coming up the long drive on the lane from the third-story nursery windows, came pelting down to greet them. The two Lady Nevilles arrived at a slower pace, with Sarah Yorke following them.

"Why, Philip, I had not expected you back so soon," Violet said, looking puzzled. "I was just telling Miss Yorke that it would probably be two weeks before you returned. Now you have made me out to be a liar."

"Hello, Mother. Grandmother." He greeted both his mother and grandmother with a peck on the cheek. "I am sure Miss Yorke will understand that the untruth was caused by my erratic nature, not your lack of veracity. We simply finished our business much sooner than expected." He turned toward Sarah. "Miss Yorke. How are you?"

"I am in excellent health and spirits, Sir Philip. As are all the boys. They will be very happy to hear that you are back. I must go now. I am sure you wish to visit with your family. I just came over for Lady Neville's recipe for blancmange."

"No, wait, don't leave yet, Miss Yorke," Philip said persuasively. "You are practically one of the family, and I have an announcement to make. 'Tis easier to do it all at once."

Everyone turned interested eyes on him at these words. Cassandra suspected what he was about to say, and she went pale, her stomach clenching. She should not have let it go this far, she knew; she should have convinced Philip that he did not have to marry her. *It had been sheer self-ishness on her part to let it go on.* She was certain that his mother would be appalled at the engagement, and his stiff-backed grandmother even more so!

Philip took her arm, pulling her forward.

"Philip, no! Wait!" she whispered frantically, but he only smiled.

"Don't be silly. Now is the perfect time." He turned back to Violet. "Mother, Grandmother." He bowed toward the younger set, who were all watching, wide-eyed. "Everyone. I have asked Miss Verrere to be my wife, and she has graciously given me her consent."

There was a moment of intense silence. Cassandra wished that she could sink into the ground. Then Lady Violet held out her arms to her son, saying, "Oh, Philip! I have waited so long for this day. I can't tell you how happy I am."

Violet hugged him, and Georgette let out a shriek and ran to him, jumping on him as soon as their mother released him. "I knew it! I just knew it! What took you so long? I told Olivia two days after they got here that I had never seen you so gone on a girl."

The rest of the two families crowded around, offering their congratulations. Philip's mother hugged Cassandra and welcomed her to the family, and even old Lady Neville offered Cassandra her cheek to kiss and told her that her grandson had excellent taste.

"But I—I mean—" Cassandra realized that she could hardly tell Philip's mother and grandmother that she did not intend to hold Philip to his offer of marriage, that, indeed, there hadn't actually been an offer. She certainly was not about to admit that she and Philip had been caught in a compromising position. Finally she smiled. "I was afraid that you wouldn't approve."

"Not approve?" the older Lady Neville said with a sniff. "Why ever not? Verrere has always been a good name. Sister to Lord Chesilworth and all that. Quite appropriate, I think."

"Thank you."

Georgette hugged Cassandra, telling her that she was perfect for Philip and that she, Georgette, looked forward to being her sister. "Best of all, now Olivia can live with us all the time! I've been dying for years to have a sister, and now I have two. And two more brothers, as well!" She cast a laughing look at the twins. "Who will make excellent brothers, being such pests as they are on occasion."

The twins, needless to say, took exception to her jest and paid her back by untying the sash of her dress, with the result that all four took off on a shrieking game of chase. Cassandra turned to find Sarah Yorke standing quietly at her side.

"Miss Verrere..." Sarah held out her hand. "I wanted to offer you my best wishes. I am sure you will make a lovely bride."

She was smiling, but Cassandra detected a glimpse of sadness in Sarah's eyes. Cassandra thought that she had been right about Sarah's hidden liking for Philip, and she felt sorry for the woman.

"I hope that you and I will become good friends, now that I will be living here," Cassandra told her sincerely.

"Yes, I do, too." Sarah smiled at her again and turned away to offer her congratulations to Philip.

When she moved on, bidding him farewell, Philip came to Cassandra's side. Smiling, he slid his arm around her shoulders, pulling her up against him. "I thought that went rather well, didn't you?"

"Philip, I feel guilty about deceiving your mother—"

"Deceiving? In what way? We are engaged."

"Not really. You never asked me. You just said that to appease Aunt Ardis."

"Cassandra, I thought we had gone through all this before. I have intended to marry you from the moment we went down to the gazebo that night.''

''You have?''

''But of course. I knew what it would do to your reputation if it got out. What the consequences would be. When we left the garden, I knew I would offer for your hand.''

But what about love? Cassandra wanted to cry out, but of course she did not. She refused to press him for something that was worthwhile only if given freely.

''But it's not necessary,'' she said instead. ''I knew what I was doing. I went into it freely.''

''So did I.'' He looked down into Cassandra's face, frowning. ''Do you— Are you saying that you don't want to marry me?''

Cassandra supposed that she ought to lie and tell him that she did not. But she could not bring herself to say it. ''No,'' she replied softly. ''I do not mean that.''

''Good.'' He bent and kissed her on the temple, murmuring, ''One thing, my love, do not let my mother persuade you to name a wedding date very far away. I want to be married as soon as possible.''

She looked up into his gleaming eyes, and an answering heat started up in her loins. Perhaps she was wrong to marry him, knowing that Philip did not love her, but she knew that she was not strong enough to resist. She would marry him, hoping that she could bring him to love her, hoping that he would not regret it.

They set out the following morning on foot, Cassandra and Philip and their four siblings, map in hand and leading a pony cart carrying several digging tools. Cassandra had drawn a new copy of the combined maps, which Philip carried now in his shirt pocket. She wore her oldest dress, as did Georgette and Olivia, and Philip had put on the sort of rough trousers and collarless shirt that the local farmers wore. Cassandra wondered what it was about the attire that made all her nerve endings come alive just looking at him. She had never had a similar reaction to any farmer she had met. But it did something to the pit of her stomach to see his bare forearms beneath the rolled-up sleeves and the V of chest that showed at the neck.

"There is Littlejohn Creek." He gestured toward the brook in the distance.

"It looks much closer on the map," his sister put in doubtfully.

"I don't think Margaret Verrere drew the maps to scale," he told her lightly. "But she put in the distances. That should make it much easier."

The copse of trees was not where it was supposed to be, and they decided that it must have been felled by man or disease since the map was drawn. They continued along the road, but after some time they still had not found the large stone beside the road that was the last mark before the peat-cutter's hut.

"Could the stone have been removed since then, too?" Cassandra asked worriedly.

"I don't know. I don't recall anything like that beside the road." Philip frowned, shading his eyes with his hand to peer into the distance. "No sign of an old hut, either."

"Don't you think there would be ruins of both it and the wall? Perhaps we should strike out fifteen paces to the side of the road and search up and down until we come to the ruins."

"We may have to."

After a few more minutes of fruitless walking, they stopped again. "I don't think it could be farther than this," Philip said flatly. "She would have put some more landmarks in, like that huge old oak tree over there." Philip pointed across the road.

"Why don't we do what Cassandra suggested?" Georgette interjected.

Philip nodded. "All right. Fifteen paces is a little vague, but we can spread out in a line and make a sweep down. One of us ought to stumble across the ruins."

Philip paced out fifteen long steps, and the other five spread out on either side of him, a few feet apart. Philip led the pony, with its trailing cart, over the rough terrain. They began walking slowly back the way they had come, keeping on a line with the road. As they walked, their eyes searched the ground, looking for any sign of a former hut or stone wall.

The walk seemed endless. Cassandra's neck began to hurt from looking down at the ground, searching for signs of the hut, and a throbbing ache was growing behind her eyes. She was tired, thirsty and hungry, and she knew that if she felt that way, the younger ones were probably doubly so.

"Let's stop and rest. Eat the lunch that Henri sent."

Philip nodded his agreement, and they sat down together in a clump of trees and devoured the lunch. Afterward, they leaned back against the trunks of the trees and rested. The twins even dozed off.

Rejuvenated, they got up and began their tedious search again. Hart found a circle of rocks, and they got excited, but it turned out to be only the traces of an old campfire. On and on they plodded until finally they could see the steeple of Saint Swithin's rising above the trees in front of them.

"We're back to the church!" Olivia cried out in disappointment.

Philip nodded. "Nearly. I fear that we have missed it somehow."

They sat down again and tried to regroup.

"What happened to it?" Olivia cried out in frustration. "How could the place just disappear?"

"It has been a long time," Cassandra reminded her. "If the hut was wood and thatch, it could have rotted away or been taken for lumber."

The twins were sunk in gloom.

"We'll never find it, will we?" Crispin asked, and Cassandra could tell that he was doing his best not to cry.

"We'll try again," Philip promised. "Maybe we're looking at the map wrong somehow. Cassandra and I will go over it again tonight. And tomorrow I will go talk to Jack Everson. He and his father before him lived in that house we saw on the other side of the road. I'll see if he remembers anyone ever mentioning a peat-cutter's cottage on the other side of the road."

"But unless we can find those landmarks," Crispin persisted, "we have no hope of finding the treasure, have we?"

"I don't see how," Philip admitted.

It was a sad group that straggled back to Haverly House.

Cassandra sat in front of the mirror at her vanity, listlessly brushing out her hair. She felt bone weary. Even the long, hot bath she had taken when she got home had not done away with the soreness in her muscles from the day of hiking. Worse than that was the tiredness in her mind—no, she reconsidered, the tiredness was in her very soul. She had been chasing the Spanish dowry for years, all her life it seemed, and her father before her. For the past year, since she had read the diaries, finding the treasure had been her primary goal. It had become not only a means of reestablishing the family fortunes but a way of vindicating her father, and even the long-dead Margaret Verrere, as well.

Now, it appeared, they would not find it. It seemed the final bitter irony to have proved that her father had been right about the existence of the treasure, yet the treasure was still lost.

She laid her forehead on her crossed arms on the vanity top, hot tears seeping from her eyes. She felt as though she had let everyone down: her brothers and sister, her father, even Margaret Verrere and a long string of ancestors. *What was her family to do?* True, they no longer had to worry about living on Aunt Ardis's charity. Philip would take in her siblings, and she knew he would be generous. Still, it would chafe them, especially Crispin, to be living on anyone's charity, even Philip's, and they could hardly expect Philip to go to the huge expense of putting Chesilworth in order.

Something parted her hair in back, and warm, velvety lips brushed across the nape of her neck. A shiver ran down through her. "Philip…" she breathed, suddenly revived, and raised her head. She looked up at his reflection in the mirror and smiled. "How did you get in?"

"The usual way—the door." He was standing behind her, dressed in only trousers and a shirt. He gazed back at her in the mirror. "Brooding?"

"A little." Cassandra nodded.

"Try not to worry. We will do our best to find it. And if we cannot, you must know that I will take care of your brothers and sister. Olivia shall have her coming out and dowry. The boys will go to Eton. Chesilworth will be restored to its former glory. I will make it my special project."

Tears welled in Cassandra's eyes. "You are too kind. But I don't want my family to be a burden to you."

"They are no burden. And I do not want you worry about them. From now on, you are only to worry about getting ready for our wedding."

Cassandra smiled tremulously. She hated to admit how eager she was to think about only that. "Your mother wants a grand wedding."

"I know." He caressed her hair, admiring the shimmer of light on the pale strands. "I told her she can have as grand a wedding as she wants, as long as it happens no longer than a month from now."

"A month! But, Philip, you cannot plan a grand wedding in only a month. Why, there would barely be time to get out invitations."

"Believe me, Mother trotted out all the arguments." Philip lightly trailed his fingertips down the sides of her neck, watching in the mirror. There was something fascinating in watching his movements and Cassandra's reactions in the mirror, almost as if he stood apart from them and observed, both feeling what he did and seeing it as a stranger.

"She said that anything less than six months was simply absurd and, moreover, would give rise to all sorts of speculation and salacious rumors," Philip continued. "I told her, not as many rumors as would be caused by the infelicitously early arrival of a babe three or four months after we were married."

"Philip! You didn't!"

"I did." His hands moved down to caress her shoulders and upper arms, then spread out across her chest. "There is no hope that I could wait six months to have you in my bed again. Why, look at me. Three nights since my vow not to come to your bedchamber, and here I am, sneaking down the hall to your room."

He grasped her shoulders and pulled her up unresistingly. Moving close behind her, he slid his arms around her waist and bent to kiss her shoulder. "You are so beautiful," he breathed. "I cannot stay away from you. It seems as if all I can think about is you. All day I look at you and imagine you unclothed."

He slid his hands up and down her bare arms, then moved to cup her breasts through the cloth of her chemise. He stared, heavy-lidded, at their reflection, and Cassandra did, too, leaning back against him and going limp at the exquisite sensations pouring through her. Her chemise was thin, and the dark circles of her nipples were visible through the cloth. As he gently kneaded and caressed them, the nipples hardened visibly, thrusting against the material.

Letting out a sound that was half sigh, half groan, he nuzzled into her neck, his hands roaming over her body hungrily. He breathed her name as Cassandra turned in his arms, pressing herself into him. They kissed, slowly working their way across the room to the bed, stripping off articles of clothing and letting them drop where they were. Philip lifted Cassandra into the bed and lay down beside her. They made love tenderly at first, their desire growing more and more fierce as they went, until finally they could wait no longer, and he thrust deeply into her. Trembling under the force of their emotions, they rode out their passion, climaxing finally in a burst of raw pleasure.

Collapsing onto the bed, Philip wrapped his arms around Cassandra, holding her close against him. Their eyes drifted closed and, exhausted, they slept.

It was a few hours later, in the dead of the night, that the coolness of the air on Philip's skin awakened him. He opened his eyes slowly, pulled up out of a panicky dream in which he kept running from windmill to windmill, searching desperately for Cassandra. He wrapped his arms a little more tightly around her to reassure himself that she was safely here in his arms. Then he blinked, his mind clearing.

Suddenly he sat up. "Oh, my God! That's it. Cassandra, wake up. I figured it out!"

21

Cassandra opened her eyes sleepily. "What? What are you talking about?"

"I know why we couldn't find the treasure. It's because of the fens! They were drained after Margaret Verrere left England. At that time there were big areas of marshland that are now viable pasture. Don't you see?"

"Of course!" Cassandra sat up excitedly, her mind clearing. "It must have changed the landscape drastically. Remember how the creek seemed closer on the map?"

"And I just shrugged it off as poor map drawing. But we might have been looking in entirely the wrong place."

"How can we find out what the landscape used to look like?"

Philip was already out of bed, pulling back on his clothes, and Cassandra quickly jumped out and followed suit. "The library. There must be old histories of the area that might have a map. Or maybe some sort of record of how the draining of the fens changed the landscape. If worse comes to worst, we'll have to go back to Aunt Liliane and ask if she remembers people talking about where things were before the fens were drained."

Philip lit a candle, and Cassandra opened the door to

peer out into the hall. Seeing no one, she stepped out, gesturing for Philip to follow her. They glided softly along the hall to the back stairs and down to the library. There they closed the door, lit the lamps and began to search.

Cassandra vaguely remembered having seen an old book that appeared to be a vicar's reminiscences of life in the parish in the middle seventeenth century, so she looked for it on the second floor of the library. Philip went to a section of shelves that contained several histories. They worked steadily away for some time before Cassandra found the vicar's recollections she had remembered and pulled the book out, calling to Philip.

Unfortunately, when they looked through it, they found no map anywhere in it. Philip set it aside. "Don't put it back up. Perhaps if we read through it, it will describe the area around Saint Swithin's so that we can reconstruct the way it must have looked. But, first, let's look for a map."

Philip found a history of the shire, but it was written after the draining of the fens, and the only map in it showed the area in its present state. They continued to look, even though their initial excitement was wearing off into sleepiness. The room was turning light with the dawn when Cassandra pulled out a narrow black book that she had almost missed at the end of one shelf.

"'A True Account,'" she read, "'of the Draining of'— Philip! This book is about draining the fens." She opened it as he strode quickly over toward her. "Look! A map! A map of the area before it was drained. There are three of them, of different parts. See?"

"Yes. There's Saint Swithin's. And the road. But look." His forefinger jabbed at a large shaded area on the left side the map. "That is a fen. That's where we were today. That couldn't have been the road Margaret drew on the map. This road makes a big bulge around the fen."

Cassandra nodded. "No doubt, once the fen was drained, the way we went today was much closer, so the road shifted over here. We were on the wrong road entirely." She glanced up at Philip, frowning. "Do you think that this old road still exists?"

"There might be traces of it. It's probably overgrown, but we might be able to follow it to the wall and the peat-cutter's hut." He grinned at her, excitement effectively chasing away his weariness. "Well? Do you want to try?"

"Now?"

"It's light outside."

"All right. I'll get my bonnet." She turned and looked back at him. "Should we wake the children?"

Philip hesitated, then shook his head. "No. I'm afraid of getting them excited and then disappointing them again. We may not be able to locate it, you know."

Cassandra nodded her agreement and hurried away on tiptoe to get her bonnet. They stopped in the kitchen to grab a quick breakfast, startling the servants, then went down to the bottom of the garden, where Philip pulled a shovel out of the gardener's shed. He propped it on his shoulder, and they set out once again for Saint Swithin's.

This time, when they reached the church, they did not follow the existing road but walked along in the general direction in which the old road was drawn. Soon, a little to their surprise, they found themselves on a narrow trail.

"Do you think this is it?"

"It corresponds to the map. Look, the creek is much closer now. I suppose people continued to walk along here, and it didn't become completely overgrown."

There were places, they found out as they moved on, where the path did disappear for a time, but if they continued to walk in the right direction, after a while the trail would reappear.

"There's the copse of trees!" Cassandra pointed out, her voice rising. "Oh, Philip, we really are on the right trail."

They reached the stone landmark beside the road and launched in search of the peat-cutter's hut. At first they walked past the remains of the hut, but on their second sweep they found it. There was little left except a rectangle of tumbled rocks, hidden by weeds and shrubs.

Cassandra and Philip looked at each other. Her heart was pounding in her chest. They were only five paces away from the dowry's hiding place. Cassandra drew in a deep breath. She was scared. *What if they failed again?* Philip raised his eyebrows in inquiry. She nodded.

He turned back around and looked down at the jumble of rocks. "It's hard to tell exactly where the corner was. It would be quite easy to go a little off."

He positioned himself in what he hoped was the right direction and walked away from the corner. When he reached five paces, he stopped and began to dig. After a while, he had a hole, but no sign of a small casket. He began to dig out in a straight line on either side of the hole, creating a narrow trench. By the time the sun was climbing toward the center of the sky, he had dug a trench three feet to one side of the hole. He moved back and began to dig in the opposite direction.

Within minutes, his shovel clunked into a hard object.

Philip looked up at Cassandra. She moved closer, nerves leaping in her stomach. "Do you think that's it?"

"It could be almost anything." Carefully he began to dig away around the object, finally getting down and brushing aside the earth with his hands. Cassandra joined him, heedless of her dress and hands. The rounded metal top of a box appeared. They dug away from its sides, and began to rock and pull. Finally, as they tugged, it popped free, startling them. Philip pulled it the rest of the way up and set it on the ground beside the hole.

They looked at it for a moment, breathing hard from their exertions. It was a heavy box, despite the fact that it was only a foot and a half long and two-thirds as wide. It resembled a miniature humpbacked trunk, with little ornamentation and a hasp close secured by a heavy lock. It had held up well through the years.

Philip brought the shovel down hard on the lock several times until the lock broke and fell off. Scarcely breathing, Cassandra knelt beside him in front of the casket. Her heart was pounding. Philip gestured toward the little trunk.

"Go ahead. It is your chest, after all."

Cassandra drew a long breath and pushed the lid up. It fell back, revealing a box full of little velvet bags and stacks of coins. On the top lay a large object swaddled in velvet. Philip reached in curiously and took out one of the bags and spilled out its contents into his hand. Several large uncut jewels fell into his palm, including sapphires, rubies and a very large uncut emerald. Another small bag revealed several jewels of antique cut and setting.

"These are worth far more than they were at that time," he commented. He poked in the box beneath the bags. "Loose gold coins on the bottom, I believe. Yes, a tidy sum for our Lord Chesilworth." He paused, then added, "Aren't you going to unwrap that?" He nodded toward the large object.

"I'm scared," Cassandra admitted. "I have imagined the gold leopard for so many years that I'm a little afraid to see what it really looks like."

But she reached out her hands and picked up the heavy object. She set it in her lap and carefully unwrapped it. As the velvet fell away, a large gold leopard was revealed. It gleamed in the sun, an object of expert craftsmanship, each spot an indentation, its crouched stance so real that it seemed about to spring. Around its neck was a collar of small rubies. Its eyes were brilliant dark emeralds.

Cassandra could do no more than stare for a moment. It was so beautiful, so expertly wrought, that it quite took away her power of speech. "Philip..." she breathed at last, stroking a hand along its back, almost as if it were a real cat. "It's beautiful. Have you ever seen anything like it?"

Before he could answer, a voice behind them said cheerfully. "*I* certainly have not."

They swung around, Cassandra instinctively cradling the leopard to her chest. Standing several feet away from them was Mr. Simons. He was smiling, looking as jolly and avuncular as ever. The only thing that spoiled the image was the rather large shotgun in his hands, which he held pointed directly at Cassandra.

"Mr. Simons!" Cassandra stared, slack jawed.

"It was you, then?" Philip asked, his eyes hard and dark. "All this time? The break-ins? Everything?"

"My, yes. As soon as Mr. Miller brought those diaries to me, I could see the possibilities. If anyone could find the maps and the treasure, I knew it was Miss Verrere. She was always a sharp one, a better mind, really, than her father, even. When she dealt with me for a book, I rarely got much profit out of it." He seemed quite happy to talk, rather proud of his actions. "At first I couldn't bear to wait for her to find it. I was too greedy. I sent someone to get the maps, but I quickly realized how futile that was. Far better to let the two of you locate the maps for me."

"And, of course," Cassandra said disgustedly, "we played right into your hands by inquiring about the prayer book."

"My yes. I had not seen it before, but it wasn't hard for me to find out who had bought it from Sir Richard and where it had wound up." He pulled the small prayer book from his coat pocket and held it up, almost as if he expected to be applauded for his cleverness.

"So you stalled us by sending us to places you knew it would not be while you searched for it—and had your man break in to steal the map we had."

"Yes." He sighed and repocketed the book. "Unfortunately, I could not seem to get either map. When I got the book and there was no map, I knew that you must have retrieved it from Bigby. Well, I had no choice but to follow and see what you came up with. I must tell you, I was quite disappointed by the results yesterday. All that tramping about fair wore my man out, having to hide as he did. That's why I set about watching your house today. Thank God I did."

"What about David Miller? Was he in on it? Your partner?"

Simons laughed, and Cassandra wondered why she had never noticed before that there was an ugly undertone to his laughter. "That innocent? Heavens, no. Of course, it was rather handy when he showed up again and wanted to visit you. I heard a good deal of useful gossip from him after he returned to London. But help me pull off such a scheme? Not likely. He would be shocked, I assure you."

Cassandra shot Philip a triumphant look. "I told you he was not the sort to steal the dowry."

"Since you also told me that Mr. Simons was not the sort, I can hardly give you much credit for prescience," Philip replied sourly.

"Now, now, children, that's enough. Time to end the chitchat. Miss Verrere, please be so good as to bring that lovely objet d'art over here to me. Remember, I will have the gun on Miss Verrere the entire time, so please don't try anything foolish, Sir Philip."

"I won't." Philip's voice was grim.

Cassandra rose slowly, cradling the heavy statue in the crook of her arm. She started toward him, walking deliberately. He held his gun on her the whole time. As she grew close to him, she tripped and stumbled forward, flinging out her arms. The elegant golden leopard went tumbling to the ground. Instinctively Simons reached for the falling statue, his shotgun lowering. Philip, who had been watching closely, certain that Cassandra would not meekly hand over the fortune she considered her family's, leapt forward and grabbed the gun.

The two men wrestled over it. Cassandra rolled out of the way and rose lithely to her feet. She glanced around for the leopard, thinking to pick it up and bash Simons over the head with it, but the two men were struggling right over it. It did not matter, anyway, for at that instant Philip wrested the gun away from Simons and tossed it away. Simons started after it, but Philip grabbed his arm and whirled him back around, sending a fist crashing into the other man's chin. The rotund little man was no match for Philip's strength, and in a few more moments he was facedown on the ground, with Philip's knee planted in the small of his back and his arms crossed behind him.

Cassandra quickly tore off the sash of her dress and tied it around Simons's wrists. He moaned and fussed that she was tying it too tightly, but Cassandra merely let out an unsympathetic grunt. She reached into the pocket of his coat and pulled out the prayer book.

"This belongs to Mr. Bigby, I believe."

They made an odd little group, walking back down the track to the church and then to Haverly House. Mr. Simons walked in front, his hands secured behind his back, and Cassandra marched a few feet behind him, shotgun trained on him. Philip brought up the rear of the procession, carrying the small casket of treasures on his shoulder. They passed a farmer on the road between the church and Haverly House, and he stared at them oddly but only tugged at his cap and offered them a good day.

When they reached Philip's house, he turned both the gun and their prisoner over to his gamekeeper, instructing him to deliver Simons to the constable in the village and to assure the man that Sir Philip would be down shortly to inform him of the crime that had been committed.

With that responsibility taken care of, he and Cassandra walked into the house and up the stairs to the nursery. They found the twins and the two girls there, all looking rather glum. All four of the youngsters looked up at Cassandra and Philip, goggling at their dirty and tousled appearance.

Philip marched solemnly over to the window seat, where Crispin sat. The other three instinctively moved closer. He set the chest down in front of the window seat and with a grand gesture flung open its top, revealing the glittering leopard recumbent on the bags of jewels and coins. "Lord Chesilworth—the Spanish Dowry."

The rest of the day was spent in celebration: showing off the contents of the box to the other residents of the house, retelling their story time and again, laughing and talking, dreaming with the twins and Olivia about what they would do with the money. True to his word, Philip had given the Verreres the entire contents of the strongbox. When Cassandra protested that half of it was his, earned by his efforts many times over, he had simply shaken his head and smiled, saying, "No. 'Twas your scheme from the very start. I would not even believe you at first. If it had not been for you and your persistence, that box would have lain in the ground forever, unless some lucky farmer

happened to plow it up one day. Besides, it was the Verreres' treasure to begin with. Margaret did not marry a
Neville, and I cannot see that the Nevilles have any claim
on it.''

"Margaret wanted it divided between the two families.''

"Margaret wanted the rift healed between the two families," he corrected. "She thought that the only way to do
it was to split the treasure. But you and I will heal the rift
by marrying. The money is unnecessary.''

"You are a kind and generous man," she told him, going up on tiptoe to kiss his cheek.

He smiled, placing a hand on her back to keep her close.
"I am glad you think so. I fear that when you are Lady
Neville, you will cease such accolades.''

Cassandra felt a warmth stir deep inside her in response
to the gleam in his eyes as he gazed down into her face.
"Indeed? Do you intend to be such an ogre of a husband
that I shall stop thinking you are kind?''

"Not an ogre." His grin broadened, and he leaned
closer by degrees, whispering, "Just very demanding.''
His lips brushed hers, leaving no mistake as to his meaning.

"Philip!" Cassandra put her hands between them, flat
against his chest. "Your mother could come in at any moment." They were in the sitting room downstairs, unexpectedly alone for the time being.

"Then she would be shocked." He kissed her again,
more lingeringly. "However, I think she already suspects
that I cannot keep my hands off you.''

Cassandra could not deny a thrill of pleasure at his
words. Philip was quite open about his desire for her, and
his passion both stirred and pleased her. However, she
could not help wishing that his desire had a basis in love.
Passion, she suspected, could easily die, probably would,

in fact, and then what would be left between them? *Would Philip resent her then? Would he wish that he had never married her?* Cassandra did not think that she could bear it if Philip turned away from her. She was falling more and more in love with him by the hour.

She had not told him, of course, except once or twice, when he had fallen asleep. She was scared to say it to him, afraid that he would think she was pushing him, trying to coerce him into responding that he loved her, too—but even more afraid that he would not say the words in return.

The lack of Philip's love was not the only worry that niggled at her that day. After all the initial excitement had died down and the treasure had been stored away in the study safe, after Philip had set off for the village to inform the constable about Simons's wrongdoing, Cassandra had begun to reflect on the events of the past few weeks. One thing kept recurring: it made no sense for Simons to have had her locked her in the windmill.

She simply could not see how hurting or killing her or even delaying them for several days could have helped Mr. Simons. Until she and Philip came to London and told him about the book they were searching for, he had had no idea where the second map was. Delaying their search in that way would have gained him nothing. Besides, there was the fact that had made her suspect Philip of having locked her in there—the note had told her to meet Philip at the abbey. *How would Mr. Simons, who had never even been around them, have known that their favorite destination on their rides was the ruined abbey?* It made no sense, and things that didn't make sense bothered Cassandra.

Like a tongue to a sore tooth, Cassandra's thoughts kept returning to the illogical attack on her. It bothered her so much, in fact, that the next morning she set out for the village herself, heading straight for the jail. It took a little persuading, but finally she cajoled the constable into letting her see their criminal.

"Ah, Miss Verrere," Mr. Simons said, smiling just as if they were meeting on the street or in his shop. "It's a pleasure to see you."

"Mr. Simons." She stood for a moment, looking through the bars at him, wondering how to begin.

In the end, it was he who started the conversation. "I trust you realize, my dear, that it was never my intention to harm you."

Cassandra looked at him in some astonishment. *Apparently, he had forgotten the fact that he had held a shotgun aimed at her the day before.*

"I have always been fond of you," he was saying. "And your father, too." He sighed. "It was greed that was my downfall, of course. Once I had read about the dowry, I simply had to see it, possess it. I hope you will forgive me."

"I hope I will, too," she replied levelly. "But at the moment my feelings are a trifle too fresh." She paused, then continued, "If you did not intend to harm me, then why did you have me locked up in the windmill?"

The older man stared at her blankly. "I beg your pardon? The windmill? My dear Miss Verrere, I have no idea what you are talking about."

"I'm talking about the fact that you had someone knock me over the head, drag me into the windmill and lock me in. It was sheer happenstance that anyone found me."

The book dealer looked at her in dismay. "But my dear…how could you possible think that I had anything to do with that?"

"You seem to be the only possibility," she replied bluntly.

He continued to gape at her, unable to come up with any sort of argument. It was his stymied look that convinced her more than anything. He was very good at creating trust where it was not deserved, of course. In proof of that, she had his seeming kindness toward her when all the while he was plotting behind her back to steal the Verrere treasure. Still, she could not believe that his astonishment was feigned. It seemed to her that he knew nothing about the windmill incident.

Her mind buzzed all the way back to Haverly House. *If Mr. Simons had not locked her into the windmill, who had? And why?*

Surely Joanna or Aunt Ardis could not have been so jealous, so afraid of her spending time with Philip, that they would have hatched up this scheme to stick her out of sight for a while. Greedy they might be, and definitely foolish, but Cassandra did not want to believe that either of them was wicked enough to have done that to her.

She came up to the house through the side garden, so deep in thought that she was almost upon Sarah Yorke before she saw the woman walking toward her through the garden.

"Miss Verrere!" Sarah cried in delight and hurried forward. "I had just called at the house and was so disappointed to find that you were not there. I had been hoping to talk to you."

"Really?" Cassandra did not feel like talking to Sarah or, indeed, anyone, right now, but she tried to put a good face on it. She did, after all, like the woman.

"Yes. I—" Sarah glanced around, almost as if she were looking for something. "Why don't we take a walk? Would you care to stroll through the garden?"

Cassandra sighed inwardly, but said only, "Of course, if you would like."

"Yes, I think that sounds like an excellent idea."

They turned and started across the garden, moving past the fragrant roses and down into the lower part of the garden.

"What did you want to talk about?" Cassandra prompted when the other woman did not say anything more.

"What?" Sarah glanced at her blankly.

"You said that you had hoped to talk to me. I thought you meant that there was something in particular..."

"Oh! Oh, no, nothing in particular. That is, I was hoping, you know, that we might have a chance to chat, to— to get to know one another better."

It struck Cassandra that Miss Yorke was acting in a most peculiar manner. Her speech was vague, and she kept darting looks around her, as if she were hoping to see—or avoid—something. She seemed unusually nervous, and Cassandra thought that her eyes had a rather odd, wild look to them.

"Miss Yorke...is something the matter? Something that I can help you with?"

"Help me!" Sarah whirled on her, her eyes flashing, and Cassandra took a step backward. "Help me! How can you say that?"

Cassandra stared at her, puzzled and rather alarmed by the young woman's odd demeanor. She didn't know what to do, but she was aware suddenly that she did not want to walk any farther away from the house with the woman.

"Why don't we turn back?" Cassandra suggested, starting to follow her words with action.

"No!" Sarah grew even more agitated. "No! We can't go back. It's too late!"

Suddenly everything fell into place in Cassandra's mind. "Sweet Lord in Heaven!" Cassandra breathed. "It was you, wasn't it? You were the one who locked me in the windmill!''

"Yes! Yes!'' Sarah hissed, and, taking Cassandra completely by surprise, she stuck her hand into her reticule and pulled out a pistol. She pointed it straight at Cassandra.

It occurred to Cassandra that she was growing quite tired of having guns pointed at her. "Miss Yorke, please, why don't you put that thing away, and we can talk? There is no need to tell everyone that you were responsible for the windmill incident. I am sure you regret it.''

"I didn't want to hurt you,'' Sarah agreed earnestly. "I liked you. I truly did.'' She waved the pistol at Cassandra, motioning her forward. "But we have to walk. You have to walk.''

The pistol in Sarah's shaking fingers made Cassandra exceedingly nervous, so she did as the woman asked, starting once more down the path.

"You have to turn down there and go out to the trees,'' Sarah instructed, once again motioning with the firearm.

"Of course, if that is what you want.'' Cassandra strolled along as slowly and as calmly as she could. The last thing she wanted to do was to set Sarah off. She needed time to try to figure out how she was going to get out of this nightmare. "But, you know, it really would be more comfortable to talk in the house. We could have a cool drink. That would be nice, wouldn't it?''

"Don't condescend to me,'' Miss Yorke snapped.

"No, I would never…''

"Yes, you would, you all would—although you seemed better than the others. Like that cousin of yours, Miss Moulton.'' She made a noise of disgust. "I thought it was she whom he liked when you first arrived here. She was so pretty, and she hung on his arm, as if he were her property.'' Jealousy dripped from every word. "She looked at me as if I were nothing, a worm, not even worthy of her notice. I knew she would take him away from me."

"Joanna is like that," Cassandra admitted. "However, she is like that to everyone. She thinks herself so beautiful that everyone else should fall down in admiration."

Sarah let out a small, twisted smile. "She fell all right. I thought if I pushed her in, she would get scared. That she would go back where she came from. It didn't hurt her. She wouldn't even have gotten so wet if she hadn't floundered about. But then she just got him to carry her out of the water, and she leaned against him so brazenly and flaunted her body in those wet clothes, and I thought that I had just made it worse."

She paused as they reached a path leading away from the garden and into the more untamed reaches of the estate. Cassandra was reluctant to go, but Sarah motioned impatiently with the gun, and Cassandra started along the path.

"Then I saw that I had been all wrong. It was stupid of me, really. I should have know that Philip could not be interested in a vain, feather-headed chit like that. Whenever I was there, I could see that he avoided her. But he was spending all his time with you!" She glared over at Cassandra.

"We were working on something together," Cassandra tried to explain. "It wasn't preference for my company, it was just the project. We were trying to find the Spanish Dowry, you see."

"Stop it! Just stop it! Do you think I'm feebleminded? Of course, it was a preference for you. *He is marrying you!*"

Cassandra realized that Miss Yorke had a point. There was little possibility of convincing this jealous woman that Philip did not care for her when he had proposed marriage to her. She decided to keep her mouth shut on the subject and hope that Sarah would move on to something else more easily dealt with.

"I didn't want to hurt you," Sarah rambled on. "I *liked* you. You seemed much nicer and more intelligent than other young ladies of quality. You took an interest in Silverwood, too. The boys liked you."

"Thank you. I like them, as well. And I like you, Sarah. Don't you think that we could be friends?"

"Friends! How can we be friends? You have everything I want. I can't stand by and watch you marry him!" They walked a little farther, and Sarah said again, "I didn't want to hurt you. I didn't mean to. I knew that they would find you at the windmill in a little while. If they hadn't, I would have come and let you out. I just wanted you to get scared, to decide to leave Haverly House. Why couldn't you simply have left? Then we would never have had to come to this point."

"We still don't have to come to it," Cassandra soothed.

"Yes! Yes! You wouldn't leave. You wouldn't leave, and now the only thing to do is to stop you from marrying him."

Cassandra didn't want to ask how Miss Yorke planned to stop her. "You know, Miss Yorke, just because you get rid of me, it doesn't mean that you will have Philip to yourself."

"But I would! He would have turned to me sooner or later, I know he would. He would have come to see that I loved him more than anyone else possibly could. He was so good to me, so kind to give me the position at Silverwood. I know it must have indicated some degree of affection on his part. Don't you see?"

"Yes. I am sure that Sir Philip is very fond of you. But he won't be if you—if you—" She balked at the words.

"He won't know!" Sarah crowed. "That is the beauty of it. It will look like an accident. No one will ever know."

"Of course they will. Someone is bound to have seen us from a window of the house. They will know that we left together, that you were the last person to see me."

"Shut up! Shut up!" Sarah shrieked, and Cassandra wisely did not say anything. It was obvious that the woman's control was hanging by a thread.

They continued walking, but they did not say much now. Cassandra hoped that someone had indeed seen them from the window, but it would be sheer happenstance. She could not count on it. And even if someone had seen them, they would think nothing of it, just that the two of them were going for a walk.

"There!" Excitement filled Sarah's voice, and Cassandra glanced around for whatever object had occasioned it.

She saw nothing except a stand of trees and, off to one side, a well. Sarah motioned her toward the well.

"Over there. Go stand over there."

Cassandra did as she said. She understood now how Sarah intended her death to look like an accident. She would somehow force her down the old well, and people would assume that she had fallen in by accident. Although... She looked at the well as she came to a halt beside it.

"Sarah, this is not going to work," she began reasonably. "This well is covered, and it stands almost waist high. It would be very difficult to fall into it accidentally."

"It *will* work," Sarah insisted obstinately. "You take off the cover."

"No." Cassandra faced her calmly, crossing her arms across her chest.

"What? You have to. I'll shoot you!" Sarah waved the gun for emphasis.

"Go ahead. However, you can rest assured that if I am shot, no one will think it was an accident. Everyone will know that I was murdered. I can also guarantee that Philip will find out who did it. He won't rest until he knows who murdered the woman he was about to marry. *The woman he loves.*" She spoke each word separately and loudly, pushing them into Sarah's face. She wanted to make the other woman mad, wanted to put her in such a rage that she would do something foolish.

"Stop it!" Sarah came forward a few steps, her entire body rigid with rage. "Don't say that. It's not true!"

"Why else would he be marrying me?" Cassandra asked. "Everyone knows that the Verreres have no money. Only love would bring him to marry me. And when Philip loves, he is unshakable. You know that. He loves me, and he will always love me. *Only* me. No matter what you do, you can never make him love you."

Sarah came closer, her eyes wide and furious, her hands shaking so badly that Cassandra was afraid she would set the gun off accidentally. Cassandra swallowed, hoping that she would not push the woman so far that Sarah simply dropped her with a shot. Taking her courage in her hands, she added, "When he finds out that you are the one who killed me—as he will surely do—he will hate you forever. Go ahead, Sarah, shoot me. See how long it will be before Philip knows all about you—and despises you forever."

Sarah snapped. With a wild shriek, she rushed at Cassandra, raising her hand to bring down the pistol on Cassandra's head. Cassandra ducked and lunged forward, hitting Sarah in the chest and knocking her backward. They staggered back, then forward, swinging and kicking and fighting for purchase. Cassandra dug her fingers into the other woman's arm and hung on, struggling desperately to keep her from bringing the pistol down and firing it. The gun went off, the noise reverberating in the air, but the bullet went harmlessly upward.

Cassandra was bigger than Sarah, but the other woman was more muscular from years of having to physically deal with rambunctious young boys, as well as cooking pots and desks and chairs—and she seemed possessed of an almost superhuman strength. Cassandra could understand now how Sarah had been able to haul Cassandra's unconscious body onto a horse and then into the windmill.

Cassandra stumbled back, catching her heel on her skirt and falling heavily against the wall of the well. Pain slammed through her back, stunning her, and for an instant she felt herself weakening, as though she might pass out. Sarah raised the pistol high and slammed it down. Cassandra was able to turn her head only a fraction of an inch, evading it, and the handle slammed into the well. Sarah let out a cry of frustration and dropped the pistol. She grabbed Cassandra tightly around the neck and began to squeeze. Cassandra struggled against her, already weakened by the blow to her back. She could not get any air. She clawed in vain at the other woman's hands.

Suddenly there were noises, a voice shouting, and in the next instant Philip ran up behind Sarah, his face contorted with fear and anger. Clasping his hands together, he swung them down hard on the back of Sarah's head. Her hands loosened around Cassandra's neck, and she swayed on her feet.

Philip slammed his clenched fists down again, and Sarah crumpled to the ground.

He shoved her aside impatiently, grabbing Cassandra and pulling her into his arms. "Cassandra! Oh, God, don't tell me I'm too late. Cassandra, please, say something, look at me."

He wrapped his arms around her, rocking, babbling frantically. "My love, my love, please don't die. You can't leave me. Damn it, Cassandra, say something." Cassandra could hear the tears in his voice.

She made a croaking noise. He peered down into her face. "What? Are you all right?"

Cassandra nodded. "I think so." Her voice came out in a whisper.

"Thank God!" He clutched her to him again. "I was so worried. I saw you talking to Sarah, and there was something odd about it, so I stopped and watched, but I still couldn't understand what troubled me. Then, as you were walking out of the garden, I saw her wave the gun. I've never been so scared in my life. I thought I couldn't get out of the house and across to you in time."

He rained kisses all over her face and head, telling her again and again how glad he was. "Why did she do it, Cassandra? Why did Sarah attack you?"

"Because she was in love with you." Cassandra smiled up at him, feeling better by leaps and bounds.

"In love with me!" he repeated in astonishment. "But how—I never—"

"I know. It hurts to love and not be loved in return."

He nodded, cuddling her to him. "But how could she think— I could never love her. You are the only woman I love. The only woman I could ever love."

A thrill ran through Cassandra, so hard and sizzling that she thought she would have collapsed had Philip not been holding her up. "Do you?" she asked, gazing up at him. "Do you love me?"

He looked astounded. "Of course I do. Why do you think I asked you to marry me?"

"Because Aunt Ardis found us in a compromising position."

Philip snorted. "As if I cared for that. I was already

determined to marry you. You know that. I knew I loved you when I took you down to the gazebo. We would not have gone, else.''

Cassandra swallowed. ''Oh, Philip!'' She flung her arms around his neck. ''I love you, too.''

''It's about time you admitted it. I was beginning to think I would have to wait until we were married to hear you say so.''

He bent and kissed her.

''Well, I promise you that you won't have to wait again to hear it.'' Cassandra threw her arms around his neck. ''In fact, I fully intend to say it at least ten times a day. I love you.'' She punctuated the words with a kiss. ''I love you. I love you.''

Philip laughed and wrapped his arms around her. With a contented sigh, Cassandra melted against him. She realized that now she had truly found the treasure she had been seeking.

Epilogue

～⌢⌣⌢○⌢⌣⌢～

"It is absolutely beautiful." Cassandra gazed up at the walls of Chesilworth from where she sat in the garden, and a smile curved her lips.

Philip had insisted on restoring the old mansion himself, telling Cassandra that it was his wedding present to her. Now, a year and a half after their wedding, most of the renovations were complete. There was still scaffolding all over the west wing, where the damage was so drastic that it would take more than a year to fully repair. But the roof had been replaced, and the old dilapidated carpets and threadbare draperies had been ripped out and replaced with new ones. New paint gleamed on the interior walls, except where wallpaper was hung. Stairs had been repaired, and squeaking floorboards had been replaced. The fireplaces had been fixed so that they no longer smoked, and the vast kitchen had been brought up to date.

It was beautiful outside, as well. A full-time staff of gardeners, under the watchful eye of old Chumley, had pulled weeds, trimmed hedges and planted flowers until the gardens were prettier than Cassandra could ever remember them. Even the maze in the back had been restored.

She turned with a smile toward the man who sat in the chair beside her. "Thank you for doing so much for Chesilworth."

Philip shrugged off the thanks. "They have done an excellent job with the place. I think we shall find it quite pleasant to spend part of the year here."

It was another kindness on Philip's part. As lovely as Chesilworth was becoming, it was not his home, and Cassandra knew that his offer for the family to spend part of each year there was for Olivia's and the boys' sakes, especially Crispin. He did not want them to have to grow up entirely cut off from their home just because he had taken them in.

"It is lovely," Joanna piped up, and Cassandra turned to stare at her cousin, who sat on the other side of the small wrought iron garden table. "I never could understand what you saw in the moldering old place, but now it's actually quite attractive," she added, sounding more like herself.

Joanna was lovely today, as always, in a gown of pale pink that set off her porcelain beauty. Her fiancé, a quiet man given to stuttering when he talked, looked at her with admiration. His name was Anthony Gordon, and his father was a Scottish peer whose title Anthony would one day inherit. Cassandra found him a trifle boring and even dim at times, but his admiration of Joanna was obvious, and he seemed content to sit and listen to her self-centered babble for hours, murmuring only an occasional, "Yes, dear."

He was an acquaintance of Philip's, and Philip himself had introduced the two of them at his and Cassandra's wedding. When Cassandra had mildly teased him about his matchmaking efforts, he had said, "I suspected he would be perfect for Joanna—not too bright, quiet, an admirer of beautiful things—and, best of all, his family seat is far away in Scotland, which means that we shall have the pleasure of your cousin's company only rarely.''

It was Joanna's wedding that had brought Philip and Cassandra and all their family to Chesilworth this week. Even Violet had come with them, though the elder Lady Neville had declined, citing old age as an excuse to stay at Haverly House. Privately, she told Cassandra, who was becoming more and more a favorite of hers, that she was sure that Joanna Moulton's wedding would be an insipid bore.

''Cassandra!'' Crispin and Hart called to her from the other side of the garden, then waved and dashed off around the corner of the house, engaged in some boyish pursuit. It seemed to Cassandra that they had each grown at least two inches this past year. Soon, she knew, they would be sprouting up to the height of full-grown men. It was a thought that brought a curious pang of both pleasure and pain. In just another year they would go off to Eton. Cassandra was afraid that she would feel like a mother hen without her chicks.

At the thought, she glanced over to the shady bower where Georgette and Olivia were sitting on a blanket, playing with the baby, tickling his stomach and listening to his delighted laughter while his rosy-cheeked nurse looked on. Cassandra and Philip's son was five months old now and a constant delight to his parents and everyone else in the family. Blond-haired and blue-eyed, he was a healthy, chubby baby possessed of a sunny disposition.

Of all those who spoiled him, perhaps the worst were his two young aunts, Georgette and Olivia. They were bent over him now, the dark head and the blond one close together. Their instantaneous friendship had only grown closer in the last year and a half. Though Georgette would be due to make her debut this next season, she was insisting upon waiting until the next year so that she and Olivia could make their coming out at the same time. Since both girls seemed to grow more lovely every day, Cassandra suspected that they would take the polite world by storm.

Philip reached over and touched her arm. "Would you care to take a stroll with me in the garden, Lady Neville?"

Cassandra smiled. "Indeed, I would, Sir Philip."

She took his hand and rose to her feet, picking up the lacy blue parasol beside her, which matched perfectly the blue of her dress. She was dressed, as always, in a simple dress of excellent cut. Dressing well was still new enough to her that it sometimes surprised her to see herself in her mirror. Both Lady Nevilles had supervised a massive infusion of new clothes into her wardrobe from the time she and Philip first became engaged. Violet had taken her on marathon buying sprees to London, and Cassandra had been amazed by the languid woman's stamina and energy when it came to selecting and purchasing clothes.

Cassandra opened her parasol and propped it on her shoulder, then took her husband's arm, and they strolled in a leisurely manner through the garden.

"Have you heard anything about Miss Yorke?" Cassandra asked after a moment.

"Yes. Miss Emmings writes that she is doing much better."

Neither Cassandra nor Philip had had the heart to have Miss Yorke arrested and tried for her crimes. When she had come to, she had been a sobbing, incoherent wreck. Philip had placed her in a home close to the seashore, where a kind, firm woman by the name of Emmings cared for several individuals whose minds were no longer functioning properly and whose families could not bear to send them to a place like Bedlam.

Under Miss Emmings's care, Sarah had improved and even helped Miss Emmings work with the other patients in artistic endeavors and schoolroom matters. Of course, Miss Emmings said that Sarah also still told people that she was Sir Philip Neville's secret wife, but at least she no longer exhibited any sort of violent behavior, and her life seemed to be as happy as one could hope for.

"You know," Cassandra said, "I was just thinking. I don't believe that things could be any more perfect."

"I'm glad." Philip took the hand curled around his arm and raised it to his lips. "Certainly you have made my life perfect."

"Only you would say so—being pursued and threatened by thieves, having a whole family of children put in your care, being burdened with an old, decaying house."

"And having more fun than most men have in a lifetime," he added to her list. "Hunting for secret maps and buried treasure, having children around to make me laugh, being handed a project to keep me entertained, having a handsome and intelligent baby with a smile like an angel...most of all, being given the most beautiful and intelligent of women for a wife. I think that I have had the best of the bargain."

Cassandra smiled.

"My only problem is getting you to myself. It seems that there are always people around."

They had left the garden and were now strolling across the green yard. "Where are we going?" Cassandra asked.

"I thought that we might explore the reconstructed maze."

Cassandra lifted her brows. "I'm not sure that I remember how to get out of it anymore. We could be trapped in there for hours, and no one would be able to find us.''

Philip bared his teeth in a wolfish grin. "My dear, that is exactly what I had in mind.''

Cassandra laughed and lifted her skirts above her ankles. "What are we waiting for, then?'' she asked and took off at a run for the maze, with Philip right behind her.

New York Times **bestselling author**

E L I Z A B E T H

LOWELL

takes you to the Andean Cloud Forest,
Ecuador. Mysterious and hauntingly
beautiful—a dangerous land despite its beauty.
A land to be feared. And respected.

Trace Rawlings is a man who lives by his own rules.
Ruthless, domineering, he takes what he wants.

Cynthia Ryan is used to others trying to manipulate her—
especially her powerful father. So she can handle this man—
after all, he's been hired to guide her through the
treacherous forest.

Thrown together by her father's ruthless ambition, first as
adversaries, then as lovers, Trace and Cynthia force their
way through the cloud forest—transformed by a passion as
wild and steamy as the forest itself.

D A R K   F I R E

On sale mid-August 1998
where paperbacks are sold!

MIRA®

MEL453

Look us up on-line at: http://www.romance.net

THREE OF AMERICA'S FAVORITE WRITERS
OF ROMANCE FICTION,

JILL BARNETT,
DEBBIE MACOMBER
and SUSAN WIGGS

WELCOME YOU TO
RAINSHADOW LODGE—WHERE LOVE IS
JUST ONE OF THE AMENITIES....

Rainshadow Lodge may be on a secluded island with
blue skies and crystal waters, but surely that's not
enough to make three utterly mismatched couples jump
over their differences and into each other's arms. After
all, what could a socialite and a handyman have in
common? How could a workaholic and a free spirit ever
compromise? And why would a perfectly nice woman
overcome a bad first impression made by a grumpy
stranger? Must be something in the air...

That SUMMER Place

MIRA

On sale mid-August 1998
where paperbacks are sold!

Look us up on-line at: http://www.romance.net

MANTHTSP

Take 2 of
"The Best of the Best™"
Novels FREE
Plus get a FREE surprise gift!

Special Limited-Time Offer

Mail to The Best of the Best™

3010 Walden Avenue
P.O. Box 1867
Buffalo, N.Y. 14240-1867

YES! Please send me 2 free novels and my free surprise gift. Then send me 3 of "The Best of the Best™" novels each month. I'll receive the best books by the world's hottest romance authors. Bill me at the low price of $4.24 each plus 25¢ delivery per book and applicable sales tax, if any.* That's the complete price, and a saving of over 20% off the cover prices—quite a bargain! I understand that accepting the books and gift places me under no obligation ever to buy any books. I can always return a shipment and cancel at any time. Even if I never buy another book, the 2 free books and the surprise gift are mine to keep forever.

183 MEN CH74

Name _____ (PLEASE PRINT)

Address _____ Apt. No. _____

City _____ State _____ Zip _____

This offer is limited to one order per household and not valid to current subscribers.
*Terms and prices are subject to change without notice. Sales tax applicable in N.Y.
All orders subject to approval.

UBOB-98   ©1996 MIRA BOOKS

You won't want to miss the newest
hardcover novel that will be on
everyone's lips this summer...

TALK

All of America is tuning in to talk-show diva
Jessica Wright, including a dangerously devoted
secret admirer—a stalker who has planned a finale
even more sensational than any of her shows....

**A novel of intrigue and suspense
from national bestselling author**

LAURA
VAN WORMER

Available in July wherever hardcover books are sold.

Special offer—Take advantage of our $2.00 off
coupon for *TALK* in the back pages of the
paperback release of *JUST FOR THE SUMMER* by
Laura Van Wormer, available in June, from
MIRA® Books.

MIRA

If you enjoyed this story of
passionate adventure and romantic
intrigue by award-winning author

CANDACE CAMP

Don't miss the opportunity to receive her other
titles from MIRA® Books:

#66035	SUDDENLY	$5.99 U.S.☐	$6.50 CAN.☐
#66166	SCANDALOUS	$5.99 U.S.☐	$6.99 CAN.☐
#66264	IMPULSE	$5.99 U.S.☐	$6.99 CAN.☐
#66297	INDISCREET	$5.99 U.S.☐	$6.99 CAN.☐

(quantities may be limited)

TOTAL AMOUNT	$
POSTAGE & HANDLING	$
($1.00 for one book, 50¢ for each additional)	
APPLICABLE TAXES*	$ _____
TOTAL PAYABLE	$ _____
(check or money order—please do not send cash)	

To order, complete this form and send it, along with a check or money order for the
total above, payable to MIRA Books, to: **In the U.S.:** 3010 Walden Avenue, P.O. Box
9077, Buffalo, NY 14269-9077; **In Canada:** P.O. Box 636, Fort Erie, Ontario L2A 5X3.

Name: _____

Address: _____ City: _____

State/Prov.: _____ Zip/Postal Code: _____

Account Number: _____ (If applicable)   075 CSAS

*New York residents remit applicable sales taxes.
Canadian residents remit applicable GST and provincial taxes.

**The Brightest Stars
in Fiction.™**

**MIRA
BOOKS**

Look us up on-line at: http://www.romance.net

MCCBL4